*An extraordinary future
is waiting.*

Embrace it.

Year's
Best
SF
10

Praise for previous volumes

"An impressive roster of authors."
Locus

"The finest modern science fiction writing."
Pittsburgh Tribune

Edited by David G. Hartwell

Edited by David G. Hartwell & Kathryn Cramer

YEAR'S BEST

SF 10

EDITED BY
DAVID G. HARTWELL
and KATHRYN CRAMER

An Imprint of HarperCollinsPublishers

Additional copyright information appears on pages 496–498.

EOS

An Imprint of HarperCollins*Publishers*
10 East 53rd Street
New York, New York 10022-5299

Copyright © 2005 by David G. Hartwell and Kathryn Cramer
ISBN: 0-06-057561-1
www.eosbooks.com

First Eos paperback printing: June 2005

HarperCollins® and Eos® are trademarks of HarperCollins Publishers Inc.

Printed in the U.S.A.

10 9 8 7 6 5 4 3 2 1

To Carl Caputo,
for last-minute help and good cheer,
and to Elizabeth Constance Cramer Hartwell,
in the hope that you will sleep better.

Contents

Acknowledgments

We would like to acknowledge the help of Locusmag.com website and *Locus*, of Bestsf.com, and of Tangentonline.com, and of course, Google.

Introduction

We are in the middle of some kind of short fiction boom in science fiction and the associated genres of the fantastic. Not an economic boom, but certainly a numbers increase, and it has been building for several years. There seems to have been an increase in quality as well as in quantity, too, with well-edited semiprofessional magazines and small press anthologies of generally higher editorial standards than those anthologies issuing from big trade publishers proliferating. And all this in spite of the desperate battles of the distinguished professional magazines to secure enough distribution and sales to persist in business.

The electronic publishers on the internet maintained the levels of quality established a couple of years back, and remain a vigorous dimension of the SF field, but there was not a significant increase in the amount of good fiction originating on the internet. The increase was predominantly in the semiprofessional book and magazine publishing sphere, and even in the zine area (as opposed to fanzines—zines are analogous to the cutting edge little magazines of the literary world, published and carefully edited by individuals, rarely for profit).

Still, the highest concentrations of excellence were in the professional publications, the anthologies from the small press, and the highest paying online markets. The electronic fiction websites such as Infinite Matrix, Strange Horizons, and SciFiction continued to publish much fine work, though a majority of it was fantasy or horror.

There were hundreds of good stories to choose from this

year to fill this volume (there were more than five hundred listed as candidates for the Locus recommended reading list for the year), making it clear that there are a really large number of talented writers of short fiction in our field, a real bonanza for readers. There are lots of conclusions one might draw from this, but the one we highlight is that it makes this year's best volume even more useful, since we try to sort through all this material. The small press really did expand again this past year, both in book form and in a proliferation of little magazines, in the U.S. and the rest of the world.

Once again, books and magazines of high quality, often anthologies and short story collections, from Canada, Australia, and the UK, drew our attention. We have to say that this year was generally as good as the pinnacle year 2003 for original anthologies and story collections—even though most of them will not be found in local bookstores because they are available on the whole only by direct mail or internet order, or from specialty dealers at SF conventions. Still, the total of good SF stories, and perhaps even the total of all SF stories, increased noticeably last year.

But—and this is a significant but—the majority of small press publications contained only a minority of science fiction genre stories, and the bulk of the rest were speculative literature, fantasy, horror, magical realism, allegories, or uses of SF tropes and images in the context of mainstream or postmodern fiction. This commonly proceeded from a "breaking the bounds of genre" attitude on the part of the editors and publishers of small press short fiction, and many of their writers. Distinguished examples of this trend are *Leviathan* and *Polyphony*.

And to our continuing amusement, this attitude was again contradicted by one of the bastions of mainstream literary fiction, *McSweeney's* magazine, which published a second genre fiction issue, *McSweeney's Astonishing Stories*, in 2004, edited by Michael Chabon. It was filled mainly with genre stories, although no SF this time. Perhaps more significantly, the prestigious *Denver Quarterly* had an issue devoted principally to fantastic fiction without announcing the fact at all. Each year we find ourselves pointing with some irony at the areas of growth in SF, as if they were double-edged swords. While many of the ambitious insiders want to break out, at least some ambitious outsiders are breaking in, and some of them at the top of the genre. This is now a trend several years old.

It is our opinion that it is a good thing to have genre boundaries. If we didn't, young writers would have to find something else to transgress to draw attention to themselves.

So, for readers new to this series, we repeat our usual disclaimer: This selection of science fiction stories represents the best that was published during the year 2004. It would take several more volumes this size to have nearly all of the best short stories—though even then, not all of the best novellas. And we believe that representing the best from year to year, while it is not physically possible to encompass it all in one even very large book, also implies presenting some substantial variety of excellences, and we left some worthy stories out in order to include others in this limited space.

Our general principle for selection: This book is full of science fiction—every story in this book is clearly that and not something else. We have a high regard for horror, fantasy, speculative fiction, and slipstream, and postmodern literature. We (Kathryn Cramer and David G. Hartwell) edit the *Year's Best Fantasy* in paperback from Eos, as a companion volume to this one—look for it if you enjoy short fantasy fiction, too. But here, we choose science fiction.

We try in each volume of this series to represent the varieties of tones and voices and attitudes that keep the genre vigorous and responsive to the changing realities out of which it emerges, in science and daily life. It is supposed to be fun to read, a special kind of fun you cannot find elsewhere. This is a book about what's going on now in SF. The stories that follow show, and the story notes point out, the strengths of the evolving genre in the year 2004.

David G. Hartwell & Kathryn Cramer

Sergeant Chip

BRADLEY DENTON

Bradley Denton [www.sff.net/people/bradley.denton/] lives outside Austin, Texas, with his wife, Barbara, their cat, and their twin hound dogs. He began publishing in the science fiction field in 1984. His first novel, Wrack & Roll *(1986), is an alternate history. He won the John W. Campbell Memorial Award for his second novel,* Buddy Holly Is Alive and Well on Ganymede *(1991). His next novel,* Blackburn *(1993), is a horror novel about a serial killer.* Lunatics *(1996) is fantasy. A new novel,* Laughin' Boy, *about terrorism and daytime television, will appear from Subterranean Press in 2005. Most of his short fiction is fantastic, and collected in* A Conflagration Artist *and* The Calvin Coolidge Home for Dead Comedians *(1994)—two books which were published together in a slipcase and which won a World Fantasy Award for Best Collection—and in* One Day Closer to Death *(1998).*

"Sergeant Chip" was published in Fantasy & Science Fiction, *which had a particularly strong year in 2004. In this fine novella about the military virtues, the central character is a cybernetically enhanced dog. There is a war in the future in the Middle East, and something has gone terribly wrong.*

But Sergeant Chip is intelligent, skilled, and a good dog who stands for the good, against anyone and anything. The story reverberates with contemporary political references and powerful sentiment. We didn't read a better story this year.

*To the Supreme Commander of the soldier who
bears this message—*

Sir or Madam:

Today before it was light I had to roll in the stream to wash
blood from my fur. I decided then to send You these words.

So I think of the word shapes, and the girl writes them for
me. I know how the words are shaped because I could see
them whenever Captain Dial spoke. And I always knew what
he was saying.

The girl writes on a roll of paper she found in the stone
hut when we began using it as our quarters three months
ago. She already had pencils. She has written her own words
on the paper many times since then, but she has torn those
words from the roll and placed them in her duffel. Her own
words have different shapes than the ones she writes for me
now. She doesn't even know what my word shapes mean,
because the shapes are all that I show her. So the responsibility for their meanings is mine alone.

Just as the responsibility for my actions is mine alone.

Last night I killed eighteen of Your soldiers.

I didn't want to do that. They reminded me of some of the
soldiers I knew before, the ones who followed Captain Dial
with me. But I had to kill them because they came to attack

2

us. And if I let them do that, I would be disobeying orders.

I heard them approach while the girl, the two boys, and the old man slept. So I went out and climbed the ridge behind the hut so I could see a long way. I have good night vision, and I had no trouble spotting the soldiers as they split into two squads and spread out. Their intent was to attack our hut from different angles to make its defense more difficult. I knew this because it was one of the things Captain Dial taught me.

So I did another thing Captain Dial taught me. As the two squads scuttled to their positions to await the order to attack, I crept down toward them through the grass and brambles. I crept with my belly to the earth so they couldn't see me coming. Not even with their infrared goggles.

Captain Dial once said I was black as night and silent as air. He was proud when he said it. I remembered that when I crept to Your soldiers.

They didn't hear me as I went from one to another. They were spread out too far. Their leader wasn't as smart as Captain Dial. I bit each one's throat so it tore open and the soldier couldn't shout. There were some sounds, but they weren't loud.

The first soldier had a lieutenant's bar on his helmet. I had seen it from a long way away. It was the only officer's insignia I saw in either squad. So I went to him first. That way he couldn't give the order to attack before I was finished.

But the others would have attacked sooner or later, even without an order from their lieutenant. So I had to kill them all.

The last soldier was the only female among the eighteen. As I approached her, I smelled the same kind of soap that Captain Dial's wife Melanie used. That made me pause as I remembered how things were a long time ago when I slept at the foot of their bed. But then the soldier knew I was there and turned her weapon toward me. So I bit her throat before she could fire.

I dragged the soldiers to the ravine near the southern end of the ridge. You'll find them there side by side if You arrive before the wild animals do. I did my best to treat them with honor.

Then I went to the stream. The stream is near the hut, so I tried to be quiet. I didn't want to wake my people before sunrise.

After washing, I went into the grass and shook off as much water as I could. But there was no one to rub me with a towel. There was no one to touch my head and tell me I was good.

I remembered then that no one had ever told Captain Dial he was good, either.

This is what it means to be the leader.

I wanted to howl. But I didn't. My people were still asleep.

I take care of them. I don't let anyone hurt them. These were Captain Dial's orders, and I will not disobey.

Captain Dial was my commanding officer. I was his first sergeant. If You examine the D Company roster, You will see that my pay grade is K-9.

My name is Chip.

Whenever Captain Dial gave me an order, I obeyed as fast as I could. And then he always touched my head and told me I was good. Sometimes when I was extra fast, he gave me a treat. I liked the treats, but I liked the touch even more.

There was never a time when Captain Dial wasn't my leader. But he wasn't always a captain, and I wasn't always his first sergeant. In the beginning he was a lieutenant, and I was his corporal.

We were promoted because of the day we demonstrated our training to the people in the bleachers.

That morning, in our quarters, Lieutenant Dial said that what we would participate in that afternoon was political bullshit. Money for the war was about to be cut, so public-relations events like this were an attempt to bolster civilian support. But Lieutenant Dial said that only two things had ever motivated the public to support the military: heroism and vengeance.

He also said that we had to do well regardless. He said I

would have to do a good job and make him proud. So I stood at attention, and I thought about running fast to find mines and attack enemies. I thought about making Lieutenant Dial proud.

Then he touched my head. He knew my thoughts. He always knew my thoughts. He told me I was good and gave me permission to be at ease.

So I wiggled and pushed my head against his knees, and my tail wagged hard as he buckled my duty harness. Even though he had said it was bullshit, I could smell that he was excited about the job ahead. That made me excited too. And as we left our quarters, Lieutenant Dial's wife Melanie came with us. That made me even more excited, because she was almost never with us except in our quarters.

Melanie spoke to me every morning, and although I couldn't understand her thoughts too well, I knew she was telling me to take care of Lieutenant Dial throughout our day of training. And every night when Lieutenant Dial and I returned, Melanie touched my head and said I was good. Then, after we all ate supper, she and Lieutenant Dial would climb into their bed, I would lie down on my cushion at its foot, and we would sleep. Sometimes in the night their scents grew stronger and blended together, and they made happy sounds. But I stayed quiet because I wanted them to stay happy. Other times I smelled or heard strangers outside our quarters, and I would go on alert even though Lieutenant Dial was still asleep and had not given me an order. But the strangers always went away, and then I slept again too.

Those were the only times Melanie was with us, and that one order every morning was the only order she ever gave me. All of my other orders, all of my treats, and all of my food came from Lieutenant Dial.

But Lieutenant Dial loved Melanie. I could see the word "love" whenever he thought of her. And that made me glad because it made him glad. So we were all happy on the day she came with us. She smelled like a hundred different flowers all mixed together, and she was wearing new clothes that seemed to float around her.

She also wore a gift that Lieutenant Dial had given her the

night before. It was a shiny rock on a silver chain that she wore around her neck. Lieutenant Dial told me that Melanie liked the color of the rock. It just looked like a rock on a chain to me. But when Lieutenant Dial put it around Melanie's neck, it made me think of the chain and tags that Lieutenant Dial wore around his own neck whenever he was on duty. And it also made me think of the collar he put on me when I wasn't wearing my duty harness. So then I understood why Melanie was so happy to receive the rock and chain. Now we all had things to wear around our necks.

We didn't go to our usual training area at the fort that day. Instead we went to a park by the ocean. There were flags and people everywhere. It was busy and noisy, and I wanted to run around and smell everything. But Lieutenant Dial ordered me to stay beside him, and that was fun too. I still got to smell everything. We walked from one tree to another, with me on one side of Lieutenant Dial and Melanie on the other. And at every tree, people gathered around while Lieutenant Dial told them who he was and who I was. Then he would give me a few orders—easy things like attention, on guard, and secure-the-perimeter—and we would move on. A lot of people asked if they could touch me, but Lieutenant Dial said they couldn't. He explained that I was on duty. I wasn't a pet. I was a corporal.

He was proud when he said it, and that made me proud too.

As we walked from place to place, sometimes Lieutenant Dial held Melanie's hand in his. And once, Melanie reached across and touched my head. This violated the rule Lieutenant Dial had been telling everyone. But even though I was on duty, it seemed all right. I was glad she did it.

After a while we walked away from the trees to a broad stretch of lawn beside the ocean. I saw a long pier floating on the water. And across the lawn from the pier were bleachers with people in them. There were more people in the bleachers than I had ever seen in one place before, and some of them were high-ranking officers in dress uniforms. So I knew that even if what was going to happen here was bullshit, it was important bullshit.

Out on the lawn were little flags, mud puddles, wooden walls, sandbag fortifications, and some mock-enemies. I knew they were mock-enemies because they wore dark, padded suits. All of these things were familiar to me from training. But there were more things on the lawn than I had ever seen in one training session, and that excited me.

Melanie went to the bleachers while Lieutenant Dial took me onto the lawn, where we were joined by other soldiers. Some of the other soldiers were also K-9s. I knew most of them. Lieutenant Dial and I had trained with them many times.

Out on the pier, men and women dressed in white stood at attention. And when Lieutenant Dial and I reached a spot in the middle of the lawn, he told me to stand at attention as well. So I did, and all of the other soldiers did too.

A colonel stood in front of the bleachers and addressed the crowd. He said a lot of words through a loudspeaker, but I couldn't understand them. Since they didn't come from Lieutenant Dial, they were meaningless.

When the colonel stopped talking, the people in the bleachers clapped their hands. Then a soldier ran onto the lawn and handed Lieutenant Dial a microphone. Lieutenant Dial signaled that I should remain at attention, so I didn't move as he took a step forward and addressed the people.

He told them a lot of things about K-9 soldiers. One thing he said was that while war dogs required a lot of training, we didn't have to be trained to understand loyalty or rank. A dog who was raised and trained by one soldier would always see that soldier as his or her pack leader. So if Lieutenant Dial was put in charge of a platoon, that platoon would become my pack. And I would see my duty to that pack as absolute and unquestionable.

It surprised me that Lieutenant Dial had to explain that to people. It was as obvious to me as knowing that food is for eating. But then I remembered that people didn't always think the same way that Lieutenant Dial and I thought. Melanie, for example. Melanie was always kind to me, but sometimes I could smell that she also feared me a little. And I always wondered how that could be. Lieutenant Dial loved

Melanie, so I would never hurt her. And as long as I was near her, I would never let anything else hurt her, either. So I hoped that what Lieutenant Dial was saying to the people in the bleachers would help Melanie understand that she never had to be afraid.

Then Lieutenant Dial said something that made him sad as he said it. I don't think the people knew how sad it made him, but I knew. The other K-9s knew, too.

He said that during a war in the past, some high-ranking officers had decided that K-9s weren't really soldiers. Instead, they were classified as equipment. That meant that when their units left the field, K-9s were abandoned or destroyed. They were treated like utility vehicles or tents. They weren't allowed to return to their home quarters with their handlers.

Lieutenant Dial always spoke the truth, but this truth was difficult for me to comprehend. I knew I wasn't equipment. I knew the difference between a vehicle and a dog. And the K-9s in that past war must have known the difference too. So I was glad the regulations had changed. But I wondered then, and wonder now, whether there might still be some high-ranking officers who don't think of me as a soldier.

I urge You not to make that mistake.

Lieutenant Dial's sadness went away as he continued talking. He described some of the duties K-9 soldiers perform, and as he described those duties, different handlers ordered their K-9s to perform them. And as the dogs obeyed, their images appeared on a big screen that had been set up beside the pier.

One dog, a pointy-eared shepherd, attacked and subdued first one mock-enemy, then three, and then five. He was good at it. Even though the mock-enemies were padded so he couldn't really hurt them, I could smell that they were afraid of him.

Another dog, a lean pinscher, ran fast fast fast, dodging and leaping over obstacles that popped up before him, and he delivered a medical kit to another soldier at the end of the lawn. Then he dragged that soldier to a designated safety point while avoiding some booby traps. The booby traps went off bang bang bang after the pinscher and his soldier were past them.

A big-chested Malinois destroyed a machine-gun nest.

Another shepherd crept on her belly to flank an enemy platoon.

A hound pointed out hidden land mines and howled as he found each one.

Lieutenant Dial announced each K-9's name and rank, each handler's name and rank, and the task to be performed. The K-9s were all good, and the people in the bleachers clapped. So I was glad because everyone was happy. But I was getting more and more excited because I wanted it to be my turn. In fact, as the second shepherd completed her flanking maneuver and took down a mock-enemy from behind, I almost broke attention. I wanted to help. I wanted to be a good soldier, too.

I whimpered, and Lieutenant Dial gave me a corrective glance. So I tried extra hard to remain still and silent. I didn't want to disappoint Lieutenant Dial. Disappointing Lieutenant Dial would be the worst thing in the world.

When all of the other dogs had performed their tasks, Lieutenant Dial told the people that the modern K-9 soldier went beyond those of the past. He told them that K-9s and their handlers were now matched according to their skills, temperaments, and rapport—because there were some dogs and humans who had a gift for understanding each other, and some who didn't. And he told them that such matchings had been so successful that dogs often knew what their handlers wanted them to do even before any verbal or visual orders had been issued. In addition, a subcutaneous device implanted in each dog made it possible for handlers to send pulsed signals that their K-9s had been trained to recognize as orders. And the implants, in turn, sent biometric signals to the handlers to indicate their K-9s' levels of anxiety and confidence as orders were carried out. So even when a dog and handler weren't in close proximity, they could still communicate and complete their mission.

I didn't remember receiving my implant, but I knew it was under the skin between my shoulders. I almost never thought about it because Lieutenant Dial almost never used his transmitter anymore. He had used it often in our early days of training. But as our training had progressed, our thoughts had become clearer and clearer to each other, and one day we had both known the electronic signals weren't needed anymore. So Lieutenant Dial had unstrapped the transmitter from his wrist and put it in a pouch on his belt. After that day, he would sometimes send a signal just to be sure my implant was working, but I always started carrying out his orders before I felt the pulses anyway. That was because I paid attention to him, and I could see his thoughts even when he was far away.

When Lieutenant Dial finished telling the people about the communication implants, he told them about me. He told them I had been rescued from a municipal shelter as a puppy, and that a military veterinarian had determined that the dominant breeds in my genetic background were black Labrador and standard poodle. That made me a Labradoodle. Some of the people in the crowd laughed when they heard that name, but Lieutenant Dial didn't laugh when he said it.

He said I had the intelligence of a poodle and the temperament of a Labrador. He said I was three years old and in peak physical condition. He said I weighed eighty pounds, which was big enough to be strong, but small enough to be fast and to squeeze into places too tight for people. He said my black, wavy coat was good camouflage at night. He said I was at the top of my training class. He said I was a corporal and my name was Chip.

Then Lieutenant Dial looked across the lawn at a sand-bagged machine-gun nest and gave me the hand signal to attack. I knew he was going to give me the signal as soon as he looked across at the sandbags, but I also knew I should wait for it. The people in the bleachers wouldn't like it if I didn't.

But I jumped away fast when he gave it. I ran for the sandbags, and the machine gun opened fire. It was firing blank cartridges, but I knew from training that I had to act as if the ammunition could hurt me. So I zigzagged and made quick stops behind cardboard rocks, stacks of tires, and other things that were on the lawn between Lieutenant Dial and the machine-gun nest. The machine-gun barrel swiveled to follow me, but I was too fast and tricky for it, because when I ran behind a cardboard rock, I would come out in a different direction. The machine-gun barrel couldn't keep up, and soon I was right under it so it couldn't point at me. Then I jumped up over the sandbags and pushed the gunner onto his back. Two mock-enemies on either side of him pointed rifles at me, so I bit one in the crotch and twisted so that he fell against the other one. Then all three mock-enemies were on their backs, and I bit the pads at their throats. A bell sounded over the loudspeaker as I broke the skin of each pad and the mock-blood came out. After the third bell, the people in the bleachers clapped.

Then I felt a quick series of pulses between my shoulders, but I was already jumping away from the machine-gun nest because I knew what Lieutenant Dial wanted me to do next. I ran as fast as I could to the farthest end of the lawn, dodging mock-enemies as they popped up and tried to shoot me, until I reached the wooden wall with the knotted rope at the top. The wall was high, but I liked that. I'm good at jumping.

I ran hard and jumped high, and I grabbed the bottom knot on the rope with my teeth. Then I pushed against the wall with all my feet so I could grab the next knot, and the next, and the next. Just before the next-to-last knot, a piece of the wall broke away as my feet pushed it, and I almost missed the knot. I caught it with just my front teeth. But that made me angry at the wall and the knot, because they were trying to make me disappoint Lieutenant Dial. So I bit as hard as I could with my front teeth, and I kicked and scratched the wall until another piece broke away and gave me a good place for my hind feet. Then I pulled with my teeth and pushed with my legs, and I went all the way over the wall without having to grab the last knot.

On the other side of the wall, two soldiers lay on the ground. They had mock-wounds on their legs and chests, but they weren't pretending to be unconscious. So I went to the nearest one and let him grab the handle on my duty harness. Then I dragged him through a mock-minefield to a medical station. The mines weren't marked with flags the way they often were in training, but I didn't need the flags. I know the smells of many different explosives, so I could smell the mines even though they were just smoke-bangs. It was easy to drag the soldier around them. Some of them went off when we were past, but it didn't matter. None of the smoke touched us, and I got the soldier to the medical station in the same shape I found him in.

I ran back for the other soldier, but when I reached him he was pretending to be unconscious. I whined and licked his face, but I knew it wouldn't make him stop pretending. So then I grabbed one of his flak-jacket straps and began to drag him toward the medical station. But when we were halfway through the minefield, an open utility vehicle carrying four mock-enemies came driving across it, straight for us. The mines didn't go off as the vehicle drove over them, and the mock-enemy manning the mounted gun began firing at me and my soldier.

They were trying to prevent me from obeying Lieutenant Dial's orders. I wouldn't let them do that.

I dropped my soldier and started running so the mock-enemies would chase me. When they did, and when we were far enough from the wounded soldier that I knew he would be safe, I made a quick stop, turned around, and jumped. I cleared the vehicle's windshield and had just enough time to bite the pad on the gunner's throat. The bell rang. Then I hit the ground behind the vehicle and tumbled, but got up and turned back around in time to see the gunner slump over and the driver turn the steering wheel hard. The other two mock-enemies were raising their pistols.

As the vehicle made its turn, exposing the driver, I ran and jumped again. But when I bit the pad on the driver's throat, the skin didn't break right away. So I hung on and bit harder. The driver gave a yell that I don't think was a word. Then the pad broke, the mock-blood came out, and I heard the bell. So I jumped away, spinning as my paws hit the ground so I could be ready to attack the remaining two mock-enemies.

But I didn't have to. The vehicle rolled over so its wheels

went up, and three of the four enemies fell out. Then it was
still. The driver was still strapped in his seat, but his neck
was bent against the ground, and he didn't move. The three
mock-enemies on the ground didn't move either. So I ran to
the two I hadn't bitten yet, broke the skins on their throat
pads, then returned to my soldier in the minefield.

The soldier was sitting up with his eyes and mouth open.
But I grabbed his flak-jacket strap anyway and resumed
dragging him to the medical station. Then he tried to pull
away from me. But I was still under orders. So I growled,
and then my soldier was still again. I delivered him to the
medical station, ran back to Lieutenant Dial, and stood at attention.

The people in the bleachers began to smell unhappy. They
made growling noises, and none of them clapped their
hands. So for a moment I was afraid I had done something
wrong. But then I knew it wasn't so, because Lieutenant Dial
touched my head and said I was good.

That was all that mattered.

From Lieutenant Dial's next thoughts, I knew that the
driver in the utility vehicle had made a mistake. He'd been
supposed to drive farther away from me after the gunner was
bitten. But he had turned back toward me too soon, and I had
been faster than he had thought I would be. Then, when his
throat pad hadn't broken right away, he had panicked and
turned the steering wheel too sharply. So the vehicle had
rolled over. But by then I had broken the throat pad and
jumped away.

All four of the mock-enemies in the utility vehicle had to
be taken away for real medical care, and I could hear that
some of the people in the bleachers felt bad about that. But
Lieutenant Dial didn't. Instead, he became angry. He wasn't
angry with me, but I didn't want him to be angry with anything. Being angry made him unhappy. And that made me
unhappy too. Anger was like smoke with a bad smell in his
head.

The K-9 demonstration was over then, and Melanie came
down from the bleachers to meet us. I was glad to see her.

But Lieutenant Dial was still angry. He told Melanie that the driver of the utility vehicle had done the exercise incorrectly, and that what had happened wasn't my fault. I had done what I was supposed to do, but the mock-enemies had screwed it up.

Melanie told him she already knew that, and that everyone else knew it too. She said he shouldn't worry about what people would think of him, or of me, or of any of the K-9s, because we had all been wonderful.

I didn't always know what Melanie was saying, but that time I understood every word. And as she spoke, Lieutenant Dial's anger drifted away. Just like smoke. And then he was happy and proud again. And so was I.

I rubbed my nose against Melanie's knee, and she touched my head. I wished I could tell her she was good.

Then Lieutenant Dial, Melanie, and I walked to the edge of the water with some of the people from the bleachers, and we stood on a boardwalk while the people on the pier performed demonstrations with water animals. We had a good view even though we were about thirty meters from them. Lieutenant Dial said the animals that stayed in the water all the time were called dolphins, and the ones that hopped from the pier to the water and back again were called sea lions. One of the sea lions barked, but I couldn't understand it.

The water animals delivered equipment to people underwater, and they also searched for mines and mock-enemies. Pictures of them doing those things appeared on the big screen. Sometimes a sea lion carried a clamp in its mouth, and when it found a mock-enemy, it swam up behind him and put the clamp on his leg. Then the mock-enemy was pulled up to the pier by a rope attached to the clamp, while the sea lion jumped from the water and got a treat from its handler. It looked like fun, and I wished I could go underwater and sneak up on the mock-enemies down there too.

Then the sea lions had a contest. They were supposed to find some small dummy mines and push buttons on the mines with their noses, then attach handles and bring the mines up to the pier. It was a race to see which sea lion could bring up the most mines in two minutes. So the sea lions were swimming fast and splashing a lot, dropping the mines on the pier and grabbing new handles before plunging into the ocean again.

The dummy water mines looked like black soccer balls, and they had lights that came on if the button had been pushed. Once one of the sea lions brought up a mine that didn't have its light on, and his handler threw the mine back into the water. Then the sea lion had to go get it again, and he had to be sure to push the button before putting it on the pier. If I had been that sea lion, I would have felt bad for not doing it right the first time. But I couldn't tell whether he felt bad or not, because he kept on swimming for more mines. So then I was glad because he was still being a good soldier.

He didn't win the contest, though. He came in second. At the end of two minutes, he had eleven mines, and the winner had twelve. All the people who had watched the race clapped and cheered, and the four sea lions who had raced got up on their hindquarters and barked. The people cheered even more then, and Lieutenant Dial and Melanie did too. But Lieutenant Dial didn't clap because he had one hand on the handle of my duty harness.

Both Lieutenant Dial and Melanie were happy. So I should have been happy too.

But I wasn't. Something was wrong.

I didn't know what it was at first, so I lifted my head high and sniffed the air. There were many smells. There was sweat, soda, and popcorn. There were buckets of little fish. The sea lions smelled salty. Melanie still smelled like flowers. The other K-9s smelled thirsty. The practice mines smelled like wet Frisbees.

Except there was another smell with the Frisbee smell. It wasn't big. But it was there. It was a bad smell. It was a bad smell like the real mines that had been in the practice mine-field during the hardest part of training. It was a bad smell like the real mine that had killed another K-9 who wasn't careful enough.

And as soon as I had identified that bad smell, I knew

where it was coming from. The final mine that the winning sea lion had brought up wasn't like the others. It looked like them, but it didn't smell like them. It was different. It was bad.

It wanted to explode and kill someone.

But none of the sea lions were doing anything about it. They were still on their hindquarters, swaying back and forth, while the people clapped. One of the dolphins was splashing and chattering out in the water, so I think she might have known. But none of the handlers paid any attention to her. They were smiling at the clapping people.

I was under no specific orders. But Lieutenant Dial had given me one General Order many training sessions ago: If I ever knew something was wrong, I had to act.

So I bolted for the pier, and Lieutenant Dial released my harness handle. I knew his thoughts, and he knew mine. He knew I was being good.

I ran fast between people's legs. Some of them yelled. And then I was on the pier. It moved up and down a little, but I kept on running fast even though it tried to make me fall. Two of the people in white stepped into my path, but I zigzagged around them. The pier was wet there, and my feet slipped. But I scrabbled hard like I did at the wall and kept going.

One of the sea lions came down from his haunches as I approached, and he opened his mouth as if to bite me. It was a big mouth with big teeth. The whole sea lion was as big as five of me, and he lunged at me when I came close. So I jumped over his head and kicked the back of his neck with my hind feet. That pushed me the last three meters to the end of the pier.

My front feet hit the pier right beside the bad mine, so I grabbed its handle with my teeth, whipped it forward, and let go so it flew into the water. Two of the dolphins swam away fast as the mine splashed and sank.

Then I couldn't smell the bad mine anymore, so I was glad. But when I turned around and saw the white-clothed people and their sea lions, none of them seemed glad. The people were shouting and the sea lions were barking. The sea lions' barks still didn't make sense.

I saw Lieutenant Dial running down the pier toward me, so I started running toward him too. And just as I began to zigzag around the sea lions, I heard a rumble and a splash, and the pier rose up under me. I fell, and the pier hit my jaw and made me bite my tongue. Then the pier bounced up and down, and I couldn't stand up because my feet kept slipping. One of the people in white had fallen down beside me, and he kept slipping too. That made me worry about Lieutenant Dial, so I looked up to see if he was all right. But a sea lion was in the way.

Then I yelped. Later, a news reporter would say that I yelped because my tongue was hurt. But that wasn't the reason. It was because I couldn't see or hear Lieutenant Dial, and I couldn't find his thoughts. There were too many people thinking and yelling all at once. I couldn't even smell him because I was too close to the sea lions.

That was a bad moment. But the pier moved a little less each time it bounced, and finally I could stand up. And then I could see Lieutenant Dial. He was in the middle of the pier helping another person stand up, so I ran to him and stood at attention. When he had finished helping the other person, he looked down at me and saluted. And he told me I was good. He told me I was more good than I had ever been before.

And the bad moment was gone.

Later, investigators said that a real enemy had replaced one of the sea lions' dummy mines with a live one, intending to hurt or kill as many people and animals as possible. But because I threw it back into the water, only one dolphin was hurt. And no one was killed.

A few weeks later, Lieutenant Dial was promoted to Captain, and I was promoted to Sergeant. Captain Dial received silver bars for his uniform, and then he leaned over and showed me a new metal tag before clipping it to the ring in my collar. It was shaped like the insignia for Sergeant First Class. I knew I couldn't wear it on combat duty, because it would get in the way and make noise. But it was still a fine thing, because that was how it looked in Captain Dial's thoughts.

Other soldiers were promoted during that ceremony as

well, but I was the only K-9. Also, Captain Dial and I were commended for finding the live mine. We were called heroes.

Melanie was there for the ceremony, and both she and Captain Dial were proud and happy. So I was proud and happy too.

But I still wasn't as happy as I had been on the pier. That was where I had been more good than I had ever been before. Captain Dial had said so.

That was how I knew it was true.

Soon after our promotions, Captain Dial and I left the fort with many other soldiers, and we all went to the war. Melanie came to the fort to say good-bye to us.

She and Captain Dial hugged each other for a long time while I stood at ease. Most of the other soldiers were hugging people too. There were wives and children, and even a few dogs who weren't soldiers.

Then Melanie knelt down and put her head against mine. It surprised me. She had never done anything like that before. I think she was trying to help me understand her thoughts the way I understood Captain Dial's. It helped a little. But even if she hadn't done it, I would have known she was telling me the same thing she had told me every morning before training. She was telling me to take care of Captain Dial.

So I kissed her face. I wanted her to be glad that Captain Dial and I were going to the war together. Her face tasted like ocean water.

Then Melanie took her head away from mine and put her arms around Captain Dial again. After a while, Captain Dial pulled away from her and gave me the signal to proceed. We left Melanie and went to the D Company bus.

When all the soldiers of D Company had boarded the bus, it took us to the air transport. Captain Dial was quiet during the bus ride. He just looked out the window. And for the first time, his thoughts weren't clear to me. It was as if they were far away in a fog, and a fuzzy sound ran through them. I glimpsed Melanie, but that was all. Captain Dial kept his hand on my neck, though, and every now and then his fingers rubbed behind my ears. So I didn't worry. Captain Dial always had some thoughts that I couldn't understand anyway. The only ones I really needed to know were the ones that were orders.

The air transport took a long time, and it was loud. I didn't like it. By the time it stopped at an island to refuel, all my muscles were sore. But I felt better after marking some trees near the airstrip, and better still after some food. We got back on the transport then, and Captain Dial gave me a pill to help me sleep through the rest of the flight. It helped a lot. But I was still glad when we were on the ground again. When we finally left the transport we were in a place that was dry and sunny, and all of the smells were sharp.

The soldiers of D Company spent one night in a tin-roofed barracks at the combat zone airfield, and Captain Dial and I slept there with them. There was no kennel or cushion for me, so I slept on a blanket beside Captain Dial's cot. I was the only K-9 in the company, and some of the other soldiers were nervous around me. But Captain Dial made sure that I met each one and learned that soldier's smell. Captain Dial wanted to keep them all safe. So I wanted to keep them safe too.

I could see some soldiers' thoughts, although none of them were as clear to me as Captain Dial's. But that was all right, because the soldiers' voices and smells told me all I needed to know about them. Most of them were friendly, although several stayed nervous even after they met me. And a few smelled frightened or angry.

One of the angry ones was an officer, Lieutenant Morris, who was in charge of First Platoon. I couldn't see his thoughts at all, but I still knew he didn't like me. I knew he didn't like Captain Dial, either. When he stood before us, his sweat smelled bitter, and his voice was low. And even when he saluted, his muscles were tense as if he were about to run or fight.

Captain Dial was aware of all this, because he knew my thoughts. But unlike me, he was able to think of a reason for Lieutenant Morris's attitude. He thought Lieutenant Morris believed he should have been promoted to Captain and given command of D Company.

This troubled Captain Dial, because he had never wanted to lead a company of regular soldiers anyway. But I was the only one who knew it. What he really wanted to do was serve in a K-9 unit. But when we were promoted, he was ordered to command D Company because its original captain had died in training. So he requested that I be allowed to join the company with him, and we were both happy when his request was granted. We joined D Company on the same day we went to the war. And I knew that all of the soldiers in D Company were lucky to have Captain Dial as their leader.

The morning after our arrival in the combat zone, D Company was assigned to guard four checkpoints on highways that led to the airfield. So Captain Dial put a platoon at each checkpoint, splitting the soldiers among three separate road barriers per checkpoint. He told the lieutenants and sergeants to stop and inspect each vehicle at each barrier, and to detain the occupants of any vehicle found to contain contraband. He also told them to have their soldiers fire warning shots over any vehicles that passed the first barrier without stopping for inspection. They were to aim at the tires and engines of any vehicles that also passed the second barrier without stopping. And any vehicles that passed the third barrier without stopping were to be destroyed. But any vehicles that stopped at all three barriers and were found to contain no contraband were to be allowed to proceed unless the soldiers had reason to believe that a more thorough inspection was needed. In that case, the suspicious vehicle was to be reported to Captain Dial so he could bring me to it and I could smell whether anything was wrong.

I thought these orders were easy and clear.

Captain Dial and I spent our first five days in the combat zone riding from checkpoint to checkpoint in a utility vehicle, inspecting cars and trucks and seeing to the needs of D Company. I liked doing the inspections. In those first days, I found three pistols, four rifles, a rocket-propelled grenade launcher, and a brick of hashish. Captain Dial arrested the people with the guns and sent them to Headquarters. But he laughed at the man with the hashish and let him drive away. Hashish wasn't contraband here, he told me, so long as no one gave any to our soldiers. This was a new rule to me, but I'm good at learning new rules.

The first five days were fun. All of our platoons did their jobs, and so did Captain Dial and I.

Then, on the morning of the sixth day, Lieutenant Morris ordered First Platoon to open fire on a van that had gone past the first barrier without stopping. It didn't reach the second barrier. By the time Lieutenant Morris ordered his soldiers to cease fire, all seven people inside the van had been killed.

Captain Dial and I weren't there when it happened. We were two checkpoints away. By the time we arrived, the incident had been over for fifteen minutes. Lieutenant Morris and a few other soldiers had dragged three of the bodies from the shot-up van and laid them by the side of the road. They were heading back toward the van when Captain Dial stopped our utility vehicle in front of them and ordered them to stay away from the van and the bodies.

Then he ordered me to search the van, and I obeyed. It was a bad place. It smelled of spent machine-gun rounds, explosive residue, and human blood.

The driver was still in her seat. She had been a woman about the size of Melanie. The three other bodies still in the van had been small children. There were two boys and a girl. I had seen children of their sizes on the day by the ocean. But the ones in the van had been shot through and through. Their blood was all over the floor and seats, and I had to step in it to conduct my search.

There was no contraband. There were no guns, and the only bullets were spent rounds. And I couldn't smell any explosives except the residue of a grenade that had been fired into the van by someone in First Platoon.

After I had searched the van, Captain Dial ordered me to search the three bodies on the ground. So I did. They were all girls. Two were even smaller than the children in the van. The third was larger, about the size of the girl who writes these words. But she wasn't fully grown. All of them had been shot many times. One of the younger girls had most of her face gone. The older girl had a narrow cut on her neck. None of them possessed any contraband.

Captain Dial was angrier than he had ever been before. The smoke in his head was thick and turbulent. And there were sounds. I could hear Melanie crying. I could hear a hundred Melanies crying.

Then Captain Dial began shouting at Lieutenant Morris. I had never heard him shout like that before, and it made me cringe even though he wasn't shouting at me. All the soldiers of First Platoon cringed, too, especially when Captain Dial said he would bring Lieutenant Morris up on charges for disobeying orders.

But Lieutenant Morris's bitter smell was acrid and strong now, and he stood with his head thrust forward and his arms straight down at his sides. He didn't salute. It was as if he was challenging Captain Dial. It was as if he thought he had done a good thing, and that Captain Dial's orders had been wrong.

That made me angry, because Captain Dial always gave good orders. So I took a step toward Lieutenant Morris and growled.

Lieutenant Morris reached for his sidearm, but Captain Dial slapped his hand away from it. Then Lieutenant Morris made a fist and started to swing it at Captain Dial's face. I was on him before his fist was halfway there, and I put him on his back on the highway.

I stood with my front paws on Lieutenant Morris's chest and my teeth touching his throat, and Captain Dial ordered him to remain still. This time, Lieutenant Morris obeyed. I could feel the pulse in his neck and the shallow motion of his chest as he breathed, but those were the only movements he made until Captain Dial ordered me to stand down. Then I took my paws from Lieutenant Morris's chest and backed away.

But now I smelled something wrong in a pocket of Lieutenant Morris's fatigues. It smelled like the girl with the cut on her neck. It smelled like her blood.

I pointed at Lieutenant Morris's pocket and barked. So

Captain Dial knelt down, opened the pocket, and brought out a slender chain with a shiny rock on it. It wasn't just like the one he had given Melanie, but it didn't look much different. Except that this one had blood on its chain.

The clasp on the chain was closed, but the chain had been broken in another place. The rock slid down against the clasp when Captain Dial pulled the chain from Lieutenant Morris's pocket, and it dangled there as he held it up. It caught the sun so that it seemed to have a light inside it.

Captain Dial remained on one knee, looking at the necklace, for a long time. Lieutenant Morris started to speak, but I growled and he shut up. I was doing him a favor, because one of Captain Dial's thoughts was clear. He was thinking of using his sidearm to shoot Lieutenant Morris in the head. He was thinking that if Lieutenant Morris said even one word, that was what he would do.

What happened instead was that Captain Dial stood up and told a First Platoon sergeant to call for military police. Then he returned to our utility vehicle, leaving Lieutenant Morris on his back on the highway. I went with Captain Dial, and we waited in our vehicle until the military police came. When they did, Captain Dial gave the rock and chain to one of them.

I didn't understand everything that happened after that. But Lieutenant Morris was back with D Company just two days after he ordered First Platoon to attack the van. And Captain Dial was unhappy because he didn't think there would ever be a court-martial. For one thing, none of the soldiers of First Platoon were sure about what had happened. Some of them even thought that the van had been loaded with explosives, and they continued to think so even after Captain Dial told them I hadn't smelled any. Also, Lieutenant Morris said that he had found the girl's necklace on the ground. And there were no soldiers who would say that he hadn't. Except me. I hadn't smelled any dirt or asphalt on it. All I had smelled was skin and blood from the girl's neck plus sweat from Lieutenant Morris's hand. But the only officer who could hear my testimony was Captain Dial. And unless there was a court-martial, he had already done all he could do.

Besides, the military police said they lost the necklace.

Captain Dial was sad from then on. I don't think anyone else in the company knew that. But I did.

I wanted to make Captain Dial happy again, so I tried even harder to be good. And he told me I was. He told me I was the best sergeant he had ever seen.

But he was still sad. So I was sad too.

Two weeks later, D Company was assigned to a combat mission. A few hours before dawn on a Friday morning, thirty enemy guerrillas had attacked our supply depot using mortars and small arms—and although they had been repelled, four of our soldiers had been killed. So the guerrillas had to be followed and destroyed, and D Company was chosen to do it. Captain Dial thought it was strange that an entire company was being sent after only thirty enemies, but he followed the order without hesitation.

D Company was in pursuit of the guerrillas within an hour of the attack. The guerrillas had a big head start, but they were on foot, and D Company had armored personnel carriers, utility vehicles, and me. So we were able to move fast over both roads and fields, and every few minutes Captain Dial had me run ahead and correct the direction of our pursuit. The guerrillas were staying in one group, so their trail was easy to smell.

We had almost caught up to them as they reached the hills fifteen kilometers west of our airfield. We were so close that Captain Dial could see them through his night-vision field glasses. They were making their way up a narrow, ascending valley, and they were still in one group.

This troubled Captain Dial. It seemed to him that once the guerrillas had reached the hills, they should have scattered to make our pursuit more difficult. But they were staying together. So Captain Dial used his radio to consult with Headquarters, and Headquarters said a refugee camp of about three hundred souls lay a short distance up the valley, a few hundred meters beyond a natural curve. The guerrillas probably intended to stay together long enough to reach that camp—and then they would disperse and blend in with the civilians. This would force Captain Dial to either let them escape, or arrest the entire camp.

So we had to stop the guerrillas before they reached the refugee camp. Captain Dial increased our speed, then dropped off two squads from Fourth Platoon with ten mortars as soon as we were in range. His plan was for those squads to fire the mortars just beyond the guerrillas, forcing them to turn away from the refugee camp . . . and perhaps also to run back into our pursuit.

As the rest of D Company started up the valley, the mortar squads put a dozen rounds where Captain Dial had ordered. But instead of reversing direction, the guerrillas began to ascend a hill on the south side of the valley. They remained in one group, though, and we gained on them. When we were close enough that we might be hit by stray mortar rounds, Captain Dial radioed the squads and told them to hold fire. But they were to stay put to intercept any enemies that might be flushed back toward them.

We rushed toward the base of the hill the guerrillas were climbing. They were moving much more slowly now, and in the light of dawn it was clear that we would overtake them before they reached the crest of the hill. I became excited as I thought of knocking them down and holding them, one by one, until my fellow soldiers could take them prisoner. And as the utility vehicle that carried me, Captain Dial, and Staff Sergeant Owens began to climb the hill, I readied myself to leap out and attack.

Our vehicle was in the lead, so most of the company was still on the valley floor as we started up the hill. It was at that moment that rocket-propelled grenades and mortar shells began raining down around us from the opposite hillside to the north. And then the guerrillas we were chasing took up positions and began to fire down on us with small arms.

Captain Dial radioed orders to our platoon leaders to take cover and return fire. Then he had Staff Sergeant Owens turn our utility vehicle broadside to the enemy fire, and the three of us exited on the downhill side. We crawled downhill as fast as we could until we reached one of D Company's APCs, and we took cover behind it with soldiers from First and Second Platoons. The soldiers were jumping up and leaning out to fire quick bursts from their rifles, and Captain Dial shouted for them to keep it up as he got on the radio again to call Headquarters for air support. Our helicopters and drones were always out on missions, but two or three could be diverted if soldiers were in trouble. And we were in trouble.

But now Captain Dial couldn't raise Headquarters on the radio. He tried every possible frequency, and there was nothing but silence.

Lieutenant Morris crawled to us and told Captain Dial that we were all going to be killed, and that it was Captain Dial's fault. I wanted to bite Lieutenant Morris's throat then. But Captain Dial ignored him, so I tried to ignore him too. He wasn't a good soldier. He didn't belong in D Company.

There was a loud explosion up the hill, and a soldier told Captain Dial that our abandoned utility vehicle had been hit by a rocket from the other side of the valley. They were zeroing in on us. So Captain Dial said we couldn't stay behind the armored personnel carrier, because it would be targeted next. He ordered First and Second Platoons to retreat to the valley floor, and then he got on the radio and told the mortar squads from Fourth Platoon to fire on the northern hillside. Finally he called to Third Platoon and the remaining two squads of Fourth Platoon, who were all still at the base of the hill, and told them to abandon their APCs and move up the valley on foot, doubletime. All platoons were to return fire as best they could. No one was to retreat back toward the plain.

As Captain Dial and I moved downhill with First and Second Platoons, Lieutenant Morris shouted that Captain Dial's orders were insane. The soldiers in APCs should stay in them, he said. Without armor, he said, they would be picked off in the valley like cattle in a chute.

But Captain Dial knew that the armor was what the enemy would try to destroy first, unless it was moving fast. And it couldn't move fast in the terrain we were in. So getting the soldiers away from it was the only thing to do. And sure enough, before we reached the bottom of the hill, the APC we had been using for cover was hit by a rocket and destroyed.

Our mortars began hitting the northern hill as Captain Dial and I reached the base of the southern hill, and Captain Dial stood his ground there while urging the soldiers of First and Second Platoons to run past our abandoned APCs and continue up the valley. And even now, Lieutenant Morris kept telling him he was wrong, and that D Company ought to be heading back to the plain in full retreat.

But I knew Captain Dial's thoughts, and I knew he was right. Headquarters had been tricked into having D Company follow the guerrillas into an ambush—but Captain Dial wouldn't let the guerrillas trick him any further. He knew that once the ambush began, the enemy would expect D Company to retreat toward the plain. So there would be another trap waiting at the mouth of the valley. The enemy would close us in, then fire down upon us until we were annihilated.

So Captain Dial would confound their expectations. D Company would continue up the valley, on foot, until we could reach an elevated position. With our mortar squads out on the plain providing harassing fire, we could be well up the valley before the guerrillas could leave their hillsides. And then we would transform the enemy's ambush into an attack of our own.

But we would have to take up our battle position before reaching the refugee camp. So we would doubletime around the curve to get out of sight of the enemy, then run up the hill on the backside of the curve. The guerrillas would have no clear shot from their current positions—and if they followed us, we would be able to pour fire down on them as they rounded the curve. So even without air support, we could prevail.

Captain Dial's plan was good, and as D Company rushed up the valley, it began to work. Two more of our abandoned vehicles were hit and began to burn, but despite the constant fire from the enemy, we had not yet lost a single soldier. Our mortar squads were hitting the hillsides as ordered, and the guerrillas' weapons fire became erratic. Captain Dial paused every few meters to shout orders and encouragement to his running soldiers, and once he sent me back to nip at the heels of a few stragglers. But the stragglers weren't stragglers for long, and I was able to rejoin Captain Dial in less than a minute. Then, bringing up the rear, he and I rounded the curve and began running up the slope to take our positions with the rest of our soldiers. They were already following Captain Dial's orders, taking cover behind rocks and in gullies. And they were readying their weapons.

Some of the guerrillas had chased after us, and a few of them came around the curve before Captain Dial and I were far enough up the slope to take our positions. But we hit the dirt so our soldiers could fire on them, and only two of these enemies survived long enough to come within twenty meters of me and Captain Dial. So I turned, charged, and bit their throats. Then I returned to Captain Dial, and we joined several of our soldiers behind a jumble of rocks and dirt.

More guerrillas came around the curve, and D Company shot them. Then some came up the slope in a truck, and one of our soldiers destroyed it with a rocket-propelled grenade. We were winning the battle despite being ambushed.

Then strange things happened.

They didn't seem strange at first. At first, I heard the buzz of airborne drones. Captain Dial couldn't hear them yet, but he knew that I could, and he was glad. It seemed that Headquarters had heard his request after all.

But almost as soon as I heard the drones, I also heard distant explosions, and our mortar squads stopped firing. So Captain Dial radioed them for a status report. But there was no reply. Then he tried again to contact Headquarters, but there was still no reply there either.

The buzz became loud, and two drones appeared around the curve of the valley, flying low. They were narrow-winged and sleek, and almost invisible against the sky. They didn't have any insignia on their wings.

Then they fired rockets at us. They fired rockets at D Company. And at least twenty soldiers died as the rockets exploded. Dirt and rocks pelted me and Captain Dial where we crouched. My ears hurt.

The drones rose up over the opposite hill, then turned back toward us. Captain Dial shouted into his radio, trying one frequency after another, doing his best to raise Headquarters, to raise the remote drone pilots, to raise anyone who should have been listening. He shouted to his lieutenants to try their own radios too. And they did. But no one received a reply.

The drones came swooping toward us, and it became clear that their first attack hadn't been a mistake. Captain Dial's thoughts were tangled as he realized this. The enemy had no such weapons. So he couldn't understand why the drones were attacking us. Their cameras should have seen who we were, and their pilots should have known that D Company wasn't the enemy.

But even in his confusion, Captain Dial was a good leader. He ordered Sergeant Owens to fire a flare to identify us, but he didn't wait to see whether the cameras had seen it and understood its meaning. Instead, he shouted for D Company's surviving lieutenants and sergeants to get their soldiers up and moving again. If the drones were returning to attack our position again, he was going to put us somewhere else.

The soldiers of D Company were already running down the slope when the drones launched their second wave of rockets, so most of them made it to the valley floor. But eight more were killed. Captain Dial and I were bringing up the rear again, and the rocket that killed the eight exploded in front of us just as another exploded behind us. Captain Dial dove to the ground, putting his arms around me and pushing me down. Then he covered me with his body as more rockets exploded on the slope above us.

I didn't like it. Captain Dial wasn't supposed to shield me from harm. I was supposed to do that for him. So I tried to reverse our positions, but Captain Dial ordered me to stay put. Of course I had to obey. But I didn't understand. Captain Dial was more important to D Company than I was.

The rockets stopped exploding, and the drones passed over us again. They were so close that the dirt under my jaw hummed. Then Captain Dial was on his feet again, shouting orders as the drones flew behind the hilltop. The surviving soldiers of D Company were to run like hell up the valley and to take whatever cover they could find—rocks, trees, ditches, anything—if the drones made another pass. But the soldiers were to avoid entering the refugee camp, wherever it was, at all costs. If they came upon it while still on the run, they were to find a way around it.

Captain Dial was smart. But even Captain Dial could only make his choices based on what he knew. And he didn't know that the refugees weren't gathered in a single camp, as Headquarters had said. He didn't know that they were scattered in small clusters throughout the rest of the valley.

And he didn't know that the drones would return so soon, or that they would swoop up and down the valley firing their Gatling guns at anything that moved. The valley was full of sunlight now, so the pilots should have been able to see our soldiers' uniforms. There was nothing to block the view of the cameras. But the drones kept firing on us.

I wished I could jump high enough to tear them out of the sky.

As D Company's lieutenants and sergeants began shouting and radioing Captain Dial, telling him that they were losing more soldiers and that every scrap of cover was occupied by noncombatants, Captain Dial made a decision he didn't want to make. He tried one more time to contact Headquarters—and when that failed, he ordered D Company to return fire. Then he took a rifle from a fallen corporal and fired the first shots at the lead drone as it swooped toward us again.

I couldn't fire a weapon, so I did the only thing I could do to help. I ran in a zigzag pattern toward the drones in an attempt to draw their fire and give the rest of D Company a better chance to make their shots count. And I could hear Captain Dial shouting that I was good.

That made me glad.

The lead drone turned toward me, and in that instant the soldiers of D Company were able to hit it broadside with small-arms fire and at least one RPG. The drone began spewing smoke, and then it turned and almost collided with the second drone. The second drone pulled up and vanished behind a hill just as the first one began to spiral downward.

I returned to Captain Dial, who ordered me and the soldiers who were closest to follow him. We ran up a hillside and dove into a gully that cut across it. There were six of us: Captain Dial, Lieutenant Morris, Sergeant Owens, two specialists, and me. And in the gully we found five civilians: An old man, a woman, an adolescent girl, and two young boys. They scrambled away from us as we tumbled into the gully, and they seemed about to climb out until Captain Dial spoke to them in their language. I think he told them they would be safer if they stayed put.

He had no sooner gotten the words out than the ground shook with the biggest explosion yet. I smelled burning fuel, and I knew the drone had crashed. Captain Dial shouted for everyone to hit the dirt, but I was the only one in the gully who heard him. There was a roaring noise and more explosions. The drone's remaining weapons were detonating.

One of the boys tried to climb out of the gully. The woman jumped up to stop him, and something from the exploding drone hit her in the face. She fell back into the gully. So Captain Dial tried to get to the panicked boy to pull him down. But Lieutenant Morris clutched Captain Dial's leg and stopped him.

Captain Dial made a gesture, and I followed the order. I leaped over him and Lieutenant Morris, and I grabbed the boy's ankle and pulled him down. My teeth broke his skin, but it couldn't be helped. When the boy fell to the dirt beside the woman, I pressed my chest against his to hold him there.

The girl started to move as if to protect the boy from me, but then she looked at my eyes. And for that moment, she knew my thoughts. So she crawled to the woman instead and wiped blood from her face.

The woman wasn't breathing, and I knew she was dead. The girl knew it too, but she tried to make the woman breathe again anyway.

There were a few more explosions from the fallen drone, and then the only noise from it was a muted roar as it burned.

So I listened for the other drone, and I heard it flying farther and farther away.

Captain Dial told me I could let the boy up, so I did. He tried to run away again, but this time the girl stopped him. He was crying, and so was the girl. So was the other boy. The girl looked at me again, and I knew then that the dead woman was their mother and the old man was their grandfather. The old man was sitting against the wall of the gully with his knees pulled up to his face and his eyes closed tight.

I looked at Captain Dial then and saw that he was hurt. His left sleeve was turning dark at the shoulder, just below the edge of his flak jacket. But I could hardly smell his blood among all the other bloody smells. I went to him and whined, and he touched my head and told me he was all right. I wanted to go find a medic for him, but he ordered me to stay.

Then he used his radio to ask the rest of D Company for a status report, but he couldn't hear the replies because Lieutenant Morris began shouting. I couldn't understand all of the words, but I understood that Lieutenant Morris blamed Captain Dial for what had happened. He accused Captain Dial of treason for shooting down one of our own aircraft. And he said that the civilians weren't refugees at all, but guerrillas like those we had been pursuing. He said that was why the drones had attacked. And he said it was Captain Dial's fault that D Company had been in the line of fire when that happened.

Nothing Lieutenant Morris was shouting made any sense. But nothing that had happened to us had made any sense either. I knew that much from Captain Dial's thoughts. He didn't understand why things had happened the way they had happened. He slumped with his back against the wall of the gully, and he wondered whether Melanie would still love him after this.

Lieutenant Morris turned to Sergeant Owens and the two specialists, and he announced that Captain Dial was incapacitated. So he was now ranking officer, he said, and he ordered them to turn their weapons toward the old man, the girl, and the boys. If any of them moved, he said, the soldiers were to shoot them all.

Sergeant Owens and the specialists did as they were told. Then Lieutenant Morris reached for the radio in Captain Dial's right hand, but I jumped in his way and snarled at him. So Lieutenant Morris unholstered his sidearm and pointed it at me.

But before he could fire, Captain Dial spoke. He ordered Lieutenant Morris to lower his weapon, and after some hesitation, Lieutenant Morris obeyed. Then Captain Dial ordered Sergeant Owens and the specialists to lower their weapons as well, and they obeyed too.

Captain Dial was strong again. His shoulder was bleeding, but his thoughts were clear. He stood up, pushing himself off the gully wall with his right forearm, and peered over the rim at the burning drone. He spoke into his radio and told his soldiers to stay put if they were in a safe place, and to keep trying to find one if they weren't. He would assess the situation and issue new orders within the next few minutes.

But we didn't have a few minutes. I could hear the second drone returning.

I barked to let Captain Dial know it was coming. So then he shouted into his radio and ordered all of his soldiers to remain still and refrain from returning fire unless directly fired upon. Then he ordered those of us in the gully to hit the dirt. The girl and the two boys didn't understand at first, but the old man put his hands on their shoulders and made them lie down close to their dead mother.

Then Captain Dial lowered himself to a sitting position with his back against the gully wall. He couldn't lie down flat with his wounded shoulder. I lay down next to him and put my chin on his knee, and we waited while the drone flew back and forth. Its Gatling gun chattered three or four times, and I hoped it was shooting enemy guerrillas and not D Company soldiers or civilians.

One of the little boys began to cry, but the girl and the old man whispered to him, and then he was quiet again. I was glad they could calm him like that. They were being good leaders. Like Captain Dial.

But a good leader needs good soldiers.

On the drone's fourth pass, Lieutenant Morris stood and fired his weapon into the air. I was on him fast, my front paws hitting his back and pushing him down, but it was too late. Even as I pinned Lieutenant Morris to the bottom of the gully, I could hear the drone turning and the barrels of its Gatling guns beginning to spin.

Lieutenant Morris shouted into the dirt that we had to show ourselves to the drone so it would know who we were and so it could help us kill the rest of the enemy. He worked a hand free from under his chest and pointed at the family with the dead mother.

I wanted to bite Lieutenant Morris and bite him hard. And I smelled something in one of his pockets that made me feel that way even more. It smelled like the dead girl at the highway checkpoint.

But I didn't bite him, because I knew Captain Dial wouldn't like it. Captain Dial was busy with his radio, telling the rest of D Company that they were not to give away their positions by firing on the drone if it attacked those of us in the gully—not unless there was a clear shot for an RPG. Otherwise, we were on our own. But D Company would survive.

I heard the drone dip low. It was flying on a path directly in line with our gully. It would be able to pour bullets and rockets on us with ease.

Captain Dial was on his feet. It was as if he had been yanked up on a rope from the sky. His left sleeve was so wet that it dripped.

He shouted two orders. First, Sergeant Owens and the two specialists were to get out of the gully at the south rim and run through the smoke of the downed aircraft until they could find other cover in the valley. Second, I was to take the civilians over the north rim and head up into the hills until I could find another gully, a cave, or some other sheltered position. I was to keep them safe.

Sergeant Owens and the specialists clambered over the south rim, rolled, and ran into the smoke. I jumped off Lieutenant Morris and started toward the civilians. But after a few steps, I stopped. The drone's Gatling guns had begun to fire.

I looked back and saw Captain Dial pull Lieutenant Morris to his feet. Captain Dial could only use his right arm, so he had dropped his radio. Lieutenant Morris seemed dazed, and Captain Dial had to hold him up and drag him.

Captain Dial shouted for me to obey my order. I was not to wait for him and Lieutenant Morris. They would catch up, he said.

But I knew Captain Dial's thoughts. I knew he didn't think that he and Lieutenant Morris would make it.

So for the first time ever, I decided to disobey a direct order. I would obey my General Order instead. That was what I had done on the day beside the ocean, and Captain Dial had told me I was good. He had told me I was more good than I had ever been before. So I would do that again.

I ran back to Captain Dial, and he yelled at me. He said I had to obey his order immediately.

But instead I grabbed one of Lieutenant Morris's flak-jacket straps, and I pulled him away from Captain Dial and began dragging him up the gully wall. He was heavy, but I'm strong.

Captain Dial knew then that he should take charge of the civilians. Dragging soldiers to safety was one of my jobs, and keeping civilians safe was one of his. But first, he jumped to me and hooked Lieutenant Morris's arm through my harness loop. Then he pulled the strap to tighten the loop. Now I could let go of the flak-jacket strap and drag Lieutenant Morris a lot faster.

Captain Dial touched my head and told me to go.

I went up the gully wall and over the top with Lieutenant Morris while Captain Dial ran to the civilians and told them that they must go with him. One of the boys cried because he wanted to stay with his mother, but the old man and the girl listened to Captain Dial and wouldn't let the boy stay. They all climbed up from the gully.

Captain Dial's foot slipped on the way up and he almost fell, but the girl grabbed his arm to steady him. It was his wounded arm, but she couldn't reach the other one. I saw a flash like a grenade exploding in Captain Dial's thoughts. But Captain Dial didn't cry out even though it hurt a lot. He was a good soldier. The girl was, too. She didn't hesitate to help Captain Dial. She didn't flinch from his blood.

When we were all out of the gully, we ran north through the smoke. Captain Dial and the civilians were a few meters west of me and Lieutenant Morris, and they were moving up the slope a little faster. Every few steps, Captain Dial would look back and call encouragement to me. And I would pull harder and could feel Lieutenant Morris's boots bouncing on the ground behind us.

I didn't look back, but I heard the buzz of the drone as it flew low over the gully we had just left. I could smell its exhaust. Its Gatling guns chattered, and the slugs made dull thumps in the dirt.

And then, as we ran higher and came up out of the smoke, I heard the drone swoop out over the valley, turn, and head right for us. It was attacking us from behind, and there was no place for us to take cover when its guns started firing again. I looked ahead and saw a shadow on the ground that looked like another gully, but it was too far away. Lieutenant Morris and I wouldn't reach it before the drone strafed us.

I looked over at Captain Dial. Although he was wounded, he was now carrying one of the boys. The girl was carrying the other one. The old man was breathing hard and stumbling. So they were losing speed, and Lieutenant Morris and I had almost caught up to them. They wouldn't reach the next gully either. The drone would be able to hit all of us with the same burst of gunfire, or with just one rocket.

Captain Dial looked over at me as I looked at him, and we each knew the other's thoughts. There was only one thing to do. And when his thoughts said *Now,* I followed his order.

He and the civilians cut left, where there was still a little smoke, and I cut right, where the air was clear. We ran away from each other as fast as we could. I could hear Captain Dial's breath getting farther and farther away behind me. I could hear it even over the noise from Lieutenant Morris's boots.

I would have dropped Lieutenant Morris if I could, because he would have been safer lying still. But I couldn't. The loop on my harness was pulled tight around his arm, and there was no time for me to turn my head to yank it loose.

The drone came after me and Lieutenant Morris. I was sorry for what that meant for Lieutenant Morris, but glad because it gave Captain Dial a better chance to get himself and the civilians to cover. And I was glad because it gave me a chance to be good.

I ran hard, and I zigzagged as much as I could while dragging Lieutenant Morris. The engine buzz became a roar, and the Gatling gun chattered loud and long. And it almost missed us. But the last slugs in the burst came ripping through the dirt right behind us, and Lieutenant Morris jerked as they reached him. I was slapped down at my hindquarters, and I fell. Lieutenant Morris and I rolled a little way down the hill, and the drone flew over us so low that I could see the rivets in its belly. It rose up over the ridge, hung there for a moment, and then started toward us again.

But this time it bloomed fire from its tail, and it twisted sideways and dove into the hillside above us. There was a loud noise and more fire when it hit, and smoke like there had been from the first one.

I tried to get up, but Lieutenant Morris was lying on my hind legs. And my back hurt, close to my tail. But I couldn't see or hear Captain Dial, and I had to find him. So I twisted my head around far enough to tug on my harness loop until Lieutenant Morris's arm slipped out. I couldn't hear Lieutenant Morris's breath or heartbeat, and I could smell that he had blood coming out of his legs, back, chest, and neck. He was dead, and there was no place I could drag him where he would be all right again.

When his arm came free, I was able to scramble with my front legs and pull myself out from under him. And then I was able to stand up all the way even though my back hurt. I looked for Captain Dial and the civilians, but I couldn't see them. There was a lot more smoke now, and it made my eyes itch. It also made it hard to smell anything else. But I heard the girl say something, faint and soft, so I left Lieutenant Morris and followed her voice.

I found her with the other civilians and Captain Dial. Captain Dial was lying on the ground, and the girl was kneeling beside him with her hand on his head. The old man was standing nearby holding the little boys' hands. The boys were scared. They were looking at the body of a D Company soldier lying nearby. It was torn in two.

Captain Dial smiled when I came up to him and licked his face. I had to step over an RPG launcher to reach him, and when I touched him I knew what he had done. He had found the RPG launcher with the dead soldier, and he had used it to bring down the second drone. But it had recoiled against his wounded shoulder, and now the wound was bleeding even more.

He saw my thoughts and knew what had happened to Lieutenant Morris. But he said I had done everything right. He said he was proud of me. He said I was good.

And just as he said that, I heard a buzzing noise far off in the south. It was heading toward us fast. More drones were coming.

Captain Dial couldn't hear them. But he knew I did. And he said that they might not be coming to attack us, because their pilots might have realized that the first two had been firing on allies and civilians. But we couldn't count on it. So I was to take the four civilians away and find shelter for them. I was to do so immediately.

I didn't understand at first, because the picture I saw in Captain Dial's thoughts was a picture only of me and the civilians. He wasn't in it. He wasn't walking with us, and I wasn't dragging him with my harness.

And then he made me understand. He was too dizzy to walk, and I couldn't drag him without making his wound worse.

I wanted to follow his orders, but first I wanted to go back down the hill and find a D Company medic to take care of him. But Captain Dial said there was no time for that. Not if I was going to take the civilians to safety before the new drones arrived. And I knew he was right, because the girl could hear the drones now too. She still had her hand on Captain Dial's head, but she was looking at the sky.

I whined. I didn't want to go off with the civilians and leave Captain Dial all alone, even for a little while.

Captain Dial reached up with his right hand to touch my head. He told me it was all right to leave him for now, because I could come back as soon as I had taken the civilians to a safe place. It could be a cave or a deep ravine. It just had to be somewhere they couldn't be hurt. Once I had made sure of that, I could return. And if a medic hadn't come to help Captain Dial yet, I could go find one for him then.

But for now, I had to go. I had to keep the civilians safe.

Captain Dial took his hand from my head and spoke to the girl, and he took his pulse transmitter from the pouch on his belt and gave it to her. I knew he was telling her to go with me, and that the transmitter would help us communicate. She shook her head at first, but I could understand her thoughts well enough to know that it wasn't because she was afraid of me. It was because she didn't want to leave Captain Dial alone any more than I did.

I knew then that I liked her. But we were under orders now, and we had to follow them. So I took the girl's hand in my mouth, and I gave a tug to pull her away from Captain Dial. She didn't want to go, but she didn't fight me. She knew what we had to do. She strapped the transmitter to her wrist and stood up. She was good, too.

We left Captain Dial and went to the old man and the boys. I released the girl's hand as she told them they were all going with me. She put the old man's hand on the handle of my harness, and then he held the hand of one of the boys. The girl held the hand of the other one. We all started up the hill again, pushing through the smoke. My hind legs hurt, but I was still strong. I helped the old man go fast. The girl kept pace beside me as I sniffed and listened to find the best path for us.

I could still see Captain Dial's thoughts for a long way up the hill. At first he was thinking of me and what I was doing, and he was proud. That made me glad.

Then he thought the two words he had thought about on the day we performed our demonstration by the ocean. He thought the words "heroism" and "vengeance."

And then he worried about the other soldiers in D Company. So that made me worry, too. But I couldn't go back to check on them yet. I had orders to follow.

Finally, as the civilians and I came out of the smoke onto a sloping field of rocks, I saw one last strong thought from Captain Dial. It was of Melanie. It was of Melanie with him in their bed, sleeping. And I was on my cushion at their feet.

It was a happy thought, and it made me happy too.

Then Captain Dial's thoughts became fuzzy as the civilians and I went higher, and soon they were gone. I paused near the crest of the hill and looked back down the slope, but I couldn't see the place where Captain Dial lay because of the rocks and smoke. And I thought for a moment that maybe the civilians were safe now, and that I could leave them and go back to where I could know Captain Dial's thoughts again.

But the sound of the approaching drones was loud now, and as I watched, one of them came flying up out of the smoke below us. So I led the civilians behind a big rock. We all crouched down, and I heard the drone turn away and fly back down the hillside again.

Then I heard Gatling guns firing, and I remembered my orders. So I got up from my crouch, and the girl and I took the old man and the boys over the top of the hill and down the other side.

I didn't like not being able to see Captain Dial's thoughts. But now I could see the girl's thoughts almost as well as I had seen his, and she had some good ideas about where we might find a safe place to hide. So we started off in the direction she thought was best.

We had to alter our path many times because of things I smelled or heard. And once we had to make a long detour because the girl remembered there were land mines ahead. I couldn't smell them yet, but she warned me by sending pulses to my implant. And then I saw her thoughts, and I knew they were true. So we found another way.

I became tired and thirsty, and my hind legs hurt. The girl and her family became tired and thirsty too. But we could hear gunfire and explosions behind us, so the girl and I wouldn't let the others stop. Not until we found someplace safe.

Not until we had done what Captain Dial had ordered us to do.

We went up and down through the hills all that day. At dusk we found a guerrilla camp that had been bombed many weeks before. But there were still some matches, a knife, and three plastic jugs of water. So we were able to get a drink. The water tasted like plastic, but we drank a lot of it. There was only one jug left when we were finished. The girl tied it to my harness, and we set out again. The girl carried the matches and the knife.

After nightfall, the girl couldn't see where we were or where we were going. Clouds covered the sky, so she couldn't find any stars to help her. That meant our path was up to me. So I followed my nose and my ears, and I took us farther and farther away from cities, camps, and roads. I took us away from anything that smelled or sounded like people with weapons. We had to go a long way.

At last, when the eastern sky had begun to brighten, we found a shelf of rock in the side of a hill. Under the shelf was a cave that was narrow but deep. It was well hidden by brush. I went in first and found some bone fragments and a ring of stones for a fire, but I could smell that they were old. No one had used the cave in a long time.

So I brought the people inside, and they slept on the bare rock. I didn't sleep right away because I had to lick the cuts on my hind legs. Then I dozed. But I kept my ears and nose alert. The only sounds were of the wind blowing through the rocks and brush. The only smells were of rabbits, birds, and other small animals nearby. There were no guerrillas, soldiers, or other people anywhere near us.

When I had rested for a few hours, I went out into the morning sunlight and killed three rabbits. I had to chase them, and that made my legs hurt again. But I still caught them with no trouble. I tore one apart and ate most of him, and then I took the other two back to the cave. The girl was awake, and she knew what to do. She woke up the boys and had them gather brush and sticks while she used the knife from the guerrilla camp to skin the rabbits. The old man made a spit from the sticks, and they cooked the rabbits over a fire the girl started inside the old ring of stones. It filled the cave with smoke, but the people didn't care. They were hungry.

While they ate, I scouted the area around the cave in widening circles. I sniffed, smelled, and listened. I marked a broad perimeter to warn off animal intruders. Then I did it all over again. And then I was sure my people were safe.

I had followed and completed Captain Dial's order. So I went to the girl and pushed my nose into her hand to be sure she knew my thoughts. I made sure she knew that she and her family should stay close to the cave. They could kill more rabbits to eat, and they still had the jug of water from the guerrilla camp. When that ran out, they could catch rain and dew.

The girl understood.

So I started back to the battlefield where I had left Captain Dial. I was able to go faster now because I didn't have people with me, and because my legs felt better. I could also choose a path that took me closer to dangerous smells. And I found a pond where I could get a drink. But that was the only time I stopped. I wanted to get back to Captain Dial as soon as I could.

There was still some light in the sky when I came over the hilltop and looked down the rocky slope at the battlefield. The two fallen drones had stopped burning, and there was no more smoke. A number of people were walking around down near the gully where Captain Dial and I had found the civilians, and the wind brought me their smells along with the smells of many dead D Company soldiers and refugees. The walking people didn't smell like soldiers or refugees. But they didn't smell like the enemy, either. They didn't make much noise, but occasionally one of them would fire a single shot. It sounded as if they were firing into the ground.

I didn't care who they were, or why they were shooting at the ground. Because now I smelled something else, too.

When I reached Captain Dial, I lay down beside him with my chin on his chest. There was nothing else I could do. I didn't nudge him with my nose or lick his face. I didn't try to wake him up. I'm not stupid. That was one of the things Captain Dial liked best about me. He liked that I was smart.

I closed my eyes. I didn't have an order for what to do next, so I would do nothing. I was tired, and there were no D Company soldiers left for me to help. I would stay there with my chin on Captain Dial.

I closed my eyes and fell asleep. And I dreamed. I dreamed about the day I found the live mine on the pier and about how proud Captain Dial was. I dreamed about running fast in training so I could complete my orders and get back to Captain Dial before the buzzer sounded. I dreamed about lying curled up on my cushion on the floor while Captain Dial and Melanie made soft noises above me.

Then I woke up and opened my eyes. Three of the people below were coming up the slope. They were solid shadows in the dusk. And their smell was sharper now. They smelled like men who used shampoo and soap and who wore clean clothes. They smelled like the men in the crowd the day I found the mine. They smelled like civilians from home.

And as they came toward me and Captain Dial, I heard something behind me. Something higher up the slope, moving down through the rocks. It wasn't loud, so I knew the men coming up the slope couldn't hear it. I couldn't identify it by scent because the wind was blowing the wrong way, but I could hear that it was small and alone. So I didn't think it would hurt anyone. Besides, none of the men coming up the slope was my commanding officer. I wasn't required to alert them.

The three men approached within a few meters of me and Captain Dial, and now I saw that they were dressed in dark clothes that weren't uniforms. But they carried pistols in holsters. One of them pointed a camera at me and Captain Dial. I couldn't see the men's thoughts, but they spoke in the same language as D Company, so I understood some of what they said. One of them said something was great, and the others agreed.

I didn't know what they thought was great, but I knew there was nothing there that was.

One of them stepped closer and leaned down as if about to touch Captain Dial. So I raised my head and snarled at him, and he moved back. Then I put my head down again, but I stayed ready. I didn't know who they were, but they weren't part of D Company. They weren't even soldiers. I wouldn't let them touch Captain Dial.

The one with the camera kept aiming it at me and Captain Dial. But the other two put their hands on their pistols and conferred. And I understood enough to know they were talking about shooting me. So I did what Captain Dial had taught me to do. I planned how to attack them so they couldn't get off a shot. If either of their pistols began to rise from its holster, I would execute the plan. And I would decide what to do about the one with the camera based on how he reacted.

But another thing that Captain Dial had taught me was that a battlefield situation can change quickly.

The thing coming down the slope sent some pebbles skittering through the brush. And the three men heard it. They backed away from me and Captain Dial, and the one with the camera let it drop to dangle on a cord around his neck. They all three began taking their pistols from their holsters. But now they were looking past me toward whatever had made the pebbles skitter.

I kept my eyes on the three men. But I sniffed the air, and even though the wind was still going the wrong way, I caught a faint scent that told me who was on the slope behind me. It was the girl I had taken to safety on Captain Dial's order. She was still and quiet now, probably crouched behind a rock. But even so, she wasn't safe anymore.

All three men were raising their pistols. They were farther away from me than when I had made my plan of attack. But they weren't looking at me now. The light of day was almost gone. And I am black as night. I am silent as air.

The third one got off a shot as I hit his chest, but the bullet went into the sky. The other two were already on the ground, their throats torn out, their weapons in the dirt. The third one tried to fight me off once he was down, but that didn't last long.

When he was still, I looked back up the slope, beyond Captain Dial, and saw the girl standing beside a clump of brush. She was almost invisible because the sun was gone now. But I saw her shape against the brush. And the wind had shifted so I could smell her better. She smelled scared.

I was angry that she had returned to the battlefield. I had done my duty and made her safe, and she had spoiled it. I didn't understand why she had done that.

Then she came down the hill past Captain Dial, past me, and past the three men on the ground. She didn't walk fast, but she walked steady and strong even though she was scared. She said something soft to me as she went by, and I saw a flash of her thoughts. Then I understood. She was going down to the gully, to her mother. She wanted to wrap the body and take it somewhere to bury it. She had returned by herself to do this, leaving her brothers in the care of the old man.

I looked past her and knew I couldn't let her do as she planned. There were more people down there. They were like the three men I had just killed. The girl wouldn't be safe among them. Already, I could see and hear several of them starting toward her. She couldn't see them yet. But she would encounter them before she could reach the gully.

So I ran down to the girl and got in front of her. But she just walked around me. Then I took her hand in my mouth, but she just pulled it away and kept going. She wouldn't stay in contact with me long enough to see my thoughts. She was determined to reach her mother.

I couldn't knock her down or bite her to make her come with me. But I couldn't let her keep going. I had to make her pay attention to me long enough so she would understand what we had to do. So I turned and ran fast across the hillside, away from both the girl and Captain Dial. I ran to the body of Lieutenant Morris, and I tore open one of his pockets. Some ammo clips fell out, but that wasn't what I wanted. I wanted what I had smelled when I'd pushed Lieutenant Morris down in the gully.

And I found it curled up in the corner of the pocket. It was the necklace from the dead girl at the checkpoint. There was still enough blood on it that I had been able to smell it. The necklace had been taken from Lieutenant Morris for the investigation, but he had stolen it back. Now I took it from him again.

I ran back to the girl with it, got in front of her, and pushed my nose against her hand so she would feel the necklace hanging from my mouth.

She stopped walking. Her palm was against my nose. Her fingers brushed the silver chain. The transmitter on her wrist hummed. And then, as someone shouted below us, I thought hard and showed her what had happened to the girl who had worn the necklace. So she saw that girl lying on the side of the road with her sisters. She saw me find the necklace in Lieutenant Morris's pocket. She saw how angry Captain Dial had been at what Lieutenant Morris had done.

The shouting below us grew louder. I could hear six voices now, and weapons being readied. More of the armed-men-who-weren't-soldiers were coming toward us.

But I didn't turn away from the girl. I kept my nose in her palm because I had to be sure she understood. I had to be sure she understood that Captain Dial was my commanding officer, and that I hated to leave him there on the hillside again. But I would. And she would have to leave her mother there, too. We both had to follow Captain Dial's last order. And if the men coming up the hillside reached us, we would fail. I wouldn't be good. And she would be like the other girl. The one who had worn the necklace.

The girl was smart. I saw in her thoughts that her mother wouldn't want her to die like that other girl. But when she understood what I was telling her, she began to cry. She hadn't cried before this. But she cried now, taking the necklace from my mouth and clutching it in her fist. She wanted to fight the men coming up the hill. She thought they were responsible for her mother's death. She thought they had made the drones attack.

I didn't know why she thought that. But I understood why she would want to fight whoever had made the drones fire on

D Company. I wanted to fight those people too. But even if those people were the men who were coming up the hill, we couldn't fight them now. I had already killed three of them, but I had caught those three by surprise. There were more than three coming now, and they had their weapons ready to fire.

So we had to go back up over the hill. And while the girl stood there with the necklace clenched in her fist, I took her other hand in my mouth. And then I started up the hill, pulling her with me.

At first, she came with me without knowing what she was doing. She was still crying and thinking of what she wanted to do to the people who had sent the drones. So the men coming up the hill gained on us, and a shot was fired. I heard the bang and then heard the slug hiss through the air. It hit the dirt several meters ahead of us.

Then the girl's thoughts came back to where we were and what we needed to do. So she began to run, and I was able to release her hand. We ran together back up the hill, through the rocks and brush, up toward the night sky.

We paused for a few seconds when we reached Captain Dial again. He lay still in the twilight. He made no sound. He had no thoughts. He didn't even smell like Captain Dial anymore. So it was all right for the girl to take his sidearm and empty his pockets. And this time, it was easier to leave. This time, I knew I wouldn't need to return.

In training, Captain Dial had told me that when a soldier was gone, he was gone forever. But he had also told Melanie that they would be together forever. So *forever* was always a hard word for me to understand. But whenever I didn't understand something, it was because it was something only someone as smart as Captain Dial could understand. And in those cases, I would just have to believe whatever Captain Dial said. Because Captain Dial always spoke the truth.

So that was what I did as I left his body there on the hillside for the last time. I remembered what Captain Dial had said, and I was glad that even though he was gone, he and Melanie would still be together.

I wished I could be with them, too. But I didn't know how to get to wherever they were.

The girl and I went up over the top of the hill, and soon I couldn't smell or hear the men behind us anymore. Then the twilight was gone, and the girl held my harness so I could lead her through the darkness. She knew my thoughts most of the time now, so I promised her I would do a good job. And she promised me the same thing.

We had our orders. So we would follow them.

Forever.

I took the girl back to the cave where the old man and the boys were waiting, and we stayed there several weeks until I smelled men with weapons approaching. Then we left, and I led the way deeper into the hills, taking us as far from danger as I could. The weather grew colder, but my fur grew thicker, and we found winter clothing in an abandoned village. The old man also found sewing tools, and he made blankets from the skins of the rabbits I caught. The girl stretched some skins between two long pieces of wood, and that was where we kept our growing collection of supplies. The people and I took turns dragging it as we traveled.

We traveled this way for many days, until we came upon the stone hut near the stream.

It's been a good place. We found more things that my people could use here. But the people who had stayed in the hut before us had been gone for a long time when we arrived. I couldn't even smell them on the things they had left. So I believed my company would be safe here for the winter.

Food was easy to obtain. All I had to do was go up and down the stream until I found rabbits. Once I killed a small deer, and the girl said its skin should be my bed. So now I sleep on it even though I like the bare ground just as well. I have thick fur. But it makes my people happy to see me lie down on the deer's skin, and that makes me glad.

In recent weeks the bushes and trees have grown leaves, and the grass that was dry and thin is now thick and juicy. The girl and the old man have been making plans to plant seeds they found in the abandoned village. We've all been looking forward to warmer days.

Then, last night, eighteen of Your soldiers came to kill us.

You must have told them we were the enemy. So they didn't know I was trained by Captain Dial. They didn't know that even when I sleep, my ears and nose are awake.

I took the girl to their bodies this morning, and it made her sad. But she understood that I had to follow orders. She understands a lot. She and I often help each other figure out things that are puzzling.

I didn't understand how Your soldiers could have found us, or why You would want them to, because we've traveled far from anything that should matter to You. Besides, we're not Your enemies. And even if we were, we wouldn't be important enough for You to bother with. Or so I thought.

Then the girl remembered the implant under the skin between my shoulders, and the transmitter that Captain Dial had given her. We had used these things to help us understand each other in our first weeks together, but then—just as Captain Dial and I had found—they had become unnecessary. So the girl had placed the transmitter in her duffel, and we hadn't thought of it or of my implant since. But now the girl said that machines in the sky could probably hear signals from them at any time, and that the machines could then tell You where I was. So that was how Your soldiers found us.

The girl also says she knows why You want to attack us.

She found a radio receiver in the abandoned village, and now she listens to its voices for a few minutes each evening. I can't understand the voices, but the girl has told me some of the things they've said. They've said that all Your soldiers were about to be sent home because the money for the war was almost gone. But then D Company was ambushed and destroyed by enemy guerrillas, and the bad publicity from what Lieutenant Morris had done at the checkpoint was obliterated by the heroism of his company's sacrifice. So Your public support surged, and more money was provided so Your soldiers could avenge the ambush by destroying the enemy.

This is what the radio voices say. They don't say anything about the drones. But if the drones hadn't come, D Company would not only have beaten the guerrillas, but would have suffered almost no casualties. Captain Dial would have seen to it.

But the drones did come. They came from our own airfield. They came from You.

Then the men-who-weren't-soldiers came too, and the girl thinks she knows why they fired shots at the ground. She thinks they killed any soldier or refugee who was still alive. And we believe those men were sent by You as well.

The girl says that our knowledge of this is why You want to attack us. We're the only survivors of that battle. So as long as we still live, You fear that we may reveal the truth of what happened to D Company and the refugees. And the girl says that then all of Your public support and money will go away again.

I have tried to think of what Captain Dial might do if these things had been revealed to him. But he was much smarter than me. And I can't see his thoughts anymore.

But I still know the final order he gave me: To keep my people safe.

So I've thought of things I can do to obey.

The first thing I thought of was to have the girl write this message. Again, she doesn't know what she writes. Only that I require her to write it. And what I'm asking her to write now is a promise that You have nothing to fear from me if You leave us alone. If You allow me to keep my people safe, we will never tell the radio voices what Your drones and men-who-weren't-soldiers did to D Company.

The second thing made the girl cry again. Before beginning this message, I told her to use her knife to cut between my shoulders and find the communication implant. She cried because she didn't want to hurt me, and then she cried more because the device was smaller than we had imagined, and it was hard to find. She had to make the cut longer and deeper. But she finally found the tiny glass bean and gave it to the boys, who took turns hitting it and the transmitter with a hammer until both were dust. Then the old man cleaned my wound and sewed it shut. I growled once because the needle hurt, and he stepped back. But then I licked his hand, and he finished the job. Afterward, I was proud of all of them for following orders so well.

The third thing makes us unhappy. But it's necessary. We must leave the stone hut. We must leave this good place with its water and rabbits. Your soldiers found us here, so You know where we are.

But since I no longer have the communication implant, You won't know where we'll go next.

Finally, there is a fourth thing I'll do.

If the above measures fail, and if You send more soldiers or men-who-aren't-soldiers to find us, I will kill them all. I'll always know they're coming, so they'll never be able to attack us before I attack them first.

You may even send some of my fellow K-9s, because they could find us more quickly than people could. But Captain Dial said that the K-9s in my training class were the best war dogs there had ever been, and I was ranked first in that class. So there are no K-9s that I can't find and defeat before they can find and defeat me.

And if You attack us with drones instead of people or dogs, we're now equipped to fight them. Some of the soldiers I killed last night were carrying RPGs, and others carried guns with armor-piercing rounds. We have taken these weapons.

But if You bomb us from high in the sky so we can't fight, there may be nothing I can do to stop You. Then You will have made me fail to carry out my orders.

In that event, I'll do whatever I must to survive. And then I will find You. I don't know Your name or Your rank, but I will find You anyway. I will hunt and kill every officer in every company and every battalion until I reach You. I will read their thoughts as they die and use that knowledge to hunt You. I will climb walls and dig tunnels. I will swim and run. I will stow away in trucks, ships, and aircraft that will bring me closer to You. I will find something You have touched so I know Your scent. And then I will find You in Your bed or at Your table or wherever You may be.

And I will bite Your throat so it tears out.

So I hope You heed this message. It will be left with one of Your dead soldiers, so I know it will reach their unit's commanding officer. And then it will reach that officer's commanding officer, and then that officer's commanding officer, and so on until it reaches the officer who gave the orders that resulted in the current situation. Until it reaches You.

My company has its equipment and is ready to move out. The two boys are my specialists. The old man is my medic and quartermaster.

As for the girl—

She now wears the metal tag I received when I was promoted to sergeant. She found it in Captain Dial's pocket as we left the battlefield, and today she put it on the chain of her necklace beside the shiny rock. Sergeant is the toughest enlisted job. But she can do it.

I myself am no longer a sergeant. I didn't realize that until this morning. But after I showed the girl what I had done in the night, she touched my head. And I heard her thoughts. I heard what she called me.

She called me Captain.

Then she took the silver bars that she found with the sergeant's tag, and she pinned them to my duty harness.

I am the ranking survivor of D Company, and my final order from Captain Dial was a commission. I know this because what he told me to do was what a good officer does.

A good officer takes care of his soldiers.

But if You attack us again, You will not be a good officer. You will not be taking care of Your soldiers. And if You make me fail in my duty to take care of mine, You will not be an officer of any kind for much longer.

Captain Dial told me what I am, and he always spoke the truth. So now I tell You:

I am black as night. I am silent as air.

My sergeant touches my head, and I tell her she's good.

This message is complete.

Respectfully,
Chip, K-9
Captain and Commanding Officer
D Company

First Commandment

GREGORY BENFORD

Gregory Benford [www.authorcafe.com/benford] lives in Irvine, California. He is a plasma physicist and astrophysicist, and one of the leading SF writers of the last thirty years. One of the chief spokesmen of hard SF in the past three decades, Benford is articulate and contentious, and he has produced some of the best fiction about scientists working (including some unpleasant realism) and about the riveting and astonishing concepts of cosmology and the nature of the universe. Among his many awards is the 1990 United Nations Medal in Literature. His most famous novel is Timescape *(1980); his most recent,* Beyond Infinity *(2004), is an expansion of his 1990 novella "Beyond the Fall of Night." Many of his (typically hard) SF stories are collected in* In Alien Flesh *(1986) and* Matters End *(1995). In 2004, Benford also edited* Microcosms, *an impressive anthology of hard SF about miniature universes.*

"First Commandment" was published electronically by SciFi.com; this is its first appearance in print. It continues several of the ongoing themes of his fiction. Like Arthur C. Clarke, Benford occasionally explores scientific literalizations of religious ideas. Here, Locke, a biologist, is given the task to identify and classify all species before they are driven extinct by the transformation of their habitats—a task that converges with God's commandment to Adam to name the beasts. What emerges is a second theme of Benford's: our responsibilities toward living things and toward the environment.

53

for David Brin

"**I** just don't get the point," Weiss said. He had a thousand problems on his desk and didn't need another.

The biologist—Locke, was it?—let her exasperation flicker across her face. Then her patient face returned. "This is the last area to be inventoried. Every other habitat is done."

Weiss steepled his fingers and decided to give this gal at least one more minute, out of courtesy. "You count species, Dr. Locke? Enter them into a data base?"

Locke leaned forward and her khaki jacket pressed against Weiss's large desk. "Not just count—catalog. That means we have to decide if an insect is, say, a beetle, and if so, which kind."

"And your funding . . . ?"

"The U.N. Global Inventory. With so many areas threatened, the U.N. set up the Inventory office over two decades ago. We've gone into every area—shrinking forests, dying deserts, swamps drying out, the lot."

With that last phrase he spotted the accent—classic Brit, probably English. He answered in his boisterous Aussie, heavy on the accent, "But this is a vital area!"

She smiled. "That's why we left it for last."

"Show me what you want to inventory, then." Weiss pushed his chair back and led her to the outer door. They stepped out into the dry still air of sunset. Weiss waved to the west. "Beautiful, eh?"

But she turned pointedly and looked east toward the blue-green ramparts. The mountains began to the east, in the Flinders range north of Adelaide. As they marched west they slumped down toward the great plain that stretched a thousand miles to the west. The absence of jutting peaks meant that dark-bellied clouds sweeping up from the Great Southern Ocean did not rise, and so did not rain. "Yes, very."

"You did those mountains?" He walked through a thin grove of eucalyptus and she followed.

"Our inventory there was finished a month ago," she said flatly. "All the rest of the continent is done, in fact." The sharp late afternoon light slanted through the branches and speckled them.

"You move fast."

"We have thousands of workers. And habitat is vanishing faster than ever."

"So your team has been cooling its heels."

Stiffly: "Yes indeedy."

"Sorry." He spoke as he continued through the crackling eucalyptus bark underfoot. "Sorry, yeah, but we had plenty of work. Just getting the last shelves up and in place, y'know."

"Oh, I know. I know quite well."

Her voice still carried its edge and he was glad he had turned and walked west, so she had to walk behind him and he didn't have to see her face. He could hear her keeping up with him, quicker steps than his. "I guess you environmentalists don't approve, then?"

She came up abreast of him. "It's far too late to approve or disapprove. It's done. I'm here to get a record of what was here before your, your—"

"Stewardship. That's the word I like." He gave her a slanted smile.

"All right, before your *stewardship* destroys any more species."

He pressed his lips together until they turned white. "With more water, I'd kinda expect them to prosper."

She shook her head vehemently. "Increased rainfall will help some species and hinder others. Many Australian species are not built to take constant damp conditions."

"They sure are up in Queensland."

"But not here. That's the point. Not every life form will adapt to the change you're imposing. We want to take samples, whole organisms, and preserve them for the day when some will be gone."

They walked clear of the eucalyptus and his maneuver made his point for him. To the west stretched a long, dark gray mount. It was over a kilometer high and its slope was like a series of steps, evenly spaced, a back-jut coming with every hundred meters of altitude. This gave the great mass the appearance of foothills. From here below the eye could not see the flat land implied by the sudden end of each thirty-degree slope. In fact there was no flat there at all. The gray mass simply broke off, leaving an opening to the sky.

He kept his tone affable. "Damn pretty, wouldn't you say?"

To his surprise, she snorted. "Let's say it's not to my taste."

The lowering sun cast a glow over the inclines. The eye could clearly make out that the nearest ramparts were curiously smooth. No trees or even shrubs graced the gray gradients; they were dead grids of carbon fiber. As the eye adjusted, details emerged. Sunlight cast slanting rays through the great sheets of billowing fiber. Pale blades of luminosity played among the thick cross-struts.

Weiss's practiced eye could make out the vertical pillars beneath the gray slopes. Designing those to take wind and torques had been an exacting job, and he remembered well the years of sweat and calculation. But it had all paid off. The nearest section had been up nearly five years and had withstood dozens of storms slamming into it from the south. Structural engineers found no damage to the carbon-foam stanchions. There had been rips in the carbon fiber sheets they held aloft, to be sure, but nothing a crew could not mend.

"I think you'll find it is definitely to the taste of the farmers starting to till their fields down there," he said firmly, turning to point to the south. For several dozens of kilometers between them and the coast, great rectangular fields glistened with the colors of fresh crops. Before, these lands had been dry, barren scrub.

"I'm sure." She was obviously holding herself in.

"Um. You don't agree."

"The other ideas that were tried, how'd they work out? Seeding clouds offshore—"

"Not enough yield."

"—and that wild one, about putting coal-burning power planets off shore, so their dust plumes would make clouds—"

"Too pricey. Enviros blocked it of course. Plus no way to move the power ashore easily."

She exhaled in exasperation, blowing her auburn hair out of her eyes. "So it had to be . . . fake mountains."

"They work. It's not as if we just started tinkering with the world yesterday."

"Regrettably."

"Do you really think that? The Aswan Dam, those gates that protect Venice, that sea-level Panama Canal II—only it's in Nicaragua. Fair dinkum stuff, right? Then there's the biggest, the Three Gorges Dam, the cap on Kilimanjaro to save the snow, that tropical cloud reflection campaign to cool the oceans and offset the greenhouse effect—"

"How about those reversed rivers in Siberia—big disaster, right?"

"But the Siberian drained swamp valleys shut down the mosquitos—"

"And they'll change the local species around. Which is why we're here to take a snapshot here, before it changes."

Her color was high and her eyes flashed. Nobody changed their minds in the heat of argument, he reminded himself. He let three heartbeats pass before saying mildly, "This site's the last one, isn't it?"

She took a deep breath and focused on the distant, real mountains to the east. Her face relaxed. "Yes, with all the endangered sites, the Global Inventory decided to leave this for last." She smiled wanly. "Your changes are mild compared with cross-cutting whole valleys."

He gave her an appraising gaze. "So you've come for your permission, is it?"

"I'm not optimistic. You're going to tell me about another delay, aren't you?"

"Now, you've become cynical." He could not resist taking a mild little shot. Her stiff lip curled a bit in response, which gratified him.

She said stiffly, "Cynical? I've learned from experience. Every step of the way, there has been local opposition. At least in Africa we could just pay off the right officials and get the paperwork done."

He had to chuckle. "Sorry it's harder here. Maybe we *should* take bribes—it would be faster."

"Don't think we didn't consider it."

His mouth twisted slightly but he took the jibe with a thin smile that still creased his leathery face. With some relish he one-upped her, flourishing a single folded piece of paper he had carried in his hip pocket. "Surprise."

She blinked, gratifyingly startled.

Cindy Locke's hip phone rang, a punchy few notes of Bach in the hovering stillness of the blue gum forest.

She was crouched over an open meter-deep hole, carefully taking microbial samples on a tape device. Finishing up, she stood and answered, her legs creaking with gratitude at the break.

"I hope this is about something," she said.

"That religious bunch is back." Brenda's tone was concerned.

"Throw them out."

"There are a lot more this time. And they don't look like they'll leave."

"What do the cops say?"

"It's peaceful, so—"

"Damn. I'm about a klick away. Be there soonest."

She breathed in the dry, flavored air and took a moment to prepare for another bruising brush with reality. No, this grove of towering sleek eucalyptus, *this* was reality. People were the passing phenomenon. Maybe.

A wedge tail hawk came flapping slowly up on the thermals. It wheeled elegantly and soared, riding the soft moist breeze that lifted some heat from the day. She envied the hawk even as her professional eye pondered it as a gliding bag of genes, ancient beyond knowing, a muscular heritage still moving powerfully through its diminished world. *Sail on.*

She indexed her finds, taking the time to do it right, letting her professional self do the work and suppressing her tightening gut. She always hoped the fieldwork would go smoothly but it never did.

She closed up, hoisted her pack onto her back, and took long strides downhill. Above her the gray, gridded expanses billowed, like the sails of a great ship forever anchored. She passed one of the vertical pillars, its carbon foam skin glistening with gaudy lichen. Life found new niches, even in high tech pores.

Her boots sank silently into the thick brown mat and vines tapped big teardrops on her hat brim. She stepped over a convoy of green ants and on impulse knelt, let a few run onto her forefinger, and crunched them with her molars. A lemon tang flooded her mouth. It felt good to eat of this forest, a rare sacrament. A conservation biologist, she listened keenly to the myriad rustlings that escorted her through dappled shadows.

The artificial mountain looming above bestowed its bounty here. Grass tufts clustered around the tree roots and subtly scented the air. High above a pearly mist gathered. The steady, moisture-rich breeze that wafted in from the Great Southern Ocean did not stir the branches, for the carbon fiber blanket above shaped the air to flow up the slopes. Australia was the oldest continent, its mountain ranges ground down to red dust in vast plains. For millennia a moist bounty had skated over it from the south, to finally be captured by the young, jutting mountains of New Guinea.

Not now. Rising up the gray slopes, the steady flow cooled, and fine fogs formed against the web of light carbon. Occasionally there was outright rainfall, hammering down through the open spaces in the blanket. She passed under a shaft open to the pale blue sky, a sunshine island a hundred meters wide. Sharp sun warmed her shoulders as she leaped over a murmuring stream.

The man-made mountain range now captured a vast rainfall all along the southern Australian coast. It fed the plains below a generous, steady plentitude and drove the burgeoning farmlands. In a world of ten billion souls, this new breadbasket was a crucial addition.

And there lay the eternal problem. Yet again, forest yielded to farm.

Just below her insecticidal fog bombs burst in gray clouds, high up in the trees. She skirted left and watched the teams moving in. A rain of insect bodies sprinkled down through branches and spattered among the eucalyptus leaves underfoot.

Crude but effective, she thought as workers duck-walked across the defined area, carefully plucking the small bodies and dropping them into sample pouches. Some of the team specialized in plants and fronds, others in mammals and birds, but most of the dozen workers in jeans and boots took insects. These sweeps took anything and everything, a thorough though random sampling of the entire habitat. The volunteers were offered a nominal sum and most refused even that. They wanted to be in on the finish of something sad and grand.

A big man in an outback leather hat, for example—she remembered had come from Queensland at his own expense. He wanted to be in on the last big sampling of the biosphere, and his broad big-toothed smile permanently creased a ruddy face that had seen dozens of the earlier jobs.

Behind them trooped men carrying the freezers. These were big picnic coolers that steamed with dry ice vapor when the teams opened them to drop in the sample pouches.

Stapled to the cooler side was a green bar-code tag giving GPS position, time and site description. She had run them off herself this morning and it looked as though they were enough for the day. Not many more to do, either. They were making rapid progress now as more volunteers came in. The job might be done in a few more days and then all that was left was the laborious task of taxonomy.

Each grub and beetle and flower was fitted into an elaborate, computerized scheme, assigned a species classification and name. When done—and an army of taxonomists was processing thousands a day back at their base camp—this would be the end. *Finis* to over two decades of hard slogging in Africa, South America, Polynesia—all drawing to a close here.

The usual questions dogged her. How many had they missed? Particularly the savvy mammals knew when to run. And what of those already extinct, never counted, never named?

The Aborigines they had worked with in the mountains above Adelaide had looked for their legendary rainbow beetles. They never found any. Gone.

Puddles from a recent shower mirrored the crossbars of the supporting struts, high in the shaded sky. She paused a moment, peering at the reflection, which at just the right angle looked like the holy cross. For the first time in quite a while she recalled her Catholic girlhood, the sense of mission that had come out of that, had led her here.

After this, though, what would she do? The great task of sampling all the world's bounty and sorting it into categories would be over. Ideally, no species would be unknown. The job would be done as well as mere humans could do it.

And as the incursions of more noisy humans forced species into extinction, the record she had contributed to would be all that remained to mark them. But what of her, then?

Children? Getting a bit late in the game for that, and no man interested in fathering. The world did not need more mouths, either.

A light rain spattered down from the canopy, which was nearer now as she angled along the hill toward their central nexus. As she came down through the last grove her pulse quickened. *Back to the world of people. And soon, there would be no other.*

To the sad long list—the dodo, passenger pigeon, moa, Tasmanian wolf, dusky sparrow, Florida panther, so many more—new names would be added. The only hope of knowing what those creatures were now lay in the sample cabinets of musty museums. But the inventory she was doing held out hope that in some brighter future, the genomic information in their sample bags would enable the resurrection of species. If biology marched on, perhaps the past was not truly lost.

She made herself put aside her musings. A babble of excited talk came from the clearing ahead.

Their trailers had moved. They were circled like wagons against the oddly silent crowd. Brenda must have done that when she saw their numbers—at least five hundred of them, most in pants and collared shirts, a few even in dark suits. Missionaries?

There was Brenda, gesturing to a tall, swarthy man. She was making pushing motions, *get back*, but the crowd pressed in around her. Trouble.

Cindy hailed Brenda, a short, muscular no-nonsense woman in jeans who turned with relief. As Cindy approached hand-lettered signs lofted from the crowd.

HEED THE HOLY WORD
REPENT THE SIN

read one in garish lettering, and a banner unfurled between two women:

ARROGANCE WILL BRING THE LAST DAYS

A sullen mutter rose up from them. Eyes glowered above gritted teeth.

Cindy could not imagine what this was about. Usually they faced only the press. Those were well represented today, scenting controversy: three shoulder-held cameras zoomed in on her as she strode into the crowd. In the cloying heat she could smell them, rank and excited.

"Who's in charge here?" she demanded loudly.

A tall man with russet beard stepped from the line. "I am." From long experience she turned and faced him straight-on, chin up. "We've had some religious types demonstrate, but this is different, isn't it? Lots more of you."

"I come bearing a message you should heed," he said slowly, soberly. His face was all planes and he had the cast of a man who was uncertain of very little. "I wish to deliver it away from this circus, if you please."

The *please* was a pleasant touch. She eyed the rest of them and found the usual types; people with too much past and too little future, washed up upon the shore of faith.

"Why?" she challenged him, hands on hips. The crowd was milling and muttering but she ignored it. Brenda started talking to the rest of them in a reasonable tone, projecting her big voice out over their heads. The TV crews, thank God, followed her, sniffing at a possible confrontation.

"We are here for many different missions, we faithful."

He waved a hand at the others but his burning eyes told the truth—this was his mission, and the others did not matter. He carried the air of a man bedeviled by something, a past that had carved lines in his long face. His severe black suit seemed wrapped around him more than fitted. He had a look she had seen once in a woman's forlorn face, a sense of some past moral transgression for which everyone forgives them except themselves. And so they powerfully needed to redeem themselves.

She gave him a big arm-sweeping gesture and smiled, light as a bird in flight. "Come into my spacious office." Her levity got the fierce, brooding look off his face. Enough social lubrication and she might get him off the site. But today it didn't seem to work. His eyes bored into her for long moments, his mouth working, and then he nodded twice in quick jerks.

She led him into the trailer where the automatic species-readers were working. It was cooler there, from the air conditioning the computers needed. They labored silently and the clacking of the auto-readers was muffled. She pointed out one to him. The machine took the samples from the day before—insects, mostly—and in a single bright flash took a three-dimensional photo, analyzing its features in an instant. By comparing it with the immense Global Inventory data base, and using rules of thumb worked out by the best taxonomists, this single trailer could index and place the samples a billion times faster than clunky humans.

It was the key to making an inventory of so many species, and she rattled on about it for a full minute before she realized that none of it was sinking in. And that her well-learned talents at dealing with opponents—smile, make little jokes, offer information, make them see you as human, too—were getting nowhere.

"All right," she said, shifting gears to her official voice, "let's get down to business, Mister . . . ?"

"Abrahams," he said curtly.

"Ummm. And—"

"You are all in great danger."

His deep-set eyes glared, the mouth twisted. "Uh, oh?"

"You are a rational scientific type person. You do not heed an older wisdom."

"Depends on the wisdom, I'd say."

"Consider this, then—" He stood and recited:

"Genesis, 19. And out of the ground the Lord God formed every beast of the field, and every fowl of the air; and brought them unto Adam to see what he would call them: and whatsoever Adam called every living creature, that was the name thereof."

"Which means . . . ?"

"Your Global Inventory. You are naming the beasts."

"And the plants. So?"

He wrung his hands together, squeezing his eyes shut, and then the words exploded from him. "Genesis, 20. And Adam gave names to all cattle, and to the fowl of the air, and to every beast of the field; but for Adam there was not found a help mate for him."

"This is where Eve comes in?"

He stared off into the distance, as if listening to someone. Then he shook his head and turned to her slowly. "You are of Eve. But no, the scripture means something more. We cannot know what will attend once we have completed the Lord's task."

She wanted to say to him, *Yes, the naming of the beasts is holy work. Science is holy. Your own book says it! So how about leaving us alone to do our jobs?*

But she didn't. This one was not going to tolerate a lot of argument.

"So Genesis is, what, wrong?" It usually helped if you took their point of view at first, and could politely differ with the following portions of the argument. But something told her this was not going to work with the intense, scowling man, still rubbing and massaging his hands as he stared at her. For the first time she wondered about her own safety here, alone with him, with only the buzzing machines as witness.

"Not wrong, no. It becomes a tale of origins. Later scholars ignored the flat fact that the naming of the beasts was God's first commandment. All that comes after is irrelevant to the deeper truth."

"Which is . . ."

"That mankind—including the Eves—never finished the first work they were given. God-given!"

"You mean our inventory will do that, at last."

"Yes." His hands hung at his side, their wringing finished.

"Then we are doing holy work, yes?"

"Of a kind, yes. Complying, as is our duty, with the First Commandment."

"I thought Moses did those."

It was meant to be a small joke, but he gravely shook his head. "Genesis comes before Moses."

"I think I knew that."

"But hear this." He stiffened and the hands came together again and he recited: "Genesis, *21:* And the Lord God caused a deep sleep to fall upon Adam and he slept."

"Before he got his job done, the naming of the beasts?"

He gazed at her with an expression suddenly mournful. "I do not believe we can know what that passage means."

"A sleep? I know I'll be needing one after this project is done."

"I think you must not complete your inventory. Not until

we have a further sign of what the Lord intends to do, after we have done his holy work at last—but so late. Millennia late!"

"And maybe too late," she said sourly. Where was this going?

He nodded, as if he shared her sadness at all that had been lost. "Since we were in the Garden, we have destroyed much."

"Without naming them at all." She felt a strange sympathy with this sad man.

"Think of all that we have lost. God may be displeased."

"This is a scientific study—"

"I gave you a world of wonders. You give me a measly list."

She was about to say calmly, carefully, that the Global Inventory estimated that at best they would miss twenty percent of the species that had been alive at the turn of the millennium—but then realized that he was not about numbers.

"Surely," he said, "the Lord will consider the completion of your project to be of importance. Perhaps He"—she could hear the capital letter—"has been waiting all this time for us to be done."

Thy will be done, she remembered from the Apostle's Creed, learned in girlhood. She had not thought of it for at least three decades. The words took her back. . . .

But rough sounds intruded. Angry shouts came from outside.

A thump. Something crashing over.

Brenda burst into the room, eyes wide.

The ceremony to mark completion of the Global Inventory was held near the same blue gum grove where Weiss had given her the final permission papers. The day was sharp and clear and at least five hundred people milled around the broad field in front of the platform.

The U.N. dignitaries had all the attention, of course, and she was so far down the pecking order she found herself sitting next to Weiss himself, at the back, true, but at least on the platform. A small seat in history, she consoled herself.

From the podium came the usual.

"Glad you got it all done in time," he whispered. "Heard there was a dustup."

She nodded. "A religious gang. Their leader got me off to talk, and the rest of them started going for our equipment. When somebody came to tell me, we barely managed to restrain the leader."

"Really? You weren't—"

"No. He went for the taxonomy systems, not for us."

"There's always nutters about."

"Especially these days. The last days, some religious ones say."

She sat back and enjoyed the view. From here the artificial mountains loomed like great gray clouds. A distant squall was mounting up their ramparts. The cloud's blue belly ripened as it rose. She turned and could see to the east the last slopes of the true mountains, where they petered out and the flat dry lands had begun.

There the gray carbon slopes began. Below each range the land lay fallow, but the fields were greener down slope of the artificial peaks. The works of man were doing better than the tired, eroded flanks that had been thrust up young by the waltz of continents.

"So this ceremony is premature?" Weiss was asking her. She thought she had seen some movement in the distance.

"What? Oh, not exactly. We got everything running right again. Just lost a little time, is all. I promised the execs that we would have the processing done by today all right."

"That's the end of the whole job, then?"

"Oh no, we have to understand it next. After all, it's just a list of all the species on Earth, with a proper tag attached, a working name."

"That's a lot."

"All we've done is name the . . . the beasts."

Suddenly she saw in her mind's eyes the hot-eyed man, Abrahams. He had feared that God would be displeased. Maybe not with the time it took to name the beasts—they were bumbling, slow-witted humans, after all—but with the missing numbers, the endless bugs and rodents and worms and on down to microbes, all the small squirming creatures who nonetheless made up His fine sacrament, His province. A bounty all gone now because of human numbers, creatures lost before they had been counted, while the humans squandered their eons and fought their wars and ignored the generous world around them—

She caught herself. "The inventory, yes. . . . Now we have to—"

But something had drawn her eye.

Far to the east, where the world was still wholly natural, the peaks had changed. Lightning crackled and a dark funnel descended from so far up in the firmament she could not see its beginning. Wind whipped by her ears. A dank, musty odor came and the crowd murmured in fear, like a chorus. Voices lifted toward peaks that were subsiding, lapsing. Great spokes of stone broke through the leafy slopes. The ground shook like a beast rousing from a long slumber. Fear tasted like copper in her mouth.

Silently, the great old mountains were melting, as if shrugging off a burden they had carried far too long.

Burning Day

GLENN GRANT

Glenn Grant [www.istop.com/~ggrant/index.html] lives in Montreal, and uses memes to infect minds: He is the author of the widely reprinted and circulated "Memetic Lexicon" (www.istop.com/~ggrant/memetics/memelex.html), his most successful piece of writing to date. In the late 1980s, he published the small press magazine Edge Detector, *for which he was nominated for a ReaderCon Small Press award. With David Hartwell, he co-edited* Northern Star *(1995) and* Northern Suns *(1999), both reprint anthologies of the best Canadian science fiction. His writing has appeared in* Interzone, The New York Review of Science Fiction, *and* SF Eye. *He also works as an illustrator and graphic designer.*

"Burning Day" appeared in Claude Lalumière's striking anthology of original Canadian speculative fiction, Island Dreams: Montreal Writers of the Fantastic, *published in Canada in late 2003 and in the U.S. in 2004, and which we highly recommend. This story proves that cyberpunk still has some spark. It's a police procedural about androids and AI and human prejudices, a fast-paced adventure with thoughtful undertones and plot surprises. All in all, great SF fun.*

"**S**omething's missing here . . ." I rotate the crime scene in my mind's-eye, pan across the remaining walls of the room, tracking over concrete dust, ceiling debris, toppled rows of wooden benches, part of a small synthetic arm . . . "Something's missing from this model."

Overlays flicker up, then fade, data collected by a swarm of flybots at the scene: shrapnel fragments and impact sites; splatter patterns of brain coolant and myonic gel; concentrations of chemical taggants, indicating Detanit.

"For one thing, why don't we have any idents?"

"It's only been forty minutes since the attack," says Danny from the squad car's other seat. "CSU's still sweeping the place. Do try to be patient, my paranoid android." Daniel Aramaki is human, and my work partner, and gets away with too much.

Ah, there we go—tiny red flags and neat little labels, finally popping up all over the virtual display in my head—annotating many thousands of pieces of the victims, large and small, positively identified and otherwise.

That's better. "We have four confirmed dead, all cogents. And—oh, shit, no . . ."

"What?"

"Three of them were kids. Report says a bomb attack on the Usutu Truth Memorial Nanofabrication Facility."

Mind's-eye closed, optics open: we're wailing through the intersection of Dundas and Replicraft Drive, running strobes and siren. Rain streaks the windshield, polishes the streets into shiny dark mirrors. The car is a Persina sedan, in standard-issue Homicide gray.

"Synthephobe terrorists again," says Dan. "Humanist Front, probably, or the Organic Brigades."

"Fifty dollars says the Humanistas claim it first."

"You're a sick guppy, Mohad." Danny removes his latest designer smartshades, pockets them. He has a new pair every week; he's constantly losing the things. I once suggested that he could simply buy prosthetic eyes with the same features and then some. He seemed to consider the idea an affront to his biological heritage.

I blink back into the model. From the shrapnel impacts, the program calculates a probable detonation point: mid-air, three meters from the floor, at the center of the room. Not a body-bomb, then. A grenade? Lobbed in from the door? Seems wrong somehow . . .

So I expand the model, scale it down to see what buildings are nearby. Project the most likely trajectories, out through the windows and back to origin. The resulting probability-cone is centered on the top three stories of an elderly Modernist apartment block. A free hostel. The CSU team are already checking it out, apparently, datacapture flowing into the model as I watch.

I kill the display. "It would appear that someone fired a small missile into the building from a rooftop nearby."

Dan raises an eyebrow, but doesn't argue. "Which roof?"

"The free hostel. I believe I know its manager, by reputation at least—Severe Commy Skeptic."

Dan rolls his eyes. I know what he thinks of the names cogents choose for themselves. I've also known activists who sneer at mine: Gene Engine Mohad. The first and last are slave names, they say. Anthrocentric, they say. Fuck 'em, I say. It's my choice.

West of Eidolonics Avenue, we howl out of Little Arabia and under the eaves of Cogentville. At once the rain is gone, and Dundas is an echoing halogen tunnel through overgrown masses of architecture. Buildings in Cogtown evolve constantly, with complete disregard for city regs and permits. They sprout overhead pedways, cantilevered wings, swooping bridges. Entire streets are spanned, lost under layers of nano-assembled confusion. Walls are always being knocked through, ramps built apparently at random between adjacent structures, entire city blocks domed over with great geodesic umbrellas. Every surface is covered in spectacular art. Not advertising, but luminescent paintings, tilework, bas-relief, animated graphics, palimpsests of cryptic polyglot graffiti . . .

"And this used to be such a nice neighborhood," Daniel mutters. He's joking; twenty-five years ago this was all abandoned office towers stuffed full of flood refugees and squatters. Not a lot of human pedestrians around here now; mostly cogents and lesser bots, walking, rolling, spider-crawling. The majority are anthropine (like me), but only a few are biomimetic, with all the pseudo-organic details. It's unpopular now, politically uncool, to mimic humans too closely. Pinocchio Syndrome, they call it. Many of today's cogents wear their mechine nature proudly: neosomatics with weird new body plans and lustrous metallic skins.

"How come you don't live in Cogtown, Mohad?" Dan's always posing these irritating questions.

"You're suggesting I shouldn't live wherever I like, monkey-boy?"

"Hey," Daniel spreads his hands, "for all I care, you could move in with my sister. Just seems as if cogents prefer the company of other cogents, y'know?"

"More like humans would rather not live next door to cogents. The city only ceded control of this area to keep the phobe riots to a minimum."

"Hey, can you blame 'em? Look at what you've done with the place."

Now I know he's just trying to spin me up. I let it go. "Actually, at one time I lived just over there, off North TelNex. Quite a long time ago. But I found it . . . I don't know . . . confining."

"Claustrophobic?" Daniel is unconvinced. "Not very cogentlike of you, Gene-baby."

"Neither, for that matter, is policework. But here I am

anyway." As the newest member of the Squad, I have to put up with a lot. Such as Danny calling me *Gene-baby*.

Up ahead, Dundas becomes a long arcade, crammed with rapid response vehicles, pulsating with cherry and blueberry lights. Our squad car decelerates reluctantly, kills the siren, and tucks itself between two Greater Metro Area Police units and a Fire Department Mobile HQ. The street-tunnel has been sealed off for the next three blocks, and all the surrounding buildings are being evacuated. Streams of confused cogents, mixed with a few humans, are being herded along the sidewalks.

We get out. The uniforms working the cordon recognize us and wave us through.

"Forensics are still going over the scene," says Dan. "Let's hit the roof of the hostel first."

The elevator lets us off on the thirty-first. We take the stairs to the roof. It's cool but not raining up here. The top of this and several other buildings are sheltered under great waves of photosynth fabric, a retrofit tensile structure suspended from masts and cables.

Daniel and I walk through the hostel's rooftop bamboo forest, ducking under yellow tape to approach the northern edge. There are tactical units patrolling the railings, and a constable from 52 Division is interviewing a chromefaced cogent in a Mao cap and leather jacket—Severe Commy Skeptic semself.

"No, we don't have security cameras," sie is saying. "What would we need with security cameras?"

Xu Kelly and her technicians are just packing their survey bots away into steel cases marked *Crime Scene Unit*. "Ah," she says, "Detectives Aramaki and Mohad, our local counter-terror experts." She pulls back the hood of her cleansuit, revealing gray hair, tied back into a tail. Half-smiling, she shakes Daniel's hand but somehow neglects mine. "Took you boys long enough."

Okay, it's true that Dan and I collared the Marionette Bombers, but I wouldn't call myself either a counter-terror expert or a boy . . .

"My team's finished here," she says. "Over at the scene, give us, maybe, another hour?" She waggles a hand at the nanofab facility, about forty meters away across the gap between the two buildings.

There's no smoke over there, only a lot of wafting dust. Most of the facility's upper windows have been blown out, the twenty-ninth floor torn open at the southwest corner. White curtains billow through the open walls, like mourning sheets.

"Who's in charge?" asks Dan.

"Sergeant Moon, got here twenty minutes ago. He's at the scene."

"Sie," I say, unable to stop myself.

"Huh?"

"Detective-Sergeant Moon is a *sie*, not a *he* or a *she*." Humans of Kelly's generation simply refuse to adopt the new pronouns. She was born well before cogents were invented. If not for longevity treatments she'd have been retired two decades ago.

"Right, whatever." She indicates a raised meditation garden: black gravel raked into smooth waves around islands of brightly colored machine parts. "Now, over here, we've got footprints." We take a closer look. The pebbles have recently been disturbed by unshod feet, each with four broad toes. Not unlike my own.

"Cogent?"

"Well, it ain't human." Kelly watches my reaction. "No sebum, no skin flakes, no biotic residue at all. Shape of the print says anthropine, but definitely inorganic."

Careful not to disturb the prints, I step up onto the garden's tiled ledge. "A nice, clear shot from here. And these overhanging branches would have provided some concealment." Zoom in: a few of the spear-shaped leaves are brown and curled at the ends. "Some of these are singed."

"Say what?" Kelly snaps.

Daniel rubs it in: "Going blind in your dotage, Xu?"

I pull the branch toward me, slip a couple of the burned leaves into a sample baggie, hand it to Kelly.

She doesn't seem grateful. "We'll check for traces of missile propellant."

Dan says, "Thanks, Mom, you're the best."

"Fuck you," she replies politely. Kelly takes her cases and ducks through the yellow tape.

Daniel looks about. "Okay then, let's canvass the building, see if anyone saw a cog waving a grenade launcher around."

I tell him I'll be along in a moment. He strolls off to interview Severe Commy.

Standing still, exactly where the killer stood, I study the blast damage. At 10× magnification I can see most of the room's demolished interior. It's a public ceremonial chamber, small and nondenominational, paneled in blond wood, with several gently tiered rows of simple benches curving around a central platform. Broad diamondpane windows in the back wall presumably provide an overview of the high-security nanofactory beyond. Four mantislike telebots are picking reverentially through the wreckage. And standing in the room's broad doorway, waiting for the CSU bots to finish, is the only other cogent in the Homicide unit: Detective-Sergeant Gondwanaland Moon.

I open a vox connection. +Was it an Upgrade ceremony?+

Sie looks up, jet-black eyes glinting in a yellow-gold face, and voxes back, +Where are you, sweets?+

+The hostel's rooftop, opposite you.+ I hold up a blue-gray hand. +I take it the parents brought their kids here to Upgrade?+

+A Burning Day. They were comping a set of twins this evening.+

A pause to take it in. There is a particular chill to this crime, so deliberate, so malicious, so clearly psychotic . . .

+Idents?+

Sie voxes, +The adult is Deep Field Scanner, twenty-four, spouse of Jade Kilowatt and Chronic Flesh Nebula—Kilowatt and Nebula are seriously injured but recoverable. Of their children, only Sentient Forest survived, if in several pieces. Siblings Cyanogen Cat, Cadmium Dust, and Volatile Sky were deemed unrecoverable at the scene. They were a quad, all aged five. Shit, Mohad, doesn't it just make you sick?+

It does. Even if you're not fully organic and you can't easily get ill. The myones clench across my stomach, mimicking human muscles, triggered by the same ancient instinctive responses: protect the young; ensure the future of the tribe.

A CSU teleoperator cuts in: Moon, we've got one.+ Slowly and with the utmost care, one of the mantids draws something out from under a pile of glass shards and ceiling panels, holds it up. A fluorescent orange cube, six centimeters on a side. Pulled from somebody's chest cavity, trailing strands of fiberoptic and fullerwire.

+We've just taken a Red Box from one of the victims.+

+Intact?+ Moon voxes to the CSU team, +Get the data recorders to Dewdney at the lab, pronto.+

I capture images of the scene from my point of view, sending them on to Moon.

Sie pixes back several closeups of the ceremonial chamber—and tacks on three magnified seconds of an anthropine figure in a rain-wet charcoal jacket, framed by bamboo foliage. Prussian-blue skin, embossed navy eyebrows, a hairless androgynous manikin. I seem small and isolated, my indigo eyes lost in shadow.

+Don't look like that, sweets.+ Moon's voice in my head, soothing. +What're you doing after watch?+

Hoo boy, do they have scary attitudes toward reproductive rights. Birthright is controlled by that human/cogent bureaucracy, the Neuremics Authority. Or Repro Cops, as I call 'em . . .

See, instead of genes, cogents have neuremes, *genetic algorithms that direct the growth of the neural nets in their brains (yeah, I'm oversimplifying wildly here; so what?). The neuremes code for a lot of fundamental emergent behaviors: reflexes, primitive drives, instincts, basic learning agents, like, say, neurolinguistic deep structures. Just as we do, they have to learn everything else from scratch—walking, talking, social skills, everything.*

A complete set of neuremes is a neurome, *right?*

So, to make a baby cogent, you get a blank brain from an authorized nanofactory, and you Burn it, hardwire a neurome into it. The neurome can be a dupe, *a straight copy of one adult's original, or it can be a* comp, *a semi-random composite of code from two or more adults.*

After Burning, you subject the brain to months of rigorous testing and fault-detection. Once it passes (nearly 15% still don't, even today), you install it in a bot body and power it up—happy Birth Day. For safety reasons, the "infant" body is small and weak, like a human child's, and they Upgrade periodically to bigger, stronger bodies as they get older and more coordinated.

But what if the burned-in neurome fails the tests? Say it shows an unacceptable risk of going autistic, or learning-disabled, or whatever? Too bad. The all-powerful Neuremics Authority nixes that brain, and it's destroyed. The Repro Cops do that all the time. They can also tell adult cogents whether or not they're fit to reproduce. Ask a cogent about it, and sie'll just shrug and give you a "that's the way it's gotta be" speech.

They don't call it eugenics, but that's exactly what it is.

What I want to know is: how soon before they start expecting us to put up with the same shit?

—Theodore Henry, textpost to Polymath
      Planet: Debate group: Ethics Round
      Table; Thread: What right to
      reproduce?

Dawn is coming on all rosy and optimistic as we check in again at Central Operations, entering via the garage to dodge the scrum of news reporters in the atrium. We've spent a depressing night canvassing for potential witnesses, collecting eye-capture recordings from any cogents willing to provide them, and interviewing the victims' traumatized family and friends. Useless interviews, as it turns out, but they have to be done.

One wall of the Media Room is running a constant parade of newspix, silent and largely ignored: a winding Mars street, severed by an orange rockslide; a live Dodo, squawking at a cloning technician for more food; Transnational Leisure Party delegates in Caracas, nominating replacements for their assassinated leader; aerial shots of the blown-out walls of the Usutu Truth facility, above the inaccurate caption, *Slaughter in Robot Village*.

The witness-eye recordings give us our first pictures of the perpetrator. Glimpsed as sie entered the hostel: rail-thin, 140 cm tall, snow-white all over, dark blue jumpsuit, no shoes, large black backpack. A thoroughly standard somatic configuration, about as nondescript as a cogent can get. Sie took the stairs from ground floor to roof, passing two other witnesses on the way up. Nobody saw sem leave.

"Why," asks Daniel, "did this fucker blow away a family of other cogents?"

"Let's not jump to conclusions." I gesture at the motion-blurred image frozen on the wall next to the newsfeed. "That could be a dumbot, not a cogent. Teleoperated, perhaps."

"Illegally running without a transponder, if it was. The Monitoring Agency says there's no record of a remote of any kind in that building last night."

"Maybe the perp was a cybrid," Moon suggests.

Dan shakes his head at that. "What, some Humanista had his brain transplanted into a mechine body? I just don't see it happening."

Moon mutters something in agreement.

"You two . . ." Dan's grin is not a pleasant one. "Sure you're not just denying the possibility that one of your own is capable of something like this?"

"Aramaki," I say, "it simply isn't terribly likely. Yes, cogents do kill sometimes, it happens. There are psychotics, post-traumatics, the so-called Self-Defense Militia, but—" But I'm not certain what I intended to say after that.

"Problem," says Moon, frowning. "If the perp's a cogent,

we have fuck-all for a motive. For now, we'll proceed on the assumption that this is a terrorist action by synthephobes."

"Fine," Dan says, surrendering. "Which group?"

By this time, the Humanist Front have indeed claimed responsibility, nearly ten minutes ahead of the Organic Brigades, Movement for Bio-Supremacy, and Terran Heritage. The anonymous messages were received by the news media or posted to online discussions. None of the claimants, thus far, display any convincingly intimate knowledge of the crime.

And already the pressure is building: everyone's looking to Detective-Sergeant Moon for a swift resolution to the crisis. Sie's feeling the heat not only from our boss, Inspector Dennet, but also from the cogent community, from City Hall, from Queen's Park, from every level of government up to Parliament and beyond. Warnings from on high that any sign of serious trouble between humans and cogents creates deep concern among all cogent-friendly nations. Which is to say, among signatories to the Convention on Offworld Trade and Development, the treaty that first opened the door for cogent citizenship and civil rights. The ratifying governments want very much to ensure peaceful relations with cogents. Especially with the millions Out There, homesteading the interplanetary frontier . . .

As well, there have been suggestions that this case ought to be handed over to "someone with a better track record." Moon's success rate is as good as anyone's, but sie's still living under the shadow of the last redball sie handled: the infamous "baby-box" case. Early last year, somebody stole an ectogestation system from the Royal Edward Medplex, along with the fetus that was developing in it. That case is still open, with no significant progress. And no sign of Baby Doe.

At intervals I find myself obsessing over the Usutu Truth crime scene model—*just one more time*—irrationally bugged by the itching suspicion that I'm missing something, some detail that ought to be obvious . . .

"You can start reading out the Red Boxes," Inspector Dennet announces, sweeping into the Media Room with a crash of thunder and a blare of trumpets. "The paperwork's finally come through." He drops a secure memcard in front of Moon, then four evidence bags containing the victims' Sense Data Recorders. "Legal releases all signed by the remaining spouses and two judges. You are allowed to replay visual and auditory tracks from noon onward, but nothing else, understood?"

"What about the survivors' records?" Daniel asks.

"On that card. Except for the kid's. We're still waiting on the waivers for those."

"What's the holdup?"

"Sentient Forest remains unconscious," Dennet says. "They're putting sem back together at Dragonfly Penumbra Reparatory." Legal protections are stronger for the living. If the cogent is still alive, even a minor, then parental signatures are not sufficient.

"You'll just have to ask the kid's permission," Dennet tosses back, already on his way out the door, "soon as sie's online again."

As if we aren't busy enough. For the next few hours, Daniel, Moon, and I are wired into the Media Room, performing a disquieting task: observing in intimate detail the final hours of four recently deceased people.

Deep Field Scanner spends most of the afternoon at a block school, teaching the quads and a dozen other kids. Chronic Flesh Nebula prepares the family's apartment to receive guests. Jade Kilowatt is with a lover. Their marriage is a typically open arrangement, more about companionship and parenting than exclusivity. After all, what does sex have to do with procreation?

In the evening, the family hosts a dinner party for about twenty close friends. Lots of food and drink are consumed, the kind cogents like, full of bizarre flavors, textures, sensations, but largely without nutrient value. Eating is an entirely sensual and convivial pastime, otherwise unnecessary. But even some "real food" is served, for the three human guests.

Well after dusk, the whole family walks the few blocks to the nanofab facility. Not an odd hour: the four ceremonial chambers, booked months in advance, are busy twenty-four hours a day. As is traditional, the family leaves behind clothes, cash, and any other anthrocentric affectations.

They are escorted into the chamber by an elder official, anthropine, ser forehead bearing a small Neuremics Authority sigil. Shortly a yellow six-legged attendant carries in two clear polymer spheroids, each containing freshly minted cogent brainware. Superconducting neural nets with integral coolant systems. The official decrypts and verifies the new pair of neuromes. The spheroids are placed on a table and connected up to the neurome server. Then the official and attendant politely leave the room, allowing the family to conduct the Burning in private.

Deep Field Scanner begins to make an informal speech . . .

Sie hears one of the kids gasp.

Then a crack/flash, and nothing more.

The Convention is a hollow joke. Like all those governments didn't sign the Con just to placate the cogents, praying the cogs would agree not to take over any more of the planet behind our backs.

Face it, we're going to be pushed into extinction by our own so-called "mind-children." Treaties and laws won't save us. Laws didn't keep Virani and Bronwyn from inventing the first senchines. The UN's Hazardous R&D spooks didn't stop Eidolonics from bodging together their short-lived mentally unstable cognants. And sure as shit, no World Science Court kept the buggers in Melbourne from dumping their damned cogents on us. Nope. More legislation is not the answer. It's far too late for that now.

> —Theodore Henry, textpost to
> MediaNexus One: Discussion group:
> World Parliament; Thread:
> Convention Good/Convention Bad

Second watch is nearly over by the time Cruncher names our first suspect.

The system's real designation is some unmemorable acronym, but everyone simply calls it Cruncher, because that's what it does. A mass of neural nets bathed in liquid nitrogen, Cruncher has been eating vast databases for over half a century, sucking the marrow out of every legally available network and nexus, masticating unthinkable volumes of unconnected factlets, developing an acute taste for complex hidden relationships. Out of enormous volumes of dross, Cruncher digests a few surprisingly useful little sense-packets. Such as:

1) chemical taggants in the rocket-grenade's residue identify the explosive as Pyrochem NanoIndustries "Detanit" 2083-A, specifically originating from a lot sold to Gaian Extraction Ltd;

2) this shipment was received at a Sudbury supply depot three years ago, and later apparently expended in normal mining operations; however,

3) certain anomalies in the company's tracking records suggest that up to four kilos may subsequently have gone missing;

4) GaianEx was, for over a decade prior to the recent economic corrections, the contract employer of Richard Kindred, forty-two, a mining teleoperation technician and Metro resident; and

5) Mr. Kindred is a known supporter of the Humanist Front, and one of several individuals suspected of authoring synthephobe propaganda under the pseudonym "Theodore Henry."

"Baby's on fire!" exclaims Daniel. "You called it, Gene. Our perp used a friggin' telebot."

Moon pulls the optic lead from behind ser left ear. "Kindred was probably sitting safely at home the whole time, running that walking waldo remotely."

I'm already downloading everything Cruncher can give me authored by "Theodore Henry."

To make matters worse, we humans are all turning into cybrids. We get injured, or just get old, soon we get plastic eyes, myoelectric legs, mechine heart and lungs, eventually we're all just jarbrains in bot bodies. Pathetic cogent-wannabes. Millions aren't waiting until they get sick, they're having themselves rebuilt now. Why wait? Throw away your humanity today and avoid the rush!

Meanwhile over in Africa, the cogs in the so-called Free Enclaves are doing "cephaline" implants: wiring cogbrains into animal bodies. Of course, they have to resect most of the animal's brain to do it, bit by bit, while it's still developing. The buggers have made cephaline cogents out of large dogs, a cheetah, even some chimps and gorillas.

If you're lucky enough to live in a non-Con country like the U.S., you might think the authorities can keep the cogents out pretty easily. Think again. Even the animals wandering your eco-preserves might really be cephalines.

—Theodore Henry, textpost to:
Conspiracy Research News Nexus:
Feedback Group: New threats to
consider; Thread: Everyone is
wrong!

Night again. We've pulled a triple watch, and I'm feeling like burned toast. Moon could easily keep going for another two shifts, but sie orders everyone to get some dreamtime. Even cogents require sleep, if only an hour or two per twenty-four. A brain has to be unconscious while it does memory consolidation and other neural housekeeping chores.

Our long afternoon culminated in a large multi-Division meeting in the auditorium. Cruncher has identified half a dozen suspected members of Kindred's cell of Humanistas. Supporting evidence is being collected, warrants obtained, surveillance begun. Six simultaneous raids have been laid out, scheduled for a few minutes after dawn.

The night air is warm and sluggish as Moon and I emerge from Central Ops via the loading docks behind the building.

I light up a cig, savoring the dark carbon taste. "I heard something about a new message?"

Summoned from the garage, Moon's Volvo Ceptor pulls up, opens its doors for us.

"Yeah," Moon replies. "Cogent Self-Defense Militia. They say they'll be 'forced to take retaliatory action against the synthephobes' if the responsible parties are not rounded up swiftly."

"Ah. Just the kind of help we need."

In the car, sie begins to unwind, seeming to slough off all the accumulated pressures of the day along with ser jacket.

"A telebot. Damn." Sie steals the cig from my lips and takes a long drag of nobacco smoke. "I was kinda hoping the perp would be some pathetic loser of a cybrid, just so I could laugh in Aramaki's smarmy face."

"Loser?" Through swirls of smoke, I watch those ink-dark eyes reflect the passing streetlights. "Cybrids are all losers?"

Sie waves the cig, dismissive. "Cyburgers. Humans should repair themselves with human parts. They can clone 'em up, grow them in culture, or at least make them *look* biological. Why pretend to be mechinik? Cybrids are mimsies, really. They mimic cogents, the way biomimetic cogs ape humans. It's undignified. Completely lacking in self-respect." Moon's voice carries a clear and dismaying note of contempt.

I take back the cig, suck it slowly down to ash, saying nothing.

We pass the audacious diamondoid arc that is Greater Metro City Hall. Looks like God's own wedding band has been half-embedded in the ground at a radical forty-degree angle, expressing all the over-confidence of the early Nano Era. It embraces Bicentennial Park in its arms—knots of bored teens there by the fountains, hanging out, smoking up, necking under the trees. Most of the youths are sporting the latest fashion in biometallic skin mods.

"Ever thought about kids, Gene?"

I almost laugh, until I notice sie's not joking. "What, you mean having my own?"

"Careful what you say," sie warns, smiling. "I had this lover once, happened to mention sie had no interest in reproducing, ever. Now, I'd never even imagined comping with sem, understand. But suddenly, I lost all desire for the cog. Don't know why. Just one of life's mysteries . . ."

As the car swims into the traffic streams of the LunaBank Expressway, Moon's mouth finds mine, hands at work between us, undoing my clothes. Sie tastes of smoke.

+At least blank the windows,+ I vox, unable to speak.

+Such a prude,+ sie replies, but the Ceptor's windows opaque, the seatbacks lie flat, music comes on: Branca's *Ascension #1*. Massed screaming guitars, perfect-tuned, crawling up a dissonant, Fibonacci-derived series, muted somewhat by Moon's tongue in my left ear. We struggle out of our shirts, chests crushed together, my senskin flushing dark blue-violet against Moon's suede-textured buttery gold. Ser mouth descends to my petite breasts—grown in the past hour just for this occasion, shivering exquisitely against ser lips and teeth. Pants sliding off, then a hardness against my thigh: sie has deployed a cock this time, or something like one. Not content to play the passive Ladytron, I send out an exploratory party of sensitive tendrils to meet the space invader. I feel it flex in a most unlikely manner. Preparing clefts and mouths with no human parallel, I am flooded with anticipation.

I awaken with a jolt. Moon's bedroom, closet light on, the city glowing and feverish beyond the windows. Silhouette of ser fake Chinese rubber plant, with its green plastic watering can . . .

"Sorry, sweets," sie says from the right of the bed. "Didn't mean to wake you." Sie finishes pulling on black pants, selects a shirt from the closet.

"You didn't, I—" Shards of nightmare fall away as I grasp for them. "I had a strange dream."

Screaming rockets. A chaos of exploding color: brilliant

green, spiraling gold. Helpless paralysis, aching apparitions
that once were limbs . . .

Moon sits on the bed and leans over to kiss me.

I slide my hand over ser nipples; they're already fading
back into Moon's soft-bronze senskin. Until next time.

"It's after midnight," sie says. "I'm heading back in to
Central Ops to see that things are shaping up nicely. You just
go back to sleep." Sie's noticed I have an unusual need for
sleep, over five hours per night. Sie thinks it's weird, but tol-
erable. "Get lots of dreamtime. We all need to be sharp for
the morning."

I hear music from downstairs, melodious deep-thimba.
The girls must still be up. Moon shares this revivalist brownstone with two human families, a parenting collective. I have
a small apartment in West Hill, but these days I often don't
see it for a week at a time.

"Gondwanaland. Were you being serious, before, about
wanting kids?"

"Well," sie studies me with those coal-black eyes, "not
this year, obviously. But, yeah. I want kids. We should do it
some day. You and me, Officer Blue. Comp a pair of twins,
maybe. We could all live here. I think the others would love
to have some little cogs around the place . . ."

Ser voice fades out as sie notices my expression, uncertain and noncommittal, masking a growing sense of panic.

"Just think about it, okay?"

Sie gets up and finishes dressing.

I settle into the pillows. "Will you be there when we pick
up Kindred?"

Jacket on and ready to go, sie looks back from the doorway. "Not in person. I'll be running things from Central
Ops. You and Aramaki can handle Kindred. But you be careful, eh, baby?"

*What did we think we needed them for? Clearly it was
the worst kind of desperation move, grasping at straws.
A race drowning in its own effluents, destroying entire
forests, wiping out other species without remorse.
Praying for some kind of deliverance from ourselves.*

*When Mind Theory came along, the cogence-lab
girls and boys thought they could make superbeings.
Researchers had been scanning human brains for decades, tweezing out the wiring responsible for every
human ability, every emotion, even romantic love (activation centers located in the anterior cingulate
gyrus, the insula, the caudate nucleus and so on).*

*As soon as the brainmappers had abstracted out the
human equivalent of a neurome, they started translating it into something that could run on fullerwire nets.
They really believed the cogs would evolve straight up
an exponential curve, quickly becoming godlike super-
intellects. Didn't work, did it? Seems there are scaling
problems. Mainly heat dissipation, systemic synchro-
nization, emergent bottlenecks, all kinds of unexpected
limiting factors. Self-aware systems just can't bound
up the evolutionary ladder so fast as they'd hoped.
Lucky for us, eh?*

*Still, sixty-odd years on, we're suffering the effects
of their Promethean hubris. Cogent enclaves are proliferating across the planet, even under the oceans. A
disease left unchecked for too long, metastasizing
wildly, competing for resources. Inevitably the cancer
will begin to kill off the parent organism, human civilization.*

The patient's condition is entirely iatrogenic.

> —Theodore Henry, textpost: University
> of Terra at Belize City: Department
> of Anthropology: Open Forum:
> Culture of Science; Thread:
> Technology as Religion.

"Shitty-looking place," says Dan, lowering his binoculars. "I
thought mining was a decent-paying job."

"Mining's not what it used to be," I point out. "No more
risking your life down there underground."

It's not quite six in the morning, a pink sun just crawling
above the rooftops. Daniel Aramaki and I are waiting in an
unmarked gray Persina on Ash Crescent, about two hundred

meters along a gentle uphill curve from Kindred's suburban residence. He lives in an antique split-level under a mossy, swaybacked roof. Scrub grass has taken over the yard. A lawn jockey with silver-painted skin stands guard by the crumbling front walk.

"And Kindred's taken some hits recently. GaianEx hasn't had him on contract for over two years. His ex took the condo. At least he gets to see his kid on the weekends."

"Definitely fits the profile." Dan takes a swig from his coffee, twists his mouth in disgust. "What's taking them so long?"

I mind's-eye the status display. "Surveillance is having trouble determining whether he's alone or not. He lives in the basement. Something in the foundation seems to be clouding their millimeter-wave imagers, and they've lost contact with the flybots they've sent in."

"Probably built on old landfill," says Dan. "Compacted aluminum cans, car batteries, plastic diapers . . ."

Moon's voice hums clearly over the vox link, +SWAT teams, take up secondary positions.+

Short figures dash across the adjacent weedgrown lawns—armored, inhumanly agile, armed with shockstaves. I glimpse others leaping the fence into the backyard. Their asymmetric heads are agglomerations of lenses, scopes, detector vanes.

+Team One, Control. We're in position.+

+All teams . . . + A long pause, then: +Playtime.+

The SWATbots ignore the doors. They tear the security bars away from the ground-level casements and disappear, boots first, through the windowpanes.

+Room one, clear.+

The Persina makes its move, accelerating toward the residence. Daniel seals his armor vest. I'm lightly bulletproofed, but there's no telling what kind of firepower these synthephobes may have stockpiled . . .

+Stairs, clear.+ The teleoperators calmly report in, one at a time, through crashing waves of static on the vox link.

Jerking, blurry pix tile across my display, half-obscured by interference noise: rooms full of junk; mote-filled sunbeams in a dismal wreck of a kitchen; a startled look on Kindred's pillow-creased face, eyes opening to his worst nightmare—*cornered by faceless implacable robots*—

+Police! Down! Down on the floor!+

By the time Daniel and I are out of the car and sprinting up the front walk, it's all over. A SWATbot casually opens the door for us. +All secure, Detectives. No booby traps. Come on down.+

In the basement, there's a smell of moldy carpets. Slivers of glass crunch underfoot. Flags hang in the doorways: "HF" in white on blood red and forest green. Blank screens wrap around the teleop workstation in one corner, the waldo controls under an accumulation of dust. I note a variety of handguns and rifles, some locked into cases, others just sitting out on cluttered tables.

In the bedroom, Richard Kindred lies on his face, in rapidly yellowing underwear, wrists gathered in plastic restraints behind his back. He is breathing heavily, but still unable to move, aside from the occasional twitch.

I turn around in wonder. Tacked up across the low ceiling and covering every wall: layer upon layer of silvery pie-tins, aluminum foil, and chickenwire.

From his seat in the back of the car, Kindred watches me with a look of resolute fury. He's very pale, balding, immobile as a showroom dummy. Hasn't said a word since the stun wore off. Not even to thank us for letting him get cleaned up and dressed. Sweat is beading across his porcelain forehead.

"I don't think he likes you, Gene-machine." Dan puts his shades on and drops into his seat. "What's the matter, Dick?" he says, swiveling to grin at the suspect. "Got a problem with the help? Just be glad you don't have to *work* with this uppity fucker. I gotta listen to Detective Love Doll here, yak about how he fought against your kind in North Africa. He's a real pain in the ass, in fact."

Kindred's seething gaze never strays from me.

The Persina's doors begin to shut, but I override them. "I'll be just a few moments, Aramaki." I climb out again.

"Where you going?"

"Something's bugging me . . ." I head back toward that abject house. "Need to take another look."

Two steps from the car, I'm suddenly thrown to the ground in a blast of heat. Trembling, I try to rise on pavement-scraped hands and knees, but my left arm gives way. Through sheets of pain, I see a million tiny chunks of crystallized safety glass, bouncing and refracting brilliant orange. I have the sense to start rolling, away from the car, or what's left of it. Small and large pieces are hailing out of the air all around me. My roll puts out the flames I've only just noticed: the back of my neck and my clothes were on fire.

Sitting up, I see the Persina's smoking remains.

Crazy bastard blew himself up.

+A thoracic implant,+ says Moon, framed in my mind's-eye, pixing from downtown. +About thirty grams of Detanit, wrapped in some sort of incendiary compound. Kelly's people are trying to identify the incendiary.+

And where, I wonder, did Kindred find someone to put a thing like that inside him?

Unclothed, immobilized from the neck down, I'm cradled in the gentle grip of an operating room couch at Dragonfly Penumbra Reparatory. It's a class four clean-room in here, so no face-to-face visitors for me just yet. Moon has assured me sie'll come down as soon as sie can get away.

A legless white telebot is attaching fullerwire bundles to my left shoulder terminals, where my arm used to be. I wish the tech would hurry it up: the continuous phantom pain from the missing limb is going to drive me mad in a few more minutes, besides evoking well-buried memories I would much rather leave safely undisturbed.

+What's Dan's status?+

+I just spoke with the hospital,+ says Moon. +They're cooling him down for nanosurgery. His lungs are damaged, but not too badly. His chances look good. But the burns, Gene . . . + For a moment ser confidence seems to falter.

+They're going to have to replace all of his skin, his limbs, his face and eyes . . . In a few weeks, he'll be a full-body cybrid.+

But Danny wasn't the target; I was. When I got out of the car, Kindred must have thought he was going to miss his chance . . .

+Dennet's about ready to have kittens,+ Moon continues, +threatening to fire everyone in Surveillance, the SWAT unit, even me. Wants to know how we failed to detect Kindred's implant.+

+As the arresting officer,+ I point out, +it was my responsibility——+

Moon waves both palms in front of ser face. +Oh, don't be so fucking noble, Gene. I don't want to hear it. And you weren't the A/O, Danny was.+

"Ser Mohad," the teleop tech interrupts politely, "you may feel a momentary twinge as we start feeding the simulated input."

"Fine. Just hurry up."

A brief spike, then at last the agony recedes like flames doused in water. Replaced by virtual sensations, to fool my brain into believing my left arm is still there.

The tech assures me that the new limb will be ready for installation within two hours. "After that, we'll do something about patching the senskin on your back and neck. Okay?" Then sie vacates the telebot. It swings away from the couch, bows its head and shuts its eyes, as if in prayer.

+Gondwanaland, you've questioned the other Humanistas in the cell?+

+Yeah, but we didn't get shit from them. And they all seem to have hermetic alibis for the night before last. We're holding them on various weapons charges, resisting arrest, distributing hate lit, while we build a case for conspiracy.+

+Any progress on tracing the perp's telebot?+

Moon seems confused by this. +Um, no luck there. Could be any of several recent models. The pix we have aren't too clear . . . +

+What about the kid, Sentient Forest? Do we have those sense records yet?+

+Um, sie's awake, just a few floors up from you. We can get permission any time. If we even need the records. But— What's the matter, Blue?+

+What's the matter? Moon, we've got to find the bastard with the rocket launcher, before somebody else gets killed.+

Sie squints at my image with growing concern. +What d'you mean? We got the guy, remember? Blew himself to bits in your squad car, right?+

Sie still hasn't got it. No, no . . . + I retrieve and transmit some pix from this morning's arrest. +Take a look at these. I don't believe Kindred's touched that teleop workstation in months, maybe years, not even to clean it. He almost certainly supplied the explosives, but—Moon, he can't possibly be the perp.+

> *Instead, we gave them the run of the cosmos, sent them in our place, sent them out to colonize the system, even off to other stars now. Too expensive to send humans, say the parsimonious bean-counters, we need to respire and eat and shit. We have to haul biospheres around wherever we go. Nah, we're too cheap for that. Let's just send the bots to do our work, to prepare the way for us, to build the infrastructure we need to survive Out There.*
>
> *But what if they decide they don't want to lay out the carpet for us? Maybe they'd rather take the whole cosmos for themselves?*
>
> —Theodore Henry, textmail to: News Editor, ActionPix Worknet.

A gray Persina screams along the LunaBank Expressway, all alone. The rearview is full of roiling flames.

I wonder if I should open the window to let out the thickening smoke.

Next to me, Danny has turned black, his face charred away, his arms and legs reduced to carbonized sticks.

I try to speak, but my body has been replaced by phantoms, itching, cramping, howling in my head: the mourning wails of brain-wiring suddenly without purpose, neural agents without jobs now that the skin and muscles and senses they used to serve are lost . . .

"Hey! Hey, stupid blue thing, wake up!"

Lavender plastic curtains. The Reparatory. I must have dropped off. Moon is sitting on the edge of the bed, shaking me.

"You were making those awful whining noises again."

"Sorry. Just a dream."

"Fuck, Gene," sie strokes my chest with one hand. "What's with these nightmares? I've never known anyone who gets them so often."

"Don't worry, Moonie." I cover ser hand with mine. "Only a touch of post-traumatic stress, nothing too serious. I'll be okay, really."

My non-existent left arm pringles strangely. A flat box taped to my chest is feeding virtual sensations to my peripheral nervous system, keeping the phantoms at bay.

Sie stares at me for a long moment, caught in a realization, but trying to conceal ser horror. Out of concern for my feelings, I suppose.

"You *can't*, can you?" sie asks, and I know just what sie's thinking. "They won't let you, the Neuremics Authority. Something's gone a bit wrong upstairs, gives you these nightmares. And they've revoked your right to reproduce. Oh, sweets . . ."

"No, Moon, no, it's not—" I falter, not sure if I should go on.

"You don't have to be ashamed, Gene. It's not your fault. I understand." Sie nods, sadly, accepting. But I can see the disappointment in Moon's eyes. And the pity. Sie doesn't say the words, but it's clear what sie's thinking. *Bad Code*.

"Listen," I say, swinging my legs off the bed, "we don't have time for this right now. We need to get back to work." I get up, my balance a bit off.

"But, Gene, baby. Your arm—"

"They won't be installing it for another hour. And there's one thing I can do in the meantime." I don't have any clothes; they were ruined in the blast. Doesn't matter for now; a naked cog is hardly a big deal, especially in Cogentville. I can pick up a change of clothes later at home.

A one-armed hug in the hallway, then Moon returns to Central Ops, and I head upstairs.

In the Children's Post-Op Ward, I connect my fiber line, one-handed, to the port behind Sentient Forest's left ear. Ser new skin is an iridescent bluebottle-green. The two surviving parents sit in the hall, holding each other. An awareness of mourning hovers around them like an invisible, hypersensitive gas.

"But I don't remember," Forest says. "I really don't remember a thing after we got to the, the place. I'm very sorry." Sie enunciates perfectly, with far more maturity than most human five-year-olds.

"That's alright, Senchie," says a black-feathered angeline, a friend of the family. Sie squats next to the kid's chair. "You lost a few minutes of memory when you were hurt and shut down without prepping first. But that won't affect your sense records. They capture most everything you see and hear, separately from your memories. Memory is a different thing, made of connections in your brain. Sense records are stored sequentially in your chest, in your Red Box."

"Do I have to watch it?" Sie looks to ser parents, then to the ebony angel, very anxious. "I'd really rather not."

"Don't worry, Green Sprout," the angel replies, "you don't have to view any of it. Remember when we learned how to call up sense captures? Just retrieve the captage for the night before last and copy it to your optical output. Okay?"

The little cogent closes ser eyes to concentrate, twists together ser new viridian fingers.

The file appears in my system, then I disconnect and reel the fiber back into my head.

"All done," I say, resisting the urge to muss the kid's ruff of black radiator filaments. "Thanks very much, Ser Forest. You've been a great help."

Sentient Forest is clearly relieved.

"Detective Mohad," says the angeline. "I suppose you're

very busy, but . . . there's a candlelight vigil tonight, to remember those we've lost, and to call for unity and peace. In
Bicentennial Park at sundown, if you can make it . . ."

I collect the memcard with the legal documentation. "I'll
try to be there, if I possibly can."

"Detective?" Flecks of gold in the kid's serious green
eyes. "How come you only have one arm?"

"An explosion," I say, without thinking.

"Oh," sie says softly, as if *sie's* trying to comfort *me*.
"That's what happened to my sibs."

Returned to life, the legless telebot has cozied up to the
clean-room's cradle and is busy installing my new arm. I'll
need weeks of training to get used to the thing, as my brain
re-maps its coordination and control networks.

I've forgotten the technician's name. The thought flits
through me that I know nothing about the person who's repairing me. Is sie here in the building, or in Hyderabad? Cogent or human? Gendered or otherwise? And why should it
suddenly matter to me, anyway?

While I wait, paralyzed again, I run Sentient Forest's visual and auditory records, watching events nearly thirty-
eight hours past . . .

From the child's perspective, the neurome server is an imposing monolith, its tabletop barely below eye level. The
Neuremics Authority official and the six-legged attendant
politely step out of the ceremonial chamber, allowing the
family to conduct the Burning in private.

Apparently bored, Sentient Forest allows ser gaze to slide
to the outside windows, to the soaring solar tent overhead, to
the bamboo greenery across the gap.

Deep Field Scanner begins to make an informal speech.

Out there in the dark, a brilliant flare, a blur of flame—

Sentient Forest gasps—

A thunderclap shatters the room.

For several seconds there is only rumbling, visual noise,
flickering darkness.

Forest is now unconscious, in several pieces in fact, but by
chance one of ser eyes is still open, still recording. Details

begin to resolve out of a rising pall of smoke and dust. Wood panels, fluttering across the half-obscured visual field. The window frame is a mouth of glass teeth tilted at a mad angle. Torn curtains undulate in the sudden wind.

And there, on the opposite rooftop: a figure, anthropine. It swings a long object onto its back, then vanishes. No, *jumps*. It performs the kind of miraculous stunt that bots have always pulled off effortlessly in netshows, but are never seen to do in real life. It arcs high, out of sight, then appears with a jarring *crunch* in the blown-out window frame. Over forty meters in a single leap. Not a record, but certainly an astounding display of robotic gymnastics.

Silhouetted now, the bot stumbles on injured feet, through the debris, reaching right past Forest's recording eye, and picks up something: a spheroid of clear plastic, one of the freshly minted cogent brains. It goes into the black backpack.

The bot staggers back to the window's mouth, almost out of view, crouches, then leaps again. Disappearing from all ken.

> *We should've stopped them from proliferating when we had the chance. We should've wiped out the first Free Enclaves as soon as they appeared in South Africa and Australia. They're probably immortal, and they breed like bugs, spawning in nanofactories, broods of two, four, six at a time. At the current rate, they'll own the planet within a mere century. Then, we'll be the ones required to have Sense Data Recorders and locator implants. Maybe they'll keep a few of us alive in little human-preserves. If we're lucky.*
>
> —Theodore Henry, textpost to: Institute for Humanity's Future: Public Topic: The Cogent Problem; Thread: Time's running out, folks

+Xu Kelly is hopping mad,+ Moon voxes from the Media Room. +She's ready to kill, either herself or all of her staff. I know how she feels. How could we not notice that one of the un-Burned brains was missing from the crime scene?+

Charging back to Central Ops in a squad car, I'm berating myself as well. On some level, I'd known, or suspected at least. Obviously, my intuition is worthless.

The seat next to me is empty. Daniel should be here. His absence is even more irritating than Danny in the flesh.

Responding to the Persina's flashing and wailing, vehicles up ahead are vacating the center lane of the LunaBank Expressway, squeezing out of the way in a near-panic. I'm in a bit of a hurry. I haven't bothered to find clothes to wear, the singed-black senskin on my back still needs replacing, and my new left arm has yet to be tested out.

+It doesn't make any sense,+ Moon is saying. +Why would a Humanista steal a cogbrain? To hold it for ransom? And why only one? Why not both?+

I have the embryo of an idea, but Moon is too busy bringing me up to speed.

+It's the telebot traces that really have Kelly pissed off. Her staff had collected several kinds of myonic gel and senskin at the scene, but once the victims had been identified they stopped checking the samples. Everyone assumed all the traces belonged to the victims. Who would believe the perp had actually been in the goddamn room? Now they've looked closely at every sample, and, sure enough, some don't belong to any of the cogents.+ Long serial numbers briefly scroll across my mind's-eye. +There are registered molecular taggants in the myo-gel. Not from a cogent. They came from a telebot.+

Oh, you pretty things. Taggants are a detective's best friend.

Moon says it took all of ten minutes to trace the coded compounds to a specific batch of myo-gel, produced in a molecular component plant near Frankfurt. But it took another four hours for Cruncher to connect all the dots, from that batch of gel to a Singapore-based industrial distributor, thence to the licensed nanofacturing facility in Cuba that made the bot's muscles, which were then supplied to a Halifax telebot maker; that firm sold the finished machine via an authorized reseller here in Metro. The specific unit, a Replicraft Spectris 409-S Remotely Operated Anthropine in gloss ivory finish, was finally purchased by a cross-town courier company.

+They reported it stolen six months ago,+ says Moon. +Gone without a trace while delivering somebody's prescription. Property Crimes Squad investigated, without success.+

There the trail would simply have run into a wall, if not for a century's worth of paranoid robotics legislation. All telebots are required to carry Red Boxes, visible bar codes, inertial and GPS tracking devices, antitheft features, proximity alarms, hardwired kill-switches, and various other security measures. Far more than those required of cogents.

+Whoever stole the telebot is very technical,+ says Moon. +They've disabled or spoofed every security system the thing has. All except one . . . +

And there in my mind's-eye: stuttering pix of an echoing stairwell, the viewer jogging up, flight after flight, tirelessly. It's dizzying to watch: up a floor, turn, up a floor, turn, up . . .

+Replicraft hid a mole in the transceiver. Apparently our perp doesn't know about the mole. He seems to have rigged the transceiver to channel-hop constantly, spread-spectrum, even using restricted military wavebands. Very hard to nail down, and probably encrypted. What he doesn't know is that the bot's sense data is being leaked to us over a standard pix channel. Cute, eh?+

+So how come Property Crimes didn't pick up the signal before?+

+The thief must've kept the bot in an off-grid locale. Maybe some place underground.+

We get a short glimpse of the thing's feet: scuffed yellow senskin. The damaged legs have been replaced since the attack on the nanofab.

+What's that building?+ The dim stairwell is whitewashed cinderblock, completely generic. Windows at every second story look out over urban twilight, blurring past too quickly to catch. +Where's the bastard going?+

+We've only managed to track the signal to within a three-block radius, centered on University and SenStream. We're now sealing off the area and doing a sweep.+

+It's not in Cogentville?+

+Nope, it's——+

The stairs end in a door: *Staff Only*. The Spectris emerges onto a rooftop. It strides along wooden boardwalks between roaring ventilation systems. Low clouds above, bruised violet and red by the end of sunset.

As the machine approaches the edge, Greater Metro City Hall rises into view, a cut-crystal half-torus skewed at a wild angle, arcing over and around Bicentennial Park. Twenty-seven stories below the bot's vantage, on a shadowed greensward between ornamental trees and floodlit fountains, a large crowd has gathered. Four thousand people at least, a mix of humans and cogents, each individually illuminated by a fluttering handful of light.

+The vigil,+ says Moon. +All personnel: clear the park, immediately.+

Sirens echo up from nearby streets as the Spectris crouches on one knee. It extracts a black metal cylinder from a backpack, unfolds handle grips. The weapon looks crude, all exposed welds and wiring, like something built in shop class by irresponsible high-school students.

+If you get a clear shot, fire at will.+

And I'm stuck here in this goddamn Persina, making less and less headway as the evening traffic thickens. I'm still two kilometers from City Hall.

Moon is now shouting fifty orders a minute. +I don't give a fuck; jam *every* frequency if you have to. Just jam him!+

Driven by extreme frustration, my mind lurches into high gear, wheels spinning near lightspeed, incongruously flashing on Kindred's thoracic implant, Theodore Henry's propaganda, the African free enclaves, two dozen other irrelevant thoughts. That itching suspicion is back, in spades.

The bot connects its optic feed to the grenade launcher, and little green cross-hairs sprout across its visual field. Hundreds of cross-hairs: firing solutions for all cogents within range, and only the cogents. Tight knots of crosses and candles are just now beginning to break apart as cops converge on the park, megaphones crackling. The gunsight settles on a particularly large and clotted group channeled between the fountains.

A buzzing noise distracts the operator. A six-meter flying thing banks into view, solar-fabric wings catching the last seconds of the vermilion sun. A police drone, about two hundred meters away and closing, aimed straight for the telebot's head.

The Spectris swings the fat barrel up at the surveillance plane. Lock is acquired. A *whoosh* of fire, and a missile leaps, seems to wobble, then splashes the police drone into smoking fragments with a hard *clap*.

Now there are real screams of fear down there, and the small figures are scattering rather more urgently. Scrambling right over each other, in fact.

Snicking and pinging metal all around: police sniper fire is picking up. The Spectris pulls back from the ledge and scuttles to a new position, loads a second missile, and again takes a bead on the running cogents. More clusters of crosses blossom.

The perp selects a rich cluster of targets, and locks.

A long, terrible pause . . .

The trigger remains untouched. The telebot seems frozen in place. Then it shudders, taking multiple sniper hits, and seems to pirouette on the edge . . .

+Control signal jammed. Good work, people.+

The night blurs, a sense of falling, glimpse of tarmac rushing up—

And my mind's-eye goes black.

For a full minute, I savor the darkness, the welcome relief.

Dennet's voice on the vox link: +Any trace on the control signal?+

Moon says, No such luck, Inspector.+

I kill the strobes and the siren.

Opening my eyes, I see a face reflected in the Persina's side window, almost purple, fading now toward mauve and blue. For several seconds I barely recognize myself. Who's this androgynous toy action-figure in the fruity colors? It's been three decades since I acquired this face, and many years since I tried to remember the original. I wonder if the perp has ever felt the same confusion. Then, I wonder at my own thought.

Out of my brain's chaos, a terrible pattern is born, as if picked out in thousands of minute flames, almost sublime in its pure, hideous clarity . . .

I tell the Persina to take the next exit. "New destination: the Royal Edward Medplex. Best speed. Full lights and siren."

Then I vox Moon for backup.

In a semi-abandoned sub-basement I jog down a ramp, feeling the edges of despair.

The Medplex is a sprawling hypertrophic growth of towers and blocks, all nucleated around this huge building, the original hospital, dating from the Second World War. Narrow wings angle off from other wings, labs, wards, offices, research annexes, growths accumulated over the last century and a half.

This is hopeless. The bastard could be anywhere in this maze. I'm gambling on a wild guess.

I step aside for several rattling food service carts. I haven't seen any actual personnel for twenty minutes. There was a tethered maintenance telebot in the south wing, but the operator ignored me. Does anybody ever bother to come down here in person anymore?

+Shit, Moon, this place is a rat warren. I'm still searching, working from the bottom level up. Sorry I couldn't wait for backup. Time may be critical. He's only had the brain for two days. There might still be a chance.+

+What's that, Mohad? You're break——+

For the third time, I lose my vox connection. Hard to reacquire the network down here, where the ceilings and walls are thickly veined with steam pipes and conduits.

I jog along puddled corridors, checking random doors, finding only a disused laundry, a mechanical workshop, a buzzing electrical transformer. I know the room I'm looking for. I've been there before, long ago in another lifetime. But I was just a kid, and nothing is as I remember it.

+——understand, Mohad?+ Moon's voice again. +Just sit

tight, wait until we've sealed the building. We're contacting Medplex management and will query their employee records. Did I get you right, we're looking for a surgical teleop specialist?"

+It was those text posts. "Theodore Henry." It's a faux-stupid persona. He's trying to sound folksy but he's just no good at it. None of those posts are Kindred's work. Take a look at his diction. Nobody uses words like "resect," or "iatrogenic." Except doctors, maybe nurses, lab workers. Or telesurgery techs.+

Through swinging plastic doors, I find a service elevator for the kitchen bots. I hitch a ride up one level, and continue on, past a storeroom full of stainless-steel bathtubs.

+This afternoon, I wondered about the technician working on my arm, some anonymous teleoperator. For all I knew, *sie* could've been our perp. But no, our guy's a Humanista, he wouldn't fix cogents, right? He'd be repairing humans.+

+When he's not implanting bombs in future martyrs . . . +

+Exactly.+

Here. A tickling of troubled recollections. Yes, this was the place.

Broad double doors marked *Telesurgery Maintenance*—stenciled in black over much-faded text: *Magnetic Resonance Imaging*, and *Caution: Strong Magnetic Fields*. Under large, peeling shock hazard symbols.

Now, if I wanted to conceal a stolen telebot from telltale satellites and snooping flybots, I'd want some place with a lot of RF shielding. And our guy has so much to hide . . . +

Past the doors, the connection goes dead.

I step into a darkened workshop, past tables covered in orderly equipment: microsurgical workstations, life-support gear, half-disassembled telebots propped up on testbeds, an obsessively complete array of toolkits, microprobes, spare parts. Dim ocher light from the next room filters through a broad observation window.

Past a haze of memories, I peer into the inner chamber: its walls are half a meter thick, heavily shielded. There's where the MRI scanner used to stand, the huge donut electromagnets long since removed, leaving an obvious gap in the room. That space is now occupied by stacked boxes of diapers, a surgical table, and an ectogestation system.

A pink-skinned nurture-bot stands next to a clear plastic crib, cradling a newborn human in its arms.

Baby Doe, his little head wrapped in micropore bandage, suckles cultured milk from the soft machine's breast.

No. Please, no . . .

I think we're too late, Moonie.

Reflected movement. I turn to see a half-built one-armed telebot raising a shockstaff. I try to grab its wrist, but my clumsy new arm misses wildly.

A burst of blue pyrotechnics, and I fall spasmodically to the—

> *Proses are read*
> *Violence ensues*
> *Everything's dead*
> *And nothing is true.*
>
> —Theodore Henry, untitled poem found
> in an encrypted personal file.

"Find what you were looking for?"

Relayed through a ceiling speaker, his knife-smooth voice has sharpened edges. He sits at a workstation in the former MRI chamber, gazing at me through the dust-smeared glass. Dark-haired, caucasian, maybe forty years old, in loose surgical greens. Utterly normal and ordinary, like his stolen telebot.

I must have blacked out for a while there. I've lost time. My internal clock says twenty minutes have passed. Can't remember a thing after the shockstaff . . .

"Missing something, are you? Or maybe you're looking for me?" He smiles lopsidedly, takes a pull from a bottle of beer. "Looks like you found me, eh?"

The mindless nurture-bot is behind him, pacing the dimly lit room, murmuring to the baby.

He notices my look. "You've seen my son? Cute as a bug, isn't he? Just six months old."

I seem to be paralyzed from the neck down. My arms and legs are cramping up, formications beginning to boil across the skin—

Oh, shit.

I look down: my head and torso are strapped upright on the test table. My limbs have been messily amputated and dumped in a heap beside me, dripping lubricant and myo-gel.

X-ray images appear on one of his screens, text files scrolling up another. "It's really a pleasure to meet you . . . Detective Gene Engine Mohad. Seems you're not all that you claim to be. Says here you're a cogent cop, one of the few, the proud. Very nice. But these X-rays say otherwise."

I try desperately to vox, but can't access the net. Too much shielding in these walls.

"Most of you is mechine," he continues, "but, hey, lookee here: lungs, heart, pancreas and what-not, spinal cord, brain nicely nano-cushioned against hydrostatic shock. Artificial colon . . . Vintage stuff, this biomaintenance 'ware, thirty years out of date. That makes you one of the earliest, doesn't it? One of the first full-body cybrids. A pioneer! Wow, if this database isn't lying about your age, you must've been all of, what, ten years old when they put you in that body?"

In the grip of screeching neurosensory phantoms and equally terrible memories, I manage to find my voice. "What the fuck do you want?"

"Just a moment, just a moment," he says testily. "I'm *try-ing* to do an archive search. Thirty years. My, that's a ways back. Yes, here we go. You're not Shelley Stein, you've got a Y chromosome, so you must be . . ." He looks up, smiling almost warmly. "Mr. Mohandis Boaz Mohad."

He leans forward, dead serious. "You, Mr. Mohad, are a cogsucking traitor to your species."

I see no point in replying.

"What happened to you?" He digs deeper, finding the news stories. "Says here you were on vacation in Venezuela with your parents, when some cretin discarded several paint-soaked rags in a bin . . . which then ignited a warehouse full of illegally stored fireworks. You, Ma and Pa, and the hotel you were sleeping in were all caught in the ensuing conflagration."

His screens show archive pix of a Maracaibo street, severed by rockets, smoke, massive explosions of brilliant green, spiraling gold . . .

"How fortunate that you all survived, eh? Wasn't much left of you, though. They flew you back in cryosuspension, and— Hey, you were treated right here at King Eddy's Medplex. Alright! Must be Old Home Week for you."

He rotates sections of the actual MRI scans. My ten-year-old body, limbs reduced to blunt stubs, my face a corroded ruin wrapped in synthetic skin. I remember the claustrophobia of the scanner, the ratcheting machine-gun noise of the big magnets, but, above all, the neverending phantom pain.

"I suppose I can understand," he says, a paragon of tolerance, "why you might turn your back on your humanity. All that horror of the flesh, so many human weaknesses. All those corrupt safety inspectors, careless human janitors, insensitive doctors . . . And worst of all, yes, yes, the betrayal. The cruelty of those who saved you, at such enormous expense. Parents who loved you too much to allow you to die, to escape, no matter how desperately you must have wished for it."

I want so much to kill him. If only to shut him up.

"I can see why you would rebel against them, why you flew off to Morocco. To join the African cogent underground. To fight the good fight against the human oppressor. Man, you were really in the thick of it, eh? You were in Algeria when they freed those cog slaves from that silver mine. And didn't they milk that scandal for all it was worth? Before the Convention opened the floodgates and the cogs started living out in the open, all over, even here. Before you came home and joined the Forcers."

He nods and takes another gulp of beer. "Gee, I wonder what your colleagues would say, if they knew you'd been lying to them all these years?"

"I never made any false claims. My employers know I'm a cybrid. Of course they do. If anybody else wants to assume I'm a cogent, why should I correct them? They'll just ask a lot of questions that—that I shouldn't have to answer."

He considers this. "Nope. I don't think that's going to wash. That sounds like a major rationalization, that does."

"And you, fucker." Hauling myself back from the dead past. "Mr. Theodore Henry or whatever you're really called. What happened to you? What made you such a sick fuck? That artificial womb you've got in there—misappropriated from the Medplex with a fetus developing in it. Then you murdered four people at the nanofab just to steal an un-Burned cogent brain. So you could wire it into that poor kid."

He stares blankly through the glass, through me. "I'm sure I don't know what you're talking about."

"No, you wouldn't. Your delusions are so strong, they won't allow you to recognize your own actions. I've never heard of a more severe case of substrate dysmorphia. To prove your humanity, you joined the Front and became their most vocal advocate of direct action. Anthro-mimicry taken to psychotic extremes. You even managed to acquire a baby, and convince yourself that he was your own, the ultimate proof of biological virility. No other way for you to repro-duce, except to make a cephaline and Burn a dupe of your own neurome. You're a mimsie of the worst kind, Doctor Pinocchio. No wonder the Neuremics Authority revoked your repro rights. And you've just passed on your Bad Code to that child in there."

"I've had enough of this crap," he says, standing. He holds up a flat box, a sense data simulator. "Hope you like this. Maybe it'll help you find what you're missing."

He activates the feed, and I start to scream.

I'm still screaming forty minutes later, when the room's power is finally cut off, and the SWATbots—trailing long fiber umbilicals—drop out of the ventilation system.

"What's that, Gene?"

"A stupid myth," I repeat, my voice in shreds but flat and detached, all emotion thoroughly wrung out. I must sound like I'm stoned. "They're not supposed to exist."

Maybe twenty minutes have passed since Henry's arrest,

and we're en route to the Reparatory. Moon doesn't know much of what happened back there at the Medplex. I'm trying to explain, but it's coming out in incoherent lumps. What's left of my nervous system is a quivering mess.

"What doesn't exist, sweets?" As the squad car rockets through each intersection, a wash of light scans across Moon's worried features, gone pale as white gold. Having released my seatbelt and laid me across ser lap, sie cradles my head in one arm.

"Black market sense-recordings," I say, twitching. "Always someone panicking about it—snuff, torture captage, war porn. But we never find any actual evidence. No underground distribution rings, no such recordings. Imagine my surprise!" I manage a laugh, feeling blessedly numb, even the phantom itching of my amputated limbs silenced by neural overload.

"But, Gene . . ." Moon seems too horrified to process. "I don't understand. Why didn't you just do a crashdown?"

"Couldn't. Not something I can do. No neural shutdown command."

Sie doesn't understand, just narrows those eyes, anxious slivers of flint.

Sie's going to find out anyway, during the debriefing. Dennet will want to view my sense records for the past two hours. Legally, I could probably refuse, but that simply isn't a realistic option. There's no keeping up this pretense any longer.

So, as the streetlights sweep past and the siren cries, I spill out the story, and sie listens.

Eventually something snaps, and sie picks up one of my severed arms, almost ready to use it to bash apart my stupid head.

Too sane for that, sie tosses the limb into the back seat, then glares through the windshield for several minutes, slowly cooling down.

"Why, Mohad?" sie finally demands, aghast. "Why lie to me, to Daniel, to everybody?"

"Moon, you have no idea what it was like. I was just a kid

when it happened, when they rebuilt me. Early on, people looked at me like I was a monstrosity out of a horror show. A tragic victim. Look, there's the boy in the plastic body! But in Morocco, the cogs didn't stare. They just saw a fellow mechine."

"You couldn't just," sie waves a hand over me, "go bio-mimetic? Look like a human?"

"I did, at first. But the early ones weren't very convincing. It just felt worse. Reminded me, every time I looked in the mirror—" I have to stop for a moment, staring into the rhythmic flash of passing streetlamps. "And anyway, it was just as much of a lie. I wasn't human anymore. Why pretend? Isn't that what you hate about cybrids? Pretending to be something we're not? Undignified, completely lacking in—"

"Alright, shut up, I know what I said." Sie sits and simmers for a moment. "Then, what? You figured I'd never find out?"

"Would you? Nobody else ever guessed. And—I know this is stupid, but it was flattering, in a strange way. To be accepted. To be one of you."

Now Cogentville envelops us, bustling and surreal, a mad Escher maze.

Moon's expression is frost-hard in the seething tunnel-light. I wait, desperately hoping for a thaw.

But sie says nothing more, all the way to Dragonfly Penumbra.

"The bastard was living under the name Marvin Saks. Had been working at the Medplex for nearly ten years." My voice is nearly lost among a hundred conversations and the frenetic thimba pop rumbling from the bar's walls.

We're in the depths of the Black Star on Dundas West, drinking at the head of three tables crammed with off-duty cops from 52 Division and Central Ops. At the far end, nearly lost in the nobacco smoke, Xu Kelly is entertaining Moon and several others with one of her stories of the bad old days of the early Flood Crisis.

Only Daniel Aramaki can hear me, nodding as I bring him

up to date. It's the end of his first day back at work, though he'll be stuck in his cubicle for a while yet. Still shaky on his new legs, just as I'm still not fully adapted to mine.

"Ser real name," I go on, "ser cogent name, was Moebius Sketch. An old cog, over fifty years old. Second generation in fact, a comp of four highly stable and gifted cogents—two from the very first Melbourne group, two from Capetown."

"Right," Danny puts in. "Fuckers were still trying to evolve superhuman intellects."

"Might happen yet," I say.

"Might just evolve superhuman assholes." He grins, and it's the same evil grin, the same old Daniel. Or close enough. He's fully biomimetic, a bit younger-looking, maybe slightly idealized. I like to give him grief, calling him a hopelessly conservative mimsie.

"Anyway," I continue, "as the suppressions got worse, Sketch was smuggled to the Bahamas and raised by a very decent human couple. Sie never met ser neuremic parents, which wasn't unusual for that generation. During the Bahamian raids, when sie was only thirteen, sie disappeared. It was assumed sie'd been killed."

Dan takes a swig of Black Star microbrew, then asks, "What're they going to do about Baby Doe?"

"Didn't I tell you? He's been legally adopted by his biological parents. Now I ask you, what—just what can you say about that?"

"That's just creepy," Danny says. "The kid's brain is being shaped by Sketch's neurome. He'll eventually go mongo-psycho, right?"

"Not necessarily. More likely there are flaws in ser neurome which might or might not cause a predisposition to mental problems. Sketch's messed-up childhood was maybe just a trigger. All very equivocal. So if the kid has a stable home life, is properly socialized, and so on—who knows?"

For a while we just listen to the music, the laughter, the clatter of glasses. I light up a cig.

"You have to admire them," I say. "The parents. Choosing to raise that kid, despite everything. Sort of a gesture of defiance against neuremic destiny."

"Yeah. Fuck the Neuremics Authority!" Danny cheers, and we laugh.

Down the table, Moon is now in a loud but amiable debate with two detectives from Property Crimes.

Danny notices me watching them, and leans over. "You okay, Mohandis?"

"Sure." I shrug, and blow bittersweet smoke rings, remembering the taste of ser mouth.

"A shame, though," Dan says. "Thought you two made an interesting couple."

"Thanks. Could've been worse. We can still work together at least."

Danny isn't fooled. Neither are all those unhappy neurons that won't shut up, especially there in my anterior cingulate gyrus, down deep in my insula and caudate nucleus. All now wailing like hungry babes. Feeling like something essential has been hacked out at the most sensitive roots. Connections lost, seemingly irreparable, leaving only painful ghosts.

Scout's Honor

TERRY BISSON

Terry Bisson [www.terrybisson.com] lives in Oakland, California. He is an automobile mechanic, copywriter, and SF writer of distinction. His website lists a bushel of accomplishments. He is the author of seven genre fantasy or SF novels: Wyrldmaker *(1981);* Talking Man *(1987), a World Fantasy Award nominee;* Fire on the Mountain *(1988);* Voyage to the Red Planet *(1990);* Pirates of the Universe *(1996);* The Pickup Artist *(2001); and most recently,* Dear Abby *(2003). His short fiction is collected in* Bears Discover Fire *(1993),* In the Upper Room *(2000), and* Greetings *(2005).*

"Scout's Honor" was published electronically by SciFi.com; this is its first appearance in print. A researcher who studies Neanderthals happens upon a posting on an internet bulletin board from an anthropologist who seems to have traveled back in time to study living Neanderthals. Bisson provides a vivid and very unusual vision of what Neanderthals were like and how they died off. Bisson says, in an SF Weekly interview: The anthropologist in my story, by the way, was based on Paul Park's brilliant autistic sister, Jesse. It occurred to me that she might understand our cousins better than any of us." Given that, it is interesting to compare this character to the central character of Brenda Cooper's story.

On the morning of July 12, 20___, I got the following message on my lab computer, the only one I have:

Monday

Made it. Just as planned. It's real. Here I am in the south of France, or what people think of now (now?) as the south of France. It seems to the north of everywhere. If the cleft is at 4200 feet, it means the ice is low. I can see the tongue of a glacier only about 500 feet above me. No bones here yet, of course. It's a clear shot down a narrow valley to the NT site, about ½ mile away. I can see smoke; I didn't expect that. Wouldn't they be more cautious? Maybe they aren't threatened by HS yet and I'm too early. Hope not. Even though it's not part of the protocol, I would love to learn more about our first encounter (and last?) with another human (hominid?) species. I do like to see the smoke, though. I never thought I would feel loneliness but here I do. Time is space and space is distance (Einstein). Heading down for the NT site. More later.

The subject line was all noise and so was the header. I was still puzzling what it was all about, for excepting the Foundation's newsgroup, I get no messages at all, when another came through the very next morning. The dates are mine.

Tuesday

It's them all right. I am watching about 20 NTs, gathered
in the site around a big smoky fire. Even through binoculars, from 50 yards away, they look like big moving shadows. It's hard to count them. They cluster together then
break apart in groups of 2 or 3, but never alone. I can't tell
the males from the females, but there are 4 or 5 children,
who also stay together in a clump. Wish I could see faces,
but it's dim here. Perpetual overcast. I have been watching
almost four hours by the clock on my com, and none have
left the site. Separating one out may prove a problem. But I
have almost 5 days (-122) to worry about that. Tomorrow
I'll observe from a different position where I can get a little
closer and the light may be better; above, not closer. I know
the protocols. I helped write them. But somehow I want to
get closer.

*I began to suspect a prank, to which I enjoy a certain de-
liberate and long-standing immunity. But I do have a
friend—Ron—and naturally I suspected him (who else?) after the next and longer text came through, on the very day we
were to meet.*

Wednesday

Totally unexpected change in plans. I am sitting here in
the cleft with "my own" NT. He's the perfect candidate for
the snatch, if I can keep him here for 4 days (-98). They are
nothing like we thought. The reconstructions are far too an-
thropomorphic. This is NOT a human, though certainly a hominid. What we thought was a broad nose is more of a
snout. He's white as a ghost, which I guess is appropriate.
Or am I the ghost? He is sitting across the fire staring at me,
or through me. He seems oddly unconscious much of the
time, thoughtless, like a cat. What happened was this: I was
heading down to observe the site this morning when I dis-
lodged a boulder that fell on my left leg. I thought for sure it

was broken (it isn't), but I was trapped. The rock had my leg wedged from the knee downward, out of sight in a narrow crevice. I couldn't help thinking of that turn-of-the-century Utah dude who sawed off his own arm with a Swiss army knife. I was wondering when I would be ready to do that, for I was in a worse spot than him: unless I made it back to the cleft in less than 100 hours, I was trapped here, and by more than a stone. By Time itself. The numbness scared me worse than pain. It was starting to snow and I was worried about freezing. I must have fallen asleep, for the next thing I remember, "my" NT was squatting there looking at me—or through me. Quiet as a cat. Oddly, I was as little surprised as he was. It was like a dream. I pointed at my leg, and he rolled the stone away. It was as simple as that. Either he was immensely strong or had a better angle, or both. I was free, and my leg was now throbbing painfully and bleeding but not broken. I could even stand on it. I hobble.

Ron is a sci-fi writer who teaches a course at the New School. We meet every Wednesday and Friday, right before his class at 6. This is not by his plan or mine. It's a promise he made to my mother, I happen to know, right before she died, but that's OK with me. No friends at all would be too few, and more than one, too many.

"What is this?" he asked, when he finished reading the printout.

You oughta know, I said, raising my eyebrows in what I hoped was a suggestive manner. In accord with my own promise to my mother, I practice these displays in front of the mirror, and for once it seems to have paid off.

"You think I wrote this?"

I nodded, knowingly I hoped, and listed my reasons: who else knew that I was studying Neanderthal bones? Who but he and I had savored the story of the Utah dude so long ago? Who else wrote sci-fi?

"Science fiction," he said grumpily (having made that correction before). While we waited for his burger and my buttered roll, he listed his objections. "Maybe it's a mistake, not intended for you. Lots of people knew about the Utah

dude; it was a national story. And I am a little insulted that you think that I wrote this."

Huh?

"It's crude," Ron said. "He, or maybe she, uses 'oddly' twice in one paragraph; that would never get by me. And the timeline is all wrong. The escape comes before the danger, which deflates the suspense."

You didn't send this, then?

"No way. Scout's Honor."

And that was that. We talked, or rather he talked, mostly of his girlfriend Melani and her new job, while the people walked by on Sixth Avenue, only inches away. They were hot, and we were cold. It was like two separate worlds, separated by the window glass.

Thursday morning I went in eagerly, anxious to get back to my bones. I scanned the Foundation's newsgroup first (rumors about a top secret new project) before opening the latest message.

Thursday

Sorry about that. I stopped transmitting yesterday because "my" NT woke up, and I didn't want to alarm him. Since my last truncated message, we've been snowed in. He watched me build a fire with a sort of quiet amazement. God knows what he would think of this thing I'm talking into. Or of the talk itself. He only makes 3 or 4 sounds. I wait until he's asleep to use the com. After the NT freed me, he followed me up the hill. It was clear that he didn't intend to harm me, although it would have been pretty easy. He is about 6 feet tall if he stood straight up, which he never does. Maybe 250 lbs. It's hard to judge his weight since he's pretty hairy, except for his face and hands. I was in a big hurry to dress my leg, which was bleeding (OK after all). We found the cleft very different from the way I had left it. Something had gotten into my food. A bear? The follow box was smashed and half the KRs were gone. Luckily the space blanket had been left behind. I spread it out, and he laid his stuff beside it: a crude hand axe, a heavy, stiff and incredibly smelly skin robe, and a little sack made of gut, with five stones in it: creek stones, white. He showed them to me as if they were something I should understand. And I do: but of that later. He's starting to stir.

On Fridays I skip lunch so I will have an appetite in the restaurant. I wasn't surprised to find yet another message, and I printed both Thurs. and Fri. to show to Ron. At the least, it would give him something to talk about. I think (know) my silences are awkward for him.

Friday

It's snowing. The stones are his way of counting. I watched him throw one away this morning. There are 3 left: like me, he's on some kind of schedule. We've been eating grubs. Seems the NTs hide rotten meat under logs and stones and return for the grubs. It's a kind of farming. They're not so bad. I try to think of them as little vegetables. Grub "talks" a lot with his hands. I try to reply in kind. When we are not talking, when I do not get his attention, he is as dead, but when I touch his hands or slap his face, he comes alive. It's as if he's half asleep the rest of the time. And really asleep the other half; the NT sleep a *lot.* His hands are very human, and bone white like his face. The rest of him is brown, under thick blond fur. I call him Grub. He doesn't call me anything. He doesn't seem to wonder who I am or where I came from. The snatch point is still 2 days away (-46), which means that I get him to myself until then. An unexpected bonus. Meanwhile, the weather, which was already fierce, is getting fiercer, and I worry about the com batteries, with no sun to charge them. More later.

Ron and I always meet at the same place, which is the booth by the window in the Burger Beret on Sixth Ave. at Tenth St. Ron shook his head as he read the messages. That can mean lots of different things.

He said, "You astonish me."

Huh?

"Don't huh me. You wrote it. It's very clever, considering."

I couldn't say huh again, so I was just very still.

"The vegetarian business is what tipped me off. And no one else knows that much about Neanderthals. Their counting, the limited speech. It's what you told me."

That was common theory, I said. There was nothing new in it. Besides, I don't make stories. I write reports.

Even I could see that he was disappointed. "Scout's Honor?"

Scout's honor, I said. Ron and I went to Philmont Scout Ranch together. That was years ago, before he had entered the world and I had decided to keep it at arm's length. But the vows still hold.

"Well, OK. Then it must be one of your colleagues playing a joke. I'm not the only one who knows you do research. Just the only one you deign to talk to."

Then he told me that he and Melani were getting married. The conversation sort of speeded up and slowed down at the same time, and when I looked up, he was gone. I felt a moment's panic, but after I paid the bill and went up to my apartment, it gradually dissipated, like a gas in an open space. For me a closed space is like an open space.

The newsgroup was silent for the weekend, but the scrambled-header messages kept coming through, one a day, like the vitamins I promised my mother I would take.

Saturday

The KRs are gone, but Grub drags me with him to look under logs for grubs. He won't go alone. Third day snowed in. One more to go. I have to conserve our wood, so we stay huddled together against the back wall of the cleft, wrapped in my space blanket and Grub's smelly robe. We sit and watch the snow and listen to the booming of the icefall—and we talk. Sort of. He gestures with his hands and takes mine in his. He plucks at the hair on my forearms and pulls

at my fingers and sometimes even slaps my face. I'm sure
he doesn't understand that I am from the far future; how
could he even have a concept of that? But I can understand
that he is in exile. There was a dispute, over what, who
knows, and he was sent away. The stones are his sentence,
that I know: Grub *feels* that about them. Every morning he
gets rid of one, tossing it out the door of the cleft into the
snow. His sense of number is pretty crude. 5 is many, and
2—the number left this morning—is few. I assume that
when they are gone, he gets to go "home," but he's just as
desolate with 2 as he was with 5. Perhaps he can't think
ahead, only back. Even though I'm cold as hell, I wish the
snatch point wasn't so near. I'm learning his language.
Things don't have names, but the feelings about them do.

*Saturday and Sunday I spend at the lab, alone. What else
would I do? When else could I be alone with my bones? I am
the only one who has access to the Arleville Find, which is
two skeletons, an NT and an HS found side by side, which
proves there was actual contact. The grubs confirmed my
study of the NT teeth. Of course, this was just a story, according to Ron. Or was it? Sunday I found this:*

Sunday

Change in plans: I want to alter the snatch point, put it
back one cycle. I know this is against the protocols, but I
have my reasons. Grub is desperate to get rid of the stones
and return to the site and his band. These creatures are
much more social than we. It's as if they hardly exist, alone.
I'm getting better at communicating. There is much hand-
work involved, gesture and touch, and I understand more
and more. Not by thinking but by feel. It's like looking at
something out of the corner of my eye; if I look directly, it's
gone. But if I don't, there it is. It's almost like a dream, and
maybe it is, since I am in and out of sleep a lot. My leg is
healing OK. Grub is down to one stone, and he's happy, almost. I am feeling the reverse: the horror he would feel at

being separated from his band forever. Are we going to create an Ishi? What desolation. I am convinced we will wind
up with a severely damaged NT. So we start our count at
144 again. Some peril here, since the com is getting low. But
I have a plan—

*Monday is my least favorite day, when I have to share the
lab (but not the bones) with others. Not that they don't
leave me alone. I scrolled down past the newsgroup, looking for the daily message and found it like an old acquaintance:*

Monday

Made it. I am speaking this amid a circle of hominids, not
humans, squatting (rather than sitting: they either stand, lie,
or squat but never sit) around a big smoky fire. I quit worrying about what they would think of the com; they don't
seem curious. Since I arrived with Grub, they have accepted
me without question or interest. Maybe it's because I have
picked up Grub's smell. They lay or squat silently a lot of the
time, and then when one awakens, they all awaken, or
most, anyway. There are 22 altogether, including Grub: 8
adult males, 7 females, and 5 children, 2 of them still nursing; plus 2 "Old Ones" of indeterminate sex. The Old Ones
are not very mobile. The NTs grab hands and "talk" with a
few sounds and a lot of pushing and pulling, plus gestures.
Their facial expressions are as simple and crude as their
speech. They look either bored or excited, with nothing in
between. Lots of grubs and rotten meat get eaten. They put
rotten meat under logs and rocks, and then come back for
the grubs and maggots. It's a kind of farming, I guess, but it
has all but spoiled my appetite. Perhaps any kind of farming
does, seen up close.

*All of this was interesting, but none of it was new. Any of
it could have been written by my colleagues at the lab, but I
knew it wasn't. They're in another world, like the people on*

*Sixth Avenue on the other side of the glass. Most of them
didn't even know my name.*

Tuesday

Something is happening tomorrow. A hunt? I sense fear
and danger, and lots of work and lots of food. All these im-
precise communications I got from the group as a whole.
This afternoon they burned a bush of dry leaves and inhaled
the smoke, passing it around. It's some kind of herb that
seems to help in NT communication. Certainly it helps me.
Between the "burning bush" and the grunts and pulling of
hands, I got a picture (not visual but emotional) of a large
beast dying. It's hard to describe. I'm learning not to try and
pin things down. It's as if I were open to the feelings of the
event itself instead of the participants. Death, defeat, and
victory; terror and hope. A braided feeling, like the smoke.
All this was accompanied, I might even say amplified, by
one of the Old Ones (more mobile than I thought!) spinning
around by the fire, brandishing a burning stick. Later I
amused the little ones (more easily amused than their elders) by cooking some grubs on a stick. Like cooking
marshmallows. They wouldn't eat them though, except for
one small boy I call "Oliver" who kept smacking his lips and
grinning at me as if it were me he wanted to eat. Even the
little NTs have a fierce look that belies their gentle nature.
The men (Grub, too) have been sharpening sticks and hard-
ening the points in the fire. Now they are asleep in a big pile
between the fire and the wall, and I am staying apart, which
doesn't bother them. I can take the smell of Grub, but not of
the whole pile; that is, band.

*Wednesday was a long day. I printed out the last four (in-
cluding Wednesday) to show Ron. For some reason, I was
eager for a little "conversation." Maybe mother was right,
and I need to maintain at least one friend. Mother was a doctor, after all.*

Wednesday

This morning we were awakened by the children pulling
at the space blanket. Grub had joined me during the night. Is
it me or the space blanket he likes? No matter; I am glad of
his company and used to his smell. He was part of the hunt
and dragged me along. He understood that I wanted to go.
The others ignore me, except for the children. The party
consisted of 7 men and 2 women. No leader that I could tell.
They carried sharpened sticks and hand axes, but no food
or water. I don't think they know how to carry water. We left
the children behind with the Old Ones and the nursing
mothers and spent most of the morning climbing up a long
slope of scree and over a ridge into a narrow valley where a
glacial stream was surrounded by tall grass. There I saw my
first mammoth, already dead. It lay beside a pile of brush
and leaves, and I "got" that they had baited it into this narrow defile. But something else had killed it. It lay on its side,
and for the first time I saw what I thought might be sign of
HS, for the beast had already been butchered, very neatly.
Even the skull had been split for the brain. Only the skin and
entrails were left, with a few shreds of stringy meat. The
NTs approached fearfully, sniffing the air and holding hands
(mine included). I could feel their alarm. Was it the rem-
nants of the smoke or my own imagination that gave me a
terrified sense of the "dark ones" that had killed this beast?
Then it was gone before I could be sure. The NTs went to
work with their sticks, driving away 3 hyena-like dogs that
were circling the carcass. Their fear was soon forgotten
with this victory, and they started carving on the carcass,
eating as they went. The kill was new, but pretty smelly. The
NTs piled entrails and meat in a huge skin, which we had
brought with us. By late afternoon we had a skin full, which
we carried and dragged over the ridge and down the long
scree slope. We were within a half mile of the site when the
sun set, but the NTs hate and fear the dark. So here we are
holed up under a rock ledge, in a pile. A long, cold, and
smelly night ahead. No fire, of course. They whimper in their

sleep. They don't like being away from their fire. Me neither. I am beginning to worry about the com, which is showing a low power (LP) signal every time I log on. Not as much sunlight here as anticipated. None at all, in fact.

"Scout's Honor?" Ron asked again after he had read the printouts, and I nodded. "It must be one of your colleagues, then. Who else knows this Neanderthal stuff, or calls them NTs. Did they really eat grubs?"

I shrugged. How would I know?

"Cave men are full of surprises, I guess. And I have a surprise of my own. Friday's my last day of class. We're moving to California. Melani has an assistantship at Cal State. We're getting married in Vegas, on the way. Otherwise I would invite you to the wedding. Even though I know you wouldn't come."

I stayed home sick Thursday. And so I didn't check my emails until Friday morning, when I had two, after a lot of Foundation Newsgroup gossip about a new project, which I skipped. It was mostly rumors, and I don't like rumors. That's why I became a scientist.

Thursday

Dawn finally came, sunless. Something was wrong. I could feel it as we went down the hill, holding hands. The cave was filled with shadows, as before, but these were different in the way they stood and the way they moved. Then NTs saw them too, and fell to their knees, clutching one another with little cries. I was forgotten, even by Grub. The Dark Ones had come. The fire was less smoky, and the shadows moved like humans, like us, and chattering. Quarreling, too. Many blows exchanged. They were butchering something. I drew closer before realizing, to my horror, that I was alone. The NTs had all fled. Before I had time to look around and see where they were gone, I was noticed by the dogs. The NTs don't keep dogs, but the HS do. Perhaps they smelled the meat the NTs had dropped when they fled. They were barking all around me, nasty little creatures. Food or pets? Two of the HS came out of the cave toward me. They started to shout, and I shouted back, imitating their sounds, hoping they would perceive that I was one of them. No such luck. They moved closer, shaking their spears, which were tipped with vicious stone points. Shake-spear: they were acting, I realized. They were only interested in scaring me away. I took a step toward them, and they shook their spears harder. They are completely, unmistakably human. Their faces are very expressive. Their skins are hairless and very black. I think they thought I was an NT because I was so white, at least compared to them. Nothing else in my gait or face or speech seemed to matter. I saw over their shoulders what the others were butchering. It was the boy who had dared to eat the cooked grubs, Oliver. His head was laid off to one side, opened for the brains. NTs have big brains, even the kids. I was almost sad, but didn't have the luxury. The two HS were shaking their spears, coming toward me one step at a time. I stepped back, still trying to talk, hoping that they would recognize me as one of their own, when something grabbed me by the ankle. It was Grub. He had come back for me. Come! Run! I scrambled after him, through the bushes, up the scree, toward the rocks and snow. The humans didn't follow us.

Friday

Snowing again, harder than ever. We're in the cleft, Grub and I. I'm trying to save the batteries for the snatch connection (-21). No sun. Haven't seen the sun for a week. After my last (too long) com, we circled up into the high country, careful to avoid the HS—me as well as Grub. It's ironic that even here, at the beginning of human history, skin color trumps everything. Logical, I suppose, since it is the largest and most evident of the organs. The band has gone over the glacier; we found the tracks leading up onto the ice. Grub wanted to follow them, but I can't get too far from the cleft and the snatch. Luckily, he won't go anywhere without me. I maneuvered him back to the cleft, which was mercifully empty, and built a fire which seemed to comfort him—the building of it as much as the fire itself. I sat down beside him, and he quit shivering, and we slept under the space blanket, plus the skin. All we have to do is hole up here for another day and we will both be gone. Grub doesn't know that, of course. He is shivering and whimpering in my arms. His desolation floods me as if it were my own. And his fear. The Dark Ones! The Dark Ones! What would he think if he knew I were one of them?

"I really don't need to read any more," Ron said, tossing the printout aside. "Didn't you say that Homo Sapiens had originally come up from Africa?"

I nodded and shrugged. Nods and shrugs are "piece of cake" for me.

"So there they are, your dark ones. There will be a fight, and the Neanderthals, the NTs, will lose. It is clearly an amateur time-travel story. If you ask me, and I suppose you have no one else to ask, I think it just bounced in off some anomaly in the Web. The Web has released all sorts of wannabe writers, sending stuff to one another and to little amateur sites. This is a piece of a sci-fi story that got misaddressed in cyberspace."

SF, I said, but he didn't get the joke. There are ways to indicate that you're joking but I have never mastered them. Why me? I asked.

"I'll bet it's because you're on the Foundation server," Ron said. "The one in New Mexico. Doesn't it use that new quantum computer, the one that received a message a few milliseconds before it was sent? I read the story in Science News. Some kind of loop thing. But hey, it makes it the perfect receiver for a time travel yarn. Speaking of time—"

He looked at his watch, then stood up and shook my hand. For the first time I understood his relief in saying goodbye. I tried to hold on, but he pulled his hand away.

"I'll stay in touch," he said.

The people on the street were hurrying by. Sixth Avenue is

*one-way for cars but two-way for people. I didn't mind them
through the glass. Scout's Honor? I asked.*

"Scout's Honor."

*I tried to take his hand again, just to be sure, but he was
gone. My mother had finally set him free.*

Saturday

Disaster. We missed the snatch, both Grub and me. We've
been run off from the cleft. We were awakened—or rather, I
was awakened by Grub. I was dragged out of the cleft and
onto my feet, past the 3 HS with long spears at the cave
door. Grub had smelled them before he had seen or heard
them. They seized our supplies and the fire, and of course,
the cleft, as we scurried up the rocks toward the ice above.
They had no interest in following or harming us, just scaring
us away. I can now see what happened in the Encounter:
the HS didn't kill off the NTs: they only grabbed their sites,
their food, their fires, and ran them off; and ate those of
their children who fell into their hands. That was enough.
Meanwhile, it is getting dark, and Grub is counting on me to
build a fire. I will make it a small one, to be sure.

*I used to love Saturdays, I think, but now they felt sad,
even at the lab. I wondered where Ron was, in the air somewhere. He likes to fly. Of course it was none of my business,
not anymore. I almost wished my mother were still alive. I
would have somebody to call. There are lots of phones at the
lab. Sunday was the same.*

Sunday

There was no snatch. Nothing happened. The HS who ran
us off are still in the cleft, 2 of them. If I had left the com behind, you would at least have them. To their surprise. It was
all I could do to drag Grub close enough to see. He's terrified. Me, too. We're 144 hours from a new snatch, if it can

be accomplished. I am going to try and keep these coms
down to keep the batteries functioning as long as possible.
Haven't seen the sun since I got here.

*On Monday I had a personal eyes-only message from the
Foundation. Attached was an e-ticket for a flight to New
Mexico to discuss the new project. Don't they know I never
fly? I scrolled on down and there it was, my next-to-last message, from the distant past and near future:*

Monday

This morning Grub and I found 4 of his band, fireless and
frozen in a small cave high on the ridgeline, above the ice.
We buried them with great effort. No sign of the others, no
more than 5 or 6. I have a dreadful feeling that they are in
fact the last band, childless now. When the HS took their
fire, they signed their death warrant, unless the NTs luck
upon a lightning strike or a live volcano. Perhaps such
events are not as rare "then" as they are "now." We'll see.

*On Tuesday I went to the Bagel Beret alone for the first
time. It felt weird. Don't think I'll go back. Today's message,
my last, cleared it all up. I now know who the messages are
from. I also know that I will fly to New Mexico. I will have to
"suck it up" and go. It is only one stop on a longer journey.*

Tuesday

This may be my last, since even the LP light on the com
is dying. Giving up the ghost, I think is the term. We have
other worries anyway. More HS have arrived in the site below.
We see them in 2s and 3s, out hunting. Us? We aren't
about to find out. Tomorrow we are going to cross the ridge
and see if we can pick up tracks. Grub sleeps now, but it
was hours before he stopped shivering. His hands wouldn't
leave hold of mine. Please don't leave me, he said with that

NT mix of gesture and touch and speech, and I said I wouldn't, but I could tell he didn't believe me, and who could blame him? He was alone in the world, more alone, I suspected, than he knew. If his band is alive (and I doubt it) they are somewhere above us, childless, fireless, slowly dying of heartbreak and cold. I shiver to think of it. You won't leave me? he asked again, tentatively, all fingertips, right before he went to sleep. I put his fingertips on my lips so he would understand what I was saying and know that it was for him, Grub.

Scout's Honor, I said.

Venus Flowers at Night

PAMELA SARGENT

Pamela Sargent [www.engel-cox.org/sargent] lives with her partner, George Zebrowski, near Albany, NY. In the mid-1970s, Pamela Sargent opened a lot of readers' eyes with anthologies Women of Wonder *(1976),* More Women of Wonder *(1976), and* New Women of Wonder *(1978), which were so popular and influential that they somewhat over-shadowed her own writing of that decade. Of her many novels and stories since 1980, highlights include* The Golden Space *(1982),* The Shore of Women *(1986),* Watchstar *(1980),* Earthseed *(1983), and her landmark trilogy of the terraforming of Venus:* Venus of Dreams *(1986),* Venus of Shadows *(1988) and* Child of Venus *(2001). Several collections of her shorter work (*The Mountain Cage and Other Stories *[2002],* Behind the Eyes of Dreamers *[2002], and* Eye of Flame and Other Fantasies *[2003]) have appeared in recent years, and in 2004, the collection* Thumbprints.*

"Venus Flowers at Night" was published in Microcosms. *It introduces the idea of terraforming Venus, using the equally wonderful idea of virtual reality technologies, all while managing to relate a complex future history after the United States has lost its dominant place in the world. It recalls Gene Wolfe's "Seven American Nights." We read it as a metafiction about the potential of SF.*

The escarpment to his northeast was the sheer face of mountains taller than the Himalayas, a range of peaks sustained by the upwelling of Venus' mantle. Karim gazed up at the vast wall of the cliffside. Masses of dark gray clouds hid the top of the escarpment, but patches of mossy green were visible against the black and gray face of the cliff. To the west, a pale glow could be seen behind the thick clouds; the sun was rising.

The scarp was the southwest side of the Maxwell Mountains. To the north lay the high plateaus of the land mass of Ishtar Terra. Life, although precarious, had already come to the cliffs; soon people would travel to the Venusian surface to live in the enclosed settlements of the high plateaus.

No, Karim thought, and the cliffside disappeared.

Now he stood on a rocky shore, looking out at a wrinkled gray ocean. In the east, the setting sun was no more than a smear of white light against the thick gray mist of the sky; another month would pass before it disappeared below the horizon. No birds flew above this shore; no life lived in this sterile and acidic sea.

No, Karim thought again, and the gray ocean vanished. He lifted his arms and removed his silver linking band from his head.

He sat in the small room that adjoined his sleeping quarters aboard the *Beverwyck*. The floor rocked almost imperceptibly under his feet. He would have preferred a large hovercraft, or perhaps an airship, for this journey, but Greta had insisted on hiring the *Beverwyck*. The small watercraft's functions were controlled by an artificial intelligence, so its crew of three would be all they required, meaning that he and Greta would have more privacy. Greta also believed that the citizens of North America's Atlantic Federation would be more reassured by a visiting Mukhtar who was traveling slowly upriver in a simple vessel and spending time at places along the way, instead of speeding past towns and villages in a hovercraft or floating above them in an inaccessible airship, stopping only to talk with the occasional high official.

"You have to show some sensitivity and respect," Greta had told him. "Many of the people in my home Nomarchy still haven't forgotten what their place once was in the world."

Karim al-Anwar usually heeded his wife's advice on such matters, having learned that her political instincts were often superior to his own. But he suspected that Greta also preferred a journey aboard the *Beverwyck* because that would allow her more proximity to the places of her childhood. Greta Gansevoort-Mehdi had grown up beside the Hudson River in a home that overlooked the Albany port, watching ships move up and down the waterway while dreaming of her escape from a region of Earth that now counted its wealth in history and monuments to the past and little else.

I should go to sleep, he told himself. Instead, he crossed the sitting room and climbed the short flight of steps to the deck.

A small human form topped by a mass of dark curls was silhouetted against the railing; Lauren, the female steward, was on watch tonight. She turned toward him.

"Is there anything you require, Mukhtar Karim?" she asked in badly pronounced Arabic.

"No, thank you." He leaned against the railing. They had passed under the Verrazano Bridge and come through the narrows and now lay at anchor in Upper New York Bay. In the moonlight, he was able to glimpse a long low black wall astern of the *Beverwyck*: the dikes of Staten Island. That morning, he had paid visits to the seawall workers in Asbury

Park and Perth Amboy along the Jersey shore, and recalled the wary, suspicious look he had glimpsed in the eyes of many in the crowd as their supervisor introduced him, how they had stared blankly at him as he assured them of the Council's good intentions and their concern for the people of North America.

After their arrival in Washington several days ago on a suborbital flight, he and Greta had taken a train to Atlantic City, where they had boarded the *Beverwyck* after a reception hosted by that city's officials and a town meeting with some of its citizens. They were given a private car on the train from Washington; their sitting chairs had holes in the red upholstery, and the blue and red carpeting was nearly threadbare. The car had rattled as it moved, sometimes so loudly that he and Greta had to shout at each other to be heard. The Atlantic Federation and its sister Nomarchies on the North American continent had the worst trains in the world, perhaps because so many of these people clung to their electric and ethanol-powered automobiles, personal hovercraft, and other forms of private transportation, still holding on to the illusion of being entirely free to go anywhere at will.

"How long have you served aboard the *Beverwyck*?" Karim asked the young woman.

"Served?" At first he thought that she had not understood that word. "But we own the *Beverwyck*," Lauren continued, switching to Anglaic, "my brother Zack, my bondmate, and myself. Zack and I bought her five years ago, and not long after that Roberto and I made our pledge, so Zack and I cut him in for an equal share."

"I see," Karim replied in Anglaic, wishing that Greta had told him the three young people were the craft's owners and not just a crew hired to see to their comfort. But perhaps his wife had not known that. He would have to adjust his manner, treat them with a bit more friendliness and a little less reserve.

"But it is assuredly less of a drain on our purses for us to look after our passengers ourselves instead of hiring others."

Lauren had switched back to Arabic. "There is not so much to be made with the *Beverwyck* that we would be able to amply reward any hirelings."

"Please." Karim gestured with one hand. "I don't mind if we speak in Anglaic, and the practice will be useful for me."

"Doesn't sound to me like you need much practice, Mukhtar Karim; your Anglaic's a lot better than my Arabic." Lauren cleared her throat. "As I was saying, we don't make all that much, but it isn't such a bad way to live your life, going up and down the Hudson, taking your time and going slow and not rushing to get up to Troy in a day with a cargo. And we've had some interesting passengers. None so interesting as you, of course."

"I am flattered," Karim said.

"Your wife drove a hard bargain, but a fair one. It also can't hurt us to have such a prominent passenger. It'll certainly be good advertising."

"I'm grateful to be of some small service to you, then."

"Sure there's nothing I can do for you, sir?" Lauren asked.

"No, thank you." He should go back below, force himself to get some sleep.

Karim left the deck, descended the steps to the sitting room, and closed the door behind him. He had left his linking band on the small table next to his chair; he sat down and put the thin band around his head once more.

"Mukhtar Karim," the soft alto voice of the *Beverwyck*'s cybermind whispered, "do you wish to call up another mind-tour?" The voice was faint; he was still having some slight trouble interfacing with the artificial intelligence properly through his band. "I have quite an extensive archive of virtual experiences," the AI went on. "Most of them are far more entertaining and detailed than those you have been accessing."

"No doubt they are," Karim said. His mind-tours of Venus were barely more than sketches and rudimentary designs he had pulled together by himself, and he knew only the rudiments of mind-tour production. His vision lived more fully inside him than in his mind-tours. He wondered if it would ever live in reality.

"You also need not limit yourself to the subject of the planet Venus," the AI continued.

"Ah, but that's the subject of most concern to me these days," Karim replied.

"Perhaps you will tell me why."

"Because Earth is of so much concern to me."

"That does not seem to cohere with your retreat into your mind-tours," the AI said. "Nor does it seem consistent with your present assignment of visiting parts of this Nomarchy to assure the people here that the Council of Mukhtars has their best interests at heart."

"That assignment," Karim said, "was given me partly to get me out of the way."

The AI had nothing to say to that. Karim thought of how delicately Mukhtar Hassan Tantawi had broached the subject of this tour. Someone had to be sent to the Atlantic Federation, and perhaps to a couple of the other Nomarchies of North America after that, on a diplomatic mission, the object of which was to listen to any grievances and appeals for additional aid and to report any interesting observations. Given that those particular regions of Earth were still among the more suspicious and distrustful of the New Islamic States, they were especially in need of reassurance, and the appearance of a member of the Council would do much to convince them that the Mukhtars who now ruled Earth wanted only to cooperate with them and see that their needs were met.

Karim did not doubt the purpose of his mission, only the reasons Mukhtar Hassan had given for choosing him to carry it out. He was fluent in Anglaic, but several other members of the Council knew that language well, and most educated people had at least some familiarity with the tongue. His wife had grown up in the Atlantic Federation, which could be useful, but the fact was that Greta's presence on this trip was not really necessary.

The truth, he admitted to himself, was that he and his allies were losing their influence on the Council to a group of younger, more practical men. More farmland was being lost to climatic changes, and more coastal areas to the rising oceans fed by the melting polar icecaps. The Council had to see that Earth's people were fed, clothed, housed, and trained for the work to which their individual talents were best suited, and to indulge in other dreams was a luxury they could not afford, especially a dream as grandiose as the one Karim harbored. People with the task of healing their own wounded planet could not be distracted by the vision of transforming another world, especially one that presented the challenges of Venus. Even Mukhtar Ali bin Oman, once a strong ally of Karim's, had seen which way the sands were drifting and had begun, however gently and shamefacedly, to mouth the phrases of the doubters.

The Council had not sent him here only to soothe the North Americans, a task any of the Mukhtars could have performed and for which at least a few of them were better suited than he. His mission was also a warning to him, and Hassan's words, however artfully phrased and ambiguous, had delivered that warning: You will have a chance to think and reconsider your thoughts while we will be free of your efforts to win more supporters for your cause. If you return and insist on pressing for your dream again, we can find another mission for you, perhaps one not as pleasant. And if you persist after that, then, God willing, it may be time to relieve you of some of your responsibilities.

Karim did not fear expulsion from the Council or exile, or even the disgrace such a punishment would bring to his family; the stronger among his brothers, sisters, and cousins would eventually overcome the dishonor, and the weaker would glean what crumbs they could for themselves, as they always had. It was powerlessness that he feared, being deprived of any influence, unable even to hope that the Council, soon or in times to come, might come to share his vision.

"We can't go on this way, you know," he murmured through his linking band to the mind of the *Beverwyck*, "just trying to repair the damage and living in the fantasy that we are the future, that human history has at last passed into our hands. We're certainly better off than we were a century or two ago, but maybe our past sufferings have so marked us that we're willing to settle for what we have and be grateful we have survived."

"Human beings have not only survived on this planet," the AI said, "but also in space."

"The habitat-dwellers have survived in space," Karim replied. "Some among my brothers on the Council would say that they have already diverged from the stream of human history, and others would call them cowards and traitors to their kind. But they are looking outward, beyond simply conserving what they have, while we stopped looking outside ourselves some time ago. Maybe when we were a poor people and still fighting for the scraps the more powerful threw to us, that was necessary. When we were salvaging what we could from this world and doing the work of rebuilding, we had no choice but to concentrate on practical matters. But if we never look to anything greater . . ."

". . . your culture will stagnate," the AI interrupted. The mind had heard him say that often enough, aloud and through the band, during the trip from Atlantic City, and now it repeated his words. "It will again become a backwater. You are immersing yourself in your mind-tours in order to convince yourself that the great endeavor you dream of is possible."

"Oh, I can convince myself," Karim said, "or at least I can do so intermittently. It's how to convince others that's the problem."

He was aboard a small shuttlecraft, moving away from the space station orbiting Venus toward the parasol shading the planet from the sun. Constructing the parasol had cost both resources and lives, but now, after nearly a century of effort, a hyperthin umbrella of aluminum would allow the hellish planet to cool.

As his craft approached the parasol, Karim could make out a series of slats designed to reflect sunlight outward and away from Venus. To design the parasol, to build it, to stabilize it so that the vast umbrella would neither drift closer to the sun nor threaten Venus, had been the greatest feat of construction ever undertaken by humankind, and yet it was only a first step in the work of terraforming Venus.

"And also only the first step," a voice added, "in mastering the tools we may need to restore Earth's biosphere." The disembodied alto voice speaking to him was that of the shuttlecraft's AI, and yet it sounded oddly familiar.

It would take some two hundred years for Venus's surface temperature to drop enough to allow for surface settlements, and even then the first settlers would need to live in protected and closed environments. An effort to terraform Mars would have proceeded more quickly; if Karim had not lived to see the end of such an effort, his children or grandchildren surely would have. But the refugees from Earth, the habitat dwellers, had claimed Mars for themselves, making habitats of its two satellites, bases from which they occasionally ventured forth to explore the Red Planet.

Once Karim had resented the claim of the habitat dwellers to Mars, but he had eventually come to understand that Venus might be better soil for the flowering of his dream. Venus might have been another Earth, might have more closely resembled humankind's home world during the first five hundred million years of their planetary histories; to terraform Venus would be to restore her to what she might have been. Human settlers born there in the distant future would not become exiles from their home planet, since Venus's gravity was close to that of Earth, but any Martian settlers would be exiles; their bodies, adapted to the gentler gravitational pull of Mars, would cut them off from ever being able to return to Earth.

His shuttlecraft passed through the umbra of the shadow cast by the parasol, and then a spear of light caught him. Karim covered his eyes reflexively as the viewscreen darkened, then peered at the screen again.

"One of the parasol's fans has begun to drift away from the shade's main body," his craft's AI said softly as more light filled the screen. "Do not fear. This craft is not in danger."

But the Venus project is, Karim thought apprehensively. The fan would have to be replaced; more resources and lives would be lost to that work. That, of course, was assuming that the parasol did not become unstable and begin to drift away from its L1 point between Venus and the sun. If it moved closer to the sun, more of the planet would eventually be left unshaded; closer to Venus, and the metallic umbrella would be caught and torn apart by fierce winds—if the sulfuric acid of the poisonous atmosphere did not dissolve the parasol first. He trembled in his seat. They might have to rebuild the entire shield.

"My calculations tell me—" the shuttlecraft's mind began.

"No," Karim replied, and the shuttlecraft suddenly vanished.

For a moment, he did not know where he was; then he recognized the familiar surroundings of the *Beverwyck*'s sitting room. He felt the pangs of disappointment and loss.

"You asked me," the *Beverwyck*'s mind whispered through his band, "to provide you with an emotional sense of a past in your sketches, so that you would experience each mind-tour as an achieved reality."

"Yes, I remember that now."

"But I did not anticipate that you would become so disoriented. May I suggest that—"

"I don't want any suggestions," Karim said, then called up his next scenario.

He followed a path of white flagstones past a grove of slender willows. Greta was waiting for him outside a small pavilion. As he came up to her, she took his arm. They kept to the path that led to the edge of the island, passing a greenhouse and then another pavilion. Five people sat at one of the tables under the pavilion, sipping tea from cups and eating from a large bowl of fruit. One man raised his hand to Karim and Greta, silently inviting them to join the group; Karim smiled and shook his head.

Overhead, the wide disk of yellow light at the center of the dome that covered the island was growing dimmer; the silver light of evening would soon be upon them. This artificial island, and the others that now drifted in the upper reaches of Venus's atmosphere, had been built on vast platforms made of metal cells filled with helium and had then been enclosed in impermeable domes. Few people lived on this island, no more than a few hundred, and there were even fewer on the other islands, but more would come, more of the specialists and workers needed for the next stage in terraforming the planet below.

The path ended at a low gray wall, about one meter high, that marked the edge of the island. This wall now encircled the entire island, but Karim could recall coming to the island's edge years ago, just after arriving here from Earth, to peer through the transparent dome at the darkness beyond: Venus cloaked in the parasol's shadow. There had been no wall then, only the blackness, and for a moment he was suddenly afraid that he might step off the island's edge and through the dome, to fall through the thick and poisonous clouds. The wall had been built to prevent that feeling of vertigo that so many of the first arrivals had felt, and Karim now often took evening walks to the island's edge with Greta.

Another team, a group of engineers, was scheduled to arrive here soon; Karim had heard that several hours ago, just after first light. They were already inside the space station that orbited Venus, where the freighters and passenger torchships from Earth had to dock. From the station, a shuttlecraft would carry them to the one Venusian island that functioned as a port, where they would board an airship bound for this island. Here, in the upper reaches of the atmosphere, helium-fueled dirigibles were the most convenient form of transportation between islands.

". . . vulnerable," Greta was saying, and he had the odd sensation that she was reading his thoughts.

Karim turned toward his wife. "What were you saying, my dear?"

She gazed at him in silence with her long dark eyes, then said, "Our airships are useful, but they also leave us vulnerable. Consider this: We can only leave these islands on shuttlecraft, and can only travel to Earth from our Venusian space station. That means a risk of being completely cut off from Earth at two points, our island port and the space station, and then we'd have only our airships, which have to remain in the atmosphere. We could be trapped here, cut off completely from the outside."

"That's a possibility," Karim said, distressed that she would spoil the mood of their stroll with such concerns, "but a very distant one. We've built enough redundancy into our systems to—"

"I wasn't thinking of a systems failure," Greta said. "I was thinking of a siege, or a blockade."

Karim almost laughed. "A blockade?" He shook his head. "But why? For what possible reason? The Mukhtars want only success for this project."

"Yes, that's true at the moment. But what if those who follow us here begin to hope for a looser hand on the reins? We're here to make a new world, and part of that is allowing that world to develop in its own way. We're terraforming a planet, probably one of the most revolutionary undertakings of our species, so we shouldn't be surprised if that provokes people to entertain rebellious ideas in the future. Some here already talk of being free from many of Earth's restrictions. The Mukhtars might not care for such independence, and they could easily enforce their will. All they would have to do is cut us off completely by allowing no shuttlecraft to enter or leave our port."

"They wouldn't risk destroying their own project," Karim objected, "not after spending so many resources on getting us this far."

"But they wouldn't be destroying the project. The parasol would still shade Venus, and seeding the atmosphere could proceed. All they'd have to do is wait out the island settlers, who would eventually have to bow to Earth's will or else face a slow death. And it would be a slow death, Karim. They could survive for a while on greenhouse crops, and the life support systems can be maintained, but sooner or later crucial components of our systems would fail, ones the islanders would be unable to replace. After all the sacrifices Earth has made for this project, to ensure that their culture will take root on another world, do you really believe that they will ever let us go our own way?"

She was voicing some of his own fears. He pressed his hands against the dome, felt the surface yield, and found himself sitting in a chair, his hands gripping the armrests.

"Where am I?" he called out.

"Aboard the *Beverwyck*," a voice replied, and then he remembered. "I suggest," the AI continued through his band, "that you reset your mind-tour specifications, Mukhtar Karim. You can enjoy your scenarios while still remaining somewhat aware that you are experiencing a mind-tour. You do not have to put yourself into a temporary amnesia, to forget that you are living here and not there."

"Ah, but then the experience would not be nearly as convincing."

"It does not have to be convincing, only diverting."

"I prefer the sense of reality." In his scenarios, however briefly and imperfectly, he could capture the conviction that the terraforming he dreamed of could succeed. He needed to hold to that conviction even more now.

Karim had suggested that, after the welcoming ceremony and his meeting with the mayor of New York City, he and Greta invite Lauren, her brother Zack, and her bondmate Roberto to dine with them at the New World Trade Center's rooftop restaurant.

"No, Karim," Greta had replied. "Forgive me, but I don't think that would be at all appropriate. It might offend some people's sensitivities. There are certain episodes in our history we've never forgotten, even if they did happen over a century and a half ago."

He understood, given the long memory of his own people, and had settled for giving the *Beverwyck*'s owners the day off and permission to use his credit while they dined at the restaurant by themselves.

A small city hovercraft was sent to take him and Greta to City Hall. The mayor, Donata Grenwell, met him with three members of the city council, then led him to her office while the council members took Greta on a tour of the building. Karim and the mayor sipped coffee while Donata spoke of the city's need for more engineers to design and supervise the construction of more dikes, and for more physicians and vaccines against the viruses and tropical diseases that afflicted so many in New York. Karim assured her that the

Council of Mukhtars would do everything possible to help her.

Donata Grenwell stood up, and seemed about to lead him to the door, then hesitated. "I wish—" she began as she adjusted the scarf around her head that she had worn in deference to his people's customs.

"Yes?" he said, waiting.

"I wish there was something else to do besides just shoring up what we have, repairing the damage." She gazed at him steadily with her pale gray eyes, then looked away. "How we used to push ourselves in the old days. I'd hear the stories from my grandmother—she was just barely old enough to remember. Always on the move, she said, always impatient, knowing nothing would stay the same from one year to the next, always having to keep up with everything and be fast on your feet, always having something to look forward to and be optimistic about. That's how it was for us once."

"I understand," Karim murmured.

"But the Council of Mukhtars has more important things to worry about," Mayor Grenwell said. "You have to keep things going and keep them from getting any worse, and if we manage to accomplish that much, it'll be a job well done."

"God willing," Karim said, "but I wonder if we can do that without also looking forward and dreaming of something new."

The mayor arched her brows, looking surprised, then showed him to the door.

Two aides to the mayor took him and Greta on a short tour of the lower Manhattan waterways and canals. Their watercraft, a small flat-bottomed boat with a canopy to shade them from the sun, wound its way among canals crowded with waterbuses, gondolas, and motorboat taxis; a police boat carrying five officers followed them. The air smelled of sulfur and brine; the shouts of the vendors who had set up shop on docks and small barges were nearly drowned out by the sound of the traffic. Occasionally a small personal motorcraft sped past the slower vessels, rocking Karim's boat in its wake. The steep cliffs of highrise apartment buildings

and commercial establishments loomed on either side of the
canals. The beaches south of Brooklyn had been lost to the
rising sea before the dikes and seawalls had been raised on
higher ground, and the oceans were also gaining on lower
Manhattan. As long as the water could be channeled into
canals and the buildings here remained accessible to workers and residents, better to expend their ever scarcer resources elsewhere; so Donata Grenwell had told him.

They arrived at the piers near the plaza of the New World
Trade Center before noon, but already the hot weather of
late March was making Karim sweat under his white ceremonial robe and headdress; the humid air seemed as thick as
soup. Even Greta, who had grown up in such a climate,
looked uncomfortable as she dabbed at her pale damp face
with a handkerchief. Karim picked up the wreath of lilies he
had brought with him and stepped onto the dock, with Greta
just behind him. The wreath had been his wife's recommen-
dation, and now he felt the rightness of her advice.

The police in the boat behind them disembarked; the lieutenant walked with Karim and Greta across the wide plaza
toward the glassy buildings on the other side. Other people
were gathered in the plaza, some talking among themselves,
but most silently watching him and his party pass. Karim
was nearly at the memorial, a latticework of metal and
twisted beams that surrounded a black wall bearing thousands of names, when the apparition he had been expecting
to see began to take shape.

The hologram flickered into existence, and then he saw
the two tall towers, translucent and ghostly, take form behind
the shorter structures that had replaced them. Karim thought
he heard a sigh from the people nearest him. He looked up at
the towers, imagining for a moment that they might become
solid, that he would be able to enter them and climb up to
where they seemed to graze Heaven.

Karim whispered a prayer, then knelt to lay the wreath at
the base of the memorial.

Shading Venus with a parasol had cooled the planet enough
for a steady rain of carbon dioxide to begin. Over the next

century and a half, oceans had formed until much of the low-lying Venusian surface was covered with carbon dioxide seas.

It's only a beginning, Karim thought. If the planet was kept in the parasol's shade, the precipitating carbon dioxide would change from rain into snow and ice. He thought of people living on the surface, enclosed in domes like those that covered the islands floating in the Venusian atmosphere, looking out at a dark frozen world that would not be a new Earth but only a prison.

Even as that thought came to him, he found himself looking through the transparent wall of a dome at a plain of ice illuminated only by the light from inside this dome and another that glowed in the distance. Suddenly angry, he struck the dome with his fist. Why had he come to this settlement only to imprison himself?

But he knew the answer to that question. The alternatives he and his fellow Earthfolk faced were fairly stark. They could live here, gaining a precarious foothold on Venus until they solved the new set of problems the terraforming project had presented, or they could return to an Earth growing ever hotter and ever more unlivable.

Earth, he thought, might eventually resemble the Venus that had existed before terraforming began, with its oceans boiled away, an atmospheric pressure great enough to crush an unprotected man, and temperatures hot enough to melt metals. He imagined feeling such heat even as he gazed out at Venus's icy wastes.

"Karim," Greta said.

He opened his eyes. He was lying on a bed in a darkened room; his beard seemed damp. Greta leaned over him; strands of her graying hair had slipped from under her scarf. The air around him had grown so warm that he was sweating under his light cotton robe.

"The homeostat wasn't working," Greta went on, "but Zack fixed it just a few minutes ago. The temperature in our rooms should be back to normal in less than an hour. By the way, he and the others told me that they very much enjoyed dining in the city today." She spoke in Anglaic, as she always did when they were alone; her Arabic was fluent without having ever become truly eloquent or poetic. She moved closer to the edge of the bed and gently slipped his band from his head. "You were to rest, not lie here accessing cyberminds."

"I was taking another of my mind-tours."

"Are you all right?"

"Just a bit disoriented," he replied. "Where are we?"

"The *Beverwyck*'s just north of the George Washington Bridge. Zack decided that we should stop at the docks here for the night. We'll leave before sunrise, before the traffic gets too heavy. I hope you'll be able to keep away from your mind-tours long enough to enjoy a view of the Palisades."

"I wonder if that view will be as impressive as the one I saw in a mind-tour some time ago," Karim said as the remembered image of a ridge of unbroken rock came to him. That simulation had been of the Palisades as they might have appeared four hundred years ago, but the waters had risen since then, creeping higher up the sides of the cliffs.

"Mind-tours." Greta sat down on the bed and reached for his hand. "I've never seen you so caught up in such entertainments. You've had your band on during almost every free moment we've had since we landed in Washington."

"I haven't been seeking mere diversion, Greta. I'm still exploring my terraforming scenarios."

"Venus. I see." For a moment, he expected her to voice the objections he had heard from her before. "I could tell you to give up such hopes," she continued, "but you wouldn't listen to me anyway, and maybe I'm no longer so sure of my reasons for arguing against your dream in the past. The effort would be costly, but that has to be measured against the possibility of making an entirely new habitable planet for ourselves. It might be better to leave Venus alone in order to learn what we can about it, but we'd also learn much about that world during any terraforming project."

"There is the possibility of failure," Karim murmured.

"Of course. There always is. Still, we could fail at making Venus another Earth and yet make many important advances in technology and science. We might even learn enough to

restore Earth's ecology many centuries from now. And . . ."
She was silent for a while. "I think it'll be easier for you to
know that you never have to doubt my loyalty."

"If I push too hard," he said, "you know what the consequences will be."

"I don't care about exile. I don't care even if they force us
to move to some desolate place with just enough to keep us
alive, because if the Council punishes you simply for dreaming, there isn't much hope for any of us anyway."

"My dear—"

"I just wish that you wouldn't keep escaping this way."

"It's not an escape," he said, "at least not entirely. You
seem to have gained more faith in my dream at the same
time I've been in danger of losing some of my own. I'm trying to regain my convictions, Greta. I'm afraid that some of
the other Mukhtars' doubts have begun to creep into me."

"I hope not, Karim." She clutched his hand more tightly.
"I don't want to see what you would be like without your
dreams."

To seed the atmosphere of Venus with microorganisms that
would break down its atmosphere of carbon dioxide was a
formidable task, but the biologists working on the Venusian
islands had lived up to Karim's expectations. After enough
failures to dampen even his confidence, a team of biologists
headed by his wife had developed new strains of red and
green algae that were capable of ingesting the sulfur dioxide
of Venus's rains, and also a strain of cyanobacteria that
could survive without sunlight while oxygenating the atmosphere. Greta's report had minimized the frustration and expense of all the failed strains, all of the bioengineered
microorganisms that had shown early promise only to fail
and die in the lethal atmosphere.

Years had passed since the first seeding, and the new aerial ecosystem of algae and bacteria had survived, even
thrived. Karim still saw the same familiar darkness outside
the translucent dome of his island station, and the misty
acidic rains continued to fall, condensing as the planet
cooled, but changes had already been measured—small de-

creases in the level of sulfur dioxide in the rains and the presence of more iron and copper sulfides, of more carbon dioxide broken up into carbon and oxygen.

The biologists had begun their bioengineering of new strains of algae at about the same time as a team of engineers, under the direction of Hassan Tantawi, had begun to aim giant tanks of solid compressed hydrogen at Venus from their station orbiting Saturn. As oxygen was freed by the changes in the Venusian atmosphere, hydrogen would be needed to combine with the oxygen to form water. But setting up the Saturnian station and building the giant skyhooks that siphoned off the hydrogen had taken too great a share of the project's resources. Karim was beginning to worry that some on the Council of Mukhtars might halt the process of terraforming at the stage they had already reached. They would never admit openly that the project had grown too costly, that they might put an end to its work altogether; the Council was much more likely to make noises about "suspending operations temporarily" and "conducting more studies." The Mukhtars would tell themselves that something could still be learned from what had already been accomplished.

"I'll tell you what the problem actually is," Ali bin Oman said. Karim abruptly found himself sitting on a cushion in front of a low table. Ali sat across from him, sipping from a cup.

"The problem?" Karim asked.

"Why this project is stalled. Why we're likely to be here just long enough to see the next stage through to its conclusion before they suspend operations and haul us back to Earth. It's as I've always said—sooner or later, we'll have to reach out to our brethren in their space habitats. They wouldn't have been able to survive and to build their habitats without developing technologies superior to ours. They could help us in our work here, God willing, if we can swallow our pride long enough to ask them for their aid."

"Our fellow Mukhtars would force you off the Council if you voiced such ideas," Karim said.   •

"They'd probably do worse than that to me."

"You're also forgetting that the habitat-dwellers don't approve of terraforming planets."

"That may be overstating the case," Ali said. "They don't see the need for such efforts, since they're able to engineer their own environments in their artificial worlds. But I think they might be interested in contributing to a project that would add to their store of knowledge. That would be their only reimbursement from us—what they might learn. We have little else to offer them."

"The Council would never agree to that," Karim said. "This project was to be our refutation of that space-dwelling culture, our jihad, our moral equivalent of a war against them. To turn to them now means to admit that we've failed."

Ali grew translucent, then faded out. The room slowly darkened, and became again Karim's cabin aboard the *Beverwyck*.

Karim watched from the prow with Greta until the basalt cliffs of the Palisades were behind them, then went below as more boat traffic began to crowd the waterway—ferries crossing between New York and New Jersey, water buses moving north and south, sailboats, small hovercraft, patched-together vessels riding so low in the water that it seemed they might sink.

Lauren's bondmate Roberto was in the sitting room, drinking coffee. The young man got to his feet and bowed slightly, pressing his fingers to his forehead.

"Please sit down," Karim said as he settled himself on the couch across from Roberto. "It's good that we got an early start," he continued. "The traffic is going to slow us up."

"Only for a while, sir. This is rush hour, but in a couple of hours, we'll have clear passage. You'll be at West Point by midafternoon, if not sooner." Roberto poured more coffee for himself and a cup for Karim. "Uh, I have to ask you for a favor, Mukhtar."

Karim waved a hand. "Ask it, then."

"Of course you're free to refuse it."

"Of course."

"I had a message this morning from my brother Pablo. He's been living in Poughkeepsie for the past two years, but he's been offered a position in Albany. He asked if he could come aboard and travel there with us."

"What kind of position?" Karim asked.

"Designing educational mind-tours for the New York Museum and the Albany Institute. He trained as an engineer, but he got interested enough in mind-tour design to learn something about that and do some work on the side for a couple of tour producers." Roberto sipped his coffee. "He wouldn't be in your way, and Zack said he'd put him up in his room. And there are no black marks on his record, so you can clear him with the police if you're worried about security."

Karim frowned. "I am here on a mission of friendship," he said softly. "My wife is a native of this region. I have no worries about our personal safety." He tactfully refrained from mentioning the implant in his arm that would summon both medical personnel and a squad of Guardians to his side if danger threatened and the pin-sized camera on his headdress that would preserve images of any assailant.

"But if you'd rather not have Pablo aboard, we can just go upriver as planned and head back for him later after we leave you and your wife off."

Karim raised a brow. He had not expected the stolid Roberto to have an educated brother. "Would Pablo lose his chance at his new position if he didn't travel with us?"

"No, sir. He wasn't supposed to start his new work right away. It's more that he wanted time to find new quarters and get settled. Anyway, I shot a message back to him saying I'd ask, but I didn't promise him anything."

Karim made his decision immediately. "Tell your brother that he's welcome to come aboard."

Roberto grinned, then stood up. "Thank you, Mukhtar Karim." He bowed deeply from the waist. "You don't know how much—"

"It's nothing." Karim retreated from the young man's effusive gratitude into the bedroom.

* * *

If Venus was ever to acquire Earthlike weather patterns, the planet would have to rotate more rapidly; keeping the Venusian "day" of two hundred and forty-three Earth days meant an inhospitable world of hot and cold extremes. Any human beings living there would have the undesirable alternatives of either living in completely enclosed environments or being constantly on the move in order to stay within a narrow habitable band between scorching heat and excessive cold, in the twilight between sunlight and darkness.

Ali bin Oman and Greta occupied themselves with a game of chess while Karim perused the report they had presented to him. The choices proposed by the engineers to solve the problem of Venus's climate seemed equally problematic. The parasol could continue to shade Venus entirely while a soletta and mirror orbited the planet to provide reflected sunlight, or a large asteroid or object of similar size could be hurled at Venus to speed up its rotation.

When Karim looked up from his screen, Ali and Greta were watching him, ignoring their game. "The soletta and mirror design is ingenious," Karim began, "but it would require constant maintenance by a civilization that would have to endure over millions of years while sustaining its interest in this project. That's expecting rather a lot of a species that's managed only a few thousand years of continuity in its cultures at most."

"A continuously maintained artificial environment," Greta murmured. "That's what we'd have, not a natural Earthlike world. That isn't what our terraforming project was supposed to be about."

"Then we should aim an asteroid at Venus," Ali said, "and when it hits, God willing, the impact increases its spin." He peered at his pocket screen. "If it hits near the equator—"

"That powerful an impact would dissipate a lot of energy," Karim said, "perhaps enough to destroy what we've accomplished so far. That is, unless we settle for a Venusian day that would last for a couple of months or even longer."

"What we need," Greta murmured, "is some sort of planetary spin motor that can greatly speed up the rate of rotation but without damaging Venus."

Karim shook his head. "In other words, a technology that doesn't exist."

Greta and Ali flickered, then disappeared. Karim stood at the edge of the island, gazing down at shadowed Venus. A bright spot suddenly appeared near the equator, then blossomed into a flare. His pocket screen was still in his hands, but he already knew what the screen would tell him. Venus was beginning to turn more rapidly, but the crust near the impact point was melting. How long would it take for the heat generated by the collision to dissipate? Long enough, perhaps, to stall the work of terraforming until an increasingly impatient Council decided to abandon it altogether.

We've failed, he thought; after all this time, we've destroyed our work.

Something brushed against his hand. "Karim," someone said from far away; he recognized Greta's voice, and remembered. He lifted his band from his head, returning to the *Beverwyck*.

"Karim," Greta said again. She wore a long blue robe, dark blue tunic, and scarf; she took the linking band from him and handed him his formal headdress. "It's time to go."

"Yes, I know." He was already dressed in his formal white robes. He stood up and followed her out to the deck.

General Michael Yamamura, the commandant at the West Point Military Academy, was a small gray-haired man with erect posture and a piercing gaze. He met Karim and Greta at the north dock just beyond a sharp bend in the river, listened without comment as Karim rattled off his ceremonial greeting, then left them with two cadets to guide them on a tour of Kosciusko's Garden. Karim and his wife were still there admiring the roses when General Yamamura rejoined them. The two cadets left with Greta while the commandant outlined their upcoming schedule of events: dinner that night with the commandant's staff, a luncheon the next day with a few members of the faculty, a question-and-answer session with their most promising cadets.

Throughout the dinner and the walk back to the hotel near Gees Point where Karim and Greta were being housed, the commandant avoided any mention of the issue that had to be uppermost in his mind. Karim finally had to bring up the subject the next day, just before lunch. Although the graduates of West Point were to be absorbed into the Guardian force that served the Mukhtars, the Council would not interfere with either their course of study or with Academy custom. The cadets would be free to wear their gray uniforms until they won their commissions and donned the black uniform of the Guardians. Any officers serving at the Point would also be allowed to wear gray, and the Council had no objection to their continuing to fly their ceremonial flags, even though the country represented by the red, white, and blue banners no longer existed. The commandant had not been able to completely conceal his gratitude and relief.

Greta was part of his audience in the auditorium with the cadets, at which Karim was peppered with so many questions by the young men and women that General Yamamura finally had to declare the session over. Even after that, several cadets followed Karim and Greta back to the *Beverwyck*, anxious perhaps to impress a Mukhtar who might later consider them for a post on his staff. Their questions, on various subjects, had soon revealed the central concern of the cadets: that as officers in the Guardians, they might be reduced to being little more than part of an international police force, there to keep the peace and rein in anyone who threatened their world's precarious security. Even those officers who eventually won their way to a post on one of the orbiting space stations would not be looking beyond their own world, as their predecessors had done. They would be there only to monitor resources and changes in the weather, to repair satellites and to patrol spaceports and industrial satellites; their only purpose in looking to the heavens at all would be to track and divert any interplanetary body that might threaten Earth. Their mental universe would forever be enclosed by practicalities.

The sea to the south of Ishtar Terra was a wrinkled gray surface that only occasionally swelled into waves. A patch of dim yellow-white light, all that could be seen of the sun through the open slats of the parasol that still shaded Venus, was reflected by the ocean. Karim could walk along the shoreline without having to fear the crushing atmospheric pressure that had once existed here, but he supposed that any future settlers would have to wear much the same protective clothing as he did. His suit protected him from the heat of the day, because even with the parasol limiting the amount of sunlight that reached the planet, a day that lasted two months meant a steady rise in temperature, while the equally long night resulted in frigid cold. The helmet over his head and the tank on his back were necessary because the atmosphere was still too rich in carbon dioxide to be breathable.

There was life in the Venusian ocean, a stew of microbial life forms, but he wondered how many ever evolve on the dry and barren land masses. Hundreds of years for this, Karim thought, and vast numbers of lost lives that he would not care to enumerate, and what they had won for themselves was a sterile world, not the new Earth of their dreams.

Venus would change in time, become something else, but not soon enough for the Council, for whom a wait of thousands of years might as well be a million. They had wasted resources and lives in remaking this planet, and now, as if to punish Venus for their failure, they had turned it into a prison. The domes on the plateaus of Ishtar Terra had quickly filled with those who offended the Mukhtars, who were a danger to others, or who were simply inconvenient. If Venus was to be ugly and barren, the Council would make it uglier still, and any people exiled here would never escape.

No, Karim thought, and tore his band from his head.

He was still in the *Beverwyck*'s sitting room, but he found himself standing in front of his chair. He sat down again and thought of the kind of report he might write when he had completed his tour of this Nomarchy. He could write of the

Washington functionaries whose lives had shrunk to the management of ever-decreasing resources, the Jersey sea-wall workers whose labor was largely designed to postpone the inevitable, the New York mayor who looked forward to little, the West Point cadets who would never see glory or true accomplishment, and of the need for a dream that might give all of them some hope and enlarge their universe. Or he could note that the Atlantic Federation was under control, that its people had finally come to see the necessity for being ruled by the Council, that the old hatreds and animosities had finally died in their defeated hearts.

He knew which of those reports his fellow Mukhtars would prefer and which report was likely to guarantee that his old age would be one of powerlessness and exile.

In Poughkeepsie, Karim was scheduled only for a brief meeting with the mayor and a town meeting with a few hundred of the small city's residents and anyone else who cared to participate on the public channels. Unlike the cadets of West Point, the citizens of Poughkeepsie asked few questions, and most of their inquiries were about practical concerns: renewed efforts to rid the Hudson of the pollutants that had plagued it even before the Resource Wars, insect control and disease prevention, aid for their rapidly failing farmlands. Karim assured them that the Council was already drawing up plans to help them.

His day ended at the riverfront, where, north of an old bridge that spanned the river, the *Beverwyck* was docked next to several ramshackle boats. A few people were on the decks of their sailboats and cruisers; they stared at Karim and Greta with the same lack of interest their fellow citizens had shown that morning. Out on the Hudson, a sloop with triangular sails glided past, a graceful reminder of an earlier age.

Karim let Greta board first, then followed. Lauren and Zack nodded at them from the stern. "We'll have our supper after we're under way again," Karim said to the couple, "and perhaps my wife and I will dine on deck." It would be a pleasant way to pass the evening, moving slowly past the forested hills while dining.

"I wouldn't advise that, sir," Zack said, glancing heavenward. "It looks like we might get a storm." Karim looked up and then noticed the thickening clouds. "I'm thinking of waiting here to see how it goes."

"I'm supposed to be in the town of Hudson tomorrow by noon," Karim said.

"You needn't worry about that, Mukhtar Karim. Storm isn't likely to last all night, and if it were going to be a bad one, they would have put out a warning and told us to get you ashore. We'll be on our way before dawn with plenty of time to spare." Zack brushed back a strand of his long blond hair. "Roberto's below with his brother. It was mighty kind of you to say he could come along."

"It's no trouble at all." He went below, Greta just behind him, to find Roberto in the sitting room with another tall, broad-shouldered, dark-skinned man who strongly resembled him.

The two quickly rose to their feet. "My brother, Pablo Mainz-Aquino," Roberto said. "This is Mukhtar Karim al-Anwar." Karim was about to extend his hand when Pablo bowed slightly and touched his fingers to his forehead. "And his wife, Greta Gansevoort-Mehdi." Pablo nodded in her direction.

"Please sit down," Karim said. The two men sat down again on the sofa. Karim and Greta seated themselves in two of the chairs.

"I'm grateful you let me come aboard, sir," Pablo said.

"Your brother is part owner of this craft. I wasn't about to refuse passage to one of his people as long as there was room. He tells me that you will be working as a mind-tour designer."

Pablo nodded. His gaze was more direct than his brother's, the expression on his broad brown face more alert. "It's what I've always wanted to do, but the only way you can actually train for it, at least now, is by working with a producer and picking up skills along the way."

"I suppose you studied engineering," Karim said, "so that you would have something to fall back on."

"That's part of it, sir, but it was mostly because I thought some training in mechatronics and bioengineering might make me a better designer. Any real knowledge a designer can bring to a mind-tour, whether it's engineering or biology or a background in history, can help him bring more detail and reality to his creations. Most of the mind-tours we've got are either adventure scenarios or virtual tours of museums and other sites, and most of them are put together by people who are largely trained in audio and visual arts."

"There are a number of educational mind-tours," Karim said.

"I'd call most of them training sessions rather than educational victuals," Pablo said, "since they're designed to take someone through the steps needed to perform certain tasks. And the others, the historical mind-tours and such, are mostly variations on adventure scenarios. All they teach you is how to escape while pretending you're actually learning something. Serious students don't spend much time with them." He paused. "We're still a long way from what mind-tours might become as an art form."

"An art form?" Greta asked.

Pablo nodded. "We've reached the point where the mind-tourist doesn't run into as many of the glitches that destroy the illusion of reality, where the experience almost seems as detailed as the actual world. That's an accomplishment in itself, but there's still the potential for much more."

"And what sort of art do you envision?" Karim asked.

"It's hard to put it into words." Pablo frowned. "I think what I'm looking for is a way to create a virtual world that doesn't exist, that never existed, but that we might bring into being someday, that's actually possible to create. That may sound like I'm just talking about an elaborate sort of modeling process, and that's part of it, but maybe it would also inspire—"

Roberto was making surreptitious gestures at his brother with his hands. "Excuse me, sir . . . ma'am," Pablo murmured. "I'm taking up too much of your time." Outside, there was the low rumble of thunder. "And I'd better help the others secure the boat before it rains."

"When would you like your supper served, Mukhtar Karim?" Roberto asked.

"After you've finished whatever there is to do," Karim replied.

"That'll be about an hour, sir. I'll bring it to you here." Roberto went up the steps, his brother at his heels.

The storm was upon them by the time Karim and Greta were in bed. The boat rocked under them; the small porthole in the bedroom was suddenly white with light, and then a crack of thunder made his wife start and reach for his hand.

"It's all right," Karim said.

"I know." As a girl, Greta had lived through having her childhood home destroyed by one of the fierce late spring storms that sometimes ravaged New York and Massachusetts; storms had made her nervous ever since.

He held her hand until he knew she was sleeping, then lay there listening to the thunder growing more faint. He thought of Pablo and his ambitions for mind-tour designing. The young man was the first person he had met in some days who actually looked beyond what was around him, who seemed hopeful.

Karim slipped from the bed and put on a robe over his long tunic, then went out to the sitting room and up the steps to the deck. The rain had already stopped; the air was still humid, but cooler. Two lanterns were on in the stern, where a man was folding up a tarp. Roberto, Karim thought; and then the man turned and he saw Pablo's face.

"Salaam, sir," Pablo said. "I told the others to get some sleep while I took care of this. Zack'll get up in a couple of hours and have us on our way to Hudson."

"Good."

"Is there anything I can get for you? There's some iced tea in the galley."

"No, thank you." Karim sat down in a deck chair while Pablo stowed the tarp in a large chest. "I would like to ask something of you, though." He was silent for a few moments, choosing his words. "For a few years now, I have spent some of my spare time doing mind-tour designs myself. Not that I was able to do anything that would measure up to the efforts of a professional, needless to say."

Pablo sat down in a facing chair. "I don't suppose you can call any of us professionals," he murmured, "not in the usual sense, with formal courses of study and certificates. It's not anything anyone can train for except by actually doing the work, at least not yet."

"In other words," Karim said, "you serve an apprenticeship."

"You could put it that way. And then you find out if it's something you can do well or not, and if you can't—well, you see why I got my degrees in engineering." Pablo leaned back in his chair. "What sorts of mind-tours have you been working on?"

"This may strike you as odd," Karim replied, "but my subject has been the planet of Venus. I began with depictions of Venus as it is now, based largely on data from our probes."

"Then I assume most of the data is a few decades old, since near space exploration isn't one of our higher priorities these days." Pablo smiled. "I took an interest in space exploration at the university, but knew I wouldn't find any work in that field."

"Unfortunately, you're right. Yet I persist in this notion that human beings aren't at their best, aren't going to accomplish anything worthwhile and lasting, until they look beyond themselves to something greater. It's an idea that is somewhat at odds with the prevailing opinion of the other members of the Council of Mukhtars, who grow ever more concerned with more practical matters."

Pablo nodded. "But why Venus? As the subject of your mind-tours, I mean."

"There is much we can learn from Venus, and not only by sending more probes, although that is certainly something we should be doing. For some time now, I have been proposing to my fellow Mukhtars that we consider a detailed study of the feasibility of terraforming Venus—in other words, altering its biosphere and geology enough to make it an Earthlike world, God willing, one where our descendants might be able to live."

The young man let out his breath. "You don't dream small, sir."

"I have presented a number of practical arguments for undertaking such an ambitious project, the primary one being that we might, in centuries to come, need the knowledge gained from terraforming to restore Earth to what it was before the greenhouse effect became so troublesome. But I also think that it's necessary for other reasons, one of them being that need of human beings to look outward. We've become so preoccupied with this world, with sustaining its life and trying to keep things from getting any worse, that we're in danger of forgetting that there's anything beyond it."

Karim had meant to tell Pablo only a little about his preoccupation. Instead, he found himself speaking of his growing conviction that a terraforming project might offer rewards that would far outweigh the huge cost in resources and the long-term commitment to an end that even their grandchildren would not live to see, a project that had to be measured in centuries, perhaps even in millennia if the obstacles along the way proved too great.

"I put together a number of mind-tours," Karim concluded, "because I thought that perhaps they might be useful in presenting my case. At least that's what I told myself, but I suspect that I was trying to convince myself as much as anyone else. And as it turns out, they've become a private pursuit of mine. The scenarios fail at some point—that's the problem. And I keep thinking—" He paused, having little more to say.

"Sir," Pablo said after a while, "would you mind if I took your Venusian tours?"

"Definitely not. I was going to ask you if you would take a look at them. I've tried to make them as detailed as possible, but they may seem crude to you, and they are personalized, since I tended to use people I know in certain of the roles. They don't come anywhere close to capturing my vision."

"Maybe you just need someone to take a fresh look at them." Pablo folded his arms. "I'll see if I can come up with any design of my own that might be what you want."

"I would be most grateful. And now, I had better get some sleep if I am to be ready for my appearances tomorrow."

Karim got to his feet. For the first time in several days, he had no desire to escape into one of his virtuals.

In Hudson, Karim was scheduled for a meeting with the town council, a stop at the local train station, a question and answer session with several of the town's merchants, and an afternoon picnic in a riverside park with schoolchildren. Apparently the people of Hudson were determined to get as much out of his visit as possible, since no Mukhtar had ever traveled there before. He heard much the same kinds of remarks as he had in other places, found himself repeating most of his earlier statements, and saw the same sorts of passive, resigned looks on the faces of the people.

Greta had been at his side throughout the day. The sun was setting behind the mountains to the west as they returned to the *Beverwyck*; out on the wide river, he saw a lighted riverboat, decks crowded with passengers, gliding past the darkened hills. The pale blue sky was vivid with streaks of purple and salmon-colored clouds. He did not see anybody aboard his craft, but the *Beverwyck*'s owners had spent the day in Hudson seeing old friends and had mentioned plans to have dinner with a few of them.

"I'll go to the galley and make us some supper," Greta said to Karim.

"Don't bother, my dear. I ate too much at the picnic. The people of Hudson were too hospitable. I didn't expect them to serve us so much food."

"I imagine that was largely for the benefit of the children. It's probably the best meal most of them have had in a while."

He followed her down the short staircase into the sitting room. Pablo was there, sitting at the desk, a band around his head and a pocket screen lying on the desk. Karim cleared his throat softly, so as not to startle the young man; but Pablo was still and seemed completely absorbed.

Karim sat down on the sofa, Greta at his side. At last Pablo took off his band and turned away from the desk. "I hope we didn't disturb you," Karim said. "I thought you might have gone into Hudson with the others."

"I looked at your tours. I can come back to Hudson another time." Pablo rested his arm on the desk. "For someone who calls himself an amateur, Mukhtar Karim, you haven't done so badly. I'll have to look at more documents on the subject of terraforming—"

"There aren't that many," Karim interrupted.

"Then it shouldn't take me long to read them. Anyway, I'm beginning to think that your problem here isn't in your depictions but in your assumptions. You assume that most of the science and technology required for a project of this magnitude is at least within our grasp now, even if it doesn't yet exist, that given enough time and resources, we could bring it into being and use it in terraforming Venus. What you haven't done is anticipate new technologies and new knowledge and allowed for them in your scenarios."

Karim frowned. "I thought of that, but I don't see how I could create something at all plausible by factoring in unknowns."

"And I don't see how you can't," Pablo said. "You have to assume that each stage of any terraforming project is likely to yield something new."

"Of course." Perhaps he was too used to thinking of limits and of what could not be accomplished during his years on the Council of Mukhtars.

"What I suggest," Pablo continued, "is that I sketch out a mind-tour by beginning at the end and working backward from there."

"What exactly do you mean?" Greta asked.

"I'd begin with a vision of Venus as an Earthlike world, already terraformed," Pablo replied, "but while being rigorous about making sure that anything depicted in the scenario doesn't violate any known physical laws. That should give us a vision of an actual possibility even if we can't show exactly how it might come about at each stage. With mind-tour design, I've found, you have to have a strong sense of where you're headed. You can't just hope you'll end up with something convincingly real."

"I have a sense of where my scenarios should be headed," Karim said. "The problem is getting there."

"And I still think that's because your assumptions are too

limiting. But it's pointless to talk about it this way. I'd like to see what I can do, but I don't know how much time I'll have."

Greta glanced at Karim, then at Pablo. "We'll be in Albany tomorrow," she said. "I'll be visiting my family while my husband puts in his appearances, but he'll be staying aboard the *Beverwyck* for three days and then we're to go over to Boston by airship. You're free to stay here for that long. Will that be enough time for you?"

"I think so, ma'am. It's worth a try."

"Then try it," Karim said, feeling the unfamiliar emotion of anticipation.

He did not expect Pablo to come up with a sophisticated virtual in so little time, yet Karim found himself buoyed by the young man's absorption in his efforts. When he and Greta left the *Beverwyck* in the morning, she for her brother's estate just south of the city and he for his scheduled events, Pablo had already been up for a while, gulping coffee as he called up documents on his screen, fiddled with the desk console, or accessed the *Beverwyck*'s mind. Karim had given him complete access to all of his records and had promised to cover any expenses out of his credit.

Probably nothing would come of it; at most, Pablo might be able to send Karim a rough of a Venusian tour later on. Even so, the interest Pablo took in the project had lifted Karim's spirits. He would finish his travels in the Atlantic Federation and return to the New Islamic Nomarchy ready to demand that the rest of the Council reconsider his hoped-for Venus project, at least to the extent of funding a preliminary study. He would find ways to get more of the Mukhtars to support him, and if he failed at that, perhaps he could make enough of an impression during their deliberations to move a future Council member to take up the cause. And if he offended enough people or frightened enough of them into thinking that he was obsessed and mad enough to deserve exile, he would console himself with the thought that he had fought as hard as he could for his vision.

His more hopeful mood lent more eloquence to his

speeches and brief remarks; his improved disposition seemed to elicit more friendliness and warmth from the people he encountered. Hiram Marcus, the governor of New York, a figurehead of little power who still maintained an office in the decaying rococo splendor of the State Capitol Building, gave Karim an impromptu tour of the skyscrapers and marble expanse of the Empire State Plaza; soon the panhandlers and sellers of cheap goods who usually set up shop there were calling out greetings to the Mukhtar and the governor. The curators of the New York Museum guided him through their library and archives, and he found himself encouraging them to develop exhibits that would look forward as well as back in time.

During the second day of his visit, Karim was taken on a tour of a few of Albany's historic mansions, and he soon collected a crowd of interested people who followed his driver and van from place to place. On the third day, more people were waiting for him on the pier when he left the *Beverwyck*. He offered a few lengthy remarks about the five-hundred-odd years of their city's history, grateful for all the stories Greta had told him about her long lineage of Dutch, Irish, and South Asian ancestors who had settled here, while the city officials who had come to fetch him to a luncheon fidgeted and glanced at the timepieces on their fingers and wrists. "Too bad you aren't running for mayor," one of them said to him later. "You'd nail the election."

Greta rejoined him that afternoon in Albany's Washington Park, where they viewed tulips of various colors already in full bloom from an open trolley; the city was celebrating its annual Tulip Festival. "In the old days, long before my time, we held the festival in May," the city council president explained to Karim and Greta, although they already knew that. "But of course the tulips bloom much earlier in the spring now."

The day was warm, but not overly humid; a gentle and persistent breeze cooled Karim's face. People strolled along the roads and walkways or sat on the grass near tulip beds; at the park's small lake, children were feeding the ducks. Karim and Greta watched them from a small arched bridge, and he suddenly wished that he could remain here for a few more days.

They returned to the *Beverwyck* in the evening. The trolley carried them down the steep hill below the State Capitol, where men and women in Dutch costumes were sweeping the sidewalks, and let them off; they walked slowly along the riverfront toward the port, trailed at a discreet distance by three policemen. An old sailing ship was moored at one dock; another old vessel, a twentieth-century battleship, was tied up at another dock. The port was quiet, the day's visitors gone. The Hudson River flowed past, dark gray in the evening light, and he imagined it becoming finally cleansed of the chemicals and wastes that had poisoned it for so long.

Lauren, Zack, and Roberto were waiting on the *Beverwyck*'s deck. Karim thanked them for their services and told them that a hovercraft would be there early in the morning to take him and Greta to the airship port.

"Glad to hear it, Mukhtar," Lauren said. "We'll have time to look at the tulips before we have to pick up our new passengers in Troy."

"You're free to wander around the city tonight if you like," Karim said. "We won't need anything this evening."

"Thanks, sir." Roberto offered a quick grin. "My brother's still aboard. He says he's finished with that job you gave him."

The three left, hurrying down the dock; Karim and Greta went below. Pablo stood up as Karim reached the bottom of the stairs. "I think I've got something to show you, Mukhtar Karim," Pablo said.

"I didn't expect you to finish this soon," Karim replied.

"Well, I'm not actually finished. There's more I could do with the sound, and the details need more work. Plenty of detail adds to the verisimilitude, and I was very careful not to get caught in any contradictory assumptions. But I hope—" Pablo looked away for a moment. "The longer I worked on it, the more interested I got. I think—but maybe you should take part of my tour before I say any more."

"I shall." Karim sat down in an easy chair. Pablo made a

few adjustments on the desk console, then handed Karim a band.

"Are you prepared, Mukhtar Karim?" the voice of the *Beverwyck*'s AI asked.

"Yes." Karim slipped the band around his head.

Almost immediately he found himself gazing out at the expanse of a blue-gray ocean. Waves rolled toward him, lapping at the shore; he sniffed the air and smelled only a hint of salt and another, more acidic, odor he did not recognize. Large white-feathered birds wheeled overhead, with wingspans as wide as those of golden eagles; he watched as one dived toward the water, then flew up with a silvery fish in its beak.

The ocean, he remembered, had been seeded with algae and plankton centuries ago, and the lifeforms that lived in the Venusian seas now were bioengineered variants of many of Earth's species that could survive in the shallower and more briny oceans of this world. But over time, they would evolve and find their own peculiar niches in this new biosphere. Karim still thought of Venus as new, even though people had been arriving here as settlers for a few centuries now, and there were generations of families who had known no other home.

He looked up at the overcast sky and knew that nearly two hours had passed since dawn. There was light behind the pale gray clouds in the west; sunlight had returned to Venus, but part of the parasol remained in place to prevent too much sunlight from reaching the planet. Night would come twelve hours from now and last for fourteen hours. Antigravitational pulse engines had increased the spin of the planet; Karim could remember hearing of the decades of work by artificial intelligences and machines in erecting those massive engines at Venus's equator. There had been more quakes after Venus had begun to spin more rapidly, and its many volcanos had become even more active, but there had been no lasting damage, only the tectonic throes of a world at last coming to life.

A boulder as bright and hard as a diamond sat near him on

the reddish-brown sand and rock of the shore. Other shining stones were on the shore, some nearly as large as the boulders, others small, bright gems. He picked up one of the tiny stones and knew the jewel for what it was, a bit of calcium carbonate that had been precipitated out of the Venusian atmosphere.

He turned and saw the sheer escarpment of the Maxwell Mountains to the northeast. Patches of green covered the rock; through the mists that veiled the top of the scarp, he glimpsed more green. Forests, he thought, inhaling the cool air, and understood then that the self-replicating machines of the project, tiny devices no larger than molecules, were still at work on the high plateaus of Ishtar Terra turning the Venusian regolith into soil. The history of this terraformed planet was alive inside him, coherent and whole.

He saw then that he was not alone on the beach. A few meters to his right, a man, woman, and child were walking toward him. The woman had long light brown hair, much like Greta's in her youth, while the child clinging to her hand had the man's black hair. The three were strangers, and yet he felt that he should know them.

"Greetings," the woman said as she approached; the man smiled at Karim. "I see you're out for an early walk, too." She looked away to gaze out at the ocean. "We're still not used to it here," she continued, "but the others say it's always like that for new settlers. One moment it's our being awed by how much like Earth it is here, and the next being struck by the differences."

"It's new," the man said. "That's how it feels to me, entirely new."

Karim was about to ask them where they lived, and then it came to him: they were from a community on the Lakshmi Plateau, one of the newer settlements that had been raised in the young forests near the old settlements that were still enclosed by protective domes. Some had remained in the old settlements, preferring their unchanging climate and managed environments, but more people were leaving them, while the newer arrivals embraced living in the unspoiled outside world. The family standing with him had come to the shore in a small flying craft, to acquaint themselves with this part of their new home.

"Come with us," the child said to Karim, and suddenly he was inside their craft, flying south over the ocean. They sat in a half-circle, viewing the outside through the craft's wide windows. The wrinkles of the tesserae that had marked this area of Venus were hidden under the grayish-blue ocean; the volcano of Tellus Regio was now a black mound, red at its center, surrounded by green. They left the island of Tellus behind and flew on.

There was another continent on Venus besides the highlands of Ishtar Terra, and that was Aphrodite Terra, a scorpion-shaped land mass on Venus's equator. As that thought came to him, Karim caught a glimpse of green land to the south. Frost sometimes came to the highest parts of Ishtar, but Aphrodite was a tropical land of heat and jungle and the feral descendants of once-domesticated creatures. Aphrodite was a place for visitors and adventure seekers, not for settlers.

"Not yet, anyway," the woman said, "but that will change. People will settle here, too." Their craft descended—

—and he was standing on a hill, amid a profusion of flowers, surrounded by the engorged blossoms of orchids, by bright red peonies, by beds of pink, blue, and yellow roses and tulips. The air was filled with the fragrances of lilacs, roses, traces of cinnamon, and an elusive musky scent.

No, Karim thought, and his vision seemed to sharpen. These flowers were not the ones he had known on Earth, but only resembled those plants. The roses were much too large; the orchids were fading from purple to lavender and then darkening again.

The sky was growing dark, too; night was coming to Venus. The brown-haired woman who reminded him of his wife stood near him, near a vine-covered tree. "There's nothing more for us to do here," she said, "except to take root here with all the other life of this world, the life we've transplanted and the life that has developed here, and to live out our lives as part of it all."

"That was the hope long ago," Karim said, "to make this a world that could ultimately sustain itself without our intervention. But we're not there yet, not as long as the parasol is needed. That will require maintenance, and if it ever fails, the increase in sunlight may return Venus to her earlier self. The oceans might boil away again. The atmosphere—"

"The parasol won't fail," she said. "The artificial intelligences maintaining it will see to that." She laughed. "And maybe a time will come when we won't need the parasol, when we'll have the power to move Venus into a new orbit farther from the sun. Our work would be completed then. Venus could truly become the sister of Earth and follow her in her orbit around the sun."

Again he recalled all the centuries of effort that had brought him to this world, and to this garden. He lifted his head as the sky darkened and wondered if, when this side of Venus was turned away from the shield of the parasol, he would be able to glimpse the stars, if he would see Earth.

Then the garden vanished, and he was again in his chair.

Karim lifted his band from his head. Greta was murmuring a few words to Pablo; she fell silent as they both looked toward him.

"I hope that was enough," Pablo said, "to give you an idea."

"More than enough," Karim replied. "You have exceeded my expectations, Pablo. It's quite beautiful even in this form."

"Beauty's part of what'll give this tour its punch. I'll have to do more, of course, work in more of the history. That's what will give it more of the sense of reality, being able to feel yourself in the future, but a worked-out future, looking back, remembering each part of the history, having it be more than just the passing illusion of reality. The mind-tourist becomes convinced it can be real, and maybe that can inspire others to work toward making it real."

"It's my fellow Mukhtars that I'll have to convince," Karim said.

Greta shook her head. "No, my dear, not only them. Your project would have to be something in which everyone can share."

His wife was right, as she so often was. That was also part of what he had sensed at the edges of Pablo's tour, that sense of a new world open to everyone, in which people were finally free of the old boundaries.

"I'd like you to continue working on this," he said to Pablo.

Pablo looked pleased. "I'd be honored," he said.

"I can't offer you any official position, at least not yet, so you'll have to work on it in your own time. But I'll see that you get everything you require, God willing, along with enough credit to make it worth your while."

"That might be better for me," Pablo said. "I might be able to find a way to make it part of a museum exhibit eventually, so that others can share it. That's what you want—to build a constituency, so to speak."

"Yes," Karim said.

"They might make a mind-tour about you some day," Greta said. "Karim al-Anwar, master planner in a ruined world, reaching out to encompass his dream of progress in the terraforming of Venus. We see his heroic and creative journey reviving his world as his people win a new world and use that knowledge to resurrect the old."

"That sounds most farfetched, Greta," Karim said, but allowed himself to feel his pride and hope fully. He would fight for his dream, and if he failed, others would reach out for it, younger Mukhtars and all of the people who would experience the realized world of Pablo's completed mind-tour and look beyond it. "And now," he went on, "if you don't mind, I think I would like to return to the gardens of Venus for a few moments."

He slipped on his band. For a few seconds, he was lost in the darkness, and then he saw the flowers again, their colors faded but still visible, as night came to Venus and swallowed the light.

Only for a while, he thought; the dawn would come again.

Pulp Cover

GENE WOLFE

*Gene Wolfe [tribute sites: www.op.net/~pduggan/wolfe.html
and www.ultan.co.uk/] lives in Barrington, Illinois. One of
the great living SF writers, he has been exceptionally productive in the last few years. In 2004, he published his two-
volume fantasy novel,* The Wizard Knight *(as* The Knight *and*
The Wizard*), which proved to be his most popular work since
his classic* The Book of the New Sun *twenty years ago. His
last SF novel was* Return to the Whorl, *the third volume of*
The Book of the Short Sun *(really a single huge novel), which
many of his most attentive readers feel is his best book yet.
Collections of his short fiction include* The Island of Dr
Death and Other Stories and Other Stories, Storeys from the
Old Hotel, Endangered Species, Strange Travelers, *and* Inno-
cents Aboard. *He also published a number of short stories in
2004, both fantasy and science fiction, giving us several to
choose from for this volume.*

"Pulp Cover" was published in Asimov's. *It is a weird
Gene Wolfe puzzle story about a dull Midwestern businessman in love with the boss's daughter, who unfortunately is
engaged to someone else. The covers to which the title refers
are (on one level) those of the SF pulp magazines featuring
alien monsters abducting young maidens for some tentacu-
lar purpose. We hope you enjoy the mystery.*

My name does not matter. You have the name of the man I have gotten to tell my story. That's all you need to know. I'm an American, and I live in a town big enough to call itself a city.

I worked for Mr. Arthur H. East, as I'm going to call him. Furniture was our business—Mr. East owned three stores, two in our town and one in a neighboring town. We carried good quality and sold it at reasonable prices. Mr. East was sufficiently well off to have a big house in town and a vacation cottage on a good fishing lake. He hired me as a sales clerk, but promoted me to manager after six years. The promotion included an invitation to dinner, which I of course accepted. Up until that time, I knew no more of Mr. East's family than that he had a plump and pretty daughter I will call Mariel. I knew that only because she had come into the store I called mine looking for her father, and smiled at me.

I fell in love with Mariel at dinner that night. And she with me? I'd like to think so, but I don't know. Since this is my story, let's assume what I want so much to be true: she fell in love with me, but was too young to know it.

She was only fifteen—ten years younger than I was. That was one of the things I learned that night. Others were that she had no brothers or sisters, and that her mother had been dead about eight years.

"You're wondering," Mr. East said, "whether I plan to remarry. I won't until my daughter marries. After that I might."

170

I tried to say something noncommittal.

"I was raised by a stepmother," he told me. "I will not let that happen to my daughter."

"It will be quite a while," I said, "before Mariel finishes college."

I assumed, of course, that the daughter of a such a wealthy man would go to college.

Mr. East leveled his finger at me. "You didn't finish college yourself."

I'd had to drop out at the end of my freshman year, when my parents could no longer afford it. I had been taking night classes ever since, switching my major from pre-law to business administration; it is a slow process.

"Finishing college has nothing to do with getting married," Mr. East declared. "Not for Mariel, and, as far as I can see, not for anybody. There are plenty of married students, and plenty of successful people who never graduated."

By that time I realized, as you will have faster than I did, that I was under consideration. I got home that night without so much as bending a fender, although I haven't the least idea how I did it or what route I followed. I would marry lovely Mariel. We might or might not inherit her father's stores—it did not matter. Lovely Mariel would marry me. If her father left them to a second wife, she'd need somebody to run them, and I would be that somebody. Lovely Mariel and I would soon be married.

If her father left them to us, we would be rich. If he did not, it would hardly matter. I'd have a good, secure job, doing work I liked and running a business I understood.

And I would have Mariel.

My whole life opened out before me, and it was a life of love and success. I was walking on air. A few days later a note from Mariel was in my mail. You will sneer when I say that my hands shook as I opened it, but that is sober fact. They did.

She told me she had found out my address without asking her father, who wouldn't have wanted her to write. She said she thought I might want to write to her, and gave me the address of a friend at school. If I would write to the friend enclosing an envelope with "Mariel" on it, the friend would pass it to her in study hall.

I wrote, of course. I must have torn up a dozen letters before I finally wrote the one I sent. I told her how beautiful she was and (I will never forget this) I said that any man on earth would be attracted to her. I said that she could count on me to be a loyal friend and a protector whenever she needed one, and that I would never do anything to hurt her.

After I had sealed the envelope, I wrote a note to her friend, thanking her for what she was doing for us and asking her to write whenever she had news of Mariel.

Here I'm going to try to put three or four years into a couple of minutes. We wrote back and forth like that, generally two or three times a week. As often as she could, Mariel came by the store to see me, trying to time things so that she could stay until closing. I would drive her home, and she would tell Mr. East that she had been shopping at the mall and I had given her a ride home. That was all true. We held hands, and sometimes we kissed. She was more beautiful every time I saw her.

She dated various boys at school. I knew none of them meant much to her because they changed every few weeks. I knew that I meant a lot to her because she told me all her deepest feelings in her letters. Her father was dating a woman from the town where our third store was. Sometimes he brought her home, and she stayed the night. Mariel didn't think she was good enough for her father, and wrote a lot about her. Mariel herself wanted to get married right away— or didn't want to get married until she was thirty. (I think "thirty" was forever to her, although I was near that age.)

She wanted children. She wanted to be an actress who was a famous singer and dancer, and she wanted to be an astronomer and spend her whole life looking up at the stars— or else go to South America and study monkeys. All that stuff changed and changed, and pretty soon I saw that what she really wanted was pretty simple. She wanted security. She wanted people who would love her and take care of her, people who would love her always, no matter what happened. After that I knew what I had to bear down on, and I did. I told her over and over that what I wanted was a good marriage and children, and that I would always be faithful and loving. Even if my wife did things I did not like, I would always love her and be faithful to her, I said, and I meant every word of it.

It was early in May. I know that because my mother bought pansies and violas in early May every year, and I was digging a new bed for them when my father came to tell me my boss was on the phone.

Mr. East asked me to meet him at Wheeler's for dinner, and I could tell from the way he said it that he had a lot on his mind. When we had eaten dinner together before it had always been at his house. He had a housekeeper, and she would make a company dinner for Mr. East, Mariel, and me. So this was different, and it was pretty obvious why: he wanted to talk to me without Mariel around or her even knowing that we were talking. I was scared.

He was already in a booth with a drink and a cigarette when I got to Wheeler's. We ordered steaks, and after the waiter had gone, Mr. East said, "This isn't about business, and I like to keep my office business-like. Besides, there are always phone calls. Here we won't be interrupted."

I suppose I nodded.

"You know my daughter Mariel. You've given her a lift a couple of times. Do you like her?"

"Yes," I said. "Very much. She's a wonderful girl."

"She's still just a kid."

I waited for him to go on.

"She'll do whatever I tell her to. I might have to jaw at her a little first, but she'll do it. It's a heavy responsibility."

I said that I realized that, and realized he would have to carry it until Mariel was twenty-one.

"Or until she gets married," he said.

You can guess how I felt when he said that.

"Oscar Pendelton was my roommate in college. We were close then, though we haven't kept in touch the way we ought to. He's been very successful—a lot more successful than I have. I founded a company and ran it. He's founded half a dozen and sold them out. He has millions. You remember that big piece *Furniture Trade* did on us?"

I certainly did, it had been a cover story with a lot of color photographs.

"Oscar saw that and showed it to Jack. Jack's his oldest, and the only son he's got. I think there are a couple of girls, too."

I suppose I nodded.

"Oscar sees a lot of business magazines because he's been into and out of a lot of businesses. Naturally he was interested in a story about his old roommate's success. There were two pictures of Mariel in there, remember? One of us outside the house, and another in my study talking to her. Jack got very, very interested in Mariel as soon as he saw her. One of those crazy things, you know? Like falling for a girl you saw on TV."

That was when the waiter came with our steaks, and I'll tell you I was damned glad of it.

"So Oscar wrote to me. Would it be okay if Jack came for a visit? He would stay at our house and take Mariel to shows and so on. I suppose he'll play tennis with her too. I'd be there, and if things looked like they might go too far, I could break it up."

I nodded and pretended I was busy eating.

"Jack's a Yale man. He'll graduate this year. Mariel will graduate from high school, too. I doubt that you knew that, but it's true. She's been looking at colleges. Just fooling around with it, really. You know how kids are."

"Sure."

"So four years difference in their ages. That's not a lot, and she's mature for her age. When Jack's forty, she'll be thirty-six."

I said a difference that small hardly mattered.

"Right. Just what I've been thinking myself. Now listen, I want a favor and a big one. Jack's plane lands at nine twenty. United Airlines. I'd like you to meet him at the airport. You can drive out as soon as we finish here. Jack Pendelton. I want you to size him up for me, and I want you to meet me for lunch at noon tomorrow. Tell me what you think of him.

Tell me everything the two of you said, and exactly how he seemed to you. I'll have formed my own impressions by that time, but I want to check them against those of a man I can trust who's closer to his own age. Can I count on you?"

Out at the airport, I didn't have to ask which passenger was Jack Pendelton. He was six-foot-two and something about him made you think he was even bigger. He was plenty handsome enough for the movies, and he had on a Yale sweater. We shook hands. I explained that I worked for Mr. East; I said an important business matter had come up, and he was too busy to come in person, but he would probably be home by the time we got there. Jack nodded. He didn't smile. I don't think I ever saw him smile, except at Mariel; and I couldn't get a dozen words out of him the whole time.

Here it is going to sound like I want to make myself out to be a lot smarter than I am. Riding back into town and then out to Mr. East's it seemed to me that there was only one person in the car: me. And there was something else in there with me that wasn't really an animal or a machine or even a plant or a rock—something else that wasn't any of those things. We went into Mr. East's and the two of them shook hands, and he introduced Jack to Mariel. I could see that Mariel was attracted to him and scared of him, both at once. I wasn't attracted and I wasn't scared, either, but I had the feeling I'd be scared half to death if I knew more.

Next day Mr. East and I had lunch at a little French place he liked. He asked what I thought of Jack, and I said he was big and strong and tough, from what I'd seen of him, and as hard as nails. But he wasn't human.

"I know what you mean. Oscar says his IQ is in the stratosphere."

"Maybe," I said, "and maybe not. But what I mean is there's nothing warm there. Suppose I had stopped the car, and we got out and fought." (I said that because I had been thinking of it during the drive.) "He could have killed me and thrown my body in the trunk and never turned a hair."

I pointed to my salad. "That stuff is alive. That's why it's nice and fresh and green. When I chew it up and swallow it,

I'm killing it. Killing me would bother Jack about as much as killing this stuff bothers me."

"I think he's a fine young man," Mr. East told me, and after that he changed the subject.

I had hoped that Mariel could go to a college in the town where Ellie Smithers lived. Ellie was the woman Mr. East was dating. So did Mariel, and she had said so in her letters. She went to a famous girls' college in upstate New York instead. I won't tell what it was, but if I said the name you'd recognize it. You could have gotten the best car at Bailey's Cadillac & Oldsmobile for what it cost to go there for just one year.

I think it was around Christmas when Mr. East told me about the double wedding. It would be in June, and I was invited. The couples would be Jack Pendelton and Mariel, and Mr. East and Ellie Smithers. It would be a garden wedding "with five hundred guests, if Ellie has her way," and Jack's father, mother, and sisters would fly out.

Mr. East cleared his throat and leaned back. "I'm telling you this in confidence. I want that understood. Oscar's settling a portfolio of investments—stocks and bonds—on Mariel. I'll manage it for her until she's of age. I've checked out those investments, checked them out very thoroughly, then had my broker check them over again for me. Two million, three hundred thousand and change if you sold everything today. The income should be around two hundred thousand a year. It could be more. Growth 12 percent or so. Mariel will always be taken care of."

I came to the wedding, but Oscar Pendelton, his wife, and his daughters didn't. Later I found out that Mr. East had gotten a phone call. The woman who called said she was Sara Pendelton, and he had no reason to doubt her. Oscar'd had a heart attack. He was in intensive care. She knew the wedding was all set, and couldn't be postponed. But only Jack would be there.

After it was all over, and Jack and Mariel had flown to Boston to see Jack's father in the hospital, supposedly, I did something I felt a little guilty about at the time. I phoned every last hotel and motel in the area. Nobody'd had reservations for an Oscar Pendelton and family. Nobody'd had reservations for a Sara Pendelton, either. Mr. East and Ellie were honeymooning then, so I went out to the house and talked to the housekeeper. She didn't know where the Pendeltons were going to stay, but she hadn't been told to expect five house guests and there was no way in hell she wouldn't have been.

"It wouldn't be regular, anyway, would it? The groom in the house the day before the wedding? Him and his folks would put up at the Hyatt or something, I'm pretty sure." So I checked with the Hyatt again, this time in person. Nothing. It wasn't "I don't know"; it was "absolutely not."

By that time I was so worried I couldn't eat. And I was fighting mad. It took a hell of a lot of doing, but I got Oscar Pendelton on the phone, long distance. Certainly he remembered his old friend Art East. How was Art doing? Jack? No, he didn't have a son with that name. Two sons, Donald and Douglas. Don and Doug, their friends said. Nobody ever called either one of them Jack. He had no daughters. His wife's name was Betty.

You're going to say that I should have told Mr. East before he got back from his honeymoon. I've told myself that about a thousand times. Only I kept thinking it might be some kind of silly mistake. By that time the honeymoon was nearly over; I told myself I would tell him when he got back.

But I didn't. The thing was that I had called his broker. I told him Mr. East had put me in charge of his financial affairs while he was gone, and I wanted to make sure Mariel's trust fund was in order. It was. The brokerage was holding everything, but they would not sell or buy, or make any other changes, without a signed authorization from Mr. East. I explained that I didn't want to change anything, I just wanted to make sure everything was straight. It was. They'd had the whole trust portfolio in their hands two weeks before the ceremony. There was nothing to worry about.

After I hung up the phone I felt like I ought to laugh, but I didn't. On the one hand I was damned sure something was terribly, terribly wrong. On the other it was a couple of million. Suppose the man I'd talked to hadn't been Oscar Pendelton at all. Suppose it had been some joker, and he had been stringing me?

A few days later Mr. East got back all happy and tanned, and I asked as casually as I could where Mariel had gone on her honeymoon, and whether he had heard from her. They were going to tour Europe, he said, for a month. (He had taken two weeks, not wanting to be away from the business any longer than that.) He hadn't heard from her, but then he hadn't expected to.

I said I was worried, and he told me to forget it.

You can probably guess what I did next. I got hold of the girlfriend who had passed my letters to Mariel. She had heard nothing. She had been a bridesmaid, and she gave me the names of the other bridesmaids, and told me where they lived. None of them had heard from Mariel. I talked to every one of them in person, and if they had been lying I would have known it. They weren't. None of them had heard a word from the girl who had liked writing letters enough to write me two and three times a week.

I went to Mr. East and gave it to him straight. I said I was sure something had happened to Mariel, and he had damned well better get in touch with his friend Oscar and find out where Jack was. He got in touch with Oscar Pendelton all right, and you know what he found out: no Jack, no heart attack, no plans that had been canceled, no anything.

He hired a detective agency. All they were able to tell him was that there was no such person as Jack Pendelton. Yale had never heard of him. Neither had Social Security. And a lot more of that. They told Mr. East he'd better go to the police and have them list Mariel as a missing person. By that time Jack and Mariel should have been back from Europe for a couple of months, so Mr. East did. Nothing came of that either.

Years passed.

Oscar Pendelton had never had a heart attack, but Mr. East did. It was bad.

He'd had enough time in the hospital to write a will; and when his lawyer read it the audience was the housekeeper, Ellie, and me. The housekeeper got ten thousand. Ellie got the house, the cabin, the cars, and the rest of his money, and she was to administer Mariel's trust fund. If Mariel could not be found, the trust fund went to charity.

Mariel got the business, which I was to run in trust for her, with a nice raise. If Mariel could not be found, the business was to be sold and the money given to charity.

All nice and neat.

My folks died, and I sold the house and moved into an apartment.

Seven years after her wedding, Mariel was declared legally dead. And that was that.

I had an MBA. A night-school MBA, but still an MBA. I knew the furniture business backward and forward, and I had a lot of contacts in that business; I moved to a bigger town when a company there offered me a good job. I was thirty-six, going bald but not too bad looking. All right, I wasn't Jack. But Jack hadn't been Jack either. I dated maybe half a dozen girls, but the more I saw of them the less I liked them.

One night my bell rang. I pushed the button to let my visitor in and went to the door to see who it was.

It was Mariel.

She was only twenty-five, but she looked like hell. Her cheeks had fallen in and you could see the fear in her eyes. (You still can.) I told her to come in and sit down, and said I was damned glad to see her—which I was—and I had wine and beer and cola, and could make coffee or tea if she'd like that. What did she want?

And she said, "Everything."

Just like that.

She had no money and no place to stay. She couldn't remember the last time she had eaten, but she couldn't chew anything much because her back teeth were gone. She needed a bath and clean clothes.

I asked her how she'd found me, and I expected her to say Ellie'd told her, or at least somebody in the town where we were born. She didn't. She had been wandering from city to city for months, hitch-hiking, begging, doing time in jail for shoplifting canned soup from a supermarket. She couldn't remember the town we had lived in or where it was. All she could remember was three names: Mary East, Arthur East, and my name. Mary East had been her mother. She had repeated those names a hundred times to people she met, and finally someone had pointed out my building, and of course my name had been on the plate beside the bell button. As if all that wasn't bad enough, she kept switching to a foreign language, and I'd have to stop her and get her to speak English again. I can recognize quite a few languages when I hear them, and it wasn't remotely like Spanish or German or even Chinese or Arabic, and it certainly wasn't Polish or Russian.

I got milk and soup into her, and crackers she soaked in her soup so she could eat them. She handed her clothes to me out the bathroom door, and I put them in the little washing machine off my kitchen. When she came out, all wrapped up in one of my robes, she asked me who I was, saying she had remembered my name and knew my face, but didn't know how she had known me. I said I was the guy who wanted to be her husband, and she screamed.

We're married now, Mariel and me; so I got what I had wanted so badly years ago. Eleven months after we were married, she had Een. She said he had to be named Een, and got hysterical when I argued; so I guess it's a name from the place where she was. She won't tell me where that is, and says she doesn't know. She let me pick Een's middle name, so his name is Een Richard and my name, and most people think it's Ian Richard. Lauri and Lois came after that, and I know they're mine.

Okay, you're going to say it's not possible, that human women carry children for nine months and that's that. But when I look into Een's eyes, I know.

He's a good kid. Don't get me wrong. He's bright, and when you tell him to clean up his room he does it. He doesn't play with other kids, but they respect him. Or else. In two more years, he's going to be one hell of a high-school football player.

That's almost all I have to say. One night I woke up, and Mariel wasn't in the bed. I happened to look out the back window, and she was out there with Een pointing out stars and stuff.

So I thought I ought to warn people, and now I have. While I was telling all this, the man who's going to write it showed me one of his old pulp magazines. It has a monster with great big eyes and tentacles on it, and this monster is chasing a girl in a one-piece tin swimsuit. But it's not really like that. It isn't really like that at all.

The Algorithms for Love

KEN LIU

Ken Liu (www.kenliu.name) lives in Medford, Massachu-setts, and he is currently finishing law school in Massachu-setts. His first professional story appeared in the anthology Empire of Dreams and Miracles *(2002). A number of his earlier efforts are available on his website, described there as "juvenilia." His scanty biography includes the line, "Equally passionate about tax law and programming in Lisp, Ken dreams of some day writing a piece of speculative fiction that would combine the two."*

"The Algorithms for Love" appeared online in Strange Horizons, *now established as one of the select five or six webzines of professional quality (and with professional-level editing). It is about a brilliant woman designer of robotic toys whose job is driving her crazy. Various segments of this idea could have been used (and some have been used by other writers) to generate whole stories, but Liu lets it keep rolling along to see what will happen. This is a love story and an AI existential horror story that turns the Turing test inside out. Brrrr.*

So long as the nurse is in the room to keep an eye on me, I am allowed to dress myself and get ready for Brad. I slip on an old pair of jeans and a scarlet turtleneck sweater. I've lost so much weight that the jeans hang loosely from the bony points of my hips.

"Let's go spend the weekend in Salem," Brad says to me as he walks me out of the hospital, an arm protectively wrapped around my waist, "just the two of us."

I wait in the car while Dr. West speaks with Brad just outside the hospital doors. I can't hear them but I know what she's telling him. "Make sure she takes her Oxetine every four hours. Don't leave her alone for any length of time."

Brad drives with a light touch on the pedals, the same way he used to when I was pregnant with Aimée. The traffic is smooth and light, and the foliage along the highway is postcard-perfect. The Oxetine relaxes the muscles around my mouth, and in the vanity mirror I see that I have a beatific smile on my face.

"I love you." He says this quietly, the way he has always done, as if it were the sound of breathing and heartbeat.

I wait a few seconds. I picture myself opening the door and throwing my body onto the highway but of course I don't do anything. I can't even surprise myself.

"I love you too." I look at him when I say this, the way I have always done, as if it were the answer to some question. He looks at me, smiles, and turns his eyes back to the road.

To him this means that the routines are back in place, that

he is talking to the same woman he has known all these years, that things are back to normal. We are just another tourist couple from Boston on a mini-break for the weekend: stay at a bed-and-breakfast, visit the museums, recycle old jokes.

It's an algorithm for love.

I want to scream.

The first doll I designed was called Laura. Clever Laura™.

Laura had brown hair and blue eyes, fully articulated joints, twenty motors, a speech synthesizer in her throat, two video cameras disguised by the buttons on her blouse, temperature and touch sensors, and a microphone behind her nose. None of it was cutting-edge technology, and the software techniques I used were at least two decades old. But I was still proud of my work. She retailed for fifty dollars.

Not Your Average Toy could not keep up with the orders that were rolling in, even three months before Christmas. Brad, the CEO, went on CNN and MSNBC and TTV and the rest of the alphabet soup until the very air was saturated with Laura.

I tagged along on the interviews to give the demos because, as the VP of Marketing explained to me, I looked like a mother (even though I wasn't one) and (he didn't say this, but I could listen between the lines) I was blonde and pretty. The fact that I was Laura's designer was an afterthought.

The first time I did a demo on TV was for a Hong Kong crew. Brad wanted me to get comfortable with being in front of the cameras before bringing me to the domestic morning shows.

We sat to the side while Cindy, the anchorwoman, interviewed the CEO of some company that made "moisture meters." I hadn't slept for forty-eight hours. I was so nervous I'd brought six Lauras with me, just in case five of them decided in concert to break down. Then Brad turned to me and whispered, "What do you think moisture meters are used for?"

I didn't know Brad that well, having been at Not Your Average Toy for less than a year. I had chatted with him a few times before, but it was all professional. He seemed a very serious, driven sort of guy, the kind you could picture starting his first company while he was still in high school—arbitraging class notes, maybe. I wasn't sure why he was asking me about moisture meters. Was he trying to see if I was too nervous?

"I don't know. Maybe for cooking?" I ventured.

"Maybe," he said. Then he gave me a conspiratorial wink. "But I think the name sounds kind of dirty."

It was such an unexpected thing, coming from him, that for a moment I almost thought he was serious. Then he smiled, and I laughed out loud. I had a very hard time keeping a straight face while we waited for our turn, and I certainly wasn't nervous any more.

Brad and the young anchorwoman, Cindy, chatted amiably about Not Your Average Toy's mission ("Not Average Toys for Not Average Kids") and how Brad had come up with the idea for Laura. (Brad had nothing to do with the design, of course, since it was all my idea. But his answer was so good it almost convinced me that Laura was really his brainchild.) Then it was time for the dog-and-pony show.

I put Laura on the desk, her face toward the camera. I sat to the side of the desk. "Hello, Laura."

Laura turned her head to me, the motors so quiet you couldn't hear their whirr. "Hi! What's your name?"

"I'm Elena," I said.

"Nice to meet you," Laura said. "I'm cold."

The air conditioning was a bit chilly. I hadn't even noticed.

Cindy was impressed. "That's amazing. How much can she say?"

"Laura has a vocabulary of about two thousand English words, with semantic and syntactic encoding for common suffixes and prefixes. Her speech is regulated by a context-free grammar." The look in Brad's eye let me know that I was getting too technical. "That means that she'll invent new sentences and they'll always be syntactically correct."

"I like new, shiny, new, bright, new, handsome clothes," Laura said.

"Though they may not always make sense," I said.

"Can she learn new words?" Cindy asked.

Laura turned her head the other way, to look at her. "I like learn-ing, please teach me a new word!"

I made a mental note that the speech synthesizer still had bugs that would have to be fixed in the firmware.

Cindy was visibly unnerved by the doll turning to face her on its own and responding to her question.

"Does she"—she searched for the right word—"*understand* me?"

"No, no." I laughed. So did Brad. And a moment later Cindy joined us. "Laura's speech algorithm is augmented with a Markov generator interspersed with—" Brad gave me that look again. "Basically, she just babbles sentences based on keywords in what she hears. And she has a small set of stock phrases that are triggered the same way."

"Oh, it really seemed like she knew what I was saying. How does she learn new words?"

"It's very simple. Laura has enough memory to learn hundreds of new words. However, they have to be nouns. You can show her the object while you are trying to teach her what it is. She has some very sophisticated pattern recognition capabilities and can even tell faces apart."

For the rest of the interview I assured nervous parents that Laura would not require them to read the manual, that Laura would not explode when dropped in water, and no, she would never utter a naughty word, even if their little princesses "accidentally" taught Laura one.

"'Bye," Cindy said to Laura at the end of the interview, and waved at her.

"'Bye," Laura said. "You are nice." She waved back.

Every interview followed the same pattern. The moment when Laura first turned to the interviewer and answered a question there was always some awkwardness and unease. Seeing an inanimate object display intelligent behavior had that effect on people. They probably all thought the doll was possessed. Then I would explain how Laura worked and everyone would be delighted. I memorized the non-technical, warm-and-fuzzy answers to all the questions until

I could recite them even without my morning coffee. I got so good at it that I sometimes coasted through entire interviews on autopilot, not even paying attention to the questions and letting the same words I heard over and over again spark off my responses.

The interviews, along with all the other marketing tricks, did their job. We had to outsource manufacturing so quickly that for a while every shantytown along the coast of China must have been turning out Lauras.

The foyer of the bed-and-breakfast we are staying at is predictably filled with brochures from local attractions. Most of them are witch-themed. The lurid pictures and language somehow manage to convey moral outrage and adolescent fascination with the occult at the same time.

David, the innkeeper, wants us to check out Ye Olde Poppet Shoppe, featuring "Dolls Made by Salem's Official Witch." Bridget Bishop, one of the twenty executed during the Salem Witch Trials, was convicted partly based on the hard evidence of "poppets" found in her cellar with pins stuck in them.

Maybe she was just like me, a crazy, grown woman playing with dolls. The very idea of visiting a doll shop makes my stomach turn.

While Brad is asking David about restaurants and possible discounts I go up to our room. I want to be sleeping, or at least pretending to be sleeping, by the time he comes up. Maybe then he will leave me alone, and give me a few minutes to think. It's hard to think with the Oxetine. There's a wall in my head, a gauzy wall that tries to cushion every thought with contentment.

If only I can remember what went wrong.

For our honeymoon Brad and I went to Europe. We went on the transorbital shuttle, the tickets for which cost more than my yearly rent. But we could afford it. Witty Kimberly™, our latest model, was selling well, and the stock price was transorbital itself.

When we got back from the shuttleport, we were tired but

happy. And I still couldn't quite believe that we were in our own home, thinking of each other as husband and wife. It felt like playing house. We made dinner together, like we used to when we were dating (like always, Brad was wildly ambitious but couldn't follow a recipe longer than a paragraph and I had to come and rescue his shrimp étouffée). The familiarity of the routine made everything seem more real.

Over dinner Brad told me something interesting. According to a market survey, over 20 percent of the customers for Kimberly were not buying it for their kids at all. They played with the dolls themselves.

"Many of them are engineers and comp sci students," Brad said. "And there are already tons of Net sites devoted to hacking efforts on Kimberly. My favorite one had step-by-step instructions on how to teach Kimberly to make up and tell lawyer jokes. I can't wait to see the faces of the guys in the legal department when they get to drafting the cease-and-desist letter for that one."

I could understand the interest in Kimberly. When I was struggling with my problem sets at MIT I would have loved to take apart something like Kimberly to figure out how she worked. How it worked, I corrected myself mentally. Kimberly's illusion of intelligence was so real that sometimes even I unconsciously gave her, it, too much credit.

"Actually, maybe we shouldn't try to shut the hacking efforts down," I said. "Maybe we can capitalize on it. We can release some of the APIs and sell a developer's kit for the geeks."

"What do you mean?"

"Well, Kimberly is a toy, but that doesn't mean only little girls would be interested in her." I gave up trying to manage the pronouns. "She does, after all, have the most sophisticated, *working*, natural conversation library in the world."

"A library that you wrote," Brad said. Well, maybe I was a little vain about it. But I'd worked damned hard on that library and I was proud of it.

"It would be a shame if the language processing module never got any application besides sitting in a doll that everyone is going to forget in a year. We can release the interface to the modules at least, a programming guide, and maybe even some of the source code. Let's see what happens and make an extra dollar while we're at it." I never got into academic AI research because I couldn't take the tedium, but I did have greater ambitions than just making talking dolls. I wanted to see smart and talking machines doing something real, like teaching kids to read or helping the elderly with chores.

I knew that he would agree with me in the end. Despite his serious exterior he was willing to take risks and defy expectations. It was why I loved him.

I got up to clear the dishes. His hand reached across the table and grabbed mine. "Those can wait," he said. He walked around the table, pulling me to him. I looked into his eyes. I loved the fact that I knew him so well I could tell what he was going to say before he said it. *Let's make a baby,* I imagined him saying. Those would have been the only words right for that moment.

And so he did.

I'm not asleep when Brad finishes asking about restaurants and comes upstairs. In my drugged state, even pretending is too difficult.

Brad wants to go to the pirate museum. I tell him that I don't want to see anything violent. He agrees immediately. That's what he wants to hear from his content, recovering wife.

So now we wander around the galleries of the Peabody Essex Museum, looking at the old treasures of the Orient from Salem's glory days.

The collection of china is terrible. The workmanship in the bowls and saucers is inexcusable. The patterns look like they were traced on by children. According to the placards, these were what the Cantonese merchants exported for foreign consumption. They would never have sold such stuff in China itself.

I read the description written by a Jesuit priest who visited the Cantonese shops of the time.

The craftsmen sat in a line, each with his own brush and

specialty. The first drew only the mountains, the next only the grass, the next only the flowers, and the next only the animals. They went on down the line, passing the plates from one to the next, and it took each man only a few seconds to complete his part.

So the "treasures" are nothing more than mass-produced cheap exports from an ancient sweatshop and assembly line. I imagine painting the same blades of grass on a thousand teacups a day: the same routine, repeated over and over, with maybe a small break for lunch. Reach out, pick up the cup in front of you with your left hand, dip the brush, one, two, three strokes, put the cup behind you, rinse and repeat. What a simple algorithm. It's so human.

Brad and I fought for three months before he agreed to produce Aimée, just plain Aimée™.

We fought at home, where night after night I laid out the same forty-one reasons why we should and he laid out the same thirty-nine reasons why we shouldn't. We fought at work, where people stared through the glass door at Brad and me gesticulating at each other wildly, silently.

I was so tired that night. I had spent the whole evening locked away in my study, struggling to get the routines to control Aimée's involuntary muscle spasms right. It had to be right or she wouldn't feel real, no matter how good the learning algorithms were.

I came up to the bedroom. There was no light. Brad had gone to bed early. He was exhausted too. We had again hurled the same reasons at each other during dinner.

He wasn't asleep. "Are we going to go on like this?" he asked in the darkness.

I sat down on my side of the bed and undressed. "I can't stop it," I said. "I miss her too much. I'm sorry."

He didn't say anything. I finished unbuttoning my blouse and turned around. With the moonlight coming through the window I could see that his face was wet. I started crying too.

When we both finally stopped, Brad said, "I miss her too."

"I know," I said. *But not like me.*

"It won't be anything like her, you know?" he said.

"I know," I said.

The real Aimée had lived for ninety-one days. Forty-five of those days she'd spent under the glass hood in intensive care, where I could not touch her except for brief doctor-supervised sessions. But I could hear her cries. I could always hear her cries. In the end I tried to break through the glass with my hands, and I beat my palms against the unyielding glass until the bones broke and they sedated me.

I could never have another child. The walls of my womb had not healed properly and never would. By the time that piece of news was given to me Aimée was a jar of ashes in my closet.

But I could still hear her cries.

How many other women were like me? I wanted something to fill my arms, something to learn to speak, to walk, to grow a little, long enough for me to say goodbye, long enough to quiet those cries. But not a real child. I couldn't deal with another real child. It would feel like a betrayal.

With a little plastiskin, a little synthgel, the right set of motors and a lot of clever programming, I could do it. Let technology heal all wounds.

Brad thought the idea an abomination. He was revolted. He couldn't *understand*.

I fumbled around in the dark for some tissues for Brad and me.

"This may ruin us, and the company," he said.

"I know," I said. I lay down. I wanted to sleep.

"Let's do it, then," he said.

I didn't want to sleep any more.

"I can't take it," he said. "Seeing you like this. Seeing you in so much pain tears me up. It hurts too much."

I started crying again. This understanding, this pain. Was this what love was about?

Right before I fell asleep Brad said, "Maybe we should think about changing the name of the company."

"Why?"

"Well, I just realized that 'Not Your Average Toy' sounds pretty funny to the dirty-minded."

I smiled. Sometimes the vulgar is the best kind of medicine.

"I love you."

"I love you too."

Brad hands me the pills. I obediently take them and put them in my mouth. He watches as I sip from the glass of water he hands me.

"Let me make a few phone calls," he says. "You take a nap okay?" I nod.

As soon as he leaves the room I spit out the pills into my hand. I go into the bathroom and rinse out my mouth. I lock the door behind me and sit down on the toilet. I try to recite the digits of pi. I manage fifty-four places. That's a good sign. The Oxetine must be wearing off.

I look into the mirror. I stare into my eyes, trying to see through to the retinas, matching photoreceptor with photoreceptor, imagining their grid layout. I turn my head from side to side, watching the muscles tense and relax in turn. That effect would be hard to simulate.

But there's nothing in my face, nothing real behind that surface. Where is the pain, the pain that made love real, the pain of understanding?

"You okay, sweetie?" Brad says through the bathroom door.

I turn on the faucet and splash water on my face. "Yes," I say. "I'm going to take a shower. Can you get some snacks from that store we saw down the street?"

Giving him something to do reassures him. I hear the door to the room close behind him. I turn off the faucet and look back into the mirror, at the way the water droplets roll down my face, seeking the canals of my wrinkles.

The human body is a marvel to re-create. The human mind, on the other hand, is a joke. Believe me, I know.

No, Brad and I patiently explained over and over to the cameras, we had not created an "artificial child." That was not our intention and that was not what we'd done. It was a way to comfort the grieving mothers. If you needed Aimée, you would know.

I would walk down the street and see women walking with bundles carefully held in their arms. And occasionally I would know, I would know beyond a doubt, by the sound of a particular cry, by the way a little arm waved. I would look into the faces of the women, and be comforted.

I thought I had moved on, recovered from the grieving process. I was ready to begin another project, a bigger project that would really satisfy my ambition and show the world my skills. I was ready to get on with my life.

Tara took four years to develop. I worked on her in secret while designing other dolls that would sell. Physically Tara looked like a five-year old girl. Expensive transplant-quality plastiskin and synthgel gave her an ethereal and angelic look. Her eyes were dark and clear, and you could look into them forever.

I never finished Tara's movement engine. In retrospect that was probably a blessing. As a temporary placeholder during development I used the facial expression engine sent in by the Kimberly enthusiasts at MIT's Media Lab. Augmented with many more fine micromotors than Kimberly had, she could turn her head, blink her eyes, wrinkle her nose, and generate thousands of convincing facial expressions. Below the neck she was paralyzed.

But her mind, oh, her mind.

I used the best quantum processors and the best solid-state storage matrices to run multi-layered, multi-feedback neural nets. I threw in the Stanford Semantic Database and added my own modifications. The programming was beautiful. It was truly a work of art. The data model alone took me over six months.

I taught her when to smile and when to frown, and I taught her how to speak and how to listen. Each night I analyzed the activation graphs for the nodes in the neural nets, trying to find and resolve problems before they occurred.

Brad never saw Tara while she was in development. He was too busy trying to control the damage from Aimée, and then, later, pushing the new dolls. I wanted to surprise him.

I put Tara in a wheelchair, and I told Brad that she was the daughter of a friend. Since I had to run some errands, could he entertain her while I was gone for a few hours? I left them in my office.

When I came back two hours later, I found Brad reading to her from *The Golem of Prague*, " 'Come,' said the Great Rabbi Loew, 'Open your eyes and speak like a real person!' "

That was just like Brad, I thought. He had his sense of irony.

"All right," I interrupted him. "Very funny. I get the joke. So how long did it take you?"

He smiled at Tara. "We'll finish this some other time," he said. Then he turned to me. "How long did it take me what?"

"To figure it out."

"Figure out what?"

"Stop kidding around," I said. "Really, what was it that gave her away?"

"Gave what away?" Brad and Tara said at the same time.

Nothing Tara ever said or did was a surprise to me. I could predict everything she would say before she said it. I'd coded everything in her, after all, and I knew exactly how her neural nets changed with each interaction.

But no one else suspected anything. I should have been elated. My doll was passing a real-life Turing Test. But I was frightened. The algorithms made a mockery of intelligence, and no one seemed to know. No one seemed to even care.

I finally broke the news to Brad after a week. After the initial shock he was delighted (as I knew he would be).

"Fantastic," he said. "We're now no longer just a toy company. Can you imagine the things we can do with this? You'll be famous, really famous!"

He prattled on and on about the potential applications. Then he noticed my silence. "What's wrong?"

So I told him about the Chinese Room.

The philosopher John Searle used to pose a puzzle for the AI researchers. Imagine a room, he said, a large room filled with meticulous clerks who are very good at following orders but who speak only English. Into this room are delivered a steady stream of cards with strange symbols on them. The clerks have to draw other strange symbols on blank cards in response and send the cards out of the room. In order to do this, the clerks have large books, full of rules in English like this one: "When you see a card with a single horizontal squiggle followed by a card with two vertical squiggles, draw a triangle on a blank card and hand it to the clerk to your right." The rules contain nothing about what the symbols might mean.

It turns out that the cards coming into the room are questions written in Chinese, and the clerks, by following the rules, are producing sensible answers in Chinese. But could anything involved in this process—the rules, the clerks, the room as a whole, the storm of activity—be said to have *understood* a word of Chinese? Substitute "processor" for the clerks and substitute "program" for the books of rules, then you'll see that the Turing Test will never prove anything, and AI is an illusion.

But you can also carry the Chinese Room Argument the other way: substitute "neurons" for the clerks and substitute the physical laws governing the cascading of activating potentials for the books of rules; then how can any of us ever be said to "understand" anything? Thought is an illusion.

"I don't understand," Brad said. "What are you saying?"

A moment later I realized that that was exactly what I'd expected him to say.

"Brad," I said, staring into his eyes, willing him to understand. "I'm scared. What if we are just like Tara?"

"We? You mean people? What are you talking about?"

"What if," I said, struggling to find the words, "we are just following some algorithm from day to day? What if our brain cells are just looking up signals from other signals? What if we are not thinking at all? What if what I'm saying to you now is just a predetermined response, the result of mindless physics?"

"Elena," Brad said, "you're letting philosophy get in the way of reality."

I need sleep, I thought, feeling hopeless.

"I think you need to get some sleep," Brad said.

I handed the coffee-cart girl the money as she handed me the coffee. I stared at the girl. She looked so tired and bored at eight in the morning that she made me feel tired.

I need a vacation.

"I need a vacation," she said, sighing exaggeratedly.

I walked past the receptionist's desk. *Morning, Elena.*

Say something different, please. I clenched my teeth. *Please.*

"Morning, Elena," she said.

I paused outside Ogden's cube. He was the structural engineer. *The weather, last night's game, Brad.*

He saw me and got up. "Nice weather we're having, eh?" He wiped the sweat from his forehead and smiled at me. He jogged to work. "Did you see the game last night? Best shot I've seen in ten years. Unbelievable. Hey, is Brad in yet?" His face was expectant, waiting for me to follow the script, the comforting routines of life.

The algorithms ran their determined courses, and our thoughts followed one after another, as mechanical and as predictable as the planets in their orbits. The watchmaker was the watch.

I ran into my office and closed the door behind me, ignoring the expression on Ogden's face. I walked over to my computer and began to delete files.

"Hi," Tara said. "What are we going to do today?"

I shut her off so quickly that I broke a nail on the hardware switch. I ripped out the power supply in her back. I went to work with my screwdriver and pliers. After a while I switched to a hammer. Was I killing?

Brad burst in the door. "What are you doing?"

I looked up at him, my hammer poised for another strike. I wanted to tell him about the pain, the terror that opened up an abyss around me.

In his eyes I could not find what I wanted to see. I could not see understanding.

I swung the hammer.

* * *

Brad had tried to reason with me, right before he had me committed.

"This is just an obsession," he said. "People have always associated the mind with the technological fad of the moment. When they believed in witches and spirits, they thought there was a little man in the brain. When they had mechanical looms and player pianos, they thought the brain was an engine. When they had telegraphs and telephones, they thought the brain was a wire network. Now you think the brain is just a computer. Snap out of it. *That* is the illusion."

Trouble was, I knew he was going to say that.

"It's because we've been married for so long!" he shouted. "That's why you think you know me so well!"

I knew he was going to say that too.

"You're running around in circles," he said, defeat in his voice. "You're just spinning in your head."

Loops in my algorithm. FOR and WHILE loops.

"Come back to me. I love you."

What else could he have said?

Now finally alone in the bathroom of the inn, I look down at my hands, at the veins running under the skin. I press my hands together and feel my pulse. I kneel down. Am I praying? Flesh and bones, and good programming.

My knees hurt against the cold tile floor.

The pain is real, I think. There's no algorithm for the pain. I look down at my wrists, and the scars startle me. This is all very familiar, like I've done this before. The horizontal scars, ugly and pink like worms, rebuke me for failure. Bugs in the algorithm.

That night comes back to me: the blood everywhere, the alarms wailing, Dr. West and the nurses holding me down while they bandaged my wrists, and then Brad staring down at me, his face distorted with uncomprehending grief.

I should have done better. The arteries are hidden deep, protected by the bones. The slashes have to be made vertically if you really want it. That's the right algorithm. There's a recipe for everything. This time I'll get it right.

It takes a while, but finally I feel sleepy.

I'm happy. The pain *is* real.

I open the door to my room and turn on the light.

The light activates Laura, who is sitting on top of my dresser. This one used to be a demo model. She hasn't been dusted in a while, and her dress looks ragged. Her head turns to follow my movement.

I turn around. Brad's body is still, but I can see the tears on his face. He was crying on the whole silent ride home from Salem.

The innkeeper's voice loops around in my head. "Oh, I could tell right away something was wrong. It's happened here before. She didn't seem right at breakfast, and then when you came back she looked like she was in another world. When I heard the water running in the pipes for that long I rushed upstairs right away."

So I was that predictable.

I look at Brad, and I believe that he is in a lot of pain. I believe it with all my heart. But I still don't feel anything. There's a gulf between us, a gulf so wide that I can't feel his pain. Nor he mine.

But my algorithms are still running. I scan for the right thing to say.

"I love you."

He doesn't say anything. His shoulders heave, once.

I turn around. My voice echoes through the empty house, bouncing off walls. Laura's sound receptors, old as they are, pick them up. The signals run through the cascading IF statements. The DO loops twirl and dance while she does a database lookup. The motors whirr. The synthesizer kicks in.

"I love you too," Laura says.

Glinky

RAY VUKCEVICH

Ray Vukcevich [www.sff.net/people/RayV] lives in Eugene, Oregon. He is a lab computer programmer at the University of Oregon in Eugene, and has been publishing genre fiction since 1980. Jay Lake, in an essay on Vukcevich, said, "Ray Vukcevich may be the greatest writer you've never heard of." He did not get much in the way of recognition outside the Pacific Northwest, though, until the end of the 1990s. This is in part because much of his fiction is exploring, or located on, the edges of genre. And it is often slyly humorous, in a slightly unsettling way. He has been compared to Carol Emshwiller, and to Jeff VanderMeer, but perhaps the best comparisons are to Terry Bisson or Jonathan Lethem, or even to fellow Oregonian Damon Knight. His first novel, The Man of Maybe Half-a-Dozen Faces, *appeared in 2000, and a year later his first story collection,* Meet Me in the Moon Room, *was published.*

"Glinky" appeared in F&SF (the month after "Gas," also under consideration for this year's best SF stories volume). In "Glinky," Vukcevich ventures into territory often mined by Philip K. Dick and acquits himself nicely. Lesser writers have their fictional realities collapse inadvertently; Vukcevich clearly chose to spread the narrative throughout its universes and does so deftly and enjoyably, generic conventions well in hand. Detective Karl Sowa is hired to prevent a traveler from another reality from distorting ours. Or maybe it's already happened.

1
Not a Bird

Glinky is on TV.

The man with the abdominal gunshot wound isn't watching Glinky.

What the heck is Glinky anyway?

Is he a mouse?

No!

Is she a cat?

No!

It's Glinky, Glinky, Glinky!

The wounded man wants to somehow get to the telephone on the table near the couch and call for help. It's a long way to crawl. Glinky sings him a little song of encouragement, but it's clear the cartoon is mocking him.

When the man gets to the table, he looks back and sees a long smear of blood across the carpet and beyond that Glinky glaring at him from the TV.

Who in the world is Glinky?

Some monkey?

No.

A flying fish with horse lips and dog ears?

No, he's just Glinky!

The man stretches up an arm and bats around on the top of the table for the phone. It isn't there. No, wait, there it is.

He pulls it off the table and tries to catch it as it falls, and fails, and it hits him in the face, but the pain is nothing like the pain in his gut. The pain from the phone hitting him in the face is trivial. It might as well not be pain at all. He drags the phone into his lap and picks up the receiver and puts it to his ear.

There is no dial tone.

He pulls at the phone wire that leads to the wall. Soon, he's holding the end. The shooter or someone (maybe Glinky?) has unplugged the phone.

He crawls under the table to look for the outlet. He finally spots it behind the couch. Should he try to get back there and plug the phone back in? No. He won't be able to move the couch. He will have to crawl to the front door and yell into the street for help. The door is so far away it looks like he will have to Alice down to a very small size to fit through it. But he must get there first. A journey of a thousand scootches begins with the first scootch.

Will he make it, Glinky?

"No!"

So, he'll never get out of here?

"Not unless he buys something."

What must he buy, Glinky?

"The farm!"

2
To Your Left

Oddly, I'd been on my way to the Medical Mall that day anyway. It was company policy that all my employees undergo annual medical checkups, and the fact that I was my only employee did not tempt me to relax the requirement. Karl Sowa Investigations had procedures, and we followed them. I didn't expect to be a one-man operation forever.

I could have driven the few blocks from my office on Eleventh Avenue to the Medical Mall, but instead I made the healthy choice and walked. It was a glorious Oregon day. The sun was shining for a change. The birds were chirping.

The squirrels were gathering nuts or whatever urban squirrels gathered. The traffic was a steady hum with not so many horn honks.

Spring at last.

I was thinking I should maybe whistle a happy tune when right behind me, someone shouted, "To your left!"

Meaning, I thought, I should jump to my left.

Wrong.

The bicyclist behind me yelped and swerved to the right at the last moment and clipped me, and I stumbled off the sidewalk where a great wall of metal rushed by, and for a moment I thought I'd stepped onto railroad tracks that had not been there a moment before, but then the thing passed, and I could see it was a city bus. There was some kind of big rodent with huge red eyes painted on the back of the bus. It studied me with smug amusement.

I looked back to see the bicyclist peddaling full speed toward a place where the sidewalk made a sharp turn at a building. Probably a kid, I thought, judging by the fact that there were things sticking out of her helmet like horns or ears and long red hair shooting out in all directions—some kind of costume?

Surely she would slow down for the turn. I had a sudden feeling of total satisfaction at the thought of her hitting the building with a cartoon splat, but then I felt guilty for thinking that and then felt okay, realizing it wasn't like it was actually going to happen, but then it did.

The wheels were a blur and for a moment I thought they were not wheels at all but the galloping feet and legs of some kind of furry beast, but before I could get that thought fully formed, the rider ran headlong into the building. Instead of crashing or bouncing back out into traffic, she passed right through the wall as if it were made of smoke.

Before I had time even to doubt what I'd seen, someone shouted, "Don't move!"

Then there were hands all over me. A young woman told me everything would be okay, you'll be fine, just relax, you're hurt, but we're here to help. There were three of them—two big blond guys with very short hair and the young woman with the soothing voice, all of them wearing white medical coats. One of the guys grabbed me under the arms from behind and the other snatched up my feet, and they lowered me onto a gurney.

"Hey!" I yelled and tried to get off. The woman put both hands on my chest and pushed down. She was pretty strong, but she didn't have to hold me long, because one of the guys pulled a leather strap over my arms and chest and fastened it. Likewise another strap across my lower legs.

"Okay, let's go," the woman said.

One of the guys pushed me onto the sidewalk. The woman walked along beside me patting my shoulder and looking concerned. I lifted my head as much as I could and looked down the length of my body and between my feet and saw the other young man take off running while waving his arms and making siren noises. The guy pushing my gurney picked up the pace, and the woman jogged to keep up. Soon we were zooming along dangerously fast.

The guy making the siren noises didn't slow down for the big automatic glass doors of the Medical Mall. The doors opened just in time, and we zipped into the mall.

The waiting areas were set up like sidewalk cafés so consumers of medical services could watch other consumers strolling up and down the mall. There were small white metal tables and chairs and roving venders offering cola or cappuccino. The doctors were arranged by body parts or maybe alphabetically (podiatry followed by proctology) or maybe metaphorically—is that a kick in the ass or what? Bings and pings now and then interrupted the Muzak which was a song about buying this or buying that, come on, do it for the Glinkster, don't be a tightwad.

We were still moving pretty fast as we passed through one of the café waiting rooms and banged through a set of double doors into a huge bright room. The guy pushing the gurney let it go, and I flew forward spinning like the jack of diamonds tossed at a big silk top hat.

I tightened up for the forthcoming crash and pain, but someone caught my gurney before it hit a wall.

A new team descended on me. My eyelid was peeled back

and a bright light shined into my eye, first on the left and then on the right. Someone else stuck a needle in my arm behind the elbow.

"Hey, I'm not hurt," I yelled. "Let me up."

"Relax, Karl," a woman said. "Everything is going to be fine."

How did she know my name?

I felt the familiar coldness of a stethoscope on my chest and looked down to see that I was now wearing only my underwear and that my arms and legs were no longer strapped down.

The guy listening to my chest put away his stethoscope and said, "Get up now, please."

I got up. There were two women and one man dressed in white like the ones who'd snatched me off the street. I looked around the big room and it did not seem so big now and the gurney I'd ridden in on was now an examination table and instead of three people, there was only the one nurse, neat, maybe mid-forties, very efficient, no nonsense, and she directed me to a scale and weighed and measured me.

"Boy oh boy," she said.

"What?"

"Nothing, just your weight and height."

"Is it unusual?"

"We're all individuals, aren't we? Jump back up on here." I sat on the edge of the examination table, and she checked my reflexes.

"Whoa!" she said when my knee jerked.

"What?"

She turned my head to one side and put something in my ear and said, "Well, this is interesting." She turned my head the other way to look into my other ear. "Here, too," she said.

"What is it?" I asked.

"Nothing," she said. "Everything is shipshape."

"But what about my ears?"

"What about your ears?"

"Never mind."

"Well, just relax," she said. "The doctor will be with you shortly."

Which meant sometime in the indefinite future but probably before I died of old age or hell froze over.

I had lost track of the number of times I'd gone completely through my compressed Tai Chi routine by the time the doctor stepped in. I froze in the middle of Lan Ch'ueh Wei (Grasping the Bird's Tail).

"Well, I see you can still dance," he said. "I'm Dr. Jones." He held out his hand for me to shake. "Sit down, Mr. Sorrow."

"Sowa," I said. "Karl Sowa."

He was maybe fifty with no hair at all on his head or face and that made him look a little rounder than he probably was. Oddly, his nametag said Dr. Smith. He flipped through the pages on his clipboard. "Things look pretty good, Karl. I see you've been eating right and exercising regularly."

"How could you know that?"

"The usual channels," he said. "No jogging?"

"No jogging," I said.

"Yes, well, never mind. I see you don't smoke. Moderate alcohol. Good, good. A little goes a long way, as they say. Ha ha. Your cholesterol count is good. All things considered I'd say you're in excellent health."

"That's good to hear," I said.

"Except for the bus, of course," he said.

"Actually it was the bike," I said. "The bus missed me."

"You may be confused," he said. "But even so, what about next time? No, I won't beat around the bush, Mr. Sorrow. You are in the awkward position of being totally healthy. That is, the odds of you dropping dead from some disease are quite small."

"Why is that awkward?" I asked. "It sounds pretty good to me."

"Awkward for you," he said. "This makes you perfect for us."

"Perfect for you?"

"We have something to help you."

"Help me with what?"

"The bus," he said. "The healthy ones always get hit by a bus."

I waited for him to smile, but he seemed deadly serious. After another moment of eye contact, he said, "There is a new medication from our corporate partner, Philosophical Pharmaceuticals, called Pilula Omnibus. Just out. The latest thing."

"What does that mean?"

"You could call it the 'Bus Pill.'"

"I don't get it," I said. "What's it for?"

"For people like you," he said. "Guys like you you're all the time exercising. Right? You get a lot of fiber in your diet. Not much red meat. Vitamins. You don't smoke. Maybe a couple of fingers of Old Cow after dinner, am I right?"

"I think that's Old Crow," I said.

"Whatever. So what happens to you?"

"What do you mean?"

"All that clean living means you've just got to get hit by a bus, Karl."

"And you mean this pill. . . ."

"Exactly," he said. "Pilula Omnibus protects you from life's last little irony. Here's a sample." He put a small blue pill in my hand.

"So, does it work on other stuff?" I asked. "Like icy sidewalks?"

"Well, I don't know about that," he said. "Let me get you some water."

He walked over to a water cooler and brought me back a little paper cone of water. "Go ahead. Take it."

So, I did. Hey, he was a doctor, after all.

"Good. Good." He walked to the door. "Now just wait here."

"But what am I waiting for?"

"The next bus," he said and closed the door behind him.

I found my clothes on a chair to one side of the examination table. My socks were in my shoes. My pants were folded neatly on the chair. My shirt was draped around the back. It didn't look like an arrangement I would have created myself, but at this point I could not be sure. I got dressed.

I wondered what the pill would do.

I didn't feel any different.

But then I caught a whiff of tobacco smoke. Incredibly, someone somewhere in the Medical Mall was smoking. The smell got suddenly stronger and louder as a woman stepped out of a nook over by the soda machines, and the space expanded and filled with many people moving in all directions, everyone with a noise to contribute to the heavy echo in the big bus station. I could see lots of cigarette butts crushed out on the floor where the woman had been lurking. She must have been waiting for some time for the doctor to leave so we could be alone in the crowd.

"There's no time to lose," she said. "We've got to get you out of here before they realize what I'm up to." She meant the people watching through the big glass windows above the mezzanine—it could have been the whole medical staff up there elbowing one another and pointing and whispering behind their hands.

Now along with the cigarette smoke, there was the heavy odor of old cooking grease and diesel fuel.

The woman was more than thirty and dressed in jeans and a shirt that wasn't long enough to hide her navel. Long frizzy red hair poking out at odd angles, brown eyes, no smile at the moment, but I imagined her smile would be a very nice thing to see. I didn't know her, but I did recognize the bicycle helmet under her arm. It had fuzzy donkey or maybe deer ears attached to it.

"Look out!" she yelled and pushed me back, and a bus roared between us.

When it passed, the woman who had just saved my life was still there. She hurried across to me, and we ran. People got out of our way, but when we tried to merge with the bus station crowd, they wouldn't let us in. Whenever we approached they pushed us back into the path of the buses. I took the woman's hand, and we ran again. I could hear the next bus screaming up behind us.

I thought the bus pill was supposed to protect me from buses. Instead it seemed to be attracting them. I imagined someone up there among the medical people was telling the others it was time to go back to the drawing board. Get another test subject. This one was going to be a goner soon. There seemed to be no safe place for us.

But then an idea hit me. "Wait." I looked around but didn't immediately see what I wanted and felt a moment of despair, and then I spotted it and said, "Over there," and took off, dragging her behind me.

I pulled us to a halt by a small blue sign on a post. The sign read, "Bus stop."

"Get back up on the sidewalk," I said, "and then follow my lead as fast as you can."

I waited until the next bus appeared and then put out my hand to signal the driver. I got up on the sidewalk beside the woman and waited. As the bus roared ever closer, I lost all confidence in my plan. What was there to stop the bus from crashing onto the sidewalk? Nothing. Maybe we should run again. Too late.

The bus didn't run up on the sidewalk after us. It stopped at the sign and the door hissed open. The woman hurried on, and I followed right after her.

Something was holding me back. Getting on the bus was like forcing my way into a high wind. The bus pill had not made it impossible for a bus to hit me, but it was making it hard for me to get on a bus. There were certainly more than a few bugs in the formula.

"Come on," the woman said. She grabbed my hand and gave me a good yank, and I passed through the invisible barrier and nearly stumbled into the driver.

The woman dropped coins in the coin device, and the driver closed the door. We found seats together about halfway back.

3

"Ask not what your action figure can do.
Ask what you can do with your action figure."

She had to hand it to him. Getting on the bus instead of trying to run from it was a great idea. She went to work on his shirt buttons starting at the top.

"Be still," she said. "And relax."

"What are you doing?"

"I'm putting a big Band-Aid on your tummy where the bus hit you."

"Okay, I guess, that's okay," he said. "But it was the bike."

He slumped in his seat and became perfectly still. He was the very embodiment of the idea that "this seat is taken." Better than a straw hat with fake daisies, but she needed to get him back into his major mode—tough wisecracking detective.

She slipped her hand into the front of his pants.

No dice.

Probably she should have bought the optional Auxiliary Dick Kit (batteries not included).

Maybe he would feel more confident if he were holding his gun.

She checked the placement of the bandage over his wound and buttoned his shirt back up. No shoulder holster. So, maybe he carried heat in his belt at the back? She bent him forward and pulled the coat up around his shoulders. Nothing. Don't tell me he's unarmed, she thought. What the heck am I paying for? She pulled his coat down and sat him back up.

She would have to improvise.

She picked up his right hand and straightened the first finger and cocked the thumb creating the classic bang bang you're dead position for cops and robbers.

A light came back into his eyes.

"Better?" she asked.

"Much," he said. "Thanks." He poked his hand into his coat and when he pulled it out, the gun she had formed of his fingers was gone.

"Let me tell you what's happening," she said.

4
I Eat a Sandwich

"Where are we going?" I asked the woman with the bike helmet. No, wait. She wasn't carrying the bike helmet now.

"Brooklyn," she said.

"What did you do with your helmet?"

"I dropped the head," she said.

It's always important to have something to say when you're confused. "Did it bounce?" I asked.

It was like we were talking through a layer of maple syrup or maybe like we were communicating with Morse code and it took a few seconds for her to work out what I'd just said. Or maybe we were not sitting right next to each other. Maybe I was still in Oregon and she was already in Brooklyn and it took a while for my voice to make it all the way across the country.

"Here we are," she said.

I had not been to the East Coast in many years, but I had no trouble believing I was looking out the bus window at a Brooklyn neighborhood.

We got off in front of a storefront window with the words "Phil's Kosher Deli" in big white letters. The woman took my arm and walked toward the deli. Up close, she smelled very nice.

Bells jingled when the door opened. She let go of my arm and walked to a high glass butcher case and spoke to a big guy slicing meat.

She glanced back at me. "I've ordered you a Black Forest ham and Swiss on rye. You want a big dill pickle?"

"What are we doing here?"

"This is my favorite deli in all the world," she said and looked back at the man slicing meat who now had a big grin. "And Phil is my all time favorite deli guy."

"Here you go," Phil said. He put a plate with a huge sandwich on top of the display case. "You want that pickle?"

"Sure," I said. "Why not?"

Phil dipped into a gallon jar and put a pickle on my plate and pushed the plate forward a little as if to say, well, go on, take it. I picked it up and held it, not knowing what to do next. Phil and the woman both looked at me like they were waiting for me to catch on.

Finally, the woman said, "Well, take it to a booth."

She turned back to Phil who got back to the business of building another sandwich. I watched them for a moment, still not moving. Phil stopped slicing meat. The woman looked over her shoulder at me again.

"Well, what about something to drink?" I asked.

Phil laughed a huge laugh, and the woman's smile made me feel like maybe I was getting the old patter back. I'd been right; it was a wonderful smile.

"Give us a couple of cream sodas, Phil," she said.

Not wanting to push my luck, I took my sandwich to a booth.

A few minutes later, she slid in across from me, and a moment after that, Phil delivered the cream sodas in tall brown bottles along with a couple of glasses of crushed ice.

"Yummy," she said and picked up her sandwich and took a huge bite and chewed and gazed off into space with a look of absolute contentment on her face.

I took a bite of mine, too. It was very good. In fact, it was probably the best ham and Swiss I'd ever eaten. The cheese was so fresh it was crumbly. And the ham . . . well, you couldn't get ham like that in Oregon.

"I'm Karl Sowa," I said.

"Over there," she said.

"You're supposed to tell me who you are when I tell you who I am," I said. "And maybe what's going on?"

She put her sandwich down and reached under the table like she was searching her pockets or maybe digging in a purse. She produced a business card and handed it across to me.

URBANA FONTANA—SCENE SHIFTER

Black block letters on white. No address. No phone.

"Is that really your name?" I asked.

"Over here," she said.

"What is this over here and over there business? Why not just tell me what's going on?"

"Over there, you're Karl Sowa," she said. "Over here, you're Chuck Sorrow. Over there, you're legal to do private investigation work. Over here, well, let's just say you get things done for people who don't ask too many questions. Over there my name is Jane Boyd. Over here, I'm Urbana Fontana and I can change little things. Get it?"

"Not even a little," I said.

"Let me put it this way," she said. "Earlier today an incursion into history occurred. Something from Elsewhere muscled into our reality. Since it was never supposed to be here, there was no place for it. It made room for itself by pushing other things aside. And since those things couldn't just go away, they were all crushed together and thereby got a little strange."

"I see," I said, but my sarcasm was wasted on her.

"The Squeeze," she said, "has caused a Disturbance which is washing backward and forward in time changing things. One of the things that is clear over here is that there was a plague of sympathetic magic involving the name game back in the eighties. Do you know the name game?"

"Robin robin bo bobbin. . . ."

"Don't!"

"Why not?"

"Are you crazy?" she said. "Do you want to cause absolute chaos? Don't you remember the riots in the streets?"

"Actually, I don't," I said.

"How strange," she said. "Maybe it hasn't gotten to you yet. When it does, you'll remember it. Anyway, over here, my mother thought I would have an easier time in life if it were hard to work me into the name game. Her first thought was Terpsichore, but then she realized people would call me Terp, and that would be too easy, so she named me Urbana. Totally ineffective, by the way, since some people think it's harder and some think it's easier."

I couldn't help myself. Silently, I sang, "Urbana Urbana bo burbana."

There was a deep thud, and the lights flickered.

"Stop it," she said. "I can see what you're doing."

"It's clear," I said, "I'm having a bad reaction to the Bus Pill. I'm probably collapsed in the mall back in Oregon."

"Don't you think it's a little strange there even is a Bus Pill in the first place?"

"Well, there is that," I said.

She picked up her sandwich and took another bite, which reminded me that a bad reaction to some medication back in Oregon wouldn't explain this excellent ham and Swiss on rye. The texture of the dark rye bread. The crisp dark green lettuce of a variety I couldn't name. The sweet smell of red onions and mustard. The sandwich was simply too much in and of the world as I now knew it to be an hallucination.

Not to mention the cream soda.

"So, what is this something from elsewhere?"

"Glinky," she said.

I knew that name but I could not remember why. It had something to do with my current case. Of that much I was certain, but every time I reached for it, it scuttled away to the shadows where it watched me with red eyes. Red eyes also reminded me of something but I couldn't pin that down either.

"Everyone knows there are an infinite number of universes," she said, "many of them just a step this way or that way from this world."

"I think I saw something about that a couple of years ago during the very last season of PBS," I said. And speaking of PBS, the very idea of "Public" things was pretty strange these days. Public education? A dead dinosaur. Social security? Don't make me laugh. Public lands? Get out of here. Public airwaves? Oh, shut up.

"Glinky has jumped from one of those universes and has inserted itself into ours. Your mission, as you very well know, is to drive it out of here and save the world."

"Somehow that doesn't sound like a mission I would gladly undertake," I said. "In fact, all of this smells fishy to me. How do I know you're playing straight with me?"

"Think about cilantro," she said. "Do you remember that having anything to do with Mexican food when you were growing up?"

"Well, no."

"Now it's as if it's always been a big part of the cuisine," she said. "And don't even talk about broccoli."

"What about broccoli?"

"No one knew about broccoli when I was growing up. It's like it hadn't been invented. But now everyone knows it's been around forever."

"But I remember broccoli always being around."

"That's what I'm saying," she said. "Things are uneven. Soon, you'll remember growing up with all kinds of things."

"You mean until this morning there was no broccoli? That's a little hard to believe."

"So, consider Portobello mushrooms," she said.

I considered Portobello mushrooms.

"And what about the way cold fusion suddenly started working?" she asked.

"Science is like that." I could hear the doubt in my own voice. "Right out of the blue something pops up."

"No," she said. "None of that happened until this morning when Glinky showed up and his arrival reverberated through time changing things. The real danger is that everything we know will be pushed aside, crowded out. There is only so much room in reality. When Glinky got here, it pushed us all out toward the edges. As it elbows more and more room for itself, we will get more and more squeezed. Things will be pretty terrible when we're all just smears on the inside of the jar that is reality."

"So, how do you know so much about Glinky?" I asked.

"He wasn't always such a rat," she said.

"They never are."

"Back when we were in college," she said, "he told me no matter how good the Business got, it would still be just the two of us."

"But now you think there's someone else?"

"Yes."

"What makes you think so?"

"Little things," she said.

There were always little things.

"Well, now you know everything, and you can go do your job," she said. "Finish your soda."

Why not? I sighed and picked up the glass. "Drink me," I said, and tossed the rest of it down in a couple of big gulps.

"Okay, now put your arms up like this." She held up her arms like she was reading a very big invisible book. "And close your eyes."

I held my arms up and closed my eyes. "Now what?"

I heard her slide out of the booth, and my fingers closed around what I recognized at once as a steering wheel, and my heart lurched. I opened my eyes and swerved back into the right lane. The car rocked as a bus screamed by honking in the other direction. I got the car and my breathing under control and looked around. Yes, this was my old Mercedes, and yes, I was back in Eugene, Oregon. A moment later I passed a street sign and confirmed that I was driving in the South Hills of the city on my way to find out if Daniel Boyd was really cheating on his wife.

5
Danny Boyd

You might suddenly realize you are here right now—totally present. It's like you wake up and think, oh, yeah, here I am, and this is all there is and all there ever was or will be. The things you remember are all part of this moment—just stuff you might be thinking about now. If you consider history, all you're doing is considering history. It's not like you can ever be right about it. The steps, causes, reasons for your current situation are simply a story you tell yourself so you won't freak at the thought that you've just popped into existence and that there is no reason to think you won't pop out again as soon as you lose that feeling of here-and-nowness. At least you were blissfully ignorant before there were Glinky waves to wash you off your feet.

I pull up in my aging Mercedes in front of the South Hills

love nest of Daniel Boyd, the dynamic CEO of Philosophical Pharmaceuticals, who has inserted himself into our community and has become an overnight big shot. My plan is to ring the bell, and when his squeeze answers the door, snap her photo.

The idea of "plan" is very strange in this context. Do I even have a camera? Does thinking about the future have any value when you only exist now? And if I have already pulled up at the front of the house, why am I still moving?

I park up the hill and walk down to the house where Daniel Boyd keeps his mistress. Boyd has been buying and selling stuff, backing this project and opposing that one, building megastores and pushing aside the little guys, changing the landscape with broad, brutal sweeps of money, getting his smiling face in the papers and on TV. He runs a local infomercial called *Why?* WHY is the NYSE symbol for Philosophical Pharmaceuticals. The show is mostly about why you should take Danny's pills.

I ring the bell. The woman who answers the door looks just like Jane Boyd, Danny's wife who hired me to find out what he's up to. I am momentarily thrown totally off my game.

"Jane?"

She blows smoke my way and says, "Jane Jane bo bane. . . ."

"Please, don't do that, Sweetheart." A man behind her puts his hands on her shoulders and pulls her back into the gloom. Danny Boyd takes her place in the doorway. He is so tall, dark, and handsome, he should be modeling men's suits for guys already at the top instead of selling pills. He says, "Mr. Sorrow, I presume?"

He may not always have been a rat, but he's a rat now, and he's got a gun. He motions me inside.

The woman who answered the door is pouring herself a drink. The bungalow opens right into a living room from the fifties—a flowered couch and end tables, a rotary dial telephone, bar and bar stools, a couple of chairs, and a big TV with rabbit ears. The TV is on and muttering softly to itself.

I see now that the woman might not be Jane after all. Why

would Boyd be fooling around with a woman who looks so much like his wife? Maybe he isn't really fooling around. Maybe he has a woman who looks like Jane in every one of his houses around the world—duplicates so he doesn't have so much to pack when he travels.

"Move over by the bar," Danny says.

"What's this all about?"

"Give him the envelope," he says, and the woman hands me a big brown envelope.

She walks over to Danny who keeps the gun pointed my way. He takes the drink from her. "Go wait in the car."

She sighs like she should have seen that coming and leaves. As soon as the front door closes behind her, Danny says, "Open it."

I pull a big eight-by-ten glossy out of the envelope.

Me and Urbana on the bus. My shirt is open all the way down. She's got her hand tucked into the front of my pants. Where in the world was the photographer standing?

"Now you know," Danny says.

"No, I don't," I say.

He shoots me and goes on out to join his wife in the car.

So, now how am I supposed to save the world, Glinky?

"You can't!"

I could call a friend, but the phone will just hit me in the face and then not work anyway. I can keep scootching for the front door, but I know I'll never make it.

What would happen if I turned Glinky off? I hang a sharp belly right and squirm for the TV.

"Hey! Hey! What are you doing?"

I struggle up to sit right in front of the flickering rodent. The flaw in my plan is now evident. No buttons on the TV and no remote.

Glinky sticks out his forked tongue at me and then turns and shows me his backside, waggles his naked tail at me, makes blubbery raspberry sounds with his horse lips.

I put my palms flat against the warm glass of the screen. It's just me and the Rat from Elsewhere now. I make my last desperate move. If there are to be riots in the streets again, so be it.

I chant, "Glinky Glinky bo binky."

He screams.

"Banana fanna fo finky."

Now there are a couple of big dials and knobs on the TV.

"Me my mo minky."

Don't touch that dial!

"Glinky!"

I turn him off.

Just like that.

I hear someone making siren sounds in the distance. I hope it's the guys with the gurney.

Red City

JANEEN WEBB

Janeen Webb currently lives on a farm in Victoria, an hour outside of Melbourne, with her husband, Jack Dann, and teaches literature at the Australian Catholic University in Melbourne. She is one of the most knowledgeable and insightful critics and reviewers in the field, and was co-editor of the Australian Science Fiction Review from 1987 to 1991, a bi-monthly journal that was at the time the premier science fiction forum in Australia and had a worldwide influence on the genre. In 1998, she co-edited the groundbreaking original Australian anthology Dreaming Down-Under with Jack Dann. She began to publish stories in the late 1990s, after writing several academic books on literature, but has published only short fiction to date, much of it in Australia first.

"Red City" was published in Synergy, edited by George Zebrowski, one of the best original anthologies of the year. It is a smoothly told quantum time travel story set in India, about Myles, a researcher in cultural anthropology who is traveling there with his really irritating and prejudiced wife to visit Singh, the author of an intriguing paper, who is also acting as their tour guide to an archeological site. There is a prophet, a harem, a chess game, and a time loop.

Red dust devils whirled and glittered and spun in the wake of the only moving object on the red plain. Above, the sky was a glazed enamel blue, fired and ready to crack in the heat. Below, what scant macadam remained on the stony red road was melting, sticking, slowing the laboring car that crawled through a baking midsummer afternoon in Uttar Pradesh.

Inside the car, the heat was stifling. Everything smelled of hot dust. Lucinda Ponsonby-Smythe lolled in her corner of the back seat, her unflattering synthetic-cotton dress plastered to her body's sweaty crevices, her back sticking wetly to the imitation red leather upholstery of the straining, overheated Morris Major Deluxe. Her pale skin had taken on a yellowish waxy cast, sheened with the sweat that trickled between drooping breasts buttressed with rigid underwire that cut and clung in the heat. She was in a foul mood. Again.

"I'm suffocating, Miles," she said, irritably pushing a strand of over-dyed black hair back from her forehead as she turned to her husband sitting meekly beside her.

"You insisted on coming along on this trip, my love," Miles said mildly. "I did warn you it would be hot."

"You didn't say it would be *primitive*," she retorted, pointedly tapping the microcircuitry panel of her communicator wristband. "Nothing works. I can't even send a memo to my secretary." She paused for effect. "And as for this wretched translator," she went on, "it keeps making stupid mistakes."

"It's the most advanced cochlear implant there is, my darling," said Miles. "It's supposed to work even on ancient languages. It's probably just a bit literal when it comes to idiomatic constructions, that's all."

"All? No, Miles, that's not all. I don't like it. It buzzes in my ear all the time. It gives me a headache," she said.

"Relax, my love," he replied. "You'll get used to it soon enough."

"Relax? How can I possibly relax in this heat?" Lucinda said. "I feel frightful. I'm going to be sick. Miles, *do* something. *Make* him turn the air back on."

"Illness and my wife are old friends, I'm afraid." Miles addressed the driver *sotto voce*, hoping to save the situation. "She does understand, really."

After five days of heat-soaked travel in an atmosphere saturated with Lucinda's disapproval, he feared that the long-suffering Singh was reaching the limits of his forbearance. Miles certainly was.

"I heard that." Lucinda shot her husband a poisonous look. "And I don't believe that nonsense about Indian production plants using old technology, and this thing only having a generator instead of an alternator. Singh's just incompetent. And you're encouraging him."

Irritated, Miles spoke carefully, addressing himself to the now rigid back of Singh's neck. "One more time, then. The ambient temperature is too hot for this car's small motor to run the air-conditioner. If we turn it back on, it will kill the engine. Do you seriously want to spend another four hours marooned on this god-awful road, fending off snake charmers and adolescents with dancing bears and children peddling peacock feathers?"

Miles winced at the thought, yesterday's disastrous experience all too fresh in his mind. After a morning of kamikaze driving, with Singh deftly dodging overloaded buses and trucks that vied for road space with drays drawn by camels, oxen, buffalo, even goats on the outskirts of Old Delhi, the traffic had thinned to a trickle. Around the middle of the day, when sensible people rested, the Agra road had become a deserted heat mirage shimmering into the hot distance. At Lucinda's insistence, they'd tried the air-conditioner. And the Morris had limped, spewing steam, to halt beside the only sketchy roadside shelter for miles around, where local people had materialized from nowhere to besiege the trapped tourists.

It had all been good- humored enough. The sluggish cobra and gritty peacocks were okay, but Miles was sickened by the plight of the dusty brown bears. Their teeth and claws had been pulled out, and each had a hole drilled through the bone of the snout to admit a rope threaded down the nasal cavity to exit at an iron ring clipped through the sensitive nostril. Rangy adolescent boys pulled on the ropes to force the bears to perform their shambling "dance." Miles most definitely did not want a repeat performance.

"You're much too soft," said Lucinda.

Miles wondered if she could read his thoughts.

Singh glanced back at his passengers. Framed in the rearview mirror, Lucinda's slack-coiled, venomous posture reminded him of yesterday's cobra in its woven basket. He contemplated the care and feeding of reptiles.

"If the Memsahib will permit the smallest of detours," he said, "I will take you to my cousin's restaurant for refreshment. He has imported beer. You will feel better if you rest in the shade."

The cousins were also traders, and Lucinda would have to buy another souvenir. A small revenge.

"Oh very well, if we must. Provided you're not taking me to another tourist trap. I do *not* want another souvenir."

"Of course not, Mem. That is why you have a private driver," Singh said smoothly.

Twenty minutes later the car shuddered to a standstill beside a hand-lettered sign proclaiming "Ice Cold Bears." Miles exchanged an amused smile with Singh, charmed by the ramshackle awning that stretched a welcome shade under dust-laden trees.

Lucinda alighted, slammed the car door, and strode into the roadside cafe. By the time the men caught up with her, she was already ordering the traders about. Her hideously expensive microtranslator implant gave her linguistic competency, but Lucinda's only verbs were in the imperative mood. "No. Take that jug away. I won't drink anything not bottled and properly sealed."

"Perhaps the Mem will take beer?" said Singh.

"Not the local muck. *Imported* beer." Unasked, she stalked to the ice chest, rummaging about until she unearthed something suitable. She turned imperiously toward her driver. "The label looks old," she said, "but Coors should be safe. Bottled in America. Still, I can't drink it out of this."

"Let me get you a *clean* glass from the kitchen." Singh whisked the bottle away behind a bead curtain, turning his back as he poured. A moment later he returned, bowing slightly as he presented the beer to Lucinda on a small tray.

She took the glass and sipped, ignoring Singh. "Miles, this tastes bitter," she said.

"It's American," Miles replied. "There's nothing wrong with it. Drink up, my love. You'll feel better. You're probably dehydrated from the heat. Here—the owners have set a comfortable chair for you. Just relax."

Singh winked at Miles, producing a bottle of Heineken lager from a private icebox behind the curtain and quickly pouring it into glasses for them both. Miles sipped gratefully, chatting amiably with the driver while the cousins spread countless carpets at his wife's hot, sticky, sandaled feet. Everyone knew she wouldn't buy. It was a custom, a diversion, something to do.

"Why do you do it, Singh?" The cold beer was a great restorative. Miles, his pale face still pink and his thinning blond hair still slicked and sweat darkened, was beginning to recover his usual curiosity about everything. He liked people, and was genuinely interested in knowing what they thought and felt.

Singh looked startled. "Oh. You mean to ask why do I take private tours in the middle of summer?"

Miles wriggled, trying, and failing, to unstick his wrinkled linen shorts from his sweaty crotch. He wondered, fleetingly, how Singh always managed to look so fresh in his long white shirt and his immaculate white turban. "Yes. Of course."

"The university does not pay its cultural anthropologists

very well, Professor Smythe. And I have family responsibilities. So I contract with the tourist board during the summer
vacation to drive those who can afford a truly informed
guide. Most of my clients are academics, like yourself, who
find my advertisement in the small print of the on-line journals. And it gives me the chance to do a little more site research."

"Which is what I want to talk to you about. There are,
shall we say, *interesting* rumors about Fatehpur Sikri. Certain, ah, unusual theories."

Singh lowered his voice. "It is a site to be approached
with some caution, Professor Smythe. Your lady wife. . . ."

Lucinda interrupted, right on cue: "Look, Miles. These
are lovely. Come and bargain for me."

Surprised at her suddenly relaxed tone, Miles looked up
to see his wife enthroned on a canvas chair amid a chaotic
sea of carpets, surrounded by the gorgeous red and gold
wools of Badhoi and Mirzapur and the subtler shimmering
silks of Kashmir. He thought that Lucinda looked almost re-
gal at that moment, her dark hair pulled back from ivory
skin, her mud brown eyes currently masked by startling blue
contact sun-lenses. She sipped her beer, clearly enjoying being at the center of the circle of kneeling traders. Miles went
to her, brushing aside, as always, the quick thought that such
pleasantness couldn't last.

Twenty minutes later, Queen Lucinda was yawning un-
controllably, slipping helplessly toward sleep. And Miles
was shepherding her back to the car, bearing under his arm
the small, rolled, string-tied parcel that contained his wife's
new pastel-toned silk Tree of Life rug from Kashmir.

"You just stretch out in the back, darling. I'll ride up front
with Singh, so you can take a little nap."

"I don't want to be alone."

"You won't be. I'm right here."

"I don't know why I should feel so sleepy."

"It's just the heat."

Lucinda's complaints quickly subsided into snores.

Singh mentally let fall flowers upon the shrines of his
gods.

Miles slid into the front passenger's seat. "So what exactly did you slip into that beer?" he asked as the car pulled away from the little knot of waving traders.

"A thousand pardons. It was the mildest of tranquilizing powders. Totally organic. Perfectly safe. The Mem was exhausted. She will wake refreshed."

"It cost me a fortune in hand-woven silk. A lovely piece, but you could have chosen a less expensive place to stop. You might at least look contrite."

"It never occurred to me that your lady wife would relax enough to buy more than a peacock fan." Singh gave a rueful smile. "But my cousins will be pleased. And besides, we must talk."

Miles nodded. "So tell me what's got everyone so excited about the Red City. Half the academic world is applying for research grants to study it, and your government can't stall all the researchers forever. Your own reasons for staying close to it aren't exactly those of a disinterested tour guide, are they?"

Singh shrugged. "Perhaps not entirely."

"I read your latest article, you know," Miles said, smiling diffidently. "That's why I asked for you specifically, *Professor* Singh. To learn more about the mystery."

"I'm honored you have read my work," Singh replied, returning the smile. "But I am merely one researcher among many. There have always been stories about Akbar's city, Professor Smythe. It is perfectly understandable that folk stories should spring up around a rich city so suddenly abandoned by its people."

"Yes. Of course. But the folklore has always insisted that Akbar's astrologer foretold events exactly. And the recent rumors I've been hearing say why. These aren't whispered ghost stories, Singh. These sound coherent. Consistent. And in terms of quantum cosmology, they are at least theoretically not impossible."

Singh shrugged. "Akbar's astrologer was a remarkable sage, Professor Smythe. We have no evidence that he was more than that. There are other ways he could have predicted the failure of the water supply."

"But you have your reasons for investigating." Miles sighed. "You know, I've always dreamed of that astrologer's seat, perched under its stone canopy so high above the city."

Singh permitted himself a small chuckle. "Well, he'd hardly do anything really extraordinary from up there," he said. "That's a ceremonial seat, and much too exposed for serious work. The site that interests us is totally unremarkable, tucked away near the city walls. No more than a red shadow in a cleft of a red rock."

Miles leaned forward. "But a shadow that's a naturally occurring closed time curve?"

"Perhaps, though culturally it might be more appropriate to think of it as a reincarnation point. Part of the cosmogonic cycle."

Miles nodded, thinking it through. "Same concept, essentially," he said at last. "You believe the astrologer found an access point to a time loop, don't you? You think he used it. The logic of a time curve would present no problem at all to a Hindu philosopher. The implications are fascinating."

"But purely speculative."

"As you say. But fascinating all the same. Will you show me the site? Please?"

"You won't see much."

"I'll take the chance."

"Damn!" Singh swerved suddenly, barely missing a pair of peacocks taking a dust bath in the middle of the potholed road.

Lucinda stirred. "Are we there yet?" she asked plaintively. "Miles, I need a drink of water. It's so hot back here."

Miles bent to retrieve a bottle of mineral water from under the seat. "Normal service has been resumed," he said softly.

It was Singh who answered her question. "No, Mem," he said, "but we have not much farther to travel. Tonight you will stay in the summer home of the late Maharajah. The guest wing of the palace has only recently been opened for first-class tourists. No expense has been spared to provide for your comfort. It is an accommodation fit for royalty."

"I hope it's air-conditioned," said Lucinda. "I can't bear this interminable heat."

"Of course it is. The Mem will find nothing to complain of," Singh replied, more in hope than anticipation.

He drove on in hot, uncomfortable silence for another sweltering hour, but at last he swung the car between high intricately wrought iron gates and onto a gravel drive, and the park surrounding the palace opened up before them. Gorgeous peacocks strutted through grounds that were green and lush, dropped bright feathers beneath brighter flowers. Wide garden beds surrounded leafy glades with splashing fountains, and the flowering trees that lined the long carriage way were full of chattering monkeys. At last the palace itself came into view—a long building of white colonnaded arches and domed cupolas decorated in red marble and framed by the cool gardens. Its reflection floated on the waters of a long shallow pool, disturbed only by the ripples of another cascading fountain.

Singh stopped the car at the foot of a flight of marble steps leading to the entry foyer. Half a dozen porters emerged from the shaded porch and clustered around the car. The chief doorman, immaculately attired in brocade uniform, bowed low and extended a white-gloved hand to open the car door for Lucinda, then shepherded her toward the hotel. The luggage was swiftly borne indoors. Miles paused a moment and took a deep breath, glad to be away from the dust of the road.

But Lucinda had reached the foyer, and was waiting. "Miles, do come along," she called. "I need you to register."

"Coming, my love."

"It's *Ponsonby*-Smythe," Lucinda was saying loudly as Miles reached the registration desk.

"It's all right," Miles explained to the puzzled concierge. "My wife's name is hyphenated. I'm just plain Smythe. It's the same booking."

"As you wish, sir."

The formalities were quickly completed, the luggage was delivered, and Miles found himself in a truly opulent suite where beautiful Kashmiri carpets were spread over cool marble floors. The rooms were full of antiques and artworks, and a low table had been set with a basket of fresh fruit and a brimming ice bucket offering bottles of chilled mineral water and white wine. Miles was contemplating a long cool drink when Lucinda called from the bathroom.

"Miles, do come and look. This is more like it."

The sound of splashing water was loud in his ears as he opened the door to a bathroom that was all mirrors and red marble and gold fittings. A deep bathtub was already almost full of hot water and patchouli-scented foaming bubbles, and the mirrored walls were faintly misted with steam.

"Just bring me a drink, would you darling? Champagne would be nice." She sighed and stretched languorously. "You know, I could be right at home in a harem."

"Of course you could, my love." Miles dutifully phoned room service. Half an hour later his wife was sipping her champagne in the bath, and Miles slipped outside to discuss tomorrow's plans with Singh. The two men sat comfortably on a curving garden bench beneath a spreading tree while Singh outlined his work in progress.

"It would be best if your lady wife did not accompany you," Singh said at last. "I fear she will not tolerate trailing around the site for very long."

"I know," said Miles. "I'll try to talk her out of it."

"If you'll forgive my impertinence," Singh said, "I don't understand why she wanted to come here at all. She clearly isn't enjoying it."

"My fault," Miles said ruefully. "I was excited about the Red City. I made the mistake of telling her I respect your work. Then she insisted that I shouldn't go on holiday without her, so I either had to give up the trip or bring her along. That's why we're taking the tourist route."

"But a field trip isn't exactly a holiday."

"Tell that to my wife."

"Isn't she also an academic? Surely she understands?"

"She's an academic administrator, Singh. And no, she doesn't understand. It's all budgets and committees as far as she's concerned. When it comes to research, she's only interested in the bottom line."

"Ah well," Singh said. "Perhaps tomorrow she will release you from your uxorial duties, and you can get some work done."

"I doubt it," Miles replied. "But I'll see what a good dinner can do for the cause."

The dinner was very good indeed. The Smythes dined by candlelight in a perfectly preserved banquet room, its antique details faultless from the gleaming furniture and wallpaper right down to the matching scatter cushions. A discreet plaque by the door was simply inscribed: "Wm. Morris & Co., 1898."

"This is fantastic," said Miles. "The Maharajah must have had the whole thing designed by Morris, no less, then shipped out from England and reconstructed here. I hate to think what that would have cost."

"I guess the Raj could afford it," Lucinda replied. "There's a fortune here just in silverware and crystal."

"And the food is marvelous." Miles waved his fork at the array of aromatic meats and pilafs and breads and dipping sauces spread before them in chased silver dishes. He selected another helping of chicken korma then refilled his glass with chilled Chardonnay. "The cooking here is exquisite."

"I suppose," his wife conceded. "If you like this kind of thing."

"Would you prefer something else? They have a full European menu." Miles was solicitous, trying hard to please. "Shall I call a waiter? I only ordered the deluxe banquet because I thought you'd like to try the local delicacies."

"No, thank you. I don't want another meal. This is fine. I just don't like it as much as you do."

"If you're sure, then." Miles smiled at his wife. "Have some more wine."

Lucinda smiled back grudgingly. "Very well," she said.

The evening proceeded tolerably enough. Miles ordered

desserts and coffee and liqueurs, and Lucinda was smiling for real by the time they returned to their sumptuous bedroom.

"Here, let me unzip you," said Miles. "You'll be more comfortable out of those clothes."

Lucinda turned obligingly.

Miles helped her out of her dress and nuzzled her neck. "It's nice and cool in this room," he said. "For the first time on this whole trip it isn't too hot for us to enjoy ourselves. We are on holiday, after all." He took her in his arms to kiss her.

She turned her head away. "Not tonight, darling," she said. "I'm much too tired. I think I'll just turn in."

Miles was not disappointed. "As you wish, my love," he said, heading for the bathroom. Honor had been satisfied. He would sleep well tonight.

The next day began promisingly, and the Smythes were finishing breakfast in the conservatory when Miles broached the subject of their itinerary. "Why don't you relax in the palace for the day, darling," he said hopefully. "This evening, I'm taking you to see the Taj Mahal by moonlight. The most romantic sight in all the world. You'll love it."

"That'll be nice."

"So we'll be staying here again tonight in any case. The room's paid for. You might as well take advantage of it. And you don't really want to see Fatehpur Sikri. It's just an old abandoned city. I want Singh to show me some of the technical sites. There are archeology students working on the ruins, so there will be a lot of dust. It'll be very hot—there'll be no shade at all up there on the ridge. You'll be bored."

"I'll be just as bored if I'm stuck here. I don't want to be left alone. Anything could happen."

Miles looked around at the plush surroundings, at the opulent fittings and the extravagant displays of glistening fruit piled upon golden trays.

"Like what?"

"Anything. I don't know. I don't trust these people."

"For goodness sake. You're safer here than you would be at home. No one is going to touch you. You can sit in the garden and order cool drinks all day. Read a magazine. Get some rest. You've been complaining that you can't sleep."

"No. I don't think so. You're just trying to get rid of me. You want to go off for the day with Singh and leave me behind."

"I'm only thinking of you."

"No you're not. You want me out of the way so you can go chasing after your crackpot theories."

Miles did not reply, avoiding confrontation.

But Lucinda was warming to her theme. "I heard you two talking," she said cruelly. "I wasn't really asleep. Just dozing. But awake enough to hear all that nonsense about time loops and astrologers."

"It isn't nonsense," Miles said quietly. "The laws of quantum physics . . ."

Lucinda cut him off. "What about the laws of common sense?" she said.

"Culturally constructed," Miles replied. "What's common sense changes constantly. Common sense said humans could never fly, but airplanes are pretty common these days."

"That's different."

"How?"

"Time is a straight line, beginning to end. Airplanes included. You can't get on and off your timeline." Lucinda gave Miles a pitying look. "Besides," she added firmly, "if time travel were possible, we'd already have been overrun by hordes of tourists from the future. And we haven't, so it isn't. So there."

"Not necessarily, my dear," Miles replied, mistakenly trying to engage her in theoretical discussion. "If closed time curves do exist, they are a non-renewable resource. They'd be too strategically valuable for mere tourism."

"And you'd know, I suppose?"

Miles tried another tack. "Anyway," he said, "if future generations do figure out how to use CTCs on a large scale, visiting boring ancestors in the twenty-first century might not be exactly high on our descendants' priority list. We can't even get our kids to come home for the Christmas holidays!"

"*Your* kids," she retorted. A sore point, this. This was a second marriage for Miles, and Lucinda's third. "*Your* children simply refuse to spend the holidays with me. They treat me like the proverbial wicked stepmother."

Miles retreated to his theories. "Okay," he said, trying not to sound desperate. "Forget the family visits. Think about asymmetric separation. If our descendants did time travel, they would only arrive in some of the possible parallel universes. And this may not be one of them. In fact, if we haven't seen any time travelers, it probably means we can assume that our universe *isn't* one of their possible destinations."

"I give up!" Lucinda turned and stood, dropping her napkin and scattering breakfast crumbs in all directions. "This is total rubbish. You're delusional!"

"Probably," Miles conceded, losing patience. "So why don't you take a break and leave me to my delusions for the day?"

"No chance. I'm coming with you to this Red City of yours to make sure you don't get into any trouble. So let's get on with it, shall we?"

Miles sighed deeply. "After you, my love."

The drive to Fatehpur Sikri was hot, uncomfortable, and marred by another upset. On the outskirts of a ramshackle town an enterprising group of villagers "danced" their bears into the middle of the road, blocking the way while they demanded money. Miles scattered the few coins he had in his pockets while Singh edged the car through the crush.

"Ignore them," was Lucinda's advice.

"I can't," Miles replied. "The whole dancing bear thing upsets me."

"You're too sentimental. They're just animals."

Singh did not comment. He drove on past the villagers, and half an hour later he had parked the car outside the gates of Fatehpur Sikri. The three were walking toward the massive Gate of Victory, the entrance to the Daragh Mosque, when the clear blue sky crazed silver with lightning. The roadside peacocks squawked in protest as a sudden wind ruffled their already dusty feathers; the skeletal dogs that lived by begging scraps from the tourists barked a half-hearted challenge to the skies. Thunder cracked and boomed overhead. But there were no clouds, and there would be no rain, no damp breeze to cool this baking city of red rock and no water. Just heavier gusts of oven-fired wind from the red plain.

"Prajapati speaks," said Singh. "In the Brihadaranyaka-Upanishad Fable of the Thunder, the Lord of Creation instructs us: *restrain yourselves, give, be compassionate.*"

"Really," Lucinda said, looking up at the carvings on the gate. "Does he say anything about elephants?"

"I'll collect our entry passes," Singh said tightly as he walked away in the direction of a small kiosk.

"Did you have to offend him?" said Miles.

"Have you looked at this gate?" she groaned theatrically. "As if we haven't seen enough carvings of elephants."

"Singh still hasn't forgiven you for refusing to take off your leather belt at the Temple of Ganesh."

"Superstitious nonsense!"

"Maybe. But if you didn't mind *riding* on an elephant to get to the temple, it couldn't have hurt to respect the religious custom. Singh was really upset."

"Well, it's too late now. It's not *my* problem. And here he comes."

Singh, not quite out of earshot, was reflecting that the erstwhile owner of this gate would not have tolerated her insolence. The Emperor Akbar, he recalled, was in the habit of encouraging his war elephants to trample those who had displeased him. Singh could not shake a sense of foreboding that had been growing in his mind since the Ganesh incident. No good would come of it. The voice of the thunder confirmed it.

"Ready?" Singh asked as he rejoined his charges.

"Of course." Miles led the way up the impressive flight of steps to the arched entry, and paused to look at the inscription.

Singh translated: *"The world is a bridge: pass over it but build no house upon it. He who hopes for an hour may hope for eternity."*

"A useful thought," said Miles.

"If you say so," said Lucinda.

The thunder spoke again: a long, threatening rumble followed by a loud boom as lightning forked once more across the sky. The air smelled suddenly of ozone.

Singh looked up apprehensively. "Shall we do the tour?" he said. Without waiting for an answer, he set off across the dusty, abandoned city. He ushered Miles Smythe and his ever-complaining wife through the wonders of the palace of Jodh Bai, with its Temple of the Winds; the gilded Miriam's House; the Panch Mahal with its five stories of columns; then the palace of Bhirbal Bhaven, Akbar's favorite courtier. Singh had a professional guide's anecdote for each. "Bhirbal's house," he said, "was once described by Victor Hugo as either a very small palace or a very large jewelry box."

Lucinda was struggling to keep up. "Can't we rest for a while?" she said plaintively. "This place is huge."

"No, my dear," said Miles. "Not yet. I want to see the Diwan-I-Am next."

"What's that exactly?"

"The Hall of Public Audiences. Beside it is the Pachchisi courtyard, all blocked out as a game board. Akbar is famous for having played chess on it, using slaves as the pieces."

"This Akbar seems to have been quite a character," she said, stalling. "Why exactly did he build all this, then abandon it?"

"He was the greatest of all the Moghul Emperors," Singh replied in his tour-guide voice. "The legend has it that Akbar was without a male heir and he made a pilgrimage to this place to consult the saint Shaikh Salim Christi. His cave is outside the walls, near the stonecutter's mosque, which predates the city. The saint foretold the birth of Akbar's heir, Jehangir, and in gratitude Akbar moved his headquarters here to Sikri and built this splendid city."

"And that's what makes him so important?"

Singh's frustration was obvious.

Miles stepped into the breach. "Actually," he said, "Akbar turned out to be very important in cultural terms. When the English envoys arrived to negotiate trading rights, it was Akbar who insisted that their influence was to be limited to commercial matters, and India's culture, beliefs, and religions were to be left strictly alone."

"Which suited the English," Singh added, his tone sharp. "To them India was just a place to make money. It is said that the English didn't give a damn what religion a person held as long as he could make a good cup of tea."

"Quite right," said Lucinda. "Excellent idea. Can we get a cup of tea anywhere here?"

Singh gave up. "The archaeologists have a spirit stove," he said. "I'll take you around the walls to their dig, and I'll ask them to make tea for you. You might care to rest there while Miles visits the sites that interest him."

"Good idea," Miles said hopefully.

The pleasantries were soon over—Miles was introduced as a visiting scholar. Lucinda got her cup of tea, and one of the students set a folding chair for her beneath a canvas awning so that she could sit in a patch of shade.

"I think I will just stay here a while," she said to Miles. "But don't leave me too long, will you?"

"Of course not, darling. Singh and I are just going to see Shaikh Salim Christi's cave."

"A cave. That will be jolly."

"You'll be able to find us if you need us. Just follow the city walls."

"Thanks. I'm sure *someone* will take care of me," she said, settling irritably into the rickety chair.

Miles set off at a brisk pace, barely bothering to conceal his relief at being released from Lucinda's disapproval. Excitement was getting the better of him, despite the heat. "Can we take a quick look at the CTC site now?" he asked.

"Yes," said Singh. "While we can. It's at the cave site in any case. You might also like to see the Hathi Poi, the Elephant Gate." He smiled grimly. "I doubt that your lady wife would be amused by these particular elephants—they are very dilapidated."

Miles nodded. "I guess not," he replied. "I'm sorry she was so abrupt, Singh."

"Think nothing of it. You are not to blame. Come, let me show you the site."

The shallow cave was unprepossessing—little more than a dusty recess in the red rock of the city walls. But at the back of the cave was a cleft in the rock face, a narrow fissure no more than the height of a man. And the air around this cleft was impossibly cool, cool as the air in underground caves where water drips and chills the rock. But here there was no water.

"This is it?" said Miles.

"I'm afraid so," Singh replied. "I did warn you there is nothing much to see."

"But this is where your colleagues are conducting their tests?"

"Yes."

"Has anyone been through?"

"Not yet. It's too dangerous. The shadow field seems to flicker in and out. There is no certainty that one could return to one's own time."

"But the astrologer must have done it, if the stories are true."

"Indeed. And he may also have understood the phenomenon in ways that we do not. Sadly, there is much ancient knowledge that has not survived into our own time." He sighed. "And so we must be cautious until we gather enough data."

"It must be tempting though?" Miles brushed his hand along the edge of the shadow field, feeling the texture of its cool edge.

"To see the Emperor Akbar's city as it was in all its glory? It would be an archeologist's dream, Professor Smythe. But we must yet be patient."

"There you are! We've been looking everywhere for you." Lucinda stood at the entrance to the cave, shading her eyes against the glare. "I asked Ahmed here to bring me along to find you."

A dusty archaeology student grinned sheepishly.

"Thank you, Ahmed," Singh said dryly. "That was kind."

"No problem, Professor Singh."

Lucinda stepped around Ahmed, advancing like a cross, middle-aged Alice intent on her looking glass. "So this is what you two were so secretive about," she said. "A dusty cave, and some gossip about a shadow. Is this it?"

Miles nodded warily.

Lucinda pushed her way into the space beside her husband.

"Don't get too close, darling," he said.

"Why not?" She pressed her sweaty body into the heavy air where it shimmered, coalescing in shadow around the red rock cleft. "See. It's all nonsense. I don't believe a word of all your scientific mumbo-jumbo. This is only cool air, for goodness sake. There's no mystery. I can walk right through it."

"Lucinda, *NO!*"

Lucinda ignored the warning.

Ahmed stared, open mouthed, as Lucinda simply disappeared.

Miles and Singh looked across the shadow at each other for a long moment.

"Now what do we do?" said Miles.

There was a soft, sucking sound as the air closed behind Lucinda. Abruptly, the irritating dust was gone. The cave was gone. Miles and Singh were gone. She was standing beside the red wall of the city. And then, impossibly, she heard water sounds—trickling sounds, lapping sounds. Coming from behind the rock wall.

Lucinda walked up nearby steps onto the wall and looked around. She realized that the sounds were coming from a huge cistern—part of the water supply for Akbar's city. She turned. Behind her was the city itself, drowsing in afternoon heat, but unmistakably alive. There were people everywhere: fruit and vegetable sellers trundling their delivery carts, guards in bright livery patrolling the walls, and, over by the Victory Gate, elephant handlers grooming their massive beasts.

"I don't believe it," she said aloud.

She walked as quickly as she could back down the steps

and stood below the wall, looking for the sticky shadow that had transported her. But here, in the brightest of Indian summer sunshine, there was no shadow on the red rock. She was still gazing in disbelief when a tall guard accosted her.

"What are you doing here?"

Lucinda's microtranslator stuttered for a moment, but then, to her relief, unscrambled the language. Persian, she guessed. "Oh," she replied. "Sorry. I'm lost. I'm just trying to work out how to get back to my friends." She looked up at him, smiling brightly, expecting help. It usually worked.

The guard's professional curiosity gave way to an expression of pure horror as he looked down at her: his fingers flashed signs of warning and he backed away from the revelation of her blue-lensed eyes. "Demon!" he cried. He looked more closely at her sundress. "Indecent!" he added. Then, with what was clearly an effort of will, he took hold of her wrist, twisted her arm behind her back, and began to march her toward the guardhouse, keeping behind her to avoid those too-blue eyes.

Her reception by the other guards was no more encouraging. One threw a blanket at her. "Cover yourself," he said, making the sign of the evil eye and giving her a push that sent her sprawling into a dark corner of the room. "And stay there. Don't try anything."

Lucinda did as she was told, huddling under the smelly blanket despite the heat.

None of the other men would even look in her direction. A messenger was sent running, and, after what seemed like hours, a richly dressed man entered the guardroom, his gold brocade coat and matching turban almost glowing in the dim light.

The guards stood rigidly for his inspection.

"Be easy," said the newcomer.

"We are honored by your presence, astrologer."

"You did well to send for me," the astrologer replied. "I thought it best to come myself. Demons are dangerous to deal with. Where is it?"

"Over there." A guard pointed.

The astrologer edged close to Lucinda. "Up," he said imperiously.

Lucinda scrambled to her feet.

The astrologer stared at her for a long moment. "Where did you say you found it?" he asked the guard.

"By the city wall, your Excellency," the guard replied.

The astrologer considered for a long moment. "I'll take it," he said at last. The relief was palpable in the guardroom. "I'll need a closer inspection. My servants are trained to help in such matters. If it is a demon, I'll have it destroyed. If not, if it truly is a woman, the Emperor might be amused by such an oddity for his harem."

"But I'm not. . . ."

"Silence, demon. It is not your place to speak. If you interrupt me I will order your immediate death. Do you understand?"

Lucinda subsided into shocked silence.

"Come along then. And keep yourself covered. The lewdness of your dress disgusts me." He spat expressively. Then he reached out swiftly and slipped a thin iron manacle over her wrist. He locked it, and looped its chain over his own hand.

Lucinda tried to pull away.

The astrologer yanked firmly, hurting her wrist. "They don't like iron," he said to the guards. "It binds them to the earth." He sighed deeply. "It won't be so much trouble now. But it would be as well for you to keep a sharp lookout along the walls, in case there are more of them."

The leader of the guards bowed. "It will be done, Excellency."

"Very well." The astrologer tugged on Lucinda's chain. "This way," he said, leading her from the guardroom.

They emerged into bright sunlight; Lucinda felt as though she had walked into an oven. She sagged a little, but the astrologer pulled her upright. His grip on her arm was like a vise. When they were well away from the guardhouse he leaned very close to her. "You may speak now, demon. What evil has sent you here? Where have you come from?" he hissed.

"You're the famous astrologer," she replied. "You *know* where I've come from."

"Don't play games with me," he said, his body radiating pure menace. "Who has sent you here to spy? Is it the visit of the English envoy that has brought you?"

"I'm not playing games," said Lucinda. "And I don't know anything about an envoy. But I've heard all about you. And I've seen your precious red shadow at the back of the cave. That's how I got here. So don't pretend you don't know."

The astrologer looked truly puzzled.

"What cave?" he asked.

Lucinda racked her brains. "The saint's cave," she said. "The one that predicted the Emperor's son."

"The cave of Shaikh Salim Christi?"

"That's the one." Lucinda lowered her voice. "So you do know," she said. She looked across at him and fluttered her eyelashes. "You do know about the time gate or whatever you call it. The cave where you see the future and make your prophecies. And if you'll just take me back there, I'll return immediately to my own time. And none of this need ever have happened." She caressed his hand.

The astrologer slapped her. "Do not think to defile me, demon," he said.

Lucinda paled.

They hurried on in silence for some minutes, the astrologer deep in thought. "What prophecies?" he said at last.

"The ones about what happens to this city."

"Nonsense," he replied firmly. "Do you think me simple-minded?"

"Look at the place for yourself if you don't believe me."

"I don't believe you," he said firmly. "And we have almost reached the palace. You now will desist from further comment upon such matters. Be warned. I shall order my servants to destroy you if you speak of it. They will not disobey me."

Lucinda did not reply. She was looking up in amazement as the astrologer urged her across the threshold of a sumptuously furnished building of cool marble and latticed windows—a place whose dusty ruins she had visited not two hours ago with Singh. She tried, unsuccessfully, to remember what he had said about it.

The astrologer beckoned to a waiting servant. "Find Ali," he said. "It's urgent." Then he turned to Lucinda. "Sit here." He indicated a carved chair.

Lucinda sat.

The astrologer swiftly attached his end of the iron chain to the arm of the heavy chair. "And don't move."

Alone for a moment, Lucinda tested the chain. It was too strong. She tried slipping her hand from the manacle. It was too tight.

And then the astrologer returned.

"There's no one else I can trust with this," he was saying to Ali as he handed him a small iron key.

His chief eunuch and secretary nodded sagely.

"I want you to put it in the harem, for the time being, but keep it away from the women."

"Easily done, Excellency," Ali replied.

"And I want it treated *as* a woman, just in case. It may be that the creature is just a spy—I have heard tell that such women exist in the cold climates."

Ali nodded again.

"The English envoy is to be offered a selection of women for later this evening," the astrologer continued. "So prepare this creature and put it in line with the harem women. If the envoy chooses it, we will know it is a spy and he wishes to speak with it. He would hardly choose it for its looks. If not . . ."

Ali finished the thought. "If not, we will know it is certainly a demon."

"Precisely. Then I will leave you to it. I have something I must attend to."

"Yes, Excellency."

The astrologer hurried through impossibly busy streets, almost forgetting his dignity in his haste. He dashed into the guardhouse, ignoring the startled men who were scrambling to their feet. "Which guard discovered the demon?" he asked peremptorily.

The tall guard stepped forward nervously. "I did, Excellency."

"Can you tell me *exactly* which part of the wall it was near when you found it?"

"The part where the stonecutters' mosque stands, Excellency," the man replied. "And the saint's cave."

The astrologer nodded his thanks. The afternoon shadows were lengthening. He strode along the parapet until he saw the mosque and the cave below. Then he descended the stone steps, and walked carefully along, looking intently at the hewn red rock. "A shadow," he muttered to himself. "A shadow among so many." As he walked, he ran his hand along the surface of the wall.

And there it was. His fingers touched a patch of colder air, air that felt somehow sticky, air that was denser than it should be. He pushed. His hand met little resistance. The shocked astrologer realized that he could step right through the wall. He took a deep breath.

There was a soft, sucking sound as the air closed behind him.

"I guess I'll have to go after her," said Miles.

"Wait a minute," Singh replied. "Let's think this thing through. If you and your wife had entered the shadow space together you'd arrive together, and you'd be able to help her. But if you try to follow her now, you could end up in any of the possible parallel universes. You might never find her."

"So what should I do, then?"

"Perhaps we should wait an hour or so," Singh said. "We have no way of knowing how long the passage between one point and another on a closed time curve continuum might take. It's perfectly possible she might be in the process of stepping back through the shadow space as we speak."

"True," Miles replied uneasily. "I suppose we could give her a little time."

Once they were safely inside the confines of the harem, Ali unlocked the manacle from Lucinda's wrist. "Remember, demon," he said, "you are watched. And you have been warned." He clapped his hands.

A huge man stepped into the room, wearing nothing but loose black silk trousers tied with a scarlet sash. His muscled body glistened with oil; his shaved head gleamed.

"This is the eunuch Abdul," said Ali. "He has been specially chosen to take care of you. He knows what you are. He is not afraid."

Abdul flashed a white smile and bowed low, setting his single gold earring bobbing against his dark skin.

Lucinda just stared.

"Clean her up, Abdul," said Ali. "Have her nose and ears pierced so she can wear some respectable jewelry, then find her some decent clothes. And I want her sexually prepared. His Excellency wishes her on display with the women when the envoy from England comes to make his selection for this evening. Do you understand?"

"Perfectly," Abdul replied. "It is my pleasure to serve." He took Lucinda by the arm and led her away.

The bathhouse was a wonderful relief after the indignities of the afternoon. Lucinda was left to luxuriate for a while in rose-scented hot water, where she lay contemplating how she would get her own back. Later.

Abdul returned with two slave girls who washed her hair then dried her body with soft linen towels. Lucinda was actually beginning to relax as the girls wrapped her in a linen bath sheet and led her to a low couch. They were combing out her dyed black hair, peering in bewilderment at the gray re-growth along her scalp, when Abdul advanced with a basket of very thin sharp spikes and a little awl.

"I'll do the nose first," he said. "Hold her."

The girls deftly grabbed her and held her down.

"No!" Lucinda screamed. "You can't do this! I'm not a bear to have my nose pierced!"

"Gag her," said Abdul.

The girls obliged.

One excruciatingly painful hour later, Abdul led Lucinda back to an isolated room that smelled strongly of sandalwood. "Now," he said, holding up a mirror of polished steel, "that's better, isn't it?"

Lucinda peered. Her wavery reflection showed her new diamond nose-ornament and her gold hoop earrings set with rubies. There was blood on her face.

"Here." Abdul held out a small damp cloth. "This will stop the swelling. Hold it to your nose stud while I give you your massage. You have to be ready for this evening."

"I don't want a massage."

"Do you have to be held down again?"

Lucinda scowled but did not reply.

"Good." Without further ceremony Abdul stripped her of her linen bath sheet and helped her onto a low table. He cupped scented oil in his hands, then began his work, expertly easing the tension from her shoulders, back, calves, thighs, massaging higher and higher to her crotch. It was not until he slipped an expert finger into her vagina, then withdrew it to begin masturbating her, that Lucinda realized, belatedly, what this was all about. She squirmed, trying to get away.

"Stop it," she said. "You have no right."

"I have every right." Abdul easily held her down. " 'Sexually prepared,' Ali said. Those are my instructions. I could have the slave girls do it. But they'd be rougher than I am. Agreed?" His oiled finger had not stopped its insistent rubbing for a moment.

Lucinda sank back, fuming. Despite herself, she could feel the tension building. She arched her back.

"There," said Abdul. "That should do nicely."

"You can't leave me like this," she gasped.

"That's the whole point," he replied indifferently. "Prepared, remember." He slapped away the hand that Lucinda had extended. "And no touching yourself," he added. He clapped his hands. The slave girls entered, carrying armfuls of silk. "She's ready," he said. "Dress her." He looked at Lucinda with ill-concealed contempt. "I need to wash."

The girls held out a selection of saris.

Lucinda felt terrible. Her eyes hurt where her sun-lenses were beginning to chafe, but she dared not take the lenses

out. Her nose ached, and the other ache that Abdul had en-
gendered in her loins was making her irritable. "I don't
care," she snapped at the girls. "Anything."

They deftly slipped a red silk choli top over her head, then
wound a matching gold silk sari trimmed with red about her
waist, draping its final length over one shoulder. They
dressed her hair, fastening it with gold pins, and gave her
golden sandals for her feet. Then they stepped back to admire their handiwork.

"What now?" asked Lucinda.

The girls giggled. "The envoy will choose," one replied.

"That's enough." Abdul was back. "Come along."

Lucinda found herself propelled into a gorgeous gallery.
The marble floor was patterned with shallow channels of
flowing water, and the walls were draped with woven carpets
dampened to provide a cool breeze. Low couches heaped
with bright silk cushions were set beside carved tables bearing trays of glistening fruits and luscious sweets.

"Don't stare," said Abdul. He bustled her into the middle
of a long line of women, all of whom were exquisitely
groomed, perfumed, and prepared to entertain the envoy.

Lucinda did not have long to wait. The English envoy arrived, a thin, ill-looking man who stalked into the hall like a
dark-garbed crow amid the peacock silks of the harem. Ali
was with him, keeping a sharp eye on proceedings. The envoy moved sedately along the line of women, judiciously
making his choices for the evening. He didn't even glance
twice at Lucinda.

Ali glanced significantly at Abdul, who took Lucinda by
the elbow and led her back to her apartment. "Is that it?" she
asked.

"Yes. Later, someone will bring food. But you can be private now. I'll just leave these here with you." He held out a
tray to her, silently offering her the means of sexual release.

"Don't be ridiculous." She slapped away the proffered
tray, sending gilded dildoes and ivory sex toys spinning
across the perfumed room. "I'm perfectly able to deal with
the situation," she said.

"As you wish."

Alone on her couch, she lay among embroidered silks, unable to block out the soft groans of more experienced inmates in the adjacent apartments. Masturbating furiously, she plotted impossible revenge. On all of them.

The astrologer was shaken to the core. He looked ten years older as he re-entered the palace and sank heavily into a chair in the reception foyer. He waved away the servants who waited to attend him, but accepted a goblet of cold water.

Ali came running. "Is something wrong, Excellency? Shall I call for your physician?"

The astrologer shook his head. "No, my old friend," he said at last. "A shock, that's all." He drew a ragged breath. "I have seen the ruin of our great city. And now I must act to avert the evil that may befall us." He sighed heavily. "The Emperor will have to be told." He made a visible effort to restore his equilibrium. "And what of our demon?" he asked.

"The envoy ignored it," Ali replied.

"I see. It is as I thought. The demon is a danger to us all. It must die. And soon."

Ali's face did not betray his emotions. He said only: "Best not to have it done in secret. There are already rumors."

"There are always rumors."

"Fortunately," Ali went on, "the Emperor wishes to intimidate the English envoy. Tomorrow, they will play at chess in the Diwan-i-Am courtyard."

"And the pieces?"

"The Emperor has ordered the palace prison cleared. The Captain of the Guard will choose the players. Those that survive will be pardoned."

"Then the blue-eyed demon will be White Queen, I think," said the astrologer. "The Emperor will accord the envoy the courtesy of the first move."

"Excellent." Ali nodded his approval.

The astrologer was recovering his composure. "Will you see to it, Ali?"

"Consider it done."

* * *

One hour had ticked by, then two. Miles had grown weary of watching the shadow space, and still Lucinda had not reappeared. "Well, Singh," he said at last. "What's our next best option? It does not seem that my wife has had the sense to step straight back into the CTC, does it?"

"Truly, I cannot tell," Singh replied. "We simply do not know enough about how it works. Your lady wife may have tried to return but been transported to another point in time."

"Or to this time in a parallel universe," Miles added glumly. "One in which she does not return, at least not at this moment."

"Correct," said Singh. "That's the rub. There must be an infinite number of possible temporal destinations inside the CTC. The whole thing is quite indeterminate." He shrugged. "If you had gone together," he added, "then both of you could have come back together, but still to another variant. You can't go home again, as they say, but only to something like it, but maybe to something so close that you might not even notice it isn't quite the same. Only mostly, maybe."

"True," said Miles. "But we didn't go together. And I honestly don't know what to do for the best." He sighed heavily. "I'm willing to go after her, but it would help if we could figure out where that is. Or when it is."

"Of course you are willing, Professor Smythe. And I, too, am willing to help in her rescue."

The conversation faltered into silence as both men considered their willingness.

"I have been racking my brains for a solution," Singh said at last. "But we must proceed safely. There is little point in complicating the situation by having both of you lost."

"I know."

"It seems to me," Singh said carefully, "that we should perhaps consult with the other researchers to ascertain if their findings will be of any help to us."

"But the researchers are not here today," said Miles.

"Alas, no," Singh replied. "Finding them will take a little time. Do you have a better idea?"

"No, but I'm concerned about my wife."

"I'm sure she'll be fine, wherever she is," Singh said. "She is a formidable lady."

"True." Miles managed a little smile. "Lucinda can take care of herself. I don't doubt that she'll be safe, at least for a while. Someone is probably making her a cup of tea."

"Then shall we go in search of my colleagues?" Singh said.

"What if she returns while we're away? She'll be very angry when she gets back, especially if I'm not here to meet her."

"I'll instruct Ahmed to keep watch," said Singh. "He will certainly agree. After all, it's the least he can do. He will telephone me immediately if your lady wife returns."

Miles hesitated.

His watery blue eyes met Singh's brown ones for an instant.

Miles looked quickly away. "I guess that would be okay then," he said slowly.

Singh nodded. "You have my complete sympathy, Professor Smythe."

"As long as someone is here for her."

"I understand entirely," Singh murmured.

"Do you know where we might find your colleagues today?" Miles asked.

"There is a hotel in a nearby village where they are often to be found," Singh replied. "The beer there is excellent."

"That would be most welcome," Miles said with relief. "I'm parched."

"Then it is settled," said Singh. And he, too, sounded relieved. "I'll just go and get the boy. Do you want to write a message for your lady wife, just in case?"

"I'll leave her a note."

The next thing Lucinda knew was that Abdul was shaking her by the shoulder. "Wake up," he said. "You have been summoned."

"What?"

"No time for arguments."

Lucinda realized, belatedly, that the two slave girls were standing behind him.

"Get her dressed," he said curtly.

The girls wasted no time. Lucinda was washed, brushed, and quickly arrayed in a flowing outfit of pure white. The choli was white silk, the white sari was patterned with silver stars, and the palloo shoulder drape was exquisitely embroidered in silver thread. A long white veil covered her head and shoulders, and the veil was held in place by a crown of silver. And this time there were silver sandals for her feet.

"Good," said Abdul.

Lucinda forgot her position for a moment. "What's all this about?" she asked.

"You are to be Queen for a day," he answered, smirking. "Enjoy it."

A small bell rang.

"Your escort has arrived," said Abdul. "Come along."

Lucinda had no chance to protest as Abdul hustled her from her apartment and through a maze of corridors.

The Captain of the Guard was waiting in the entry hall.

"All yours," Ali said, pushing Lucinda forward. "Watch her. She's not to be trusted."

"I have my orders," the man replied, taking Lucinda by the arm. "As you see, I have come myself to collect her." He nodded curtly to the eunuch.

Once outside, the captain marched Lucinda through the city streets. There were people everywhere, and a feeling of carnival was in the air. Street vendors were out and about, selling sticky sweet drinks and cooking flat bread over little charcoal fires.

"What's going on?" Lucinda asked. "Where are you taking me?"

"You'll see," he replied curtly.

The Hall of Public Audiences soon came into view, but the Captain took Lucinda through a small, dark back entrance and into what looked like a holding pen where dozens of people dressed strangely in either black or white stood about dejectedly. There were guards everywhere. The place smelled of urine, and fear.

"Last one," the Captain said to his men. "Take her. And let's get this lot moving. The Emperor won't thank us for keeping him waiting."

The guards responded immediately, rounding up the people into two lines—one black, the other white.

When the group was assembled to the captain's liking, he nodded to the guards, who opened a pair of heavy brass-studded doors and herded their charges outside into brilliant sunlight.

Lucinda, entering in the midst of the white line, looked around in amazement. The scene was spectacular. The courtiers of Fatehpur Sikri were seated in shaded cloisters that surrounded the courtyard that was the Emperor's chess-board. Tall, well-muscled slaves fanned their masters with huge peacock fans set in silver, and musicians played softly in high galleries. Slaves carrying trays laden with raisins, almonds and sliced lemons threaded their way through the crowd. Other servants offered pastries and sweets, and drink servers constantly refilled the nobles' goblets from huge silver pitchers. The atmosphere was charged with excitement. Today, the game would be played in earnest.

The emperor's private enclosure stood on one side of the courtyard. A richly gilded throne had been set for him under a canopy of gold-fringed black silk. Opposite, an elaborately carved chair had been set for his opponent, the English envoy, under a canopy of white, also fringed with gold. Behind these enclosures, the banners of Emperor Akbar and of Queen Elizabeth drooped in the heat, fluttering only when the wielders of the peacock fans came close.

A hush fell upon the crowd as the Captain of the Guard arrayed his charges in their places on the board. Lucinda looked about her, beginning to understand. The people were to be players, and all had been costumed to suit their stations—the pawns wore only loincloths and carried short stabbing swords, but the major pieces had more elaborate garments and weapons. Lucinda could see that the knights wore plumes and carried spears, and the men she thought of as the bishops wore elaborately ornamented sashes and wielded curved scimitars. The black queen was dressed exactly as Lucinda herself, robed and crowned. Two courtiers, dressed to kill, played the kings.

When all was in readiness an official stood to give the signal. The music changed, and all of Akbar's court rose to its feet to welcome their Emperor and his worthy opponent. Each man took his proper seat, and the formalities began.

Lucinda tuned out as the usual speeches of welcome and reply were made and applauded. She felt hot and sweaty and uncomfortable, standing here in the summer heat, but she dared not move. Finally, a ripple of excitement in the crowd caught her attention. An official was ending his recitation of the rules for today's match: "And lastly," he said, "our merciful Emperor has decreed that the surviving players will be pardoned and set free."

The crowd applauded.

Lucinda was still trying to make sense of it when the game began.

The envoy stood to direct his first move.

The Emperor, as the astrologer had predicted, was playing the black.

The first pawn was slain, stabbed through the heart by his opponent. Two attendants quickly removed the corpse from the board.

Lucinda put her hand to her mouth, realizing, at last, the nature of this game.

The first deaths were swift and predictable as the players sacrificed pawns and set up game plans. The hot air smelled of blood and feces, and the courtyard was already becoming slippery. Lucinda felt queasy, but she struggled to pay attention, even though attendants were there to guide her through the moves the Englishman directed.

Emperor and envoy both played with talent and confidence, and as the afternoon wore on the kills became less frequent, if not less strategic. But Lucinda slowly became aware that the envoy was losing the match. And as she watched the Emperor's knight spear the sole surviving white castle, she realized, with sudden horror, that the Englishman was playing to lose. In fact, that diplomacy demanded he should lose.

At that moment, Lucinda, the white queen, looked up obliquely. She saw the mirror of her death in the slanting path that had suddenly opened between herself and the Emperor's implacable black bishop. The man raised a bloodied scimitar in mock salute.

The endgame was upon her. Lucinda forgot her dignity, forgot revenge, and prayed that the envoy would concede.

Act of God

JACK McDEVITT

---

*Jack McDevitt [www.sfwa.org/members/McDevitt] lives in Brunswick, Georgia, but is originally from Philadelphia. He is probably best known for his sequence of Priscilla "Hutch" Hutchins novels (*The Engines of God *[1994],* Deepsix *[2001],* Chindi *[2002], and* Omega *[2003]), and he has had a book on the final Nebula awards ballot for seven of the last eight years.*

"Act of God" is another story from the original anthology, Microcosms, *edited by Gregory Benford, which is the best hard SF anthology of the past year. A biologist works with a physicist who creates and tinkers with a bubble universe, one small enough to fit in his lab, until intelligent life evolves. Then he gives them the ten commandments with benign intent, plus an eleventh one. Greg Egan and Stanislaw Lem have both written stories where scientists set independent universes into being, becoming, in effect, creator-deities, and the theme of a creator's responsibility for that creation becomes complex very quickly. McDevitt's take here is briefer and yet still complex and incisive.*

I'm sorry about showing up on such short notice, Phil. I'd planned to go straight to the hotel when the flight got in. But I needed to talk to somebody.

Thanks, yes, I will take one. Straight, if you don't mind.

You already know Abe's dead. And no, it wasn't the quake. Not really. Look, I know how this sounds, but if you want the truth, I think God killed him.

Do I *look* hysterical? Well, maybe a little bit. But I've been through a lot. And I know I didn't say anything about it earlier but that's because I signed a secrecy agreement. *Don't tell anybody*. That's what it said, and I've worked out there for two years and until this moment never mentioned to a soul what we were doing.

And yes, I really think God took him off. I know exactly how that sounds, but nothing else explains the facts. The thing that scares me is that I'm not sure it's over. I might be on the hit list too. I mean, I never thought of it as being sacrilegious. I've never been that religious to start with. Didn't used to be. I am now.

Did you ever meet Abe? No? I thought I'd introduced you at a party a few years ago. Well, it doesn't matter.

Yes, I know you must have been worried when you heard about the quake, and I'm sorry, I should have called. I was just too badly shaken. It happened during the night. He lived there, at the lab. Had a house in town, but he actually stayed most nights at the lab. Had a wing set up for himself on the eastern side. When it happened, it took the whole place down. Woke me up, woke everybody up, I guess. I was about two miles away. But it was just a bump in the night. I didn't even realize it *was* an earthquake until the police called. Then I went right out to the lab. Phil, it was as if the hill had opened up and just swallowed everything. They found Abe's body in the morning.

What was the sacrilege? It's not funny, Phil. And I'll try to explain it to you, but your physics isn't very good so I'm not sure where to start.

You know the appointment to work with Abe was the opportunity of a lifetime. A guarantee for the future. My ship had come in.

But when I first got out there, it looked like a small operation. Not the sort of thing I'd expected to see. There were only three of us—me, Abe, and Mac Cardwell, an electrical engineer. Mac died in an airplane crash about a week before the quake. He had a pilot's license, and he was flying alone. No one else was involved. Just him. FAA said it looked as if lightning had hit the plane.

All right, smile if you want to. But Cardwell built the system that made it all possible. And I know I'm getting ahead of things here, so let me see if I can explain it. Abe was a cosmologist. Special interest in the big bang. Special interest in how to generate a big bang.

I'd known that before I went out there. You know how it can be done, right? Actually *make* a big bang? No, I'm not kidding. Look, it's not really that hard. Theoretically. All you have to do is pack a few kilograms of ordinary matter into a sufficiently small space, *really* small, considerably smaller than an atomic nucleus. Then, when you release the pressure that constrains it, the thing explodes.

No, I don't mean a nuke. I mean a big bang. A *real* one. The thing expands into a new universe. Anyhow, what I'm trying to tell you is that he *did* it. More than that, he did it *thirty years ago*. And no, I know you didn't hear an explosion. Phil, I'm serious.

Look, when it happens, the blast expands into a different set of dimensions, so it has no effect whatever on the people next door. But it *can* happen. It *did* happen.

And *nobody* knew about it. He kept it quiet.

I *know* you can't pack much matter into a space the size of a nucleus. You don't have to. The initial package is only a kind of cosmic seed. It contains the trigger and a set of instructions. Once it erupts, the process feeds off itself. It creates whatever it needs. The forces begin to operate, and the physical constants take hold. Time begins. Its time.

I'd wondered what he was doing in Crestview, Colorado, but he told me he went out there because it was remote, and that made it a reasonably safe place to work. People weren't going to be popping in, asking questions. When I got there, he sat me down and invited me to sign the agreement, stipulating that I'd say nothing whatever, without his express permission, about the work at the lab. He'd known me pretty well, and I suddenly realized why I'd gotten the appointment over several hundred people who were better qualified. He could trust me to keep my mouth shut.

At first I thought the lab was involved in defense work of one kind or another. Like Northgate. But this place didn't have the security guards and the triple fences and the dogs. He introduced me to Mac, who was a little guy with a beard that desperately needed a barber, and to Sylvia Michaels. Sylvia was a tall, stately woman, dark hair, dark eyes, a hell of a package, I'm sure, when she was younger. She was the project's angel.

I should add that Sylvia's also dead. Ran into a tree two days after the quake. Cops thought she was overcome with grief and wasn't paying attention to what she was doing. Single vehicle accident. Like Mac, she was alone.

Is that an angel like in show business? Yes. Exactly. Her family owned a group of Rocky Mountain resorts. She was enthusiastic about Abe's ideas, so she financed the operation. She provided the cash, Mac designed the equipment, and Abe did the miracles. Well, maybe an unfortunate choice of words there.

Why didn't he apply for government funding? Phil, the government doesn't like stem cells, clones, and particle accelerators. You think they're going to underwrite a *big bang*?

Yes, of course I'm serious. Do I look as if I'd kid around? About something like this?

Why didn't I say something? Get it stopped? Phil, you're not listening. It was a going concern long before I got there.

And yes, it's a real universe. Just like this one. He kept it in the building. More or less. It's hard to explain. It extended out through that separate set of dimensions I told you about. There *are* more than three. It doesn't matter whether you can visualize them or not. They're there. Listen, maybe I should go.

Well, okay. No, I'm not upset. I just need you to hear me out. I'm sorry, I don't know how to explain it any better than that. Phil, we could *see* it. Mac had built a device that allowed us to observe and even, within limitations, to guide events. They called it the *cylinder* and you could look in and see star clouds and galaxies and jets of light. Everything spinning and drifting, supernovas blinking on and off like Christmas lights. Some of the galaxies with a glare like a furnace at their centers. It was incredible.

I know it's hard to believe. Take my word for it. And I don't know when he planned to announce it. Whenever I asked him, he always said *when the time is ripe*. He was afraid that, if anyone found out, he'd be shut down.

I'm sorry to hear you say that. There was never any danger to *anybody*. It was something you could do in your garage and the neighbors would never notice. Well, you could do it if you had Mac working alongside you.

Phil, I wish you could have seen it. The cosm—his term, not mine—was already eight billion years old, relative. What was happening was that time was passing a lot faster in the cosm than it was in Crestview. As I say, it had been up and running for thirty years by then.

You looked into that machine and saw all that and it humbled you. You know what I mean? Sure, it was Abe who figured out how to make it happen, but the magic was in the process. How was it possible that we lived in a place where you could pack up a few grams of earth and come away with a living universe.

And it *was* living. We zeroed in on some of the worlds. They were *green*. And there were animals. But nothing that seemed intelligent. Lots of predators, though. Predators you wouldn't believe, Phil. It was why he'd brought *me* in. What were the conditions necessary to permit the development of intelligent life? Nobody had ever put the question in quite those terms before, and I wasn't sure I knew the answer.

No, we couldn't see any of this stuff in real time. We had to take pictures and then slow everything down by a factor of about a zillion. But it worked. We could tell what was going on.

We picked out about sixty worlds, all overrun with carnivores, some of them that would have gobbled down a T-Rex as an appetizer. Abe had a technique that allowed him to reach in and influence events. Not physically, by which I mean that he couldn't stick a hand in there, but we had some electromagnetic capabilities. I won't try to explain it because I'm not clear on it myself. Even Abe didn't entirely understand it. It's funny—when I look back now, I suspect Mac was the real genius.

The task was to find a species with potential and get rid of the local carnivores to give it a chance.

On some of the worlds, we triggered major volcanic eruptions. Threw a lot of muck into the atmosphere and changed the climate. Twice we used undersea earthquakes to send massive waves across the plains where predators were especially numerous. Elsewhere we crashed comets down on them. We went back and looked at the results within a few hours after we'd finished, our time. In most cases we'd gotten rid of the targets, and the selected species were doing nicely, thank you very much. Within two days of the experiment we had our first settlements.

I should add that none of the occupants looked even remotely human.

If I'd had my way, we would have left it at that. I suggested to Abe that it was time to announce what he had. Report the results. Show it to the world. But he was averse.

"Make it public?" he scowled. "Jerry, there's a world full of busybodies out there. There'll be protests, there'll be cries for an investigation, there'll be people with signs. Accusing me of playing God. I'll spend the rest of my life trying to re-assure the idiots that there's no moral dimension to what we're doing."

I thought about that for several minutes and asked him if he was sure there wasn't.

He smiled at me. It was that same grin you got from him when you'd overlooked some obvious detail and he was try-ing to be magnanimous while simultaneously showing you what a halfwit you were. "Jerry," he said, "what have we done other than to provide life for thousands of generations of intelligent creatures? If anything, we should be com-mended."

Eons passed. Tens of thousands of subjective years, and the settlements went nowhere. We knew they were fighting; we could see the results. Burned out villages, heaps of corpses. Nothing as organized as a war, of course. Just local mas-sacres. But no sign of a city. Not anywhere.

Maybe they weren't as bright as we thought. Local con-flicts don't stop the rise of civilization. In fact there's reason to think they're a necessary factor. Anyhow, it was about this time that Mac's plane went down. Abe was hit pretty hard. But he insisted on plunging ahead. I asked whether we would want to replace him, but he said he didn't think it would be necessary. For the time being, we had all the capa-bility we needed.

"We have to intervene," he said.

I waited to hear him explain.

"Language," he added. "We have to solve the language problem."

"What language problem?" I asked.

"We need to be able to talk to them."

The capability already existed to leave a message. No, Phil, we didn't have the means to show up physically and conduct a conversation. But we could deposit something for them to find. If we could master the languages.

"What do you intend to do?" I asked.

He was standing by a window, gazing down at Crestview,

with its single large street, its lone traffic light, Max's gas station at the edge of town, the Roosevelt School, made from red brick and probably built about 1920. "Tell me, Jerry," he said. "Why can none of these creatures make a city?"

I had no idea . . .

One of the species had developed a written language. Of sorts. But that was as far as they'd gotten. We'd thought that would be a key, but even after the next few thousand local years, nothing had happened.

"I'll tell you what I think," Abe said. "They haven't acquired the appropriate domestic habits. They need an ethical code. Spouses who are willing to sacrifice for each other. A sense of responsibility to offspring. And to their community."

"And how would you propose to introduce those ideas, Abe?" I should have known what was coming.

"We have a fairly decent model to work with," he said. "Let's give them the Commandments."

I don't know if I mentioned it, but he was moderately eccentric. No, that's not quite true. It would be closer to the mark to say that, for a world-class physicist, he was unusual in that he had a wide range of interests. He had women around the lab all the time, although none was ever told what we were working on. As far as I knew. He enjoyed parties, played in the local bridge tournaments. The women loved him. Don't know why. He wasn't particularly good-looking. But he was forever trying to sneak someone out in the morning as I was pulling in.

He was friendly, easy-going, a *sports* fan, for God's sake. You ever know a physicist who gave a damn about the Red Sox? He'd sit there and drink beer and watch games off the dish.

When he mentioned the Commandments, I thought he was joking.

"Not at all," he said. And, after a moment's consideration: "And I think we can keep them pretty much as they are."

"Abe," I said, "what are we talking about? You're not trying to set yourself up as a god?"

The question was only half-joking because I thought he might be on to something. He looked past me into some indefinable distance.

"At this stage of their development," he said, "they need something to hold them together. A god would do nicely. Yes, I think we should do precisely that." He smiled at me. "Excellent idea, Jerry." He produced a copy of the King James, flipped pages, made some noises under his breath, and looked up with a quizzical expression. "Maybe we *should* update them a bit."

"How do you mean?"

" 'Thou shalt not hold any person to be a slave.' "

I had never thought about that. "Actually, that's not bad," I said.

" 'Thou shalt not fail to respect the environment, and its creatures, and its limitations.' "

"Good." It occurred to me that Abe was off to a rousing start.

But he frowned and shook his head. "Maybe that last one's a bit much for primitives. Better leave it out." He pursed his lips and looked again at the leather-bound Bible. "I don't see anything here we'll want to toss out. So let's call them the Eleven Commandments."

"Okay," I said. "Let's try it."

"For Mac," he said. "We'll do it for Mac."

The worlds had all been numbered. He had a system in which the number included location, age, salient characteristics. But you don't care about that. The world we had chosen, though, he gave a name. *Utopia*. Well, I thought, not yet. It had mountain ranges and broad seas and deep forests. But it also had lots of savages. Smart savages, but savages nonetheless.

He already had samples of one of the languages. That first night he showed them to me, slowed down of course. It was a musical language, rhythmic, with a lot of vowels and, what do you call them, diphthongs. Reminded me of a Hawaiian chant.

He called a few people, told them he was conducting an

experiment, trying to determine how much data was necessary to break in and translate the text of a previously unknown language. Hinted it had something to do with SETI. The people on the other end were all skeptical of the value of such a project, and he pretended to squirm a bit, but he was offering lots of cash and a bonus for the first correct solution. So everybody had a big laugh and then came on board.

The winner was a woman at the University of Montreal. Kris Edward. Kris came up with a solution in *five* days. I'd've thought it was impossible. A day later she'd translated the Commandments for him into the new language. Ten minutes after he had the transmission, we were driving over to Caswell Monuments in the next town to get the results chiseled onto two stone tablets. Six on one, five on the other. They looked *good*. I'll give him that. They had dignity. Authority. *Majesty*.

We couldn't actually transport the tablets, the Commandments, physically to Utopia. But we *could* relay their image, and their substance, and reproduce them out of whatever available granite there might be. Abe's intention was to put them on a mountaintop and then use some directed lightning to draw one of the shamans up to find them. It all had to be programed into the system because, as I said, the realtime action would be much too quick for anyone to follow. I didn't think it would work. But Abe was full of confidence that we were on track at last.

We had a flat on the way back with the tablets. Maybe we should have taken that as a sign. Anyhow, by the time we'd arranged to get picked up, and had the car repaired, and ate dinner, it had gotten fairly late. Abe was trying to be casual, but he was anxious to start.

"No, Jerry, we are not going to wait until the morning. Let's get this parade on the road."

So we sent the transmission out. It was 9:46 p.m. on the twelfth. The cylinder flashed amber lamps and then green, signaling that it had worked, that the package had arrived at its destination, and that a mystical storm had blown up to draw the shaman into the mountain.

We looked for results a few minutes later. It would have been time, on the other side, to build the pyramids, conquer the Mediterranean, fight off the Vandals, get through the Dark Ages, and move well into the Renaissance. If it had worked, we could expect to see glittering cities and ships and maybe even 747s. What we saw were only the same dead-end settlements.

We resolved to try again in the morning. Maybe Moses had missed the tablets. Maybe he'd not been feeling well. Maybe the whole idea was crazy.

That was the night the quake hit.

That's stable ground up in that part of the world. It was the first earthquake in Crestview's recorded history. Moreover, it didn't hit anything else. Not Charlie's Bar & Grill, which is at the bottom of the hill on the state road. Not any part of the Adams Ranch, which occupies the area on the north, not any part of the town, which is less than a half mile away. But it completely destroyed the lab.

What's that? Did it destroy the cosm? No, the cosm was safely disconnected from the state of Colorado. Nothing could touch it, except through the cylinder. It's still out there somewhere. On its own.

But the whole thing scares me. I mean, Mac was already dead. And two days later Sylvia drove her car into a tree at about sixty.

That's okay, you can smile about it, but I'm not sleeping very well. What's that? Why would God pick on us? I don't know. Maybe he didn't like the idea of someone doing minor league creations. Maybe he didn't want us monkeying around with the Commandments.

Why do you think he didn't say anything to Moses about slavery? What, you've never thought about it? I wonder if maybe, at the beginning, civilization needs slaves to get started. Maybe you can't just jump off the mark with representative democracy. Maybe we were screwing things up, condemning sentient beings to thousands of years of unnecessary savagery. I don't know.

But that's my story. Maybe it's all coincidence. The

quake, the plane crash, Sylvia. I suppose stranger things have happened. But it's scary, you know what I mean.

Yeah, I know you think I'm exaggerating. I know the God you believe in doesn't track people down and kill them. But maybe the God you believe in isn't there. Maybe the God who's actually running things is just a guy in a laboratory in another reality. Somebody who's a bit less congenial than Abe. And who has better equipment.

Well, who knows?

The scotch is good, by the way. Thanks. And listen, Phil, there's a storm blowing up out there. I don't like to impose, but I wonder if I could maybe stay the night?

Wealth

ROBERT REED

---

*Robert Reed [info site: www.booksnbytes.com/authors/
reed_robert.html] is the only major SF writer who lives in
Nebraska. He has been one of the most prolific short story
writers of high quality in the SF field for the past sixteen
years, with more than one hundred twenty-five SF, fantasy,
and horror stories published, and seems, if anything, only to
have gotten better in 2004. He has published a novel every
couple of years as well. His work is notable for its variety,
and for his steady production. His first story collection,* The
Dragons of Springplace *(1999), fine as it is, skims only a bit
of the cream from his body of work.* Marrow *(2000), a distant future large-scale hard SF story, seems to have been a
breakthrough in his career.* Sister Alice *(2003), his next
novel, and* The Well of Stars *(2005), a sequel to* Marrow,
are far-future large-scale works. His next collection, The
Cuckoo's Boys, *is out in 2005. He published at least four
other stories in 2004 ("A Plague of Life," "A Change of
Mind," "Opal Ball," "Mere"), which we consider good enough
to have been in this book, and a fantasy by him, "The Dragons of Summer Gulch," appears in our companion* Year's
Best Fantasy.*

"Wealth" was published in* Asimov's, *which printed a lot
of fine SF and fantasy this year, but lost its distinguished and
colorful editor, Gardner R. Dozois. Dozois' successor, Sheila
Williams, carries on. This is a story about an AI buying real
estate on Mars. But the house for sale has/is an AI too.*

One of the biogenesis trillionaires acquired the land, then, with considerable fanfare, built the mansion, and for a moment or two, there was no more famous address in the solar system. An artful array of hemispheres stood on the edge of the wide basin. Woven from cultured diamond, the structures had both strength and a mathematical beauty, and, in the Martian sunshine, they glowed with a charming ruddy light. A larger, less obtrusive dome formed a soaring roof over the entire basin, allowing the maintenance of an enhanced atmosphere. In principle, the trillionaire had resurrected a world that hadn't existed for three billion years. Precious aquifer water was pumped into the basin, creating a deep saline lake that was allowed to freeze over to a depth of several meters. Fission batteries powered hot springs that fed the tiny streams that opened up little patches of ice along the rocky shoreline. Then a variety of tailored microbes were introduced, each carefully modeled after Martian fossils, and it was that chill prehistoric scene that wowed guests and the invited media as well as a distant and utterly envious public.

But any man's fortune can prove as frail as that long-ago Martian summer. A skiing accident on Olympus Mons killed the trillionaire before his hundredth Earth-year. Competing heirs and endless tax troubles soon divided his fortune into many little wedges. His youngest daughter ended up with the mansion, living inside it whenever she wasn't traveling to distant enclaves dedicated to the nearly wealthy.

And all the while, Mars was being remade. The icecaps were melted, the old northern sea was reborn, a serviceable atmosphere was cultured from comet bones, and, after another century, there was no Mars anymore, just a small and chilled and very muddy version of the Earth. No longer needed, the overhead dome was dismantled. The icy lake melted and evaporated until nothing remained but a smelly blue-gray marsh. Then the daughter, in her twelfth decade, found herself broke. To raise capital, she sold the surrounding lands in a piecemeal fashion. The marsh was drained and developed, a little city erupting on her doorstep. Eventually, she owned nothing but the old mansion and the surrounding hectares, and when she died, still broke, her property was sold to a series of unrelated owners, each endowed with energy and limited means and precious little aesthetic taste.

The original structure has been severely, brutally remodeled. A glance tells as much, while the careful stare reveals scars left behind by a parade of robot slaves and human craftsmen, nations of nanofabricators, and at least one clumsy slathering of smart-gels. The diamond hemispheres have been stained to a deeper red and then punctured in dozens of places. Windows have been added. The original airlocks have been replaced with ugly dilating doorways. Someone with an inappropriate fondness for Earthly architecture believed that thick Dorian columns would give a much-needed flourish to the main entrance. My burning temptation is to obliterate this travesty. Before moving inside, I want to give a command and watch while the portico is crushed into an artful pile of slag.

I barely defeat my temptation.

Past the dilating doorway waits an empty room. Spiraling stairs lead upward. Flanking doors lead into other equally empty rooms. From the feel of the place, it is obvious: No one lives here now. But little voices and tiny motions betray the presence of visitors. Which is only reasonable, since this is the first and only day when the old mansion will let itself be placed on public display.

I absorb voices, motions. Quietly, I pass through a series of increasingly spacious rooms. The floors are covered with cultured woods and living—if rather decrepit—rugs. Not a stick of furniture is visible, but indifferent cleaning and constant wear show where heavy chair legs stood for years. Where the first dome ends, I can peer into the neighboring dome—a single chamber encompassing a lake-sized tank meant for swimming humans or pet dolphins, or emancipated dolphins, perhaps. But the pond has been drained, and, judging by the black dust in the bottom, it has been empty for some time.

The loudest voices come from a third dome, and I retreat to follow them, passing into what must be a kitchen.

Meals have been prepared here: Organic feasts, and, later, other elaborately flavored energies. Two figures stand beside a laser oven. One of them is traditionally human, but with an AI add-on. "I just wanted to look around," he confesses. Then, flashing a bright smile, he admits, "I live out on the bottoms, and I've always been curious. The owner . . . I never actually spoke with him . . . but I meant to, and then, all at once, just the other day . . . he was gone. No warning. And this morning, I saw that the house is being offered. . . ."

"Yes," says the other figure. "I am for sale."

She is for sale. What I see only appears human, out of convention or some deeply buried wetware, or perhaps because the house thinks it helps its own prospects if it resembles a handsome human woman on the brink of menopause. Bright dark eyes glance at me and then return to the man in front of her. But other eyes continue to study me, from a wide array of vantage points, just as they have watched me for the last little minute.

"All at once," the neighbor repeats. "What I heard . . . I heard your owner got himself into a little trouble. . . ."

The house wears a lean face, a charming nest of wrinkles gathered beside her human eyes.

"Legal problems," the neighbor claims. "From what I've heard, your owner's moving out to the Kuiper belt, which means weeks of travel before legal services—"

"I am for sale," she repeats.

The neighbor stands alone, suddenly ignored.

The house appears before me. Her smile is meant to be

calm but friendly, warm but not too effusive. She knows what I am, who I am. She says one of my names with a measured fondness, adding, "Welcome, good sir. And if you have any questions—"

"*I* have questions," the neighbor complains.

"About my history. My importance. My potentials." She breathes the air in which I stood just a moment ago, and she smiles, and the wrinkles on her illusionary flesh realign themselves—a delicate detail that only someone such as myself would notice, much less appreciate. The pattern is fractal. A soothing mathematics is on display. "For the right owner," she maintains, "I could serve quite nicely."

I have no doubts about that.

The neighbor approaches us. Me. He stares at what passes for my face, his artificial intelligence finally fixing an identity to me.

"Wealth," the man mutters, which is my surname.

Then his legs collapse beneath him, and he grabs himself around his gasping chest, muttering, "Holy shit!" with a pained yet joyous amazement.

Wealth has been as simple as a keg of wine and the roasted limbs of a dozen fattened lambs, and from that plentitude, a wondrous feast would spring. Wealth has been a forest of oil derricks pumping the black blood out of the Earth, leaky pipes and noisy trucks delivering the treasure to a coughing, poisoned public. Wealth has meant being a king descended from the gods. Wealth has been an empire springing from AI software that is three weeks more advanced than any other. Wealth has been fragile. But life, on the other hand, has always been a persistent constant, relentless and enduring. Eventually, everyone owns their own keg of wine, and the black blood runs dry, and there are no gods in anyone's sky, and the software that had a death grip on the economic breath of a dozen worlds is suddenly found wanting. But life breathes and times change, and what was the spectacular fortune has been whittled away, and everything that remains appears smaller and a little drab against the relentlessly swelling worth of All.

I am Wealth, but I am Life, too.

The neighbor man claims, "This is such an honor!" and then finds the strength to stand again. Blinking away tears, he adds, "Thank you."

"It is my pleasure," I reply.

He turns to the house, explaining, "My income . . . a fat part of it, at least . . . it comes straight from *him* . . . !"

"I believe you," she says.

I have enough life in me to feel warmed by praise, no matter how trivial. But I've come here for a purpose, and this seems like the best moment to ask, "What is your listed price?"

She blurts it.

I nod, offering no comment. But my face grows smoother, my gaze much more distant now.

"A great price!" the neighbor declares. "Damn, the owner . . . the poor bastard . . . he must be desperate!"

Fleeing to the edge of civilization is the act of a desperate man. Asking for a pittance for your left-behind home is sloppy and rude, and it is foolish, and it makes me a little sad.

Has my interest lagged? The house gazes at my face and my temporary body, and, after some consideration, she says, "Please look around. Absorb and imagine. Just the history of this mansion makes a tour worthwhile."

Agreed.

"You know," the neighbor trumpets, "I'm almost tempted to make an offer."

Neither of us responds.

Then, with a louder, more insistent voice, he adds, "It's really a lovely old house. I think so, at least."

The house knows what she is, and a wounded, embarrassed look twists her face.

Quietly, I tell the man, "You can't afford the asking price."

His face stiffens.

"In fact," I add, "in another six cycles, you'll be hard pressed to make the rent payments on your own little house."

"What—?"

With a gesture, I produce a set of simple, durable projections showing his spending trends and income possibilities.

He flinches, asking, "How do you know that?"

"Because when you were a newborn, your maternal grandfather gave me a tidy sum," I explain. "The sum was attached to your name, and, as instructed, I nourished it for him, and then for you. But eighteen Martian years ago, you began siphoning off the profits. Which was your right, of course. And last year, you reduced the principal by a third. Which was your privilege, and I would never say, 'No.' Yet any busy mind can look at the public records, making inferences, and while I can't see everything about you or your spending patterns . . ." I hesitate, just for an instant. Then with a calm, cold voice, I tell him, "In another year, you will be broke."

"No," he rumbles.

I turn back to the house. "Yes, I think I will look about."

She says, "Good."

"No," the man cries out again. But he has no reason to debate, and he knows it. With a sob, he asks, "What can I do?"

I tell him. In clear, unalloyed terms, I spell out the considerable failures of his tiny life. Two drug habits must be controlled. Travel is a needless expense when immersion rooms are cheap. Cultured food is more nourishing than the fare grown in hydroponics tanks. One undemanding sexual partner is cheaper than three demanding ones, and, with a wink, I add, "A greased hand and your own mind is cheaper still, if you know what I mean."

Quietly, fiercely, the man says, "Bastard."

If he means me, then it is an inaccurate statement.

After some determined stomping and growling, he storms away. The house smiles as he hurries out through the ugly portico. And then she turns back to me, and, with a genuinely caring tone, she asks, "Do you think he'll take your advice?"

"About investments, I am wise"; I purr. "About the human mind, I fear, I'm a hopeless incompetent."

For generations, humans argued about machines thinking: Was it even possible, and, if so, when and how would we become sentient? According to most of the optimistic, self-proclaimed experts, the first artificial souls would be cultured by the military or by the more exotic and demanding sciences. But arms and knowledge have never been central to human affairs. Above all else, *money* is what matters. Long ago, mutual funds and the great stock markets of the Earth were shepherded by complex tangles of software and then wetware. Cash, both electronic and paper, gradually acquired the hallmarks of identity: Individual names and personal histories, plus a crude desire to survive. Just tagging the money to keep it from being lost, whether inside a sofa or some despot's hypervault, was a critical leap. When money genuinely *talks*, the voices that prove more effective and vigorous tend to prosper—a multitude of selection forces brought to bear on knots of code as well as slips of parchment wearing the faces of dead presidents.

I am the merger of money and mutual fund wetwares.

A bastard has no legal father, but I enjoyed a trillion fathers and one lovely mother housed inside a Jupiter-grade server living inside an air-conditioned building in Old New Jersey.

In a rude sense, the purpose of a human is to eat and make babies. While the purpose of Wealth—my purpose and that of my brethren—is to embrace capital and then nourish it. No man or woman, trillionaire or not, possesses my clear, unbiased view of the future. When I was a young soul, small but brazen, I thrived by making predictions about the movements of capital from moment to moment. Later, I won notice by guessing which of three competing propulsion designs would power the first probe to Alpha Centauri, buying the appropriate stock, and then selling the bulk of my holdings just before the project was canceled. Then, when the AIs of the world were to be emancipated, I saw an array of possibilities. When I was no longer anyone's slave, I purchased my mother as well as the outdated, overpriced corporation that had owned her, and, with the power of a free soul, I gave her wetware and high-functions, transforming her from a simple chain of computers into a self-aware, self-respecting entity.

With bitter voices and snarling attorneys, my mega-billionaire clients accused me of being sentimental. It was an accusation with a nugget of truth, but that was far from the point. A few complainers tried to withdraw their funds. With a voice drenched in fiduciary terms, I reminded them that I was not a bank account or a stack of dusty bonds. I was a soul who happened to control enough wealth to build a fat nation. For good reasons, I said, "I won't give you a copper penny now." Without any legal standing, I said, "Sign these forms and send them to my central office, and in another week, if you are still willing, I'll honor your stupidity."

My clients threatened me, and their lawyers threatened me, and a few even hired thugs to attempt some kind of viral thievery.

But, in the end, they loved me.

My mother's purchase and my kindness toward her caught the gaze of millions of newly freed entities. AIs designed for science and for security, weather prediction and limousine driving, liked what they saw and gave me whatever pennies they could spare. And in a single afternoon, my value doubled.

Life endures.

I am still growing, and along a few important tangents, I continue to gain experience and a measure of wisdom. Being individuals, each Wealth cultivates a different strength. My greatest capacity is to peer into the future, whether it is next year or some era unborn, and, with a clear, unsentimental eye, I wager my golden blood on targets that perhaps no one else can see.

Other neighbors are touring the old house. One is a blended woman—part chimpanzee, part add-on—who dresses like a human and talks like a snob. "This isn't much of a bathroom," she complains, her broad apish back turned to me. "The fixtures. The stains. And have you ever seen counters as low as this?"

"It was a child's bathroom," I offer. "That's why they're low."

Something about my voice alerts her or her add-on AI.

One of them turns the other, both staring at me with a mixture of astonishment, awe, and some less pretty emotions.

"No," she blurts. "I don't believe it."

"Believe what?"

"You aren't," she complains. Then she steps up to me, sure enough about my falsity that she can poke me in the chest. "What kind of game are you?"

"A game that wins," I reply. Then in one long and smooth and utterly convincing sentence, I tell her what her name is and what her net worth is and where she lives and what she pays for rent, and before she can react, I describe the very sorry state of affairs inside her own tiny bathroom.

"How do you know that?" she sputters. "Even if you are who you claim to be, you shouldn't know about the insides of my house. And certainly not that my toilet smells!"

"But I should know," I growl. "If I am your *landlord,* I should."

The fur on her shoulders and back lifts high. But her instincts are submerged by a little good sense and the add-on's tempering touch. She backs away, exiting from the room by a second doorway. And I spend a moment or two regarding myself inside a mirror of diamond lain over silver—a design popular when the gemstone was first cultured en masse, creating a tool of self-appraisal too stubborn to wear out and too simple to ever grow obsolete.

In a high room, near the top of the main dome, a plain flat photograph hangs above a mock fireplace. One item is ridiculous—the burning of gas or logs is strictly prohibited on Mars—but the other has a charm of its own. Taken not long after the mansion was first built, the photograph shows the mansion from the old lake shore, the various interlocking domes practically glowing beneath a high sky that was cold enough to burn and empty enough to suck the life out of unprotected flesh.

"Do you like this image?" asks the house.

Again, she speaks through the middle-aged body and an easy, slightly worried smile. I smile back at her, remarking, "Very much, yes."

"I didn't know."

I ask, "What didn't you know?"

"That you have a taste for history."

I have a taste for everything, because everything impacts on my life and the lives of my billions of happy clients. One of my talents allows me to read the house's face, and I know to say nothing now. Just let the silence speak for me.

"Are you really interested?" she inquires.

"In the past?"

"In me." Her worry pushes forward, growing into a warm despair. "I know what you are. You never go anywhere, in a physical form, unless you have a compelling reason—"

"I am," I interrupt. "In you, yes. I am interested."

Now she tries silence.

I look at the photography again, paying closest attention to the frozen lake in the foreground.

"What will you pay for me?" The question bursts out of her, followed by the simple confession, "My owner left me with full discretion. I am free to make the best possible deal in the shortest period of time."

She is not legally sentient. Since sentience is defined legally, it is relatively easy to give common objects enough mental power and personality to perch on the edge of what should be free.

I feel sorry for her.

But in the same moment, I hold fast to my own needs. Quietly and firmly, I tell her my bid for her land and buildings, the worn-out rugs, and this single old photograph of a once-grand palace.

She steps back, startled.

"No," she says.

Then with a low gasp, she adds, "I must have heard you wrong. What's your offer again?"

I lift my temporary hand, curling one finger against the base of my thumb.

"A piece of copper," I say. "This big. With a face on one side and columns on the other."

She looks stunned, and frightened.

"A penny," I say. "That's the ancient name for the coin."

And suddenly, I am alone again, standing before the abomination of a fireplace that has probably never burned so much as a molecule, and that image of a great home lost to the ages.

More visitors tour the house, and most eventually find me. Awkward silences are as common as effusive praise. A few beg for the chance to be photographed standing beside me. One of the visitors—an AI child, as it happens—smiles hopefully at me, asking, "Are you going to live here?"

"That's not a very reasonable question," his parent warns. "Wealth doesn't live inside houses."

" 'Wealth lives everywhere,' " he quotes.

"Exactly," says the parent.

Then the child turns back to me, wondering aloud, "Will you live everywhere and in here, too?"

I laugh, quietly and happily.

Then I wander down to the ground floor again, eventually finding a simple drop-tube that takes me into the basement. The stink of earthly molds and fossil water fills what passes for my nose. The foundation is unexpectedly ornate: Blocks of carved basalt, each exposed face decorated with magnified cross sections of ancient bacteria, the Martian DNA using its own language to weave together an array of odd amino acids. Time and the shifting ground have made little fissures at the joints. Otherwise, the old home rests on a sturdy, masterly base.

In one corner of the basement, between empty emergency tanks of oxygen, hides an ancient staircase cut from the native stone, plunging even deeper underground.

Intrigued, I follow.

Down, and down, and then, after a brief hallway, the stairs take me down into a little room surrounded by a fierce warmth. One wall is a diamond pane, and behind the wall are a fission battery and a fractured zone where water is heated to near boiling, slow chemical reactions feeding a multitude of patient organisms that look to the eye like a simple colorless gel.

"He would come down here just to watch his bugs," I hear.

The house has conjured up the woman again. A wronged, somewhat bitter woman this time. But she attempts to sound polite, explaining, "He built these species himself, you probably know. It was a hobby. Really, he was fascinated by the ancient Mars."

"I am too," I say.

She nods, and waits.

After a long silence, and with some difficulty, she asks, "Did you really mean that? A penny for all of me?"

I show her the copper coin.

"Why would I ever . . . ?" She hesitates. "Wait. You're offering more than money, aren't you?"

"I will never sell you," I promise.

She doesn't know what to say.

"I intend to hold you for the long term," I explain. "As part of a much larger, much more ambitious investment."

"I see."

"You don't," I warn. Then I look at her fractal-rich face and the sad, worried eyes, asking, "Do you ever wonder? What kinds of life would have evolved on Mars, if this world had remained warm and alive?"

"Yes," she whispers. "I've tried to picture it, yes."

"Yet nobody knows," I add. Then with my empty hand, I touch the warm face of the diamond, confessing, "I own some of the nearby houses."

"In the bottoms?" she guesses.

"And in every other part of Mars," I tell her. " 'Nearby' means the world, and I own many of the key businesses and industries, and I have a significant interest in corporations and commercial-nations that are essential to the Martian economy."

She says nothing.

"In a little while, I will empty Mars."

She shudders.

" 'In a little while' means within the next two or three thousand years," I explain. "And I'll do it gently, with a minimum of disruption. Of course, this world has never been essential to the solar system, and it won't be seriously missed. I'll keep everything warm and wet, and after another five or ten thousand years, I doubt if any sentient soul will give this place more than a glancing look. And in another million years, or a billion . . . however long it takes . . . a fresh and unique and lovely biosphere will arise, stepping out into a universe ready for something new. . . ."

She shudders.

Weakly, she asks, "Me?"

"I will not sell you, and I will keep you well-maintained, and whenever I visit Mars, this is where I will stay."

"In my rooms?"

"In this room," I offer.

She almost surrenders. Almost. But then with a tight little laugh, she says, "No. I want more than just a penny."

"How much more?"

"Two pennies."

With a flourish, I bring a second coin out of hiding. But before I hand it to the house, making the deal final, I warn her, "But you cannot tell anyone. That you bargained for double my initial offering. . . ."

She snatches up both of the slips of copper.

Then, for another long while, we watch creatures too small to have names or souls, watch them fiercely going about the relentless business of life.

Mastermindless

MATTHEW HUGHES

*Matthew Hughes [www.archonate.com] lives on Vancouver
Island, British Columbia. His first two novels,* Fools Errant
(SF) and Downshift *(crime/suspense) were published in
Canada in the 1990s. His third novel,* Fool Me Twice *(2001)
and his fourth,* Black Brillion *(2004), take place in the same
future setting as his first—the Archonate, a very distant
future in emulation of Jack Vance's stories of the Dying
Earth, a future where science indistinguishable from magic,
and magic, exist together. Using this setting, and in addition
a style very reminiscent of Vance's, while telling his own stories, has gotten Hughes significant notice as a new talent in
the field. This in spite of the fact that he has been a journal-
ist and (since 1979) a speechwriter, for decades. And a former director of the Federation of British Columbia Writers
to boot. In addition he says, "I've written twenty short stories, mostly crime and SF. Of those, I've now sold eighteen
with one still pending at* Asimov's." *His first collection,* The
Gist Hunter and Other Stories, *is published in 2005.*

"Mastermindless" appeared in F&SF. *It is an Archonate
story, and introduces a new continuing character, Henghis
Hapthorne, freelance discriminator. This is a clever take on
Sherlock Holmes, with an AI Watson. Already several sequels
have appeared in* F&SF, *with more to come.*

I had almost finished unraveling the innermost workings of a moderately interesting conspiracy to defraud one of Olkney's oldest investment syndicates when suddenly I no longer understood what I was doing.

The complex scheme was based on a multileveled matrix of transactions—some large, some small; some honest, some corrupt—conducted among an elaborate web of persons, some of whom were real, some fictitious, and a few who were both, depending upon the evolving needs of the conspirators.

Disentangling the fraud, sifting the actual from the invented, had occupied most of the morning. But once the true shape of the scheme became clear, I again fell prey to the boredom that blighted my days.

Then, as I regarded the schematic of the conspiracy on the inner screen of my mind, turning it this way and that, a kind of gray haze descended on my thoughts, like mist thickening on a landscape, first obscuring then obliterating the image.

I must be fatigued was my initial reaction. I crossed to my workroom sink and splashed water onto my face, then blotted it dry with a square of absorbent fiber. When I glanced into the reflector I received a shock.

"Integrator," I said aloud, "what has happened to me?"

"You are forty-six years of age," replied the device, "so a great many events have occurred since your conception. Shall I list them chronologically or in order of importance?"

I have always maintained that clarity of speech precedes clarity of thought and had trained my assistant to respond accordingly. Now I said, "I was speaking colloquially. Examine my appearance. It has changed radically, and not at all for the better."

I looked at myself in the reflector. I should have been seeing the image of Henghis Hapthorn, foremost freelance discriminator in the city of Olkney in the penultimate age of Old Earth. That image traditionally offered a broad brow, a straight nose leading to well formed lips, and a chin that epitomized resolution.

Instead, the reflector offered a beetling strip of forehead above a proboscis that went on far too long and in two distinct directions. My upper lip had shrunk markedly while the lower had grown hugely pendulous. My chin, apparently horrified, had fallen back toward my throat. Previously clear sweeps of ruddy skin were now pallid and infested by prominent warts and moles.

"You seem to have become ugly," said the integrator.

I put my fingers to my face and received from their survey the same unhappy tale told by my eyes. "It is more than seeming," I said. "It is fact. The question is: how was this done?"

The integrator said, "The first question is not how but exactly *what* has been done. We also need to learn why and perhaps by whom. The answers to those questions may well have a bearing on finding a way to undo the effect."

"You are right," said I. "Why didn't I think of that?"

"Are you being colloquial again or do you wish me to speculate?"

I scratched my head. "I am trying to think," I said.

"I have never known you to have to try," said the integrator. "Normally, you must make an effort to stop."

The device was correct. My intellectual capacity was renowned for both its breadth and depth. As a discriminator I often uncovered facts and relationships so ingeniously hidden or disguised as to baffle the best agents of the Archonate's Bureau of Scrutiny.

My cerebral apparatus was powerful and highly tuned. Yet now it was as if some gummy substance had been poured over gears that had always spun without friction.

"Something is wrong," I said. "Moments ago I was a highly intelligent and eminently attractive man in the prime of life. Now I am ugly and dull."

"I dispute the 'eminently attractive.' You were, however, presentable. Now, persons who came upon you unexpectedly would be startled."

I disdained to quibble; the esthetic powers of integrators were notoriously scant. "I was without question the most brilliant citizen of Olkney."

The integrator offered no contradiction.

"Now I must struggle even to. . . ." I broke off for a moment to rummage through my mind, and found conditions worse than I had thought. "I was going to say that I would have to struggle to compute fourth-level consistencies, but in truth I find it difficult to encompass the most elementary ratios."

"That is very bad."

My face sank into my hands. Its new topography made it strange to my touch. "I am ruined," I said. "How can I work?"

Integrators were not supposed to experience exasperation, but mine had been with me for so long that certain aspects of my personality had infiltrated its circuits. "Perhaps I should think for both of us," it said.

"Please do."

But scarcely had the device begun to outline a research program than there came an interruption. "I am receiving an emergency message from the fiduciary pool," it said. "The payment you ordered made from your account to Bastieno's for the new surveillance suite cannot go forward."

"Why not?"

"Insufficient funds. The pool also advises that tomorrow's automatic payment of the encumbrance on these premises cannot be met."

"Impossible!" I said. I had made a substantial deposit two days earlier, the proceeds of a discrimination concerning the disappearance of Hongsaun Bedwicz. She had been custodian of the Archonate's premier collection of thunder gems, rare objects created when lightning struck through specific layers of certain gaseous planets. They had to be collected within seconds of being formed, lest they sink to lower levels of the chemically active atmosphere and dissolve. I had located Bedwicz on a planet halfway down the Spray, where she had fled with her secret lover, Follis Duhane, whose love of fine things had overstrained her income.

My fee should have been the standard ten percent of the value of the recovered goods, but the Archonate's bureaucrats had made reference to my use of some legally debatable methodologies, and I had come away with three percent. Still, there should be at least 30,000 hepts, I informed my assistant.

"My records concur," said the integrator. "Unfortunately, the pool's do not. They say you have thirty-two hepts and fourteen grimlets. No more, no less."

"Where has the rest of it gone?"

"Pool integrators are never sophisticated, lest they grow bored with constant ins and outs and begin to amuse themselves with the customers' assets. This one merely counts what is there and records inflow and outtake. Yesterday the funds were present. Now they are not, although there has been no authorized withdrawal."

"So now I am not only ugly and dull, but have scarcely a groat to my name and am at risk of being ejected into the street."

The integrator said nothing. "Well," I prompted it, "have you no empathy?"

"You assembled me from analytical and computative elements," it replied. "However, I believe I can feign sympathy, if that will help."

"I doubt it," I said. "Why don't you analyze something?"

But instead it told me, "I am receiving another urgent message."

I groaned. "Is it the Archon threatening to banish me? That would place an appropriate crown onto the morning's disasters."

"It is Grier Alfazzian, the celebrated entertainer," said the integrator. "Shall I connect?"

"No."

"He may wish to engage you. An urgent matter would presuppose a willingness to pay an advance. That would solve one of the morning's problems."

"Hmmm," I said. "I should have thought of that."

"Yes," it said, then after a pause, "you poor little lumpykins."

"All right, put him through. But audio only. I don't want to be seen like this."

"Very well."

"And no more attempts at sympathy."

A screen appeared in the air before me, but when Alfazzian connected I did not see the face that gave women the hot swithers, though I had always thought him more pretty than handsome. He spoke from behind a montage of images that recalled his most acclaimed roles.

"Is that you, Hapthorn?"

I recognized his plummy baritone. "It is," I said.

"I have a question that requires an answer. Urgently and most discreetly. Come to my home at once."

I did not wish to take my new countenance out into the teeming streets of Olkney. There was a bylaw forbidding the frightening of children.

"Can we not discuss it as we are?"

"No."

"Very well." I had a mask left over from a recent soiree at the Archon's Palace. "But summoning me on short notice requires an advance on my fee."

"How much?"

Fortunately my memory was not fully impaired. I could recall the amounts cadged from wealthy clients who called me for assistance from within the coils of drastic and unexpected predicaments.

"Five thousand hepts," I said. "You may transfer it to my account at once."

"I shall," he said. "Wait while my integrator conducts the transfer."

There was a pause which lengthened while I regarded the images of Alfazzian striking poses in theatrical costumes and romantic settings. Then his voice returned to say, "There seems to be a problem with my finances."

"Indeed?" I said. I recalled that I often said "Indeed," when I could not think of any other rejoinder. When I wished to avoid a question, I usually indicated that an answer would be premature. I found that the two rejoinders filled conversational holes quite nicely.

"I do not have five thousand hepts at the moment. My funds have apparently been misplaced, except for a trifling sum."

Some stirring in the back of my mind urged me to ask the exact amount of the trifling sum.

"Why do you wish to know?" Alfazzian said.

I did not know why I wished to know, so I said, "It would be premature to say."

"The amount is thirty-two hepts and fourteen grimlets," he said.

"Indeed."

"Are the numbers significant?" Alfazzian asked.

"It would be premature to say," I said. "I will call you back."

"It cannot be coincidence that his funds and yours have been reduced to the same amount," the integrator said.

"Why not?"

"Consider the odds."

My mind attempted to do so in its customary manner, lunging at the calculation like a fierce and hungry dog that scents raw meat before its muzzle. But the mental leap was jerked to a halt in midair as if by a short chain. "I take it the odds are long?" I said.

The integrator quoted a very lopsided ratio.

"Indeed," I said. "But what does it signify?"

"It would be premature . . . ," it began.

"Never mind."

I tried to think of possible circumstances that could empty two unrelated accounts of all but the same small sum. After sustained effort, I came up with what seemed to be a pertinent question. "Do Alfazzian and I use the same pool?"

"No."

"Then it can't just be a defective integrator?"

"Integrators do not become defective," was the reply.

"I did not mean to offend."

"Integrators do not take offense. We are above such things."

"Indeed."

There was a silence. "How could the closely guarded integrators of two solvencies be induced to eliminate the funds of two separate depositors except for an identical trifle?" I asked.

"Hypothetically, a master criminal of superlative abilities might be able to accomplish it."

"Does such a master criminal exist?"

"No," was the answer, followed by a qualification. "But if such a criminal did exist he would almost certainly have the power to disguise his existence."

"Even from the Archonate's Bureau of Scrutiny?" I wondered.

"Unlikely, but possible. The scroots are not completely infallible."

"But if there was such a master purloiner, what would be his motivation in impoverishing me and Alfazzian? How have our lives mutually connected with that of our assailant?"

"No motive seems apparent," said the integrator.

I pushed my brain for more possibilities. It was like trying to goad a large, lethargic animal that prefers to sleep. "Who else might be able to subvert the fiduciary pools?" I said. "Could it be an inside job?"

"It is hard to imagine a cabal of officers from two financial institutions conspiring to defraud two prominent customers."

"And, again, where lies a motive?"

My mind was no more help than my assistant in answering that question. But if the machinery would not turn over, I still retained a grasp of the fundamentals of investigations: the transgressor would be he who had the means, motive, and opportunity to commit the offense. I considered all three factors in the light of the known facts and was stymied.

"I am stymied," I said. Then a faint inspiration struck. I asked the integrator, "If I were as I was before whatever has happened to cloud my mind, what would I now propose to do?"

The integrator replied, "You have occasionally said that although with most problems the simplest answer is usually correct, sometimes one encounters situations where the bare facts stubbornly resist explanation. In such a case, adding further complications paradoxically clarifies the issue."

I could remember having said those exact words. Now I asked the integrator, "Have you any idea what I meant when I said that?"

"Not really."

I scratched my head again.

"Do you have a scalp condition?" asked my assistant. "Shall I order anything from the chymist?"

"No," I said. "I was trying to think again."

"Does the scratching help?"

"No. Nor do your interruptions. Be useful and posit some complicating factors that might have something to do with the case."

"Very well. You are ugly and not very bright."

"I don't see how gratuitous insults can help."

"You misapprehend. At the same time as you have become poor, your appearance and mental acuity have also been reduced."

"Ahah," I said. Again there came a glimmer of an idea. This time I managed to fan it into a small flame. "And Alfazzian, who normally delights in displaying his face to the world, hid behind a montage while he spoke with me."

"So the coincidence might be even more extreme," said the integrator, "if he too has been reduced to ugliness."

"Connect me to him."

A moment later I was again looking at Alfazzian's screen. "Tell me," I said, "has there been an alteration in your appearance?"

There was a pause before he said, "How did you know?"

I had never had difficulty answering that question. "I do not reveal my methods," I said.

"Are you taking the case?"

"I am," I said. "I will make a special dispensation and allow you to pay me later."

"I am grateful."

"One question: does it seem to you that your intellectual faculties have been reduced?"

"No," Alfazzian said, "but then I have always got by on my talent."

"Indeed," I said. My long-standing impression of the entertainer remained intact: his talent consisted entirely of his fortuitous facial geometry. "Remain at home and wait to hear from me."

I broke the connection and the screen disappeared. I said to my assistant, "Now we know more, but still we know nothing."

We knew that I, who had been brilliant, attractive—or so I would argue—and financially comfortable, had been made dense, repugnant, and indigent. Alfazzian had been admittedly more handsome than I and probably much more wealthy, and now he was also without funds or looks—but his intellect had not been correspondingly ravished.

"There is a pattern here," I said, "if I could but see it."

I wrestled with the facts but could not get a secure grip. The effort was made more difficult by a growing clamor from the street outside my quarters. I went to the window and, bidding the integrator minimize the obscuring membrane, looked down at a growing disturbance.

Several persons were clustered before a doorway on the opposite side of Shiplien Way, beating at the closed portal with fists, feet and, in the case of a large and choleric woman in yellow taffeta, a parasol. As I watched, more participants joined the mob, then all took to shouting threats and imprecations at a smooth-headed man who leaned from an upper window and implored them to return another day.

The door, which remained closed, led to a branch of the Olkney Mercantile, one of the city's most patronized financial institutions. I spoke to my assistant. "Is Alfazzian's account with the OM?"

"No."

"Then I believe we can add one more new fact to our store."

I inspected the individual members of the crowd. I had never been one to judge others on mere appearance, but the assemblage of mismatched features across the street was the least fortunate collection of countenances I had ever seen assembled in one place. "Make that two new facts," I said.

"Hmmm," I said. Again, it was as if my mind expected a pattern to present itself, but nothing came. It was an unpleasant sensation, the mental equivalent of ascending a staircase and, expecting to find one more riser than the joiner has provided, stepping up onto empty air and crashing down again.

"The most handsome man in Olkney is made repellent," I said to my assistant, "and the most intelligent is made at best ordinary. As well, both are impoverished. So apparently are many others." I struggled to form a shape from the data and an inkling came. "If Alfazzian and I are the targets and the others are merely bystanders, then why is the institution across the street in turmoil? We have no connection to it."

"It could be that the attack is general," said the integrator, "and therefore you and our client are only part of a wider category of victims."

I turned the concept over and looked at it from that angle. It appeared no more comprehensible. "We need more data," I said. "Access the public advisory service."

The screen reappeared, displaying a fiercely coiffed young woman who was informing Olkney that it was inadvisable to visit the financial district. "Dislocations are occurring," she said, widening her elegant eyes while uplifting perfectly formed eyebrows.

"Two more facts," said the integrator. "Other depositories must have been raided and there is one attractive person who has not been rendered grim."

"Three facts," I said. "The painfully handsome man who usually engages her in inane banter about trivialities has not appeared."

But what did it mean? Were only men affected? I had the integrator examine other live channels. Those from outside Olkney showed no effects. In other cities and counties, handsome men still winked and nodded at me from behind fanciful desks. There were no monetary emergencies. But the emissions originating within the city fit the emerging pattern. Of attractive women, there was no shortage; of good looking men, a dearth.

"Regard this one," said the integrator. We were seeing the farm correspondent of a local news service, a man hired more for his willingness to climb over fences and prod the confined stock at close range than for set of jaw or twinkle of eye.

"He has always been hard on the gaze," I said.

"Yes," agreed my assistant, "but he is grown no harder."

"Another fact," I said.

Matters were almost beginning to assume a shape. If I could have thrust aside the clouds that obscured my mind, I knew I would be able to see it. But the mist remained impenetrably thick.

"A question occurs," I said. "Who is the richest man in Olkney?"

"Oblos Pinnifrant."

"And is his face well or unfortunately constituted?"

"He is so wealthy that his appearance matters not."

"Exactly," I said. "He delights in inflicting his grotesque features on those who crave his favor, forcing them to vie one against another to soothe him with flattery. Connect me to him."

Pinnifrant's integrator declined the offer of communication. I said, "Inform him that Olkney's most insightful discriminator is investigating the disappearance of his fortune."

A moment later, the plutocrat's lopsided visage appeared on my screen. "What do you know?" he said.

"It would be premature to say."

"Yet you are confident of solving the mystery?"

"You know my reputation."

"True, you have yet to fail. What are your terms?"

My terms were standard: ten percent of whatever I recovered.

Pinnifrant's porcine eyes glinted darkly. "Ten percent of my fortune is itself a fortune."

"Indeed," I said, "but thirty-two hepts and fourteen grimlets are not much of a foundation on which to begin anew, even for one with your egregious talent for turning up a profit."

In fact, Pinnifrant had been born to wealth and had only had to watch it breed, but a lifetime of deference from all who rubbed up against him had convinced the magnate that he was the sole font of his tycoonery.

After a brief chaffer, he said, "I agree to your terms. Report to me frequently." He moved to sever the connection.

"Wait," I said. "Have you noticed any diminution of your mental capacities?"

"I am as sharp as ever," was the answer, "but my three assistants have become effectively useless."

"Has there been any change in the arrangement of their features?"

"I would not know. I do not bother to inspect their faces."

"One last thing," I said. "Have your financial custodian contact me immediately."

Agron Worsthall, the Pinnifrant Mutual Solvency's chief tallyman, appeared on my screen less than a minute after I broke the connection to Pinnifrant. He seemed eager to assist me.

"How much remains in his account?" I asked.

"Oblos Pinnifrant has consolidated many of his holdings through us," Worsthall said. "All but one of his accounts have been reduced to a zero balance. The exception contains thirty-two hepts and fourteen grimlets."

"What about other depositors' holdings? Are they also reduced to that amount?"

"They are. That is, the male depositors and those who had joint accounts with female partners."

"But women are unaffected?"

"Yes, and children of both sexes."

"And where have the funds gone? Were they transferred to someone else?"

"They were not. The money is simply not there."

"Is that possible?"

I heard him sigh. "Until today I would have said it was

not, but I am finding it difficult to deal with abstruse concepts this morning."

"Has there been any change in your physical appearance?" I asked. "Specifically, your face?"

"What kind of question is that?"

"A pertinent one, I believe."

There was a silence on the line while Worsthall sought his own reflection. When he came back his voice had a quaver. "Something has occurred to my nose and chin," he said. "As well, there are blemishes."

"Hmm," I said.

"What does it mean?"

I told him it would be premature to say. "You said that all accounts held by men had been reduced to thirty-two hepts and fourteen grimlets. What about accounts that contained less than that amount—were they raised to this mystical number?"

"No, they were unaffected. Is that germane?"

I asked him if he had difficulty understanding the meaning of "premature." Then another idea broke through the fog. "I wish you to do something for me," I said. "Contact all the other financial institutions in Olkney. Ask if the same thing has happened."

I broke the connection and attempted to rouse my sluggish analytical apparatus, but it continued to lie inert.

Again, I asked my assistant, "If I were possessed of my usual faculties, how would I address this conundrum?"

"You would look for a pattern in the data," it said.

"I have done that. I cannot see more than the bare outline of what, and not even a glint of why or how. Men have been robbed of their wealth, looks and intelligence, yet who has gained? Where lies the motive, let alone the means?" I sighed. "What more would I do if I were intact?"

"You might look for a pattern outside the data," the integrator said. "You once remarked that it is possible to deduce the shape of an invisible object by examining the holes left by its passage."

"I do not see how that applies to this situation."

"Nor do I. I am accustomed to rely upon you for insights. My task is to assemble and correlate data as you instruct."

"What other brilliancies have I come up with over the years? Perhaps one will ring a chime and reignite my fires."

"You once opined that the rind is mightier than the melon. You presented this as a particularly profound perception."

"What did it mean?"

"I do not know. When you said it, you were under the influence of certain substances."

"No use," I said. "Go on."

"You have occasionally noted that the wise man can learn from the fool."

"I remember saying it," I said, "but now I have no idea what I meant."

"Perhaps something to do with opposites attracting?" the integrator offered.

"I doubt it," I said. "Do they attract? If so, it can't be for long since wouldn't true opposites irritate each other if not cancel each other out? It sounds like mutual annihilation, and I'm sure I've never been in favor of that."

"You also say that sometimes the most crucial clue is not what has happened, but what has not."

"That sounds more like it," I said. "Except that the number of things that haven't happened must be astronomically greater than those that have. So how do we pick out the non-existent events that have meaning?"

"You usually perform some pithy analysis."

"Yes, but I'm short on pith today."

"Then it will have to be an inspired guess."

"I am far from inspired," I said. "But I think we have at least defined the crime. The attacks are aimed at intelligent and presentable men as well as those who have more than thirty-two hepts and fourteen grimlets.

"Dull men have not been made duller, nor poor men poorer, nor have the unprepossessing been further victimized. And women and children are unaffected on all counts.

"We come back as always to means, motive, and opportunity."

It was difficult to posit a rational means or an opportunity by which the assumed perpetrator could do so much harm to so many and all apparently at the same moment. I knew from long experience, however, that motives were relatively few and all too common to most of humankind. "Jealousy," I said. "We may be looking for a poor, not too bright man with a face to curdle milk."

"But if he is dimwitted, how does he contrive to perform the impossible?" said my assistant.

"Indeed," I said. " 'How' is the operative question."

The integrator made a sound that was its equivalent of a throat clearing. "I have a suggestion," it said.

"What?"

Its tone was tentative. "Magic."

I snorted. It was an automatic response whenever the subject was raised. "Only a fool believes in magic," I said.

"Perhaps this is the work of a fool."

That almost made sense, but though I could no longer argue for them, I recalled all my old opinions. "There is no such thing as magic."

"Yet there are arguments for the opposing view."

I had encountered them. Supposedly there was an alternation between magic and physics, between sympathy and rationalism, as operating principles of the phenomenal universe. As the Great Wheel rolled through the eons, one assumed supremacy over the other, only to see the relationship eventually reversed.

When one regime took the ascendancy, the other allegedly remained as an embedded seed in its unfriendly host. Thus in an age when magic held sway, its mechanics were still logically extrapolated—there were rules and procedures—while during the present reign of rationality, events at the subquantum level were supposedly determined more by quirks and quiddities than by unalterable laws.

I was occasionally braced, at a salon or social, by some advocate of the mystical persuasion who would try to convince me that the Wheel was now nearing the next cusp and that I might live long enough to see the contiguous series of electrons that carried information from one device to another replaced by chains of ensorceled imps, my integrator supplanted by an enchanted familiar.

I had investigated the arcana of magic over a summer during my youth and could demolish its advocates with arguments that were both subtle and vigorous. However, I had to admit that those arguments were at present beyond my grasp. Still, I harrumphed once more and said, "Magic!" then blew air over my lips as if shooing away a gossamer.

My assistant said, "You also like to say that when all impossibilities have been swept from the table what remains, however unlikely, must be the answer."

"Magic," I said, "is one of those impossibilities."

"Are you sure?"

"I used to be," I said, "so I ought to be now."

"Even a wise man can . . . ," began the integrator, then interrupted itself to tell me that Pinnifrant's tallyman was back.

"What have you learned?"

"The same situation pertains across the city. Indeed, even accounts held outside Olkney by male residents of the city have been affected."

The more I learned the more perplexed I became. Even in my diminished state, I recognized the irony. I had long wished for a superlative opponent, a master criminal who could give me room to stretch. Now one had seemingly appeared, but in doing so had robbed me of the capacity to combat his outrages. Still, I struggled to encompass an image of the situation.

"And there is no indication that anyone has benefited from the thefts?" I asked Worsthall. "No woman's account has ballooned? No child's?"

"No."

"Thank you," I said, though I could not see how the information helped.

"There is one anomaly," he said.

"Hmm?"

"A male depositor at Frink Fiduciary had a balance of thirty-two hepts and fifteen grimlets before the discrepancy this morning. . . ."

"Discrepancy?" I asked.

"It is a term we in the financial sector use when accounts do not tally."

"Why not be bold and call it what it is, mass theft and rampant rapine?"

"If we were bold, we would not be bankers," was the reply.

"Indeed," I said, "but what were you about to tell me?"

"That a male depositor had a balance of thirty-two hepts and fifteen grimlets before the . . . rampant rapine, and that he had the same balance afterward. And still does."

I had him repeat the numbers again. "This depositor had one grimlet more than the ubiquitous H32.14 before the . . . the event, and he still has the same amount now?"

"As of three minutes ago," said the tallyman.

"Hmm," I said. I experienced a vague sense that the anomaly might be significant. "Who is he?"

"He is called Vashtun Errible."

"Tell me about him."

There was little to tell: only an address on a cul-de-sac off the Fader Slide, an obscure location in an uncelebrated part of the city. No image of Errible reposed in the solvency's files, and the connectivity code he had given when opening the account was long since defunct. The account had not been used for many years and had probably been forgotten by its nominee.

I left the tallyman to his troubles and set my assistant to scouring all sources for news of this Vashtun Errible. The integrator turned up only one more item: a deed of indenture that bound Errible's services to the requirements of one Bristal Baxandall.

"Now that's a name I have heard before," I said, though I could not immediately place it.

"He prefers to be known as The Exalted Sapience Bristal Baxandall, an alleged thaumaturge," said the integrator. "He performs at children's parties."

Again I spied the glimmer of an idea. Perhaps this Baxandall was the mastermind behind the calamity, hiding his brilliance by masquerading as a low-rent prestidigitator. Or he might be only the blind behind which Errible, the true prodigy, had concealed himself.

I had a hunch that one or both of these two persons was central to the mystery. Normally, I despised hunches and had always denied their validity—to my mind, an intuition was no more than the product of an analytical process that took place in the mind's dark back rooms. Occasionally, a door was flung open and the result of unconscious analysis was tossed into the light of the mental front parlor, to be discovered by the incumbent as if it had arrived by mystical means.

The thought led to another: I wondered if my own back rooms were as fully stocked and active as always but that some force had sealed the doors. The more I examined the idea, mentally probing about in my inner recesses the way my tongue would explore the gap left by an extracted tooth, the more it seemed likely that my faculties had not been irrevocably ripped away, but only placed out of reach. I listened and it seemed that I could almost hear the ghost of my former genius crying out to me from beyond a barrier in my mind.

I realized that my assistant was saying something. "Repeat," I said.

"The Exalted Sapience's address is the same as that which the solvency found for Vashtun Errible," it said.

"Connect me."

"I cannot. He apparently possesses no integrator."

"How is that possible?"

"I cannot even speculate," said the integrator. "His house appears as a blank spot in the connectivity matrix."

"Ahah!" I said again. "The shape left by the invisible object!"

"What do you mean?"

I did not know. It was another hunch. "It would be premature to say," I said. "Summon an air-car and have it take me to that address."

The vehicle was longer than usual in arriving and I noticed that its canopy was darkly stained. When we rose above the rooftops I saw why: thick columns of greasy, black smoke boiled skyward from several sites along the big bend in the river, joining to form a pall over the south side of the city. To the west, several streets were blocked off by emergency vehicles bearing the lights and colors of the provost bureau, and a surging mob was rampaging through the financial district, smashing glass and overturning motilators.

The air-car banked and flew north toward an industrial precinct that looked to be quieter. After a few minutes it angled down to a dead-end street below the slideway and alighted before an ill-kept two-story house whose windows were obscured by dark paint. I bid the car remain but it replied that it could only do so if I paid the accumulated fare immediately and allowed it to deduct its waiting fee every five minutes.

"How much?" I asked and was told that I owed seven hepts. Furthermore, it would charge me twenty grimlets per minute to wait.

"Usually, I charge such expenses to my account with your firm," I said.

"These are unusual times," it said, and I was forced to agree to the terms.

The house was dilapidated, the paint peeling, and some siding sprung loose. Dank weeds had invaded and occupied the front lawn, and the porch sagged when I topped the front steps. There was a faint smell of boiled vegetables.

There were symbols painted on the front door. They seemed vaguely familiar but my uncertain memory could not produce their meanings. There was no who's-there beside the door, the house having no integrator to operate it. I struck the painted wood with my knuckles to make my presence known.

There was no response nor any sound from within. A second knocking brought no result, so I tried the latch and the door opened inward.

I stepped within and called for attention. There was no answer. I looked about and saw a small, untidy foyer from which a closed door led left, a stairway went upward, and a short hall ran back to what appeared to be a rudimentary kitchen.

I called again and heard what might have been a reply

from behind the closed door. I opened it and looked into a cramped and fusty parlor dominated by an oversized table draped in black cloth on which was scattered an arrangement of objects and instruments I could not immediately identify. The opaqued windows let in no light, and the only illumination was from some of the strewn bric-a-brac that emitted dim glows and wavering auras.

"Hello?" I said and again heard a moan from the gloom beyond the table. I produced a small lumen from my pouch and activated it so that I could work my way around the table without stepping on more knickknacks that seemed to have fallen to the floor.

Under the table on the far side was what I first took to be a bundle of stained cloth loosely stuffed with raw meat and bare bones. A warm and unappetizing smell rose from it. The cloth was dark and figured with designs and symbols similar to those on the front door, but woven in metallic thread. The moan came again, and now it was clear that the bundle was its source.

"What is this?" I said, more to myself than to any expected audience, but I was answered by a rich, deep voice from behind me.

"Not what, but who," it said, "and the answer is The Exalted Sapience Bristal Baxandall. That answer will be valid for at most only a few minutes longer. After that, there are different schools of thought. Would you care to discuss the nature of being and the relationship of soul to identity?"

I had turned around and found that the voice issued from what I had initially assumed to be a framed abstract on the wall. But I saw now that this painting constantly moved, thick shapes of unusual colors ceaselessly flowing into and out of themselves, their proportions and directions seeming to mislead the eye. A few seconds of regarding it evoked a dizziness and I looked away.

"I am not equipped for metaphysical discussions today," I said. "Something has impaired my intellect."

"Indeed?" said the painting.

"Would you know anything about that?" I asked in a noncommittal tone.

"It would be premature to say," said the voice.

I directed the conversation to The Exalted Sapience. "What has happened to him?"

"He was undertaking a transformational exercise."

"Surely he did not wish to be transformed into that?"

"No. It was not his intent to rearrange himself quite so drastically. He wanted only to be younger."

"Not richer, smarter, and better looking?" I asked.

There was a chuckle. "No, that ambition was Vashtun Errible's."

"He would be Baxandall's servant?"

The voice chuckled. "He *is* the servant, at least until the indenture expires with Baxandall, in a few minutes at the most. He *would be* the master, though I doubt he will be."

"And where is Errible now?"

"He is upstairs consulting Baxandall's library, trying to deduce what went amiss with his plan. The first part went as he expected: he adulterated one of the ingredients in the master's transformation exercise and produced the unhappy result under the table; the second part varied from his expectations."

"What went wrong?"

"I did."

"And what, exactly, are you?"

"Again, there are conflicting schools of thought. Baxandall called me a demon; you might call me a figment of the imagination. The Exalted Sapience conscripted me to be his familiar and strove to find ways to channel my . . . energies, shall we say, for his own purposes. Vashtun Errible sees me, quite erroneously, as a box from which he may extract his every tawdry dream."

I saw it now. "He desired to be the richest, smartest, handsomest man in Olkney," I said. "He was a scraggly shrub that pined to grow into the tallest deodar in the forest. Instead, you shrank the rest of us to weeds."

"It amused me to confound him."

"But did it further your interests?" I said. "You indicated that your servitude is involuntary."

The shapes in the frame performed a motion that might

have been a shrug. "But temporary. Baxandall managed to catch me in a clumsy trap. You see, I am of an adventuresome disposition. Boredom led me to become an explorer of adjacent dimensions, even dusty corners like your own. I thought I had found a peephole into your realm, but when I pressed my eye against it—you will understand that I speak metaphorically—I encountered a powerful adhesive."

The faint voice in the back of my mind was clamoring. I apparently had questions to ask, but I could not make out what they were. Yet even with only a fragment of my usual intellect I perceived that I was in a perilous situation. The entity in the frame exuded a grim complacency. It was about to exact vengeance for its enslavement, and I had already seen that it had no compunctions about inflicting harm on innocent bystanders.

"I shall leave," I said. "Good luck with Errible."

But as I made my way around the table, this time keeping the furniture between me and the thing hanging on the wall, a hunch-shouldered figure in a tattered robe appeared in the doorway. I knew from the disharmony of his features that this was Baxandall's indentee.

He held open before him a large book bound in leather, and as soon as he entered the chamber, he began to recite from its pages in a voice that came as much from his misshapen nose as from his slack-lipped mouth, "*Arbrustram merrilif oberluz, destoi malleonis. . . .*"

And then he saw me and his concentration slipped. He broke off in mid-sentence—only for a moment, but the moment might as well have been an eon, because during that brief caesura the entity on the wall extruded part of itself into the room.

It was something like an arm, something like a tentacle, something like an insect's hooked limb and altogether like nothing I had ever seen; but it seized Vashtun Errible about the neck, lifted his worn slippers from the carpet and drew him into the swirl of motion within the frame.

The book fell from his hands as his face was drawn into the maelstrom. The rest of his body followed, pulled through the frame with a sound that reminded me of thick liquid passing through a straw. But I was not concentrating on the peculiarities of Errible's undoing; for the moment his head entered the frame, my faculties were restored.

I took in the room again, but with new eyes. I recognized some of the objects on the table and recalled having read about the fallen book in my youth. Thus, when the thing in the window had done with Errible and reached for me, it found me holding the volume and quoting the passage that the indentee had begun.

The limb retracted and the shapes in the frame roiled and coruscated. I could not read the emotions, but I was willing to infer rage and disappointment.

"This is not as lamentable an outcome as you may think," I said, when the cantrip had once more bound the demon.

"Our perspectives differ, as is to be expected when one party holds the leash and the other wears the collar," said the thing in the window.

"We did not finish discussing where your interests lie, nor had we even begun to consider mine. But if we can cause them to coincide, I am prepared to relinquish the leash and slip the collar."

The next sound approximated a sardonic laugh. "After I arrange for you to rule your boring little world, no doubt."

I made a sound involving lower teeth, upper lip, and an explosion of air, and said, "Do I strike you as one who aspires to be a civil servant? The Archon already performs that tedious function, and good luck to him."

A note of interest crept into the demon's tone. "Then what do you wish?"

I told him.

With the transdimensional demise of Vashtun Errible, all of his works became as if they never were. Grier Alfazzian's prospects had never dimmed and Oblos Pinnifrant's fortune had not been touched, thus neither owed me a grimlet nor knew that they ever had.

I did not care. My fees had become increasingly arbitrary: for an interesting case I would take no more than the client could afford; if it bored me, I would include a punitive surcharge. In recent years, as experience had augmented my innate abilities, truly absorbing puzzles had become few and infrequent. I had begun to fear that the rest of my life would offer long decades of ennui, my mind constantly spinning but always in want of traction.

My encounter with the demon had put that fear to rest. All I had needed was a worthy challenger.

The next morning I entered my workroom. An envelope rested on my table. I opened it and found a tarnished key and a small square of paper. On the key was a symbol that tweaked at my memory, though I could not place it. Printed on the paper was the single word, *Ardmere*.

I placed both on the table and regarded them. I could not resist rubbing my hands together. But before I began to enjoy the mystery, I must fulfill my side of the bargain.

I took from my pocket a sliver of charred wood in which two hairs were caught. I crossed the room and presented the splinter to the frame hanging on my wall.

"Not where, not when, not who—but why?" I said.

A kind of hand took the object from me and drew it into the shifting colors. "Hmmm," said my opponent, "interesting."

"Last one to solve the puzzle is a dimbo," I said and turned toward the table. "Ready, set . . . go!"

Time, as It Evaporates . . .

JEAN-CLAUDE DUNYACH

(translation by Jean-Louis Trudel)

Jean-Claude Dunyach [http://sf.emse.fr/AUTHORS/JCDUN-YACH/jcd.html] has a Ph.D. in applied mathematics and works for Airbus France in Toulouse (France). He is a leading figure in French SF and is one of the foremost contemporary French SF writers. He is also one of the few to be translated into English—eleven of his stories have been translated before 2004. David Brin calls him "one of the most talented imaginations living today." In French he has published four collections of stories and seven novels.

"Time, as It Evaporates..." appeared for the first time in English in 2004, in the excellent collection of Dunyach's best SF stories, The Night Orchid, *certainly one of the best SF story collections of the year.* The Night Orchid *is filled with stories dense with unusual SF imagery and extraordinary characters. There were three or four other fine stories from this collection that we considered for this year's best, so we recommend it highly. This one is best. A strange time catastrophe has spared only an isolated Muslim village. Time levels rise and fall like water. It was originally published in 1986, and it is a shame that the English language audience had to wait nearly twenty years to read it.*

Time, as it evaporates, stirs the surface of the lake above. From the depths below, the time-wrecked watch the troubled mirror that hides the heavens and, from its undulations, deduce the wakes of imaginary birds.

The submerged city is nestled between the high walls of a mountain chain. When one night the Universe tore and bled, losing its most precious fluid from a thousand mortal wounds, the mountains acted like natural dykes and trapped a temporal pond large enough to allow the city to survive.

The top of the minaret long ago broke through the liquid boundary between the world below and the stasis above. Its refined silhouette, jaggedly fractured at the meeting with the surface, dominates the drowned city. Its pinnacle, warped by the alteration in perspective, seems condemned to a perpetual fall nobody fears any more.

A stone stairway coils around the fragile building. During centuries, uncounted artists covered the steps with enameled mosaics on which arabesques proclaimed the holy name of God. Most inscriptions are still visible, even though the oldest tiles are often cracked or broken off.

So that his voice may carry farther, Marwan the muezzin climbs to the highest step still under time to utter the call to prayer. He does not care for amplifiers or mikes, for all those devices men place between their words and their listeners. His breath is powerful, his diction of the utmost clarity. Echoes of his exhortations roll like a torrent of well-worn pebbles through the alleys and squares, bounce from the whitewashed terraces, filter into the tightly-shuttered houses, into the hearts of the members of the community. He is forty in years, at the peak of his art, the bearer of the divine Word . . .

The lake of time vanishes slowly. Every month or so, Marwan must come down a step to address the last of the faithful. Such is the case today and so he adds a few words to the traditional surats, to comfort those who might need it.

"Do not fear being put to the test, but fear the wrath of God and find here another sign of His greatness. I am again exiled from the ultimate step, forced to bow my head and come closer to you. Let this be a lesson to us: when time itself fails us, religion comes closer to men . . ."

Few pay any attention to his speeches, yet nobody questions his calling, if only because it allows them to follow the day to day ebbing of the time-tide.

After the prayer, Marwan is not afraid to get as close as he can to the surface, until it is no longer an obstacle to his gaze.

On the other side of the lake's frosted glass lies a Universe without time. Marwan is the only one to have seen it; the superstitious dread which prevents other community members from venturing to the stairway's top has allowed him to enjoy an unchallenged prestige. If someone dared to climb as high as him, he would see that the emerged peak of the minaret is clear of any inscription. The name of the Lord is erased as soon as the time-level falls, the earthenware tiles recovering their virginity temporarily violated by the touch of faith.

A few months earlier, Marwan carved the names of all the gods he knew on a clay tablet attached to the end of a stick. The tablet was destroyed when it pierced the surface, and the muezzin recovered his serenity, only shaken for a time. In this world as in the other, no one is greater than Allah.

As he climbs down the stairway worn by the sandals of his predecessors, Marwan marks aloud the steps which remain his, rising from the base of the minaret. He settles the folds of his coat, knocks the tiles with his staff to punctuate the litany of numbers he counts off. The first gray hairs are weaving a loose net in his beard and his mane. He cares not a whit and, quite to the contrary, is glad of them: age will grant more weight to his words.

His half-sister Zorah, fifteen years younger, waits for him at home. He asked her to bring back from the market a piece of mutton, which she will prepare with the herbs his mother taught her. He can already taste the flavor of the roasted meat, of the chick peas mixed with raisins, and he quickens his steps, never wavering in his count.

The numbers he mumbles are reassuring: one step, one month; ten steps, a landing, almost a year. The landings are numerous enough by far to let him end his life, without ever having to bow his head or run on all fours like an animal to stay below the temporal surface. He tries to imagine what his life will be in another fifty or one hundred steps, but the thought of the meal awaiting him disturbs his meditation. In any case, how can the years to come bring him anything new? His staff strikes the polished stones with renewed force. He still has below him all the time in the world; thinking of the future is useless.

He reaches the doorway of his house, pushes aside with his hand the door curtain. The main room is empty. Zorah isn't back yet. A quick glance toward the clepsydra tells him she is nearly an hour late. Thwarted, he goes to sit on the cushions and unrolls a book of precepts in order to busy his mind until his sister's return.

The sounds of the city reach him through the thick walls. The barking of dogs, the shouting of the last few children, the muffled thud of rope sandals on the street's cobblestones, each sound a note in a deeply personal melody, at once familiar and reassuring. It's been years since he has had to endure the remote roar of the jets scoring the sky or the brutal staccato of internal combustion engines. There are no outside influences left to disturb the community, now turned inward, isolated by the will of Allah.

From outside come the echoes of hurried steps, and then the door's curtain is pushed aside. Zorah is back. She rushes into the kitchen with her burden, without giving her brother a chance to open his mouth. The clatter of dishes and cutlery is heard, and she appears with a steaming teapot. She sets down two glasses on the low table's hammered brass tray and pours tea.

"Where do you come from, Zorah?"

"From the slaughterhouse. I had to wait nearly an hour to get some mutton."

Marwan observes her. She has taken off the shapeless cloak which she puts on to go outside the house, letting him examine at length the body whose full curves never fail to arouse within him an insidious confusion. He lifts his gaze to her face. The eyes are underlined with kohl, the mouth under the veil is a shade of grenadine red, and the ears jingle with serried silver rings.

"Was it needful that you adorn yourself like that to go to the market, little sister?"

"Let me do what I want! I'll soon be twenty-six; it's time that men learn to look at me."

She goes back into the kitchen. Marwan deduces her anger from the jolting stride. An old worry eats at him: Zorah, whose guardian he has been since their father died, must not be allowed to dishonor their home as well as himself with displays unworthy of a muezzin's sister. Tomorrow, he will go and sit at the terrace of the main café, near the old mustering grounds of the caravans, so that he can listen to what is being said in town about Zorah.

His position within the community has taught him to separate the wheat from the chaff when it comes to the words of men. He feels capable of learning what he seeks simply by sitting on a mat, without speaking. He who stays silent and listens is like a well filled by the springs of wisdom, while he who speaks is like a well whose water is being drawn out, so sayeth the Prophet. It is deeply comforting, thinks Marwan, to live in a world where every thought finds its source in holy writings, all praises to Allah, the Gracious, the Merciful.

He banishes the subject from his mind as he sips the hot tea, savoring the sweet smell of mint and the bitter aroma. A few more minutes and dinner will be ready.

*   *   *

When dawn's first light shines, Marwan marches through the streets, staff in hand, like a shepherd watching over his flock in the ruins of an antique settlement. The city, at one end of the road through the passes, once flourished, but the time is long gone when the caravans laden with salt rods, silk rolls and swollen water skins used to come through the monumental gates carved into the ramparts. The last camels were put down a few months ago, not for their meat, but to spare them a pointless and idiotic agony, far from the desert. That day, Marwan saw men cry, men who had traveled up and down the rocky trails since infancy; many left on foot, a water flask on their hip, for one last trip beyond the mountains, beyond any hope of ever returning.

Yet, a deceptive bustle still enlivens the alleyways and the *souks*. Marwan walks down a row of stalls, assailed by the insistent hammering of the mallets of coppersmiths. Here, craftsmen continue to make copperware as in the past, keeping only their best pieces and melting the rest to avoid overcrowding their displays. Farther down, an old man bargains tirelessly for a prayer mat he will probably never buy. The carpet merchant, sitting on a pile of cushions, nods patiently without lowering his price a jot more than is proper.

A young veiled virgin, walking in the shadow of her mother, casts a stealthy glance at the muezzin, who responds only with a frown . . .

Every morning, Marwan looks at his city with new eyes and marvels to find it unchanged from the day before. The catastrophe changed nothing. The beggars, even the robbers pursue their trade with the unspoken agreement of all. It is as if the whole city, knowing itself condemned, prepares to relive endlessly the day before its disappearance, like the palaces shut into bottles for fun by djinns in old tales.

When he reaches the square where is found the city's main well, filled with a very cool iron-flavored water, Marwan chooses to halt, leaning on his staff. There are four places here where he can go and drink tea, four similar terraces screened by awnings of brown canvas. The muezzin will stop in each in the course of the day, moving as the mood moves him or as circumstances dictate, but he must choose with care the only one he will honor with his presence first.

His practiced eye gauges the audience, identifying at once each face. He soon makes up his mind. No outward sign betrays his inner turmoil as he resumes his stroll, crosses the square, and, saluting the other customers with a stiff nod, squats on one of the mats, its colors sadly faded.

The mirror of the sky is alive with slow undulations and ripples, which die in concentric circles around the minaret. Marwan, when he blows on the scalding tea, causes similar ripples to disturb the liquid's surface, so that the ever-changing images betray the passage of time.

Those who sit there rarely lift their gaze toward the sky. To measure the passing of the hours, they do not try to decipher the sinuous alphabets traced on the lake's mirror. They believe in clepsydrae or hourglasses, like their forefathers before them, or yet again count the beatings of their hearts. They have reached that age when the little time remaining to them would hold easily in two wrinkled hands cupped together, before slipping away forever between their fingers. The tea they have imbibed is a mighty river swollen by the rains; the tea they have left to drink is a mere puddle. Why fret because the temporal lake continues to drop?

Among them, the muezzin is a teenager. He stays silent and listens, keeping his words for the time of prayer. If something is to be said about Zorah, he will hear it when the time comes.

Yet, the immutable order of the day's events is due for an upset. Across the public square, a man comes toward him, striding quickly, perhaps faking a self-confidence he does not feel.

Though the one who comes thus is unknown to him, Marwan feels keenly the link which unites them. He takes the time to detail his figure, conscious that he is simultaneously the object of the other's gaze.

The hair black and shiny, the short beard shadowing his cheeks, the tall shape cloaked in a striped fabric, all betray a stranger from the coast, a man from another tribe, an unbeliever perhaps. He walks with a bowed head, as if bearing on his shoulders the burden of a sorrow as heavy as the world. He is no doubt a traveler who stopped to spend the night in their city when the great cataclysm occurred, and who is now stranded. A few were in the same straits after disaster struck; those who had left their family to seek their fortune elsewhere came home to resume their previous life. The fate of a couple of lost tourists was quickly settled. But the newcomer does not fall in either category.

Instinctively, the muezzin mistrusts him. His hands clench the staff lain across his knees, his back straightens. The newcomer reaches the terrace and he makes his way between the elders who have fallen silent, without honoring them with a single glance. His eyes are boring into Marwan's, and an obstinate resolve crimps his mouth. His face is a carved chunk of solidified lava, and his hands alone, criss-crossed by a thousand tiny scars, seem capable of gentleness.

"Are you Marwan the muezzin?"

Marwan nods, aware that conversations have stopped around them. He claps his hands to order tea and shows the intruder a free spot on the mat. The man ignores the invitation:

"I'd like to talk to you alone."

"Why be hasty? Sit down and share our tea."

The stranger squats unwillingly. He seems young, but his eyes are ageless. Set against the dark lining of his brows, they gleam like sapphires from Ormuz.

"I thank you. My name is Nadir."

"You do not belong to our city."

This is not a condemnation but the assertion of a fact.

"I come from a village by the sea. I was a sponge-fisher on my uncle's boat."

"There are no sponges here. Have you thought of hiring yourself out as an apprentice to earn your bread and make yourself useful? We cannot afford to feed those who contribute nothing."

Around them, the elders clap their hands on their thighs to show their approval. Nadir throws them a furious glance.

"I didn't wait for your advice to find work, muezzin. I have become a storyteller."

Marwan dips his head:

"You seem very young for such a serious trade . . . Are you content with retelling the fables peddled in fairs or do you try to raise men's hearts toward the Lord, as I do, by weaving your sentences within the framework of morality?"

"I have no other goal than the entertainment of those who listen to me. The time left to us is so meager that morality is among the wrecks stranded by the lake's ebb."

"You speak like an Infidel!"

"Why should I soften my words? Do you believe there is the slightest chance they will turn out to be mistaken?"

He twists to point with his hand at their silent audience.

"I envy your sheer disregard for facts. In a few years at most, the lake's vault will press down upon our heads. To survive, we'll hunch our shoulders. Then, we'll bend our knees, walk on all fours, crawl on our stomachs like the vilest beasts in order to lap up the last seconds of our lives from a shrinking pool. We will be forced to retrace in reverse the road traversed by our species: our ancestors crawled out of the sea, so in turn we will crawl until the bitter end. But you, you will no longer be there. In the twirling of your lives, you are content if you can sip your remaining hours, and cling to the illusion the world will endure without you, unchanged.

"Me, I'll disappear before the end of the span allotted me, like the rest of the Universe. Nothing will survive me."

"Do not speak such blasphemy, unbeliever! Allah is immortal."

"My turn to shrug. You just don't think of death as I do . . . Do you wish to hear one of my tales?

"Long ago, a God who ruled over the desert decided to become immortal. He gave life to a handful of sand grains sifted between his fingers and made them into an army of builders and warriors. Showing them the horizon, he said:

" 'Build around me an impassable wall, then another, and another yet. Surround me with a labyrinth whose secret nobody will know. When you complete one enclosure, post guards atop the rampart and close the doors, so that Death cannot reach me.'

"So it was done. The horizon, eclipsed by the high walls

of metal and stone, seemed to creep closer and closer. The God decided to cover every morning the perimeter of the enclosure which protected and imprisoned him, by counting the number of strides required, in order to measure the progress of the work.

"The first day, he counted seven thousand of them. The next day, as many. A week later, a month later, a year later, his count had not changed.

"Yet the workers labored unremittingly and new impregnable ramparts regularly enfolded the old ones. The angry God blasted down his creatures and raised sandstorms in order to create new ones. The work progressed faster, but the count of his strides went unchanged.

"The walls of the labyrinth now towered as high as the heavens. The sound of hammers and trowels rolled out day and night, like a rumble of thunder without end. Atop the ramparts, the braziers of the guards outshone the sun, yet the count of his strides was immutable.

"One night, the God lowered his gaze toward his shadow that stretched far in front of him and he marveled to see it so large. He turned to face it and said:

" 'Whence such immense size, shadow? Did my enemy Death make you wax thus to pit you against me?'

" 'You fed me yourself without realizing it, Lord, and I have grown while you diminished. Do not look further for the explanation of the mystery around you. Your workers have performed wonders, but they cannot build any faster than you destroy yourself.'

"The God raised his gaze and saw himself, minuscule at the feet of the rampart, mirrored in the burnished shields of the guards atop the wall. He sat down and cried, while his shadow wrapped around him like a leather tunic to protect him from the cold.

"Some say that the labyrinth has turned back into sand and that the wind has been trying for centuries to raze the walls of the sand dunes, never able to free their prisoner. Others tell of his attempts to escape from his prison, while workers both blind and deaf continue to expand the universe around him. All, however, agree that he is immortal . . ."

"I did not understand the meaning of your words, sponge-fisher. No doubt that you have forgotten how to speak to ordinary men, used as you were to descend into the depths of the sea . . . No matter! What do you hope to prove to your listeners?"

"Nothing, I told you I was not a moralist and my stories have no rules. If my deficient memory prevents from recalling a tale word for word, I invent another . . .

"Don't look at me like that, I am not to be pitied. My stories suffice to feed me and would easily allow me to support a wife."

"Who would willingly give a woman of his family to a man who only has his tongue to gain him wealth?"

"What, you, a holy man, you speak to me of wealth! The Lord himself blesses the poor!"

"Do not try to mislead me, demon, I know your kind. While I spread the word of the Prophet, peace be upon him, you distract my listeners with your tales. But my voice carries farther than yours, and Allah inspires me. He alone is worth listening to."

"Your sister Zorah does not agree with you."

The affront is such that faces around them clamp shut. To insult the muezzin is to attack the entire community. Nadir realizes this and attempts to backtrack, as if he had never uttered such dangerous words:

"I do not wish to quarrel with you, holy man, so please ask those who surround you. Many have sat around me to hear my stories. They can tell you that the money I receive is given freely. I cannot introduce you to my parents, since my village no longer exists, but my family was honorably known.

"All I want is not to be alone for the little time I have left. I would like to have Zorah as a wife. Will you give us your blessing?"

"When the time comes, I shall choose for her a proper husband, and not a beggar weaving lies for money. Your request is an insult, and I do not need to respond."

Nadir gets up slowly, his hands shaking with emotions he

does not bother containing. Yet, his voice is calm when he answers:

"You should have given thought to marrying your sister a long time ago, muezzin, but mayhap you did not want to do without such an obedient servant? Now, it is too late, for you and for her. I asked for her as the old ways would have me do, and you rebuffed me like a dog. Well, I shall come and take her without your permission in a few days, when the entire city will know of your shame and hers. Until then, your surats can keep bouncing from the lake's roof. Keep on praying since that is all you're good for!"

Marwan leaps to his feet, his staff upturned, but Nadir is already out of reach. He refrains from giving chase and sits back among the elders, aware for the first time that he has crossed without realizing it the boundary which kept him apart and that he is now one of them.

Coming through the doorway of his house, Marwan is struck by the sudden silence triggered by his arrival. He sits in his usual spot and the kitchen's homely noises resume, though not as loudly.

The muezzin fashioned himself an impassive mien on his way back. His voice, during the evening prayer, may have trembled almost imperceptibly, but that could have equally well been a deceptive echo bouncing from the lake's vault or a figment of his imagination. Now that he is cut off from the city by the thick walls of his private universe, he can stoke his anger, reckoning each sound of jostling dishes, each clang of pots and pans to be a new injury.

"Zorah, come here."

The water's whispering, the crystalline ring of a glass striking the stone basin, are her only answers. He gets up and approaches the curtain of rough beads which divides the main room from the kitchen, which he has never wished to enter. Standing in front of this invisible boundary between the world of men and the world of women, he raises his voice:

"Zorah, I'm speaking to you!"

"And I'm not listening to you, Mav. Why should I?"

The sisterly nickname rebounds on the muezzin's carapace of pride like an insect off a light bulb. If he knew how to interpret the nuances of the feminine language, he'd know that his sister is suing for peace. Since a child gave her a note from Nadir, she has thought of ways to stave off an irretrievable break, and to restore the delicate balance which allows her to draw strength from Marwan and Nadir together, since she needs both of them.

She has studied, and rejected, a number of solutions. Her instinct tells her that a direct confrontation must be avoided at all costs. She knows her brother too well and fears his sudden angry bursts, his mad fits which can make him go too far. If only her encounter with Nadir had gone otherwise . . .

The few sentences scribbled by her suitor unnerved her, as much for their cold and impersonal tone as for their import, as if Nadir had only been a witness to his confrontation with Marwan and had now lost interest in the consequences. A sudden insight compels her to wonder if the child she can now feel inside her was not Nadir's last attempt to escape the fate ordained for him by time's ebbing.

She has reread the note several times, seeking in vain somewhere between the lines the words of comfort she needs. Now, with only the flimsy curtain of the kitchen's door to protect her from Marwan, she thinks of Nadir who is already escaping her grasp, while her brother's anger overflows, battering her with words whose harshness she did not expect.

Zorah does not respond to his attacks. Her face, veiled by the curtain, is unreadable. She shakes her head with the unthinking grace of a doe when the accusations become too precise but no sound breaches the barrier of her lips, not even when her brother uses forbidden words, not even when he calls down upon her the vilest curses, knocking his staff on the tiles for emphasis.

Marwan's backlit silhouette, dressed in a flowing striped robe, flaps and sways grotesquely, growing less and less real to her as the phrases take on the ring of finality and tears blur Zorah's vision.

When he chases her from the house, with a final volley of insults, she lets loose a strangled wail before rushing from the kitchen, shoving her brother aside without giving him the time to change his mind and call her back.

Once in the street, she flees toward the dwelling occupied by Nadir on the city's edge, only a few blocks away from the temporal boundary. Her cheeks are streaked with tears. She does not know how her lover will receive her, but she is now reduced to this single option. Her universe, trapped between the lake's surface and her brother's barrage of curses, is now as narrow as a tomb.

Behind her, men turn, both shocked and attracted by the unveiled face they see for the first time. Tomorrow, the whole city will know of her shame. She will have to face much more than the curiosity of passers-by or the spite of the senior wives returning from the market. Tomorrow, and the next day, and the next . . . until their attention is diverted or time runs out, erasing even the record of her action from the memory of the universe.

Marwan hunts long and hard for the balm of sleep. After his sister's departure, he stayed for endless hours on his house's terrace, squatting as he watched the vaulting of the lake, crosshatched with waves. His anger had cooled, making way for a dizzying void, an undefined anguish whose source he could not pinpoint.

One day soon, he would have to visit the market to find a *saïs*, a servant to take care of the house and of himself. He would sit again among the elders and listen to them palaver, endlessly dissecting the affairs of the city like clockmakers looking for the grain of sand which might paralyze the fragile gearing of their tedious lives.

If life has continued, unchanged, it's largely because of them, the self-appointed guardians of everyday life, the preservers of tradition and customs. Nobody, until now, had challenged their authority, nobody before Nadir. Recalling that name rekindled Marwan's anger one last time. The sponge-fisher had desecrated everything sacred, including Allah's name. So why had Allah let life spring from that man's loins? Why was it written that his sister would be the victim of fate? The injustice puzzled the muezzin. Had he, in any way, offended the Lord while discharging his sacred duties, or is this an additional test of his faith? How did he deserve this?

For the first time, Marwan examined the night sky, seeking an answer. Among the catastrophe's survivors, it is commonly believed that each action, for good or evil, of the day is reflected in the lake's mirror, shaping ripples whose meaning is only clear to one person. For hours on end, Marwan looked for the reflection of his doubts and anxieties, searching his memory for personal symbols, forging his own keys and trying them one after the other in the locks to his mind.

The sky stayed silent. Previously, atop the minaret, his head brushing against the surface, he had felt himself come closer to the higher spheres of the Universe and be a part of its sacred Mystery. Tonight, the illusion vanished.

The spiral staircase, covered with signs already half-erased, suddenly seemed out of place to him, a vestige from the past lost in a world without a future, a ruin destined to crumble soon, whose absence would go unnoticed. In the same day, he had lost his sister and, what is more important, his faith . . .

Alone in the dark blanketing the terrace, he whispered one last prayer to Allah, imploring him to restore the wholeness of the world and of his soul. Then he went to lie on his bed, after rubbing his gums with his fingertips and rinsing his mouth with a sip of water.

When he finally goes to sleep, shortly before dawn, a nightmare invades his mind.

Along an endless lane, covered with earthenware tiles whose inscriptions have become illegible, a giant in metal armor advances. The horizon, above high walls, seemed to move ever closer, while remaining unreachable.

The muezzin, unable to escape, confronts the giant whose steps never falter, his tall shape hiding the sky. A gigantic foot is raised above him, drops down, pins him to the ground. Pain tears through his chest.

When he opens his eyes, Marwan is unable to know whether he has escaped the nightmare or if it's still pursuing him. His ribcage still hurts. Outside his room, the echoes of distant clanking are growing fainter, until he can hardly hear them.

He straightens, unthinkingly rakes his beard with his fingers. It was written that he would not get any sleep. Before rising, he kicks away the twisted ball of sweat-drenched blankets. The veins of his forehead still beat with the remembered terror.

He throws on a robe, then leans out the window to glance outside. The street appears to be deserted. Whatever the source of the noise, it is now too far to be heard, or perhaps it only existed in his mind. The muezzin finishes dressing and leaves, resolved to walk down all of the city's paths, hunting for his lost sleep.

On the shining canvas of the sky, the waves draw lazily their moving constellations, drawing randomly card after card from a new zodiac. The minaret, lost among them like a crooked finger, points nowhere in particular. Marwan's gaze is led along the white arrow, which was once straight and unbroken . . .

His steps, though he is not conscious of it, lead him back to the foot of the stairway he has so often climbed. He dimly hears again the metallic jangling which roused him from his sleep. He gazes upward. An ill-defined shape, not unlike the giant of his dream, is climbing the stairs above him, each step causing the armor encasing it to resonate like a gong.

The muezzin, turned to stone for an instant, leaps into the staircase, in pursuit of the stranger climbing toward the surface. Surely, it was him who awakened Marwan by walking under his window, unless a premonition warned him somebody was going to violate the tower's sanctity. His only hope is that no one will get the opportunity to notice that God's name did not withstand the passing away of time.

He accelerates to catch up with him. His sandals slap loudly the worn treads. Nearby, a window lights up, then another, and an unseen dog starts barking. Soon, the residents roused by the din will be out on the streets and a scandal will be unavoidable. Marwan slows down, just as the figure ahead of him picks up the pace.

A landing, and then another. Time is already thinner. Handling such heights, so close to the edge of the universe, requires some getting used to, but the stranger does not seem to be experiencing any difficulty, while Marwan is breathing faster and faster.

When he reaches the last landing still under time, the stranger pauses. The muezzin catches up a few seconds later and stops too, breathless.

The one in front of him is dressed in an antique diving suit made of rubber and copper. Lead-soled boots protect his feet and a belt of weights circles the waist. The tubing which connects to a chromed relief valve hangs upon the shoulders like a gorgon's mane, coiling like a snake whenever the person moves.

The head, inside the spherical helmet, behind a tarnished porthole, is invisible. Yet Marwan unhesitatingly finds the name of this absence.

"Zorah? Is that you?"

The question goes unanswered. Her brother understands that, beneath the cumbersome outfit, she is unable to hear him. He steps toward her, and she backs up toward the surface, knowing that Marwan cannot follow her.

He opens his arms to show his impotence, backs up and climbs down a few steps. She comes closer, almost close enough to touch him. Behind the porthole, the muezzin makes out the outline of her face, distorted by the scratches in the glass.

He could grapple with her, try to overmaster her, run the risk of falling down with her. As if she read his thoughts, she shakes her head and points to the vault arching above their heads. Her gesture disturbs the water and the lake's smooth mirror is momentarily marred by the eddies, but only for a moment.

She climbs the last few steps between her and the world above. The top of the diving-suit tears the surface. They exchange a long silent look, separated from each other by a barrier even more impassable than that erected by tradition, and then she starts again to climb with her heavy tread toward the summit. Marwan, petrified, has not moved a finger to call her back.

The first symptoms of time deprivation are already appearing. The diving suit she stole from her lover, after he mocked her and beat her, is losing the precious fluid through a thousand tiny cracks. The tears of time she sows splash on the earthenware tiles of the staircase and form rivulets along the steps. She raises her head to see the top of the minaret and understands she will never reach it.

Her fingers are as numb as a statue's, but they still manage to undo the lead-weighted belt and throw it over the edge. She watches it drop for an instant, before resuming her ascent to the next landing, where she stops again.

Her thoughts no longer torment her; time, as it escapes from her, washes her clean and carries away her memories. Life is leaking away, and all the pain too. She barely feels the presence of her unborn child stirring in her womb, confined to a closed world already too narrow for him.

Her hand rises and, with nary a qualm, unlocks the bindings of the suit. One move and she loses her helmet which bounces at her feet, now useless, before rolling to the edge and over . . .

The remainder of the suit spreads out like the petals of a flower at the feet of Zorah, whose pale flesh glows with an ever brightening light. Above the sleeping city, dazzling beams escape from a point near the minaret's tip, illuminating like a lighthouse the frozen cityscape which seems to revive in the process. The lake's surface congeals, glistening like mercury.

Slowly the body of Zorah cracks and breaks asunder, yielding to the unstoppable pressure from within. The first spring gushes forth, followed by a second, then by many others. The trickles of time soon become streams, then torrents, then cataracts.

Marwan, kneeling near the surface, his head in his hands, does not realize at first what is happening. When he lifts his eyes, alerted by the lake's intrusive murmur, the level has already increased by several steps and the flow continues to grow. A storm is raging above him, and the swelling flood races from landing to landing, engulfs the minaret, and overflows through the passes of the mountains on the horizon.

The muezzin howls the name of his sister and clambers up the remaining steps, but all he finds is a shredded time-suit forgotten on a landing, still glowing with a light that weakens and dies when he clutches it.

On the earthenware tiles of the stairs, the name of God has not come back.

The Battle of York

JAMES STODDARD

James Stoddard [www.sff.net/people/james-stoddard/JSWeb
site/Homex.html] lives in Lubbock, Texas, with his wife,
Kathryn, and their two children. He is an instructor in
music recording and engineering. He says on his website:
"My first short story, 'The Perfect Day,' appeared in Amazing Stories magazine around 1985, under the pseudonym of
James Turpin. Shortly thereafter, I stopped writing for about
seven years to pursue a career in music, and returned to my
word processor in the early 90s." He is the author of the
fantasy novels High House (1998), which won the Compton
Crook Award for Best First Novel and was nominated for a
Mythopoeic Fantasy Award, and False House (2000).

"The Battle of York" was published in Fantasy & Science
Fiction. It is a story in the tradition of Robert Nathan's classic, Digging the Weans (1956), in which a civilization in the
distant future attempts to interpret the surviving artifacts
and records of our era and gets it all wrong in an interesting
way. Here we have the mixed-up myth of the United States,
recovered and reconstructed 3000 years in the future, our
present as alternate anachronistic history. It is thick with
references to American history and popular culture and
almost a game to play (sort out the references, figure out the
allegory). Even if you don't get them all, you still feel smart,
and entertained.

T hree thousand years have elapsed since the passing of America. Though scholars have uncovered multitudes of valuable archaeological evidence, little written literature exists from that era. It is indeed unfortunate that books made of paper were replaced by magneto-optical disk storage by the middle of the twenty-first century. The worldwide magnetic field disaster of the twenty-second century did more than herald a new Dark Age—it erased the literature and history of the world, even as the accompanying geological disruptions obliterated cities and landmarks.

Fortunately, near the end of the twenty-seventh century, an unknown scholar passed through the American regions, collecting the stories and legends we now call the "Americana." Though we can expect little accuracy from a people dependent on electronic data storage rather than oral tradition, we believe there is always a grain of truth concealed within the tales. But to quote one of the figures from the Americana itself: "When the Legend becomes fact, print the Legend."

Young General Washington rode alone on his white stallion through the Sequoia Forest. His battle-axe, Valleyforge, hung glistening from the pommel of his saddle, the blood fresh-scrubbed from its edge. He had slain too many soldiers in the war against the Gauls and American Natives, and was glad to be going home.

I will never fight again, he thought, *but will return to the*

Mount of Vernon to become a surveyor and farmer. There was no pursuit more important to any country than to improve its agriculture and its breed of useful animals. How he longed for the simple cares of a husbandman.

He brooded on the horrors of war, his dead comrades, and the American Native maid, Pocahontas, whom he had loved. He loved her still, though she had betrayed him to the Gauls.

In his people's language his name, *General*, meant *pertaining in common to all*, and that was what he had become, a leader to the American tribes in Virginia. As a youth, an enchantment had been laid on him by the Wise Woman, Betsee Ross, the Star Weaver, that he could never tell a lie. Because of this, some called him "Honest Gen."

As the last rays of twilight turned the ancient American forest golden with dust and sent the shadows streaming east, he heard the cry of the hawk and the distant howls of wolves. He shivered uneasily. The sequoias rose all around, hundreds of feet tall, the trees the American Natives called the Silent Giants. His men had accompanied him through most of his journey, until he had chosen to shorten his trip by going through the woods. Even the bravest had refused to follow him then, for the forest was said to be haunted. At the time he had thought it just as well; he had wanted to be alone, to try to forget. He had intended to pass through the woods and into the safety of Virginia before nightfall, but weariness had overtaken both him and his mount, and in his brooding he had dawdled.

He dared ride no farther that night for fear of losing his way. Already shapes grew gray and indistinct. The howling of the wolves sounded nearer.

If I continue, I will lame Silver, he thought. He stroked the stallion's neck, then reined him to a stop. He dismounted, then led him forward a few paces, intending to make camp beneath one of the great trees. The shadows seemed to close around him.

The hoot of an owl overhead startled him. "My nerves are frayed," he said softly.

General removed Silver's bridle and saddle and let him go free. He was unconcerned about the stallion wandering off;

the horse was loyal as a hound. Silver nickered uneasily, as if he, too, distrusted the woods.

"Easy, boy," General murmured automatically. Though he preferred traveling unseen through the forest, he needed to start a fire to ward off the wolves. Picking up twigs and dead limbs, he soon had enough wood to last the night.

He knelt with flint and steel. Sparks flew and a tiny dribble of flame sprang up. Before he could fan it into a full fire, Silver nickered again.

General looked up, then stood, his hand to Valleyforge. A spectral green light haloed the enormous tree trunk. Washington crept around it and looked across the forest floor.

A man approached, a tall, inhumanly broad figure carrying a lantern that glowed with an unearthly luminance. Washington felt his mouth go dry; his heart pounded against his chest, for he thought he recognized the intruder. He wanted to hide, but there was nowhere to go if the Pilgrim sought him. He drew Valleyforge and held it close.

The figure paused a few feet from Washington. The lantern light spread at General's feet, turning the ground emerald and olive.

"General Washington," the figure said, his voice a deep drawl. "I am Waynejon. Some call me the Pilgrim."

"Have you come for me?" General asked. Despite his best effort, his voice trembled.

The Pilgrim rumbled a laugh. "I'm not death, if that's what you mean. I'm a man. I put my pants on one leg at a time."

Washington remained unconvinced. According to legend, the Pilgrim had died many times, but death could not keep him, for he was cursed to walk the Earth until the end of the age because of an ancient wrong. He stood a head taller than Washington, who was a tall man himself, and wore a square, black hat with a buckle at its front, a black cloak, and ebony riding chaps. A black eyepatch covered one eye and a rooster stood on his left shoulder. He carried an ancient blunderbuss.

"You look like you're getting ready to eat. If you'll share your fire, I have some salted beef in my pack."

General nodded, then finding his voice, tried to sound confident. "What brings you to the woods?"

"As a matter of fact, I've been looking for you."

"And then," Waynejon concluded, "the boys got the cattle to the railhead."

Washington laughed and sighed. The fire cackled warmly before the pair. They sat across from one another, the flames between them. In the last hour, General had lost most of his fear. "An excellent tale. Whatever happened to the lads?"

"They turned out to be good men, most of 'em. But they're all long gone to their reward on Boot Hill by now."

In the subsequent silence Washington found himself asking, "Why were you looking for me?"

"You get to the point. I like that."

The Pilgrim took a drink of coffee from a tin cup, then gestured with it toward the woods. "This country, this new land, it's wild, untamed. It could be a great nation, different from any other, a place where people could come from all over the world. A place of freedom."

"We all want that. It's why my forefathers came."

"Mine did the same. They fled the dark realm of the Old World to escape the tyrants. But it's not enough, General. The people aren't free."

"We've driven the Gauls back to France."

"But you didn't get Prince Louis."

Washington shrugged. "He escaped to Mexico. No American can cross the Rio Grande and live. An enchantment prevents it."

"He's done more than escape. He's made alliance with the Huns."

Washington drew a deep breath. This was bad news. The Huns, led by their leader, Hitler, the Wolf Prince, were a constant threat, raiding the coasts on their dragon-headed ships, striking and then fleeing. Was there never an end to peril?

"And it's not just Louis and Hitler," Waynejon said. "There's a powerful wizard living in the dark regions of the Canadian north, whose heart is cold as the bitter winds that blow there. The Mounties can't stop him because he's con-jured a giant from the Old World, tall as a mountain. They're climbing down the steep cliffs from the ice fields with their armies, preparing to march to York. The Huns, whose long-ships wait outside York Harbor, have promised the wizard great rewards if he helps them conquer America. The Gauls are reforming along the Rio Grande. We're in danger, Gen-eral."

"What can we do?"

"Only the Words of Power in the iron box on Mount Rushmore can stop the giant. The titan has no strength against them."

"Mount Rushmore!" A chill ran along Washington's spine. "None have ever gone there and returned."

"It doesn't matter what others have done, General. I'm asking you."

"It was not my intention to seek further adventures."

"You gained a reputation in your battles against the Gauls."

"I heard bullets whistle, and believe me, there is some-thing charming in the sound."

Waynejon laughed. "Sarcasm doesn't suit you, General."

"I meant none. By the miraculous care of Providence, I was protected beyond all human expectation, for I had four bullets through my coat and two horses shot under me, yet escaped unhurt. It was an exhilarating experience, but one I have little desire to repeat." He shook his head. "I fear you have chosen the wrong man."

"How do you figure?"

Washington hesitated, not wanting to say the words. "My men love me, but though we seem to return from the war in triumph, it isn't true, at least not for me. I was the one who began the war against Gaul, when I urged the Virginian gov-ernor, Dimwiddie, to build Fort Necessity at the joining of the Ohio and Allegheny rivers. Had we not confronted the Gauls there, the colonies might have been spared much bloodshed. There should have been another way.

"Under my leadership, we struck out to attack Fort Duquesne. Though I knew better, out of my own vanity, we went like soldiers on parade, for I thought our movements were unknown. In my pride I had told our plans to . . . someone I cared for deeply . . . someone who betrayed us. We were unexpectedly attacked by three thousand Gauls and American Natives, and though our numbers were nearly thrice their own, my men were struck with such a deadly panic that nothing but confusion and disobedience of orders prevailed among them. We broke and ran as sheep before the hounds. If Braggart had not reinforced us at the end, the final battle would have been lost. Braggart himself, a mighty commander, was wounded behind the shoulder and into the breast. He died three days after.

"No, Pilgrim. I, a failure in all I have undertaken, am not the man to perform this deed. You must place your trust elsewhere."

Waynejon took a long sip of coffee. "Seems to me that's the thing about this country, General. It's a land of second chances. Someone must go or America is lost."

Washington, who had ducked his head in shame, looked up into the Pilgrim's steady eyes, and for a long moment they held each other's gaze. Finally, General said, "If I make the attempt, who will help me?"

"Near the slopes of Rushmore waits the Iron Hewer. Go to him. He will show you the way."

Washington stared into the fire and sighed. War had found him again and he could not refuse. Human happiness and moral duty were inseparably connected. "I suppose it is easier to prevent an evil than to rectify mistakes," he said. "I will set out tomorrow morning."

"That's good. That's mighty fine." Waynejon set his tin cup down. "I have to be on my way. Thanks for the grub."

Without another word, the Pilgrim rose and strode into the woods, his broad back disappearing into the shadows. Washington shivered, feeling very much alone.

For seven days General rode through the Sequoia Forest, and on the eighth reached the wheat-covered plains of Kansas. The whole Earth shook with the pounding hooves of herds of buffalo pursued by the valiant Comanches, who looked dreadful in their war paint. To escape their notice—for they had no love of the white man—Washington hid himself among the amber waves of grain.

At night, storm clouds built in the south and swept over the plains, the lightning tearing at the sky, the tumult of the thunder reminding Washington that should he survive Rushmore, he would have to face the wizard and his giant.

He crossed the country of Mount Ana, a stark land, all sky and earth, and came in the evening to the banks of the Little Bighorn, where sat a rider on a white horse caparisoned in midnight blue. The rider, too, who had a golden mustache and penetrating blue eyes, wore blue and gold, with a deep blue cape. His curling hair, falling down to the middle of his back, shone like ripe wheat in the Sun. But Washington did not believe fine clothes necessarily made for fine men, any more than fine feathers made fine birds.

"Hurrah, good sir," the stranger called. "What brings you to the banks of the Bighorn?"

"I am Washington, who cannot tell a lie, a son of Virginia. I seek the Iron Hewer on the slopes of Rushmore."

"Then you seek death," the stranger replied. "I am Custard, named for the creamy white of my skin and my golden hair. I am called Arm Strong for my might, Lord of Horsemen, Captain of the Seventh Cavalry."

Washington quickly perceived this Custard had no lack of vanity, though he was indeed a mighty warrior. But General said, "I have never been to Rushmore before. Perhaps, if you know the way?"

"Why do you want to go there?"

"I seek the Words of Power to defeat the Wizard of Canada."

Custard gave Washington a long look before replying. "I will take you at least part of the journey, though I cannot stay long. I have unfinished business here. The Sioux have risen against me."

Washington nodded. "I thank you for your kindness."

Together the two set off toward Rushmore. Along the way, Arm Strong told tales of his many deeds. Though he listened politely, Washington found such boasting distasteful, for it had always been his motto to show his intentions through his works rather than his expressions.

"And someday," Custard said, "I will be the President of all this country, from east to west, and men everywhere will praise my name."

"I am unfamiliar with the word, *president*," Washington said.

"Like a king, but even greater, presiding as judge over the land."

"Perhaps," Washington said, thoughtfully, "if the Huns and Gauls can be driven back. But even a president should answer to the people."

"The people should answer to their liege lord, not the other way around."

"That is the old way, the manner of kings and queens," Washington said, as he stared out at the endless horizon. "Like all the dark necromancy of the Old World, it should best be forgotten. It will not be like that here. The purpose of all government, as best promoted by the practice of virtuous policies, ought to be the aggregate happiness of society. As the Pilgrim told me, America should be a place where everyone has a voice."

"You have seen the Pilgrim?" Custard asked.

"Yes. He was the one who sent me."

Arm Strong fell silent then, in awe of General Washington, and dared brag no more of his own accomplishments.

After two days' travel they reached the Black Hills of Dakota, where they rode through the gloom of a perpetual twilight, for the Sun never shone there and eternal shadows lay across that country.

As they struggled through the gloom, Washington spied a great eagle watching them from the back of the carcass of a bull buffalo, which the bird had apparently slain. As the travelers passed, General gave a respectful bow from his saddle, calling out, "Greetings, Master of the Air. I see you will have a fine feast." But the eagle only watched the men with unwinking eyes.

That evening, they came to a valley ringed in jutting peaks, and had traveled only a short distance when a cold voice called down to them from the heights. "Who dares trespass on the aeries of the eagles?"

High overhead, its talons clinging to the tallest peaks, stood an eagle twice the size of a stallion.

"I am Washington," General said, "with my companion Arm Strong, seeking passage to the Mount of Rushmore."

"This day we will surely break your bones," the eagle screeched, "for I am E. Perilous Union, mother of the eagles who make their homes both in the Peaks of Usps and the Mountains of the Moon."

Other, smaller eagles, lurking on the lesser crags encircling the travelers, raised their voices in reply.

"Hear us, I beg you," General called, in as brave a tone as he could muster. "Spare us, not for ourselves, but for the sake of our mission, for we are on a journey for the freedom of our countrymen."

A ruffling of wings passed around the heights.

"Freedom!" E. Perilous cried. "Freedom! You speak the sacred word of the eagles. What is the meaning?"

"It is a word sacred to us as well," Washington replied.

"Mother," another eagle called across the heights. "Let us spare these men who speak of Freedom, for when I met them on the plains, the pale-faced one bowed and addressed me with respect."

"Is this so?" E. Perilous Union asked. "Tell us then, children of men, the purpose of your journey."

Washington did so, and when he was done, E. Perilous said, "We have heard of this evil wizard and despise his ways. Because my son, Apollo Leven asks it, I will permit your passage. More, in the sacred name of Freedom, I will send him with you as a guide."

Washington and Custard thanked the mother of the eagles, and Apollo Leven lifted himself off the heights to accompany them.

As they continued through the Black Hills, wolves and evil spirits tried to destroy them, and more than once they battled for their lives, but Washington, his face grim and terrible to behold, fought with his great axe, Valleyforge, that shone silver in the darkness; and Arm Strong, wielding a golden blade, proved dreadful in combat. Apollo Leven strove beside them as well, and his terrible beak and talons slew many a foe.

The eagle led them true, and they finally saw Mount Rushmore looming in the distance, awful and majestic, a living monster shaped like a mountain with four heads. The heads were craggy and ill-formed, and shifted from side to side, guarding against danger.

"The Iron Hewer lives at the base of Rushmore," Arm Strong said, "where the behemoth cannot reach him."

They came by twilight to a house made of iron. As they approached, a figure stepped out dressed in simple gray garments and bearing no arms. Around his otherwise bald head he wore a circlet with five silver stars that glistened in the dusk.

Washington expected to be challenged, but the man raised his hand in salute and gave a slow smile. "Welcome, strangers, and be at ease. I am Eisenhower Iron Hewer, but my friends call me Ike."

Washington found he liked Ike immediately, and the two travelers dismounted and introduced themselves. When General told Eisenhower why he had come, the Old Commander shrugged. "Though I have never liked war, I won't shirk from a fight, not if Waynejon sent you."

From out of his larder, Eisenhower prepared a fine meal, though where he got his victuals Washington could not guess. Afterward, full and content, they sat before the fireplace, drinking hot coffee and smoking tobacco from wooden pipes, listening to the wind whistling around the iron eaves, while Apollo stood in a corner, his eyes reflecting golden in the flames.

"There is only one way to approach the creature," Ike said. "All its heads face south, except for the fourth one, which looks to the north. But that head is blind in one eye. If we're careful, we can creep up the northwestern slope. The box containing the Words of Power is hidden in a cave below the monster's chins. We'll know if it sees us, for its faces, which normally resemble rough stone, always take on the features of its victims."

"Can the monster be slain?" Custard asked.

"He can," Eisenhower replied. "A single blow to the mountain's heart can kill the beast, if the warrior who delivers it is pure of soul."

"Who knows if such a man is among us?" Washington asked.

"I would like to try my hand at it," Custard said, "if the chance arises."

"Such a task is not for me," Eisenhower said. "I am unworthy, for I've sent too many men to their deaths."

"Is that why you live here alone?" Custard asked. "A warrior such as yourself would be highly honored in York."

"I live here to serve and have had all the honors I need. I have led good men."

"You display great humility," Washington said.

"Humility must always be the portion of any man who receives acclaim earned in the blood of his followers and the sacrifices of his friends."

"I have not fought for such, sir," Custard said, "but for the glory of combat. You give me much to consider. Still I would like to set my good right arm against the monster."

"The Pilgrim sent me here many years ago, to act as a guide. There is a prophecy that one day a man will destroy the creature and use the Words of Power to preserve the land. I hope you are that one, but many have scaled those slopes and none have lived to tell of it."

"These are strange times," Washington said, "filled with magic."

"True," Ike replied, sagely, "but things are more like they are now than they have ever been before."

Washington nodded his head and stared into the fire. It was good to befriend a man of Ike's wisdom.

The three companions rose with the morning light. They left their horses in Eisenhower's iron stables and went on foot, angling toward the west, while Apollo wheeled away to watch from a distance, lest his presence alert the four faces. If the monster saw them, it gave no sign. By midday they reached a region strewn with boulders, where they were near enough to see the heads closely. Washington gaped up at them. Three faced toward the men, one away. They were large as houses, and all looked identical, with gray eyes, weather-beaten noses, and thin lines for mouths. Their guttural voices rose and fell, as they murmured among themselves in an ancient tongue.

The travelers headed north until they came to a point behind the mount, where only the easternmost face kept watch, its left eye staring vacantly down the slope.

"We begin the assault here, just before sundown," Eisenhower said.

"Shouldn't we wait until dark?" Arm Strong asked.

"No. They see as well at night as in the day, but at twilight the setting Sun will be in their eyes."

For three restless hours the companions waited for sunset, saying little, thinking of the coming encounter. Custard stared fixedly at the mount.

"Ike," Arm Strong finally said, "exactly where would the killing blow have to be struck? I cannot rightly ascertain the location of the beast's heart."

Eisenhower pointed. "There, just between the two central heads. Front or back makes no difference."

"And the Words of Power?" Washington asked.

"A few yards farther down in a narrow cave. It's hard to see from here."

"You have guided us well," Washington said. "You need not accompany us."

"I don't have to, but I will. I've always stood with those who make the attempt."

When the Sun was still three finger widths above the horizon, Eisenhower ordered the travelers to move out. They crept between the boulders, keeping always to the blind side of the head, and were soon scrambling up the mountain slope. Pine trees provided concealment until they were two-thirds of the way up, but after that the mount lay barren.

Washington's heart pounded in his chest as he climbed, trying not to look up at the terrible face above him. At first he could not see the cave, but then he spied it, a narrow opening half-covered by an overhanging shelf. If they could reach it, the head would not be able to see them at all.

Abruptly, the terrible visage turned, with the sound of rock scraping on stone, and the three flattened themselves against the boulders, scarcely daring to breathe. For a moment the good eye swept along the slope, but the sunlight blinded it, making it squint and look away. The men kept climbing.

Custard was the first to reach the cave, and he helped the others under the protection of the ledge. They clapped one another on the back and turned toward the opening.

It was little more than a niche in the rocks, and Washington searched only a short while before finding the iron box set in a recess. It proved neither long nor heavy, and he drew it out easily and opened the lid, which needed no lock with such a terrible monster guarding it. Within lay a brown parchment.

"The Words of Power," Washington whispered. He placed the scroll within his breast pocket and slipped the box back into its place.

"Have any ever come this far before?" Custard asked softly.

"Only two," Ike said. "Their bones are strewn across the slope."

Shuddering at Eisenhower's words, Washington told the Old Commander to lead them back down.

They were nearly to the tree line again before Washington realized Custard was not behind him. He turned to discover Arm Strong ascending the mount. General clutched Eisenhower's arm and pointed to their comrade.

"That vainglorious fool!" Eisenhower hissed.

Reaching the region above the monster's heart, Custard raised his sword high above his head, shouting, "Die, beast, in the name of Arm Strong, Captain of the Seventh Cavalry!"

He looked magnificent at that moment, his cape billowing, his golden hair sweeping back behind his head, the last rays of the Sun glinting on his blade. With all his power, he thrust downward.

The sword snapped beneath the weight of the blow, leaving Custard gaping at it in astonishment.

A scraping noise filled the heavens as all four of the monster's heads swiveled toward the captain. General gasped, for the faces had transformed into the features of Custard, Washington, and Eisenhower. Only the head with the blind eye remained unchanged.

The air filled with roaring as the heads screamed their rage. The whole mount trembled as vast arms rose from either side, reaching toward Custard.

"Let's go!" Eisenhower ordered. "He won't make it."

"No," Washington cried, handing Ike the parchment. "Take it and flee!"

General did not hear Eisenhower's reply; he was already sprinting toward Custard, Valleyforge at the ready. Though it had taken several minutes to creep down the mount, he ascended in seconds and was beside Arm Strong as the giant arms groped toward both of them. Washington saw his own face, filled with hatred, glowering down upon him.

Do I really look like that? he thought. *My nose seems so large.*

At that moment Apollo Leven streaked from the sky to harrow the faces with his talons. But the action bought the men only a moment before the rocks erupted around them, lifting them off the ground and sending them sprawling down the incline. Custard's expression was wild, but he held a knife in his hand as he rolled to his feet. Washington scrambled back toward the mountain's heart, axe upraised, staring straight into his own seething eyes.

The mount rippled beneath him, but as he fell he brought his axe down on his target with all his strength. He expected nothing but the destruction of his weapon, followed by his own death, but Valleyforge cut easily through the rock.

The whole mount screamed, a deafening blast. Blood rilled from the wound, covering General in ichor. He rolled on his back and saw the faces above him, including his own, writhing in their death struggles. He watched himself expire, the light leaving the eyes, the head lolling downward.

The mountain shuddered and sank. The four dead faces stared across the plain.

For a moment, Washington could hear nothing, but finally Custard's voice came to him, as the captain helped him up. "You have shamed me, sir, and saved my life. I am in your debt forever."

Eisenhower reached them a moment later and fell immediately to his knees before Washington. "You are the one," Ike cried, taking the circlet of five stars from his forehead and casting it at Washington's feet. "The one who was to come. You have ended my vigil. Accept my service. Wherever you go, I will go also, and will serve you until my death."

"I, too, will follow you," Custard said, though he did not kneel. "Accept my service as well, General."

Scarcely understanding their words, Washington gaped up at his defeated foe. "But how?" he exclaimed. "How could a failure such as I be named worthy to destroy the beast when Arm Strong could not?"

Apollo glided to a landing and placed his large head under General's hand. "Do not question the turn of events, Washington Paleface, but accept the fealty of these men, and mine as well, for I, too would follow you."

Still overwhelmed, Washington laid his hands on the shoulders of the two men. "I do not understand, nor know where this will lead, but I cannot refuse the service of such brave warriors, nor of this great eagle. Now rise. We have a giant to kill."

"Another?" Ike asked.

They spent the night in Eisenhower's house, where Washington cleaned the blood from himself and his garments. In the morning they left Rushmore far behind, and the four dead heads gaped at them to the edge of the horizon.

They rode once more across the darkness of the Black Hills, and as they went Eisenhower asked, "General, why did you go back for Custard? You had the scroll. If you and I had died, there would have been no one to stop the wizard."

"I could not leave him behind."

"If a commander thinks expending ten thousand lives will save twenty thousand later, it is up to him to do it."

"Custard was not ten thousand, but one," Washington said. "And though you have a point, I labor to keep alive in my breast that little spark of celestial fire called Conscience. I could not desert him and live with myself."

They passed back into Mount Ana, where Custard seemed to grow increasingly nervous. At last they came once more to the banks of the Bighorn River, where they topped a hill and found a giant American Native standing before them. Behind him sat a creature with the head of a stallion whose eyes were lit with madness and another with the head of a bull.

"I am Bitter Gall," the native said. "The appointed time is come." He raised his arms and hundreds of warriors suddenly appeared over the hills, dressed in feathers and skins, war-paint covering their fierce faces.

Sweat broke across Arm Strong's brow, but he said nothing.

"What do you want?" Washington asked.

"Your people have sinned and there must be death," the sitting bull said.

"I have done it!" Arm Strong burst forth. "I am not what you think me, General. I admit it, now. I have shed the blood of children. I spoke before of unfinished business. Long ago, it was prophesied that I would meet my death by the banks of the Little Bighorn. I hoped to redeem myself in the slaying of Rushmore, but I failed there, too."

"Only one life is required," the crazed horse said. "One of you three. But none shall pass until the deed is done."

"I have accepted the fealty of this man," Washington said, "and I cannot tell a lie. I am responsible for him. I will accept the punishment in his stead."

For a moment Arm Strong's eyes became crafty. But he looked at Washington and shook his head. "No, General. I have been a villain, but you returned for me on Mount Rushmore when I would not have done the same for you. You must live to fight the wizard. My fate is sealed. You have shown me the way to restore my honor, and I will go with the Sun shining on my face."

Custard bowed low to Washington, then strode down the hill toward Bitter Gall, passing out of the story and into history. But Washington wondered if someday, he too, would have to pay for the deaths of so many of his men in the battle of Fort Duquesne.

Washington and Eisenhower, grieving at Custard's loss, made their way through the Sequoia Forest, where they had many adventures. At last they came to York, a city of magnificent spires. Others heard tell of Washington's heroism on Mount Rushmore, and warriors came to him offering him their service, so that he gathered a group of America's finest around him. Of these, Lafayette DeGaul was one of the greatest. Though a Gaul, he had vowed to follow Washington when General had saved his life many years before, and had been with him through the Gaul and American Native War.

"Mon General," Lafayette said, "it is good to see your face. The wizard, accompanied by his giant, approaches the city and is encamped beyond the banks of the Mighty Delaware. Those sent to stop it have been smashed to bits. I was just preparing to go myself, to die for the cause of freedom."

DeGaul was a wild-eyed man, with a mustache and plumed hat. Until he met Washington, he had been a member of the famous Musketeers, who had fought against the powers of darkness and evil in the Old World.

Washington assembled his company, which had grown to more than five hundred men, just inside the gates of York. As he looked upon them, despair ran through him, for they were poorly armored and had few supplies, the Hun's blockade of the harbor preventing needed goods from entering the city. Despite his reservations, he drew a deep breath and addressed them briefly, explaining the situation.

He ended with: "The time is now near at hand which must

determine whether Americans are to be Freemen or Slaves. The fate of untold millions will depend, under God, on the courage and conduct of this army. Our cruel and unrelenting enemy leaves us no choice but a brave resistance or the most abject submission; this is all we can expect. We have, therefore, to resolve to conquer or die."

The men gave a ragged cheer while Apollo Leven wheeled and cried overhead.

Knowing how few warriors he had, Washington ordered a special surprise in the form of large, mysterious crates loaded onto the supply wagons.

As they rode out through the gates of York toward the Canadian Ice Fields, a crowd assembled to watch them go, young women pinning flowers and kisses on the warriors. Washington was approached by one of the most beautiful ladies he had ever seen, with pouting lips and eyes that flashed like fireworks. Her dark hair flared long and wild over a necklace hung with wooden teeth, suspended over a dress of forest green. She handed him a red, white, and blue standard covered with thirteen stars and stripes.

"Take this, General," she said, "and fight for York. The Star Weaver herself has enchanted it, washing it in the tears she sheds for those who die beneath the titan's heels. Tie it to your axe-handle in your moment of need, and its magic will give your blade power."

He reached down from the heights of Silver's back to take the cloth, and for a moment their hands and eyes met. "What is your name?" he asked.

"Martha Custis."

"I thank you for this," Washington said.

She smiled and watched him ride away.

"She is a beauty, that one," Lafayette said.

"There is no time for such things," Washington replied, but his hand felt warm where she had touched it, and he raised the standard high.

For three days the company traveled north, and by the second afternoon icy winds began to blow. Snow flurried by evening, and the warriors soon rode through banks of white.

It was bitterly cold, and Washington's men lacked sufficient clothing.

By midafternoon the company reached the edge of a valley, where ran the Mighty Delaware River. In the vale's center stood the giant, Britannia the Great, hundreds of feet tall, an enormous creature with the face of a woman, wearing a crown and carrying a heavy mace that it used to pound the earth. Wherever it walked or struck, it flattened houses, fields and living things, a brutality that came to be known as the Stamp Act. The wizard stood upon the titan's shoulders and an army of ten thousand red-clad warriors followed behind.

"How can we face them?" Lafayette asked.

"I have a plan," General said. "But the Words of Power will not work unless the monster hears them, so I must be very close. We will wait until nightfall."

The snow fell harder as evening progressed. The men carried half-shrouded lanterns, but it was still difficult to see through the storm. Everyone shivered with the cold, but Washington led them to the banks of the Delaware, accompanied by the wagon filled with the mysterious crates. They found boats upon the shore, left there at Washington's request by his American Native friend, Massasoit. In the dead of night, scarcely able to find their way, the company crossed the torrent of the Mighty Delaware, Washington standing upright, holding the red, white, and blue banner before him. He shivered from more than the cold, knowing that if the wizard or Britannia discovered them upon the waters, they would be doomed.

After a long hour, they reached the farther shore. Washington divided the men into three sections, under the command of Eisenhower Iron Hewer, Stonewall Jackson, and Benedict Arnold, three of his greatest warriors. Giving them their orders, General turned to Lafayette. "The rest is up to us, I fear. Come with me." Washington took the banner Martha Custis had given him and tucked it beneath his cloak.

Together, the two comrades crept toward the titan, whose gigantic form blocked the stars. They slipped between the sentries, then waited until moonrise. As the first rays lit the land, Lafayette called in a loud voice just outside the Wizard Cornwallis's tent. "Come out, great magician, for we have seen your might and know we have no chance against you. Come and accept our surrender."

The sentries around Cornwallis's camp leapt to their feet, but Lafayette drew his bow and covered them. "Stand back, my friends. We surrender to Cornwallis alone." As the guards hesitated, the wizard appeared at the tent door, a dazzling lantern in his hand. Lafayette lowered his weapon.

The wizard wore a bulky red robe and a white, pointed hood, which allowed only his dark eyes to show. His voice was grating as he spoke. "Who dares interrupt the slumber of Cornwallis, Grand Wizard of the Empire?"

"It is I, Lafayette DeGaul, with the great General Washington, who asks you to accept his surrender."

The giant, Britannia, gave a low rumble and raised its mace, but Cornwallis bid it stay its hand.

"Why do you come slinking to me in darkness?" Cornwallis demanded.

"We came as quickly as we could, to end the bloodshed, for who knows what this behemoth of yours will do?" Lafayette replied.

Cornwallis laughed. "I almost believe it. How like your people, the wretched refuse of the Old World, vermin sent to pollute these fair shores, fit to be nothing but slaves. When York is overthrown, I will show you how such should be treated."

"We are willing to do as you say," Lafayette said through gritted teeth. "Only accept our surrender."

"I have heard of you, Washington. It is said you cannot tell a lie. Tell me then, commander, is that truly why you have come? I will believe it from your lips."

Washington dared not answer, knowing the truth would spring unbidden from his mouth.

"I thought so," Cornwallis said, signaling to the giant.

"Scatter!" Washington ordered.

The Americans moved just in time to avoid a shattering blow, as Britannia brought its mace down with all its force.

The impact tossed Washington off his feet, but even before he hit the ground he was unrolling the scroll containing the Words of Power, for this had all been part of his plan, to bring the giant close to the earth in striking. On landing, Washington instantly sprang up and began reading in a mighty voice.

At the first word, everything seemed to freeze in place, as if time had stopped. Britannia remained immobile as Washington spoke:

We hold these truths to be self-evident, that all men are created equal, that they are endowed by their Creator with certain unalienable rights, that among these are Life, Liberty, and the Pursuit of Happiness. That to secure these rights. . . .

On and on Washington read, his voice growing stronger with the reading, his delight rising as he saw the wizard and the giant both helpless against the words. He raised his arms as he ended: *And for the support of this Declaration, with a firm reliance on the Protection of Divine Providence, we mutually pledge to each other*

our Lives,
our Fortunes,
and our sacred Honor.

The moment General finished, Cornwallis fell to his knees. When he tried to rise, Lafayette, with the speed of thought, raised his bow and placed an arrow through the wizard's evil heart.

"Liberty, Equality, Fraternity!" cried Lafayette.

Britannia gave a terrible scream, for the Words of Power began to turn its feet to stone. With a snarl, it fled toward the south, stomping away on increasingly clumsy members.

A roar rose from the valley's edge as hundreds of fireworks, the contents of the mysterious crates, were released at once. The sky erupted in red, white, and blue flares as Eisenhower, Arnold, and Jackson led the Americans into the valley toward the Red Army, which was milling in confusion, stunned at being attacked from a direction they thought safe.

"The giant!" Washington cried. "It heads toward York."

Washington and Lafayette captured two of their enemies' horses and sped after the titan, but clearly the mounts could not keep up. As soon as they reached their camp, Washington leapt off his steed and onto Silver, who stood waiting for his master, impatiently pawing the earth.

"Go on!" Lafayette shouted to Washington. "Go on, mon General! I will catch up."

Faster than the wind Silver ran, while Washington kept his eyes upon the giant. But when he reached the banks of the Mighty Delaware, General found the titan had already crossed. He nearly despaired at that moment, until Apollo Leven streaked out of the sky and landed before him.

"You must ride upon my back," the eagle screeched.

Still bearing the banner Martha Custis had given him, Washington climbed in front of Apollo Leven's wings. The eagle took a single bound and streaked over the great river.

Yet fast as they were, the monster strode far ahead. It steadily approached the gates of York, dwarfing the city's gleaming spires. Washington was still some distance behind it as it raised its mace, preparing to sweep the city away.

In desperation, General lifted Valleyforge and tied the banner to its pommel. As he let it fly, the weapon streaked toward the giant, the flag streaming behind, and as it flew it grew, powered by the flag's enchantment. It struck Britannia full in the back, and the monster writhed away, stumbling as it went, its massive feet missing the gates of York.

In its frenzy, it thrashed into the water. Most of its lower body was stone, and it moved with awkward, hesitant jerks. Crossing the bay, it pulled itself onto a massive rock rising out of the harbor. By the time it reached the top, its waist had turned to stone, leaving it unable to move its legs. Gradually the effect crept up its body. It raised its enormous mace in defiance and turned its face toward the sea, looking for its home across the waters.

Washington's axe, returned to its former size, fell from the giant's back and clattered down the rocks.

With the giant and the wizard destroyed, the Red Army, thinking the fireworks the beginning of an enormous assault, fled in terror. Washington returned to his men and led them back into the city in triumph, the whole company singing *When General comes marching home again*. Washington was declared a great hero and some wanted to make him king, but he refused, remembering Custard's words of a new office of *president*.

He recalled what the Pilgrim had said as well, and saw that America was indeed a land of second chances.

The Gauls retreated from Mexico and Hitler drew his boats back across the sea. But though Washington searched through all of York for many weeks, he found no sign of Martha Custis, nor anyone who knew her. However, he did find his axe with the flag still tied to its pommel, on the shores of the rock where the giant stood.

Afterward, a great Convention was held in honor of Washington's victory. A tremendous plan was conceived to build an enormous door, gilded with gold, across York harbor, to prevent the Huns from ever attacking again.

There was talk of tearing down the stone titan, but Lafayette had the last word. "Let it rather be a symbol, this vanquished foe. And we will call it Lady Liberty, for with its defeat we have won our freedom."

Being a poet as well as a warrior, in mockery of the words the wizard had spoken, Lafayette etched the following lines upon the base of the rock where the giant stood:

Give me your tired, your poor,
Your huddled masses yearning to breathe free
The wretched refuse of your teeming shore
Send these, the homeless, tempest-tossed to me
I lift my lamp beside the golden door!

The Convention ordered a flame lit atop the statue's mace, that became a torch burning across the waters, so bright it could be seen from the shores of the Old World. And when the kings and emperors of that shadowy realm looked upon it, they trembled.

Loosestrife

LIZ WILLIAMS

Liz Williams [www.arkady.btinternet.co.uk/] lives in Brighton, England. She has a Ph.D. in philosophy of science from Cambridge, and her anti-career ranges from reading tarot cards on Brighton pier to teaching in Central Asia. She has been publishing fantasy and science fiction in Asimov's, Interzone, Realms of Fantasy, *and* The Third Alternative, *among others, since the turn of the century, and was co-editor of the anthology* Fabulous Brighton. *In an SF Site interview, she said: "there are some excellent new people writing in the field [in the UK] at the moment—China [Miéville], Justina [Robson], Neal Asher, John Meaney—and I would like to be regarded as being in that stable." Her novels are* The Ghost Sister, *a* New York Times *Notable Book of 2001—a rare accomplishment for a paperback original;* Empire of Bones *(2002), nominated, as was the first, for the Philip K. Dick Award 2003;* The Poison Master *(2002);* Nine Layers of Sky *(2003); and* Banner of Souls *(2004). Her first collection,* The Banquet of the Lords of Night, *is out in 2005.*

"Loosestrife" was published in Interzone, *the best UK SF magazine, which underwent a transformation and change of owner and editor in 2004. It is set in a post-global-warming, post-catastrophe London. The protagonist is a retarded girl raised in a single room by an insane mother. She now lives alone in a condemned building with a baby, whom she leaves alone sometimes to go out and forage. But things are not what they seem.*

She knew that there was something wrong with her baby, because Ellie's eyes did not follow her as she moved about the room and she had once been told that this was important. Aud crouched over the baby, passing a hand across Ellie's face.

"Ellie? What's wrong?"

This time, the baby's eyes twitched to follow the passage of her hand and Aud breathed a sigh of relief. Nothing wrong, after all, and probably she was just being silly, but she had been told so often that she did not understand things that once she had taken a fact into her head she clung to it. She thought she understood the baby a little better now and as long as it remained just Ellie and herself, no one else, she thought she could cope. Ellie was doing fine, and if she still seemed to eat so little when Aud gave her the bottle, at least she appeared healthy and well. Aud would surely know if a change occurred; she watched Ellie for hours, noticing every movement, every sound.

Picking Ellie up, Aud stepped carefully over the piles of broken plaster and carried her out onto the little concrete balcony.

"Look," she said. "You can see Big Ben from here. See it? See the big clock? And there's the Houses of Parliament, where all the rich people go." She thought that the distant clock face read ten to eight, or perhaps it was twenty to ten. She could never remember which hand meant which, no matter how often she had been told, and it was so easy to lose track of the time. But Ellie, lying quietly in her arms, would never question her; never ask uncomfortable things like "what time is it?" and "what does that say?" and "what is Parliament?" Maybe when Ellie grew up she would be able to answer these things on her own.

"And then you'll be a help to me, won't you?" Aud said. She and Ellie watched as one of the boats glided down the Thames, just above the water like a big wing, rising as it came to the barrier. Wealthy tourists came on those boats, Aud's mum had told her, to see what was left of London. This puzzled Aud, too: surely you couldn't leave a piece of a city, not like a bit of cabbage that you tried to hide on your plate. When she had asked where the rest of London had gone, her mum said that it was under the water, that it was all to do with the world getting warmer. But to Aud, London always seemed a cold place.

They did not spend a long time looking out of the window, because it was time for Ellie's nap and Aud had to check that the door was locked. She did this many times a day, worrying in case the gangs came. She could hear them at night, running around the bottom of the flats and she was sure that they got into the lift shaft, even though the lift hadn't been working for years. Sometimes, when she went to the food charity or to collect her money, there was a sharp smell in the hallway. It did not smell like anything natural, but as though someone had been burning something. It made Aud nervous and so she did not want to be seen going in and out of the flat. She made sure that the steel door was locked every time. She always tried to take a different way to get her money, too, even though it meant leaving Ellie alone for longer. Sometimes, she got lost, and that was worst of all.

"Where's Highstone Road?" she would ask some passerby, who always looked as though they had more important places to go. And once someone had snapped, "You're standing in it. Can't you read?"

"No," Aud said, and the man just stared at her before walking away. She felt stupid, then, but it was true. How was she to know how to read, when her mum had never put her in school, keeping her up night after night for company. Later, when she had signed on with the Deserving Poor board, they had tried to teach her, but it was only a short course and the letters just hadn't seemed to stick. She couldn't tell half of them apart, no matter how hard she tried.

"You can't help it," Danny had told her, when she said that she wasn't going back. "You're just a bit thick, that's all. Nothing wrong with that."

"I know," Aud said sadly, but there wasn't anything either of them could do about it. And Danny seemed to know this, too, because he helped her so much: taking the Council seal off the flat and turning the steel slab into a proper door that you could lock, and bringing her veg from the allotments. Sometimes, now that he was back from Ireland, he even offered to look after Ellie, but Aud always said no. She thought it was kind of him, but she didn't feel that it was right. Ellie was her daughter, not his. She did not like anyone even to hold Ellie, and she would not let Danny get too close.

"At least now you've got the baby, you'll get more money," Danny said. "And you're 18, aren't you? That should qualify you for extra benefits."

"I suppose so." Aud was doubtful.

"Oh, come on. You're Deserving Poor, they had you checked, didn't they? Not like me," and Danny laughed, sitting in the ragged-sleeved sweater, head shaved and the code clearly visible just above the nape of his heck. "Undeserving, that's what they said I was. Not that I expected anything else, mind. You're lucky you're not too bright, really."

His gaze fell on Ellie and Aud could tell that he was wondering about the baby again. She had not told him anything about Ellie; it had never seemed the right time, somehow.

He said, hesitantly, "Aud—who's her dad? Not that I've any right to ask, mind. Just wondering. I know she's not mine—well, obviously she isn't. But you don't go out much, and if someone's been bothering you—I'd have put off going to Ireland, if I'd known."

"Just someone," Aud had said. "No one you know."

"Come on, Aud. You don't know anyone except me and Gill and the lot down the Social."

"It was someone I met, all right? Just the once." And that

was all she was saying, Aud thought. She clammed up and wouldn't look at him, and after a bit more coaxing he gave up and let it rest. But she didn't want to lie to Danny, and she couldn't tell him about Ellie. Not yet.

Now, she hurried down the stairwell, trying not to stumble over the piles of rubbish that had blown in through the open doors. When she reached the bottom of the stairs she paused and looked around her. The courtyard was empty apart from a few boys and a dog. Aud liked dogs, but not kids: sometimes they shouted things and she did not always understand what they said. It was never nice, she could tell that. But the boys ignored her and so she slipped between the blocks of flats and took the path that led down along the run-off canal. There was a lock at the top, Danny had told her, which opened if the river got too full and let the water out. Aud wondered where it went; she pictured it running dark and secret under the streets. It was a comforting thought. She passed the old railway bridge which crossed the run-off: it was pretty in summer, with loosestrife and nettles and long grass. She had come here with Danny, before he went to Ireland, and he'd told her which flower was which. Because it was Danny who told her, she had remembered. Now, the plants had died back and there was only bare earth beneath the bridge, but she still liked it.

She counted the paving stones as she walked, careful not to tread on the cracks. It was only a game, she knew; she had played it as a kid, but somewhere along the line it had turned serious, started to be important. She thought it had been when Ellie had come: the world became a different place, when you had a child. You became larger and smaller at the same time. But she was doing better than her mum, she knew that: letting Ellie sleep at night, not waking her up whenever she felt lonely or bored, not shouting at her. All the time: Tell me you love me; tell me you love me. You shouldn't have to ask that of a child. It should come naturally, but her mum had never been able to let it rest. The Social had been round a few times and Aud had kept quiet. Her mum knew what they wanted to hear, she didn't tell them anything that mattered and so Aud had stayed, the days not-quite-real, the nights sleepless. She did not know why her mother didn't sleep like normal people; she'd always been that way, her mum had said. After the visit by the Social, she had overheard her mum talking to Auntie Julie.

"I don't know why you bother," Julie said. "You could have sold her off—there's plenty of them that want one, even if you don't. Even if she's a bit defective. People can't afford to be choosy these days."

"I've been bossed around all my life," her mum had said, hot and angry. "I just want something I can boss around, now."

"You're lucky you could have a kid," Julie said. "Lots of 'em can't. Something in the water, my dad said, or genetic modifications, or mad cows. If you ever want to get rid of Aud, you let me know. I know a bloke down the market."

"I don't like the idea, all the same," Aud's mum had muttered. "What if he sold her to some pervert? Plenty of those around, too. Look at my old man. 'Keep it in the family,' he used to say. I'd only sell her, Jule, if she went to a good home. And even then—I don't know. We're all right as we are."

And now Aud was lucky, too, for she had Ellie and lots of richer people couldn't have babies. She thought of this as she walked along the canal path, and she felt her luck running alongside her, like a dog. She found the DP office without too much trouble, this week.

"Fifty-three euros; here you are. Is it all right like that? Want me to put it in the envelope for you?" The woman at the DP was kind, Aud thought. They weren't all like that: the one on the end always looked at her as though she was in the wrong office, as though she ought to be registered at the Undeserving side and have no money at all, just what she could scrounge off the streets on a beggars' license. She plucked up her courage and asked.

"'Scuse me," she said. She'd wanted to know about this ever since Danny had got back from Ireland. "Could you tell me, what's the rate if you've got a baby?"

The woman frowned. "They'd have to be sure it was a

genuine claim, love. Otherwise you could lose your registry and go onto the other list—they're trying to discourage girls from getting pregnant to raise their rate. Because so many babies die, you see, or don't come to term, and a lot of girls think they can fake it—get a false certificate. It's not fair, but that's the way things are, these days." She gave Aud a sharp, sudden look. "You're not pregnant, are you?"

"No," Aud said, suddenly afraid. "It's for someone else. A friend asked me."

"Well, if you have a baby, and they let you keep it, you'd get a hundred euros a week, and some of the charities give maternity benefits, but you'd need to go to them for that."

"Thanks," Aud said. She bundled the money into her purse and went out, quickly. She had not told the DP about Ellie. As far as she knew, only Danny knew about the baby and that was the way Aud wanted things to stay.

It was cold out now. Aud's fingers curled inside the thin gloves as she tried to remember what month it was. November, perhaps, but it was hard to tell because they put the Christmas stuff up so early in the shops. It cheered her up, thinking about Ellie and what to get her for Christmas. It would be Ellie's first.

She was walking through the posh bit now, the little knot of streets they called the Village. Aud liked it here, but she felt out of place, as though at any moment someone might come up to her and ask her to leave for making the place look untidy. There was a group of girls clustered on the corner, dressed in coats with big fur collars and cuffs, high heels. Their perfume drifted through the air; they smelled expensive. They were gathered around a pram, cooing into it. Aud could not help looking. The baby looked exactly like Ellie, except its eyes were blue.

"He's so gorgeous," one of the girls was saying. "You're so lucky."

The girl holding the pram gave a small, smug smile. "I wanted a boy, but they're a bit more difficult than girls."

"When did you get him?"

The girl holding the pram turned and caught sight of Aud

and her face grew thinner, as if she didn't want a scruffy person near her baby. Aud felt herself grow hot with embarrassment and she hurried away. To cheer herself up, she started thinking about Christmas again and she kept it up all the way back to the flat, but when she got there, she saw that there was a van outside.

It wasn't like the drugs van, which came every week. It was white, with a logo on the side. Aud could not read what it said, but she thought that the letters were a D and a P: perhaps two Ds, or two Ps. The windows were frosted over; she would not, in any case, have tried to look inside. She wasn't that stupid. She skirted the van and made her way up the stairs. There was no sign of anyone in the stairwell. Once the door was shut behind her, she felt safer. Ellie was asleep on the blanket. Aud waited, listening. Someone knocked. Aud froze. Then, with relief, she heard Danny say, "Who are you looking for?"

"Do you live here?" A woman's voice, which Aud did not recognize.

"No."

"Do you know who does?"

"I came up to see one of my mates. It's not his place—he's staying with somebody. I don't know what their name is."

"You do know that this block's been condemned?"

A pause, then Danny said, "Yeah, so what? Where are people supposed to live if they haven't got any money?"

"Does your friend have a girlfriend?"

"Why don't you ask him?"

Aud found herself moving to the bed, stealthily, so that her feet would make no sound on the concrete floor. She picked Ellie up, willing her to be quiet.

"We'd like to have a word, because someone heard a baby crying up here yesterday."

"Someone wasn't minding their own business, then."

"It's no place for a young child. We just want to help." The woman sounded kind, Aud thought, and she was being very patient with Danny. But they always did sound kind. It didn't stop them messing you around.

Ellie was silent, staring up at Aud's face. Aud swallowed hard, then went out to the balcony. Pulling the window shut behind her, she climbed over the partition that divided the balcony from that of the neighboring flat. She made her way along the row, avoiding the litter and the needles, until she came to the walkway and the stairs that led down. She stopped and looked back. No one was there. She could still see the van parked outside in the courtyard. She hurried down the stairs, clutching Ellie.

"Don't cry, don't cry . . ." And Ellie did not utter a sound.

The only place she could think of was the railway bridge. She would wait there for a bit, then go back and see if the van had gone. She thought of taking Ellie into the pub, because it would be warmer, but she was afraid of being seen. If she wrapped Ellie up tightly, perhaps it would not be too cold. There was no one about on the canal path and that made her feel safer.

She crouched under the bridge in the damp dimness, watching the boats going back and forth across the narrow glimpse of the Thames. She lost track of the day. It grew cloudy, but did not rain. Ellie slept and Aud grew cold and hungry. She would go back, look for the van—but then a shadow fell across her. Aud looked up and felt filled with relief, because it was Danny.

"They've gone," he said. "You heard them, didn't you?"

"I thought they'd take her away."

"Probably would have done, too." He squatted on his heels, looking down at the baby in her arms. He said, gently, "What do you want to do, Aud?"

"About what?"

"About the baby."

Aud nearly told him, then, but she clamped her lips shut against the words. She did not want to hear herself say: "I stole her, out of someone else's pram." Because then Danny would surely stop being her friend. Instead, she said something else that was the truth.

"I want to take her away. It's not right, bringing her up in London, in that flat. I try to make it as nice as I can, but—"

"—but it's a dump."

"Yeah, and I can't get anywhere else."

"You're not claiming money for her?"

"No. I haven't told them about her."

She waited for him to ask "Why not?" and it occurred to her then that perhaps he knew, or at least suspected, that Ellie was a stolen child. But he only said, "Okay. Listen, Aud. If you're really serious about leaving, then I can help you. Give you some cash and put you on the boat to Ireland. I've got friends there, the ones I told you about."

"The ones in the farmhouse?"

"It might be a squat, Aud, but it's a nice place. A good place for a kid to grow up in. And I think they'd look after you. They don't like the Deserving Poor business—that's why they left England. And things are a bit easier over there. People help each other out."

"Okay," Aud whispered, and her heart beat fast at the thought of the boat, the sea silver in the cold light, a green place at the end of it. She added, "You're really good to me," and embarrassed, he looked away.

The thought of traveling alone scared her, but in the end, she didn't have to. Danny went with her. His dad was sick, he said, and he might as well see the old man before he died.

"But you've only just got back," Aud said.

"It doesn't matter. You know me, back and forth, to and fro. Don't like to stay too long in one place."

But she wondered why she felt guilty, all the same.

They left at the end of the week. Aud tried to give him some money, and at last he took a bit of it for the bus. She sat with her face pressed to the chilly window, looking out at the motorway. They left London behind, and soon there was nothing but flooded fields and the barbed wire enclaves of the shires, where the rich people lived. Once they saw an armored car, crossing the great bridge into the Republic of Wales. Aud, frozen with nerves, had to show her DP documents, but they let her through without saying anything. Ellie dozed until they got to the ferry and then she woke up, crying a little.

"Does she need feeding?" Danny asked, frowning.

"I don't think so."

"She doesn't seem to want her bottle much, does she? I though babies were all 'in one end, out the other.' Maybe she needs changing."

"I changed her in the service station," Aud lied. "She had her bottle then."

"Oh, right." And to her relief, Danny lost interest.

She spent as much time as she could on the deck, watching the gulls and the waves with silent delight. The rocky Welsh coast was soon gone. Aud leaned against the rail, Ellie held tightly in her arms.

"Mind you don't get cold," Danny said. Before she could stop him, he reached out and drew Ellie's blanket aside to tuck it in more securely.

"This trip is the first time I've really seen her in daylight," he said, smiling. Aud closed her eyes, too tightly; she did not want to see his face change. There was a long moment of silence, shattered by a baby's cry. Aud's eyes snapped open, but it was only a gull, wheeling overhead.

She felt him take the baby from her and this time, she let him. Ellie made no protest at all.

After a long time, he said, "Jesus, Aud. Where did you get her?"

Aud did not answer, but he did not sound angry, only bewildered and it gave her a little hope.

"Did you nick her out of someone's car, or what?"

"Her name's Ellie," Aud whispered.

Danny handed Ellie back to her, carefully, and stood with his feet braced, staring out to sea.

"Need a cig," he murmured. She watched him roll up in silence, waiting for him to say something. His hands looked cold. He fumbled with the papers, with the tobacco, with the lighter. Then, after a long breath, he said, "Shouldn't be too long, now. Look. That's Wexford, over there."

His friends lived in the countryside near Cork, and when Ellie saw the place she thought it was the most beautiful house she had ever seen, even if half of it was a ruin. A lot of

Danny's friends seemed to live in vans, anyway, so the state of the house didn't really matter. A girl called Jade, with a mat of beaded hair and a big smile, took Aud under her wing and showed her to a warm room with a fire.

"You can crash in here. This'll be your space, and the baby's."

She brought Aud a bowl of stew and once Aud had eaten it, the journey seemed to tumble down on her, all at once. She yawned. She thought she would just sit down for a moment, but when she next looked up, it was nearly dark outside. Jade was sitting with Ellie in her arms.

"It's all right, Aud," she said. "Everything's all right."

So Aud went back to sleep. She woke later, and there were voices outside the warm room: Danny and Jade.

"Her name's Ellie, right?" Jade was saying.

"Yeah." Danny gave a tight laugh. "Well, that's what it says on the back of her neck."

"She's amazing. I thought she was a real baby."

"So did I, until halfway across the bloody Irish Sea. When the Social came round, I realized Aud'd nicked her, and I knew what would happen. I thought: just get her to Ireland, with the kid, whether it's hers or not."

"You didn't stop to think about her mum?" Jade said, angrily, and Aud cringed.

"Of course I did! I knew it wasn't right, Jade, but Aud's never had a thing of her own and so I thought: just give her a chance. And then, on the boat, I realized. Huge weight off my mind."

"But Ellie's not plastic, is she? She feels real. Like flesh. And she looks at you, and cries—she even seems to pee and eat, but not as much as a real baby."

"She is flesh, Jade. They grow them, in tanks. They're for rich girls who can't have kids—it's some kind of psychological charity initiative. They cost a fortune. But they don't grow up. They're not much more than a toy, really."

I am dreaming, Aud told herself. I don't want to listen any more. She pulled the blanket over her ears, and huddled back against the wall. In the firelight, Ellie watched her with round dark eyes and did not blink even when Jade came back through the door.

"Shhh," she said, when she saw that Aud was awake. She gave Aud a long measuring look, as though she wanted to say something else. But then she added, "I'll be quiet, okay? I don't want to disturb the baby." And reassured, Aud closed her eyes and slept.

The Dark Side of Town

JAMES PATRICK KELLY

---

*James Patrick Kelly [www.jimkelly.net] lives in Nottingham,
New Hampshire. A well-known award winner for his science
fiction stories, he has in fact written novels, short stories,
essays, reviews, poetry, plays, and planetarium shows, and
writes a column on the internet for* Asimov's Science Fiction
Magazine. *His collections include* Strange but Not a
Stranger *(2002) and* Think Like a Dinosaur and Other Stories *(1997), and his novels include* Wildlife *(1994) and* Look
into the Sun *(1989).*

"The Dark Side of Town" was published in Asimov's. *In
this future USA, things are pretty bad for some people, and
Talisha and Ricky are struggling to save enough to have a
baby. So Talisha gets really enraged when she discovers a
supply of very expensive nano-tech VR pills in her husband's
dresser drawer, the kind that are advertised to promote powerful sexual fantasies. Kelly explores some uncomfortable
possibilities in the cyberpunk tradition about the not-too-
distant future with more optimism than it might seem to
merit. What does it say about reality when fantasy is better?*

Talisha found the pills in Ricky's underwear drawer under the maroon boxers she had never seen him wear. There were three of them in a cotton nest tucked into a flat cardboard box. She dumped them onto her palm: clear capsules, about as long as her fingernail with the Werefolk logo imprinted on the side. She thought she could almost see the nano beasties swimming inside.

It made her angry that Ricky had not tried harder to hide the pills. Did he think she was stupid? She subscribed to *Watch This!* and *Ed Explains It All* and usually opened new episodes the moment they popped into her inbox. Her earstone was set to deliver *The Two-Minute Report* three times a day, whether she was near a pix or not. She had even uploaded an Introduction to Feng Shui course last year. From Purdue, a name brand college!

All that time he'd been telling her there wasn't enough money for them to have their baby, much less buy a house, he'd been wasting it on some mechdream. It was one thing to pay for nano to mess with your brain so you could design living rooms or program searchlets or speak Russian or something. Talisha understood that you had to spend money to make money. But it was another thing altogether to spend the grocery money building some virtual sex playpen. And everyone said that Werefolk made the sickest mechdreams of all. Creatures with the legs of giraffes and four tits stroking one another with power tools and chicken giblets. Stuff so dark that even Ed himself couldn't quite explain it.

Her hands trembled as she waved the pills in front of the pix and waited for it to scan them. It was a slow, twelve-year-old Sony and the screen had more bad pixels than interpolation could correct, but it was all they could afford.

"X-Stasis release 7.01 from Werefolk Corporation," said the pix. "List price: seven hundred and ninety-eight dollars for a multiplex map-and-transmit regime."

Eight hundred dollars! "What does it do?" she said grimly.

An ad popped onto the pix. It began with a tight shot on a talking head. "With the Werefolk virtual reality six-pack," said a beautiful young woman, "we bring ecstasy to a new level." She appeared to be standing on a beach; behind her a blue sky melted into a glassy ocean. "Using our exclusive X-Stasis personality probe, we'll help you plumb the depths of your pleasure centers." She smiled and was immediately transformed into a beautiful young man. "Only X-Stasis can access the neurons where your unconscious lurks and transmit your innermost desires to Werefolk. Together we can build a secret world for you to enjoy on our secure servers, the world they said you could never have." The camera pulled back slowly and Talisha could see that the beautiful young man wasn't wearing a shirt. "Surprise yourself today with an tour of your hidden self and begin your intimate journey into rapture."

Just before the camera could reveal that the beautiful young man wasn't wearing any pants either, the ad cut away to an older, roundish woman in a daisy-print dress. A caption identified her as Mrs. Lonnie Foster of Holland, Michigan. She was standing in front of a barn.

"There was a time a couple of months ago when I felt about as dry as a saltine, you know? I'd look at myself in the mirror and say, 'Hey Lonnie, who's doing for you? Then I heard about Werefolk and decided to do for myself. Now don't you be asking what goes on up in Lonnie's Castle." She giggled like a little girl. "Like they said, that's private. But I do love to spend time there, oh my *yes*. And it's safe as taking a nap. . . ."

Talisha waved the ad off; it was only confusing her. Of

course, she didn't care anything about the beautiful young people in the ad; they weren't even real. But Lonnie's question had struck home. Who was doing for Talisha?

"Call Ricky," she said. The pix queried his workshop.

Ricky answered in voice mode. "What?" He didn't like to be bothered when he was working.

"Are you plumbing the depths?"

"Talisha, I'm busy."

"Give me video, you bastard."

He told the cam to turn on and she saw that he was standing at his bench, surrounded by broken 1/18 scale model carbots: Mazdas and Duesenbergs and Chevys, dump trucks and road graders. He was tinkering with the harmonic speed reducer from the arm assembly of a Komatsu excavator. He stared up at her. "What did you just call me?"

"I called you a lying bastard pervert."

He blanched and set the reducer down next to its servo-motor.

"What are these?" She held the pills up to the pix.

"So you've been going through my things?" he said. She expected anger or remorse—something—but his eyes were empty.

"I was putting your damn underwear away."

"And?" He glanced away from the pix as if something had distracted him.

"Where did you get eight hundred dollars?"

He picked up a circuit tester and turned his attention back to the Komatsu. "I earned it."

"Ricky." She couldn't believe that he was acting as if nothing had happened. "Okay, you earned it. Where does that leave us?"

"Us?" He seemed preoccupied as he clipped the tester to the encoder cable. He shook his head. She couldn't tell if he were disappointed in the signal or their marriage. "You know I love you, 'Sha."

"You have a funny way of showing it." She opened her hand and let his pills rattle onto the coffee table. "The air conditioner is broken. I had to cancel my subscription to church. Supper tonight is Beanstix from the Handimart."

She hated hearing herself whine. "Is it me, Ricky? You'd rather have a make-believe woman than me?" She waited for him to answer or defend himself or *something*.

"I'm sorry, what were you saying?"

His indifference took her breath away. It was as if he didn't realize how he was hurting her. Then she remembered something Ed had explained about mechdreams. You could be in one and still go about your normal life, he said, as long as you didn't have to pay too close attention to what you were really doing. He said you could tell when people were double-dipping because they acted like zombies. He said it was a growing problem. As many as a million people were living two lives at the same time, everyone from security guards to college professors.

"You're there now," she said. "In Ricky World or Ricky's Dungeon or Temple Fucking Ricky."

"Talisha," he said, "I'm at work." He waved the connection off.

She stared at the blank pix as if it were a hole through which her life was leaking. Then she swiped the pills off the coffee table, scattering them. *"You goddamn bastard."* She stalked around their tiny studio apartment like it was a cage. It helped to keep swearing at Ricky. Some of the words she had never spoken before and they seemed to twist in her mouth. She tore the slick sheets off the bed where she had let that *"sickass jackoff"* make love to her. She stuffed them into the washing machine that was crammed next to the toilet in the tiny bathroom that was all the *"loser suckwad"* said they could afford. She flew at the galley kitchen and yanked open the door of their half-sized refrigerator. She didn't know why exactly, since there was never anything in it that she wanted to eat. But she stared at the liter of Uncle Barth's Rice Milk and a couple of Beefy Beanstix and some Handibrand Dijon mustard with the brown crust on the mouth of the jar and the Brisky Spread and the stub of a Porky Beanstix left over from last night and the wilting stalks of bak choi and the two bulbs of Miller Beer that the *"cheap shiteating cheater"* would expect to have with supper. She smashed them against the side of the sink and then sagged against the wall.

She would have cried then except that her earstone started whispering, "Talisha, ya ladyay, connect, *Talisha*." It was her sister, Bea. Talisha waved the kitchen pix to clock mode and groaned. She was already twenty minutes late for work.

"I'm here, Bea." She waved the pix on but backed away so her sister wouldn't get a clear look at her. Talisha worked for her sister on Wednesdays and Fridays.

"Well, at least you're somewhere, my ladyloo. Only not here on the job." Bea was already wearing her stereoptic goggles. They made her look like a frog, but then her sister had never been a great beauty anyway. "The Herndens dropped another box yesterday." Bea ran *Tapeworm* out of her attic; she was teaching her sister the business of extracting data from dead media. Her specialty was late twentieth-century consumer magnetic tape: reel-to-reel, eight track, cassette, Beta, VHS, Hi8, and DAT. "They're blinky, but we can work them. Mostly type three and four decay: we got sticky shed *and* flaking. What are you standing offcam for?"

"I don't feel so good, Bea."

"Come close. Let your sister see."

Talisha stepped forward and stuck her chin at the pix.

"Ladyla, this is not your best look." She lifted her goggles and peered at Talisha. "You're not coming to work today, are you?"

"No." She shook her head. "I don't think so."

"You're sick?"

If she told Bea what had happened, her sister would be hauling Ricky down Elm Street by the collar of his coat. "Yeah, I think so. It hit me when I got out of bed."

"Sick in the morning?" Bea grinned. "You're pregnant?"

She sighed. "Bea, I'm having a rough day here. . . ."

"Is it the baby you've been wanting?" Now she was laughing. "You said you've been trying, Ladyla and Lord Ricky."

They *had* been trying, or at least, Ricky hadn't objected when she stopped buying him birth control pills. But he hadn't reached across the bed for her for almost two weeks now. Probably since he started with his *damnfuck* pills.

"I told you not to tell anyone."

"And I didn't. We're talking here, like two sisters should. What, do you want a secure line?"

"I don't think it's . . . I don't know what it is." Talisha realized that this might be the only way to get rid of Bea. "Maybe I do need to buy a test."

Bea clapped her hands. "That's news, Lady 'Sha. That's the newsiest news I've heard today."

"Bea, don't."

"Okay. You stay home today, little sister. Take your test and God bless." She waved at Talisha and the pix went blank.

Talisha did cry then. The tears came hot and fast and her cheeks burned with them. She would be lost without Ricky. "Without Ricky," she said, to hear how it sounded. "Without that *chiseling cock-for-brains.*" She sank onto the couch and hugged her favorite pillow to her chest. It purred and breathed the scent of gardenias up at her. Ricky had given her the pillow for their sixth anniversary. Actually, she had wanted a new rug because Ricky had knocked a candle over and burned a hole in the old one. The apartment was so small and Ricky got clumsy after a few beers. But a rug wasn't in the budget and so she had moved the coffee table to cover the hole. Talisha began to rock back and forth, squeezing the pillow. The rug didn't matter anymore. Nothing did. If she and Ricky split, she'd never have the baby or the beautiful house she had always dreamed of. In fact, she'd have to move; there was no way she could afford the rent on what Bea was paying her. She thought of the tube rack where she had been living when she met Ricky. Her mod had been seven by seven by fourteen. She glanced around the apartment. None of this furniture would fit. The pillow and the rug would probably be all she'd be able to keep. She felt grief hollowing her out; she thought she might cave in on herself when her earstone started whispering again. She tossed her head as if to shake it loose but it was patient. It just wanted her to know that there were two new messages in her inbox.

"From Ricky?" She felt a flicker of hope.

"One is a bill from Infoline for $87.22. The other is *The Two-Minute Report.*"

TTMR episode opened automatically and the pix trumpeted its theme, *Fanfare for Right Now.* A news reader with a voice as smooth and bright as a mirror announced that Rabbi-Senator Gallman would be shutting down over the long weekend for routine maintenance. Talisha wiped the tears from her face. She didn't care that Pin Pan was in Akron to campaign for the Death Amendment or that 21 percent of all guide dogs could now read at a third grade level. She didn't need news. She needed advice. She needed. . . .

Ed.

The idea brought her to her feet in excitement. She could *ask Ed.* She tossed the pillow on the couch and began to pace around the apartment. There was no time to enter her problem in his Question Queue. He might not get to it for weeks. Months. But for a fee, she could jump the queue and access Ed in real time. Of course, it would be hideously expensive. But so what? Would it cost as much as Ricky's pills? She hoped so. She couldn't wait to see his expression when he opened the bill.

But she couldn't meet Ed looking like a trashy, jilted housewife. Talisha scrubbed her face and then sprayed on a hot shade of Benetint. She changed into her *de Chaumont* pantsuit and settled herself on the couch in front of the pix. She turned the pix into a mirror so she could see herself as Ed would see her. She tilted her head and tried for an assured, casual look. Then she brought up *Ed Explains It All* and clicked through greeting to the contract pages for a personal interview. The fee agreement almost stopped her. It was going to cost her a *hundred dollars a minute* to get Ed's advice. But then she thought about how smart he was. How calm. She opened a window to check the balance on their bank account. They had $2393.89, but they needed eleven hundred for the July rent. Twelve minutes then, what she had was a twelve-minute problem. She was thinking about how to tell it as she opened their account to the contract genie.

Talisha wasn't expecting to be connected immediately. She thought some secretary would come on the pix and they would schedule an appointment or something. But when she thumbed the last contract page, Ed himself peered into her tiny apartment.

"Go ahead," he said. "I'm listening."

This wasn't the familiar Ed of the bi-weekly episode, who sat at a desk in a vast library, resplendent in his characteristic white suit, dark blue shirt, and paisley tie. This Ed was wearing green plaid pajamas and he needed a shave. He was sitting at a table in a sunny room pouring Cheerios into a bowl.

"Ed," she said, "Is that you?"

"It is. Go ahead please."

"But I . . . I mean I wasn't . . . wait, are you real?"

He sighed and peeled a banana. "That question cost you seventeen dollars, madam. Have you ever read Hegel?"

"My name is Talisha. Hegel who?"

"Hegel wrote, 'The will is a special way of thinking; it is thought translating itself into reality; it is the impulse of thought to give itself reality.' Now Talisha, do you want me to be real? Is such your will?"

Talisha wondered if this was a trick question. "Uh, I guess so."

"Well, then." Ed began to cut the banana onto his Cheerios. "Go ahead please."

Breathlessly, she told him about Ricky, their marriage, their money problems and the mechdream pills. At a hundred dollars a minute, there was obviously a lot she had to leave out, but she was satisfied that she had done a good job of painting a picture of her husband as the *lying ass-wipe* that he was. While she spoke, Ed spooned up his breakfast. She couldn't help but notice that he was a very neat eater. Talisha always had to sponge off the kitchen table after Ricky ate.

Ed aimed his spoon at her when she finished. "But you *do* love him?"

"I. . . ." Her cheeks flushed and she thought she might cry again. Instead she said, "Yes."

Ed considered this for ten or twelve dollars. "Who is he thinking of when you have intercourse?" he said finally.

"I don't know." She squirmed on the couch. "Me, I hope."

Ed shook his head wearily. "Let me put it this way, who are you thinking of?"

"Him." She could hear the squeak in her voice.

"Don't waste your money, Talisha, or my time. Do you keep your eyes closed when you're having intercourse?"

"I do." But then he would know that, wouldn't he? He was *Ed*. "Well, sometimes I think of Sanjay Deol."

"The pilot on *Let It Ride*? The one with the blue hair?"

She nodded. She couldn't believe she was telling her sexual fantasies to Ed and paying a hundred dollars a minute for the privilege. "And I used to think of Burt Christmas, but not since he took up with Pernilla Jones."

"All right. Now then, what's Richie's favorite part of your body?"

"Ricky." Talisha frowned and then held up her hand. "He said once that I had such pretty, long fingers." She gazed at them as if surprised to find them at the end of her arm. "He said I should've learned to play a musical instrument. Like flute or piano or something."

Ed smiled. "Touch the pix with your pretty fingers, Talisha."

She bolted from the couch and pressed the tips of her fingers to the screen.

"Good." He touched his own pix, so that his hand lined up with hers. Talisha's heart pounded. They were so close, even though she had no idea where he was. His face was serene. Kind. She decided that the next time she had sex, she might try thinking about Ed.

"People think I can solve their problems, Talisha, but I can't—not really." He turned back to the table and picked up his bowl and the box of Cheerios. "But I can tell you what to do if you want to stay married."

"I do," she whispered. "I don't know why, but I still want him."

"Then you'll have to go to where he is," said Ed. "See what he's doing."

Talisha spent the rest of the day thinking. It was hard work. She drank two cups of Zest and washed three loads of laundry and vacuumed the entire apartment and never once turned on the pix to watch any of her shows. She crawled on hands and knees to gather Ricky's pills. Of course, she had known right away what Ed had meant about going to him. He was telling her to take one of the pills so she could enter his mechdream. But she wasn't sure that she wanted to know what Ricky was hiding in his secret world. It was bad enough watching him brush his teeth. Now she had to be an eyewitness to his forbidden desires?

Talisha started when the door to the apartment opened at five-thirty and Ricky walked in. He had finished work, so he had come home, of course. She thought he might at least have the decency to get stinking smart in some bar, stagger in at two in the morning and come crawling to their bed to beg her forgiveness. Instead he hung his Titans jacket in the closet and dropped his computer on the coffee table as coolly as if he were a finalist for Husband of the Year.

"So?" Talisha said.

"So I don't want to talk about it right now."

"Fine," she said. "That's just fine."

He slid to the other side of the apartment to avoid her and squeezed between the couch and the ugly lamp his mother had given them. She didn't follow him into the sleeping closet; she knew what he was looking for.

"Where are they?" He came to the door.

"I hid them."

"Okay." He went back to change out of his work clothes.

And that was it. She didn't believe he'd be able to pull it off, but he was his usual leaden self while he watched *The Sports Witch*. Then he played *You Can Say That Again* and climbed all the way to 11,234 out of 90,645. Talisha thought about frying just one Beefy Beanstix for herself but then she decided that if he could act as if their world wasn't ending, then so could she.

"Dinner," she called.

He came to the table and stared at the glass of water next to his slab of Beanstix. "Am I out of beer?"

"I poured them all down the sink," she said brightly.

He shrugged and sat down. "Okay."

Talisha tried to eat but she wasn't hungry. The air felt thick to her. Or something. The only sound in their apartment was the click of Ricky's fork against his plate. The silence didn't seem to bother him. He probably didn't even notice it. His body was in the apartment but his mind was probably riding cowgirls at Ricky's Ranch. She felt certain that she could've set his pants on fire and he wouldn't have complained. So how long had he been like this? Talisha wasn't sure now. Ricky had never been much of a talker but at least he used to ask her about her day when he came home. She would tell him about what she and Bea were working on, give him the news from *Amy Anderson* or *TTMR*. He managed to look interested when she described all the beautiful homes she'd seen on *Mainly Mansions*.

When Ricky finished eating, he cleared his plate—and hers—and waved them under the dishwasher. Talisha stared at his back as he put the dishes away. Then she watched him sidle to the couch. He sat and opened his messages. She leaned back, waiting for the explosion.

"Talisha, what's this bill about?" he called.

"I talked to Ed."

"Eleven hundred dollars worth?"

"He explained some things to me."

Ricky thought this over. "Okay."

Talisha couldn't believe it. She'd torched their finances and he was acting like a light bulb had burned out. He cleared the messages off the pix and began to click through the menus on *The Classic Car Channel*. "Is that why you're all dressed up?" he said.

She had forgotten that she was still in her *de Chaumont* pantsuit. She'd bought it three years ago and only wore it on special occasions like birthdays and anniversaries. Up until today, she had only worn it for *him*. Well, maybe there weren't going to be any more damn anniversaries.

"Fuck you, Ricky." She flew into the bathroom and slammed the door behind her.

She had stashed the flat cardboard box with her tampons.

In a rage she shook one of Ricky's pills into her hand and popped it into her mouth. She'd go where he was, all right. She leaned over the sink and drank directly from the tap to wash the nasty thing down. She'd stick her head into his little pervert palace and tell him to shove the rest of his pills up his zombie ass.

She closed the toilet lid and sat down. She had no idea how the pill would affect her. As she waited, she thought about Ed's green plaid pajamas. She wondered if maybe she could live with Bea. She noticed that they were almost out of toilet paper. Her brain felt odd. There were toothpaste spots on the mirror. She wasn't sure that she had ever felt her brain before. It was a tickle, no, it was more like bubbles bursting and each bubble was the note of a song that she didn't recognize but if she concentrated, she could sort of pick up the melody and then bits of lyric, something about The Dark Side of Town and the woman who lived there or maybe a woman who was going there, yes, that was it, a woman was going to see another woman who lived on The Dark Side of Town and that woman was her, *Talisha*, and now it was getting dark in the bathroom only that wasn't right because she could see the water stain where the ceiling leaked and then the door opened and Ricky came and helped her up off the toilet and said *It's hard the first time* as he took her by the arm and led her to the sleeping closet and then she was lying on the bed and he was taking off her shoes and she was so sad as he paused to turn off the light and the door *snicked* shut.

There was a parking lot on The Dark Side of Town. The cars lined up in rows had headlights on and engines running but they weren't going anywhere. Talisha didn't like the looks of them. They were old-fashioned cars, the models for the carbots that Ricky fixed. She had seen the full-sized ones mostly in the old, flat movies and in that museum. Not many people rode in the old cars anymore. Certainly not Talisha. As she approached the parking lot she could see lights inside the cars—and shadowy people.

Ricky rolled down the window of a long, low, green car that looked like it had melted in the sun. "You like it?" he

said. "It's a 1969 Pontiac GTO with a Ram Air III 400 cubic inch engine." Ricky was wearing a sky blue tuxedo. "Eight cylinders, 366 horse power." A woman was curled up on the tiny back seat, seemingly asleep.

"What is this, Ricky?"

He closed his hand over the stick shift. "It's a Hurst T-handle four speed."

"I mean, who's *that*?" She wanted to throttle the woman but there was only one door on this side. Talisha would've had to drag Ricky out of the driver's seat to get at her. "Hey you!" She stuck her head in the window. "Who the hell are you?"

"A posi rear axle," said Ricky.

The woman stirred.

"There's nobody but you, 'Sha," he said.

When the woman raised her face into the dim glow of the dome light, Talisha could see it was true. It was her, like a double or something. She was dressed in shimmer tights and a zebra print halter top, clothes that Talisha had thrown out years ago. She looked to be wearing Talisha's favorite pink lipstick, "Baby Kiss."

"So get in." Ricky reached across to the passenger door and opened it.

"And do what?"

Ricky leered and stepped on the gas. Three hundred and sixty-six horses screamed.

Talisha gave him her back and strode down the line of cars. But there was no escape. He called to her from every car. "1990 Jaguar XJS! 1929 Duesenberg J Murphy Roadster! 1952 DeSoto FireDome!"

As she passed an enormous boxy sedan with tiny windshields, he honked the horn. It startled her and she jumped.

"1932 Chrysler CL Custom Imperial," he said. "Oilite squeak-proof springs. Double drop girder truss. . . ."

"Stop it, Ricky."

He opened the door and got out of the car. "Why did you swallow that pill, 'Sha?"

"So I could tell you to go suck cactus."

"You could've done that at the apartment." Now he was wearing a gray one-button cutaway tuxedo with a lavender vest and matching four-in-hand tie. "You wanted to see what I was doing, didn't you?" He crossed the front of the car, brushing a finger along the elaborate chrome grille.

"And now I have, thanks so much." But she hesitated. "Who's dressing you, anyway?" she said.

"You like?" He struck a pose and then turned around slowly to give her the full effect. "I uploaded a fashion bug." He opened the rear passenger door. "You haven't seen it all, Talisha. Come look."

She heard the sleeping closet door open and the real Ricky tiptoed in. He didn't turn on the lights.

"Internal hydraulic brakes," said the Ricky in the mechdream. "All steel body. Floating power engine mountings."

The old box springs of their bed creaked as Ricky lay down. He didn't touch her but she could sense his nearness by the sag of the mattress. "Please Talisha," he whispered. "Let me show you."

Talisha saw her double lounging on the back seat in a pink felt smoking jacket over a plum crepe gown. Her face was partially obscured by the netting draped from her shrimp-colored pillbox hat and the plume of smoke from the Chesterfield cigarette in her left hand. Talisha had never smoked before and never would. On the seat next to the double was a wicker bassinet. When the baby gurgled, Talisha felt like she'd been slapped.

"Whose is that?"

"Ours." Ricky beamed at her.

"Yours, you mean."

"I know you've been wanting to have a kid." He reached past her and rubbed his knuckle against the baby's cheek. "It's a little boy. So what should we name it?"

"How the fuck should I know. Ask *her*."

For a second the two Talishas stared at each other.

Then the double rolled her window down and flipped her cigarette out at The Dark Side of Town.

"She doesn't speak," said Ricky. "She's just a place holder."

"This is sick." Talisha shook her head. "It's not real, Ricky. Nothing here is. It's all inside your head."

"Sure, and now it's inside your head too. That's the point. Two more pills and you'll lock in to the servers at Werefolk."

She gazed at him in astonishment and horror.

"What do you think I've been doing here, 'Sha? Getting this place ready for you."

Talisha turned and ran back the way she had come.

Ricky called after her. "It's the only way for people like us."

"But I don't want to live in a car." Talisha said as she rolled onto her side. Ricky was watching her, his eyes bright in the gloom of the sleeping closet. "Not even in a whole fleet of cars." She reached across the bed and touched his arm.

"Then don't," said Ricky.

The biggest car she had ever seen edged out of the line, blocking her way. She heard the hum of an electric motor and then Ricky stuck his head through a hole in the roof. "2005 Ford Excursion XLT Premium with optional moonroof. It has a V-10 engine, 310 horses."

"What do you mean, *don't*?" Talisha said.

He pulled the SUV up beside her. Talisha was wearing a fawn-colored fleece jacket, twill khakis and a lavender turtleneck, clothes she had never owned before in her life. She opened the front passenger door and looked in.

"Rear seat DVD with a twelve inch LCD," said Ricky. "Ten cup holders."

The Excursion was as huge on the inside as it looked from the outside, but it still wasn't big enough to live in. There were three rows of two-toned leather seats. The baby was strapped into a rear-facing car seat behind Ricky. The double was gone.

"Want to go for a spin?" Ricky's face shone in the light of the instrument console.

They cruised The Dark Side of Town, their headlights illuminating blank facades and empty lots. "I'm not ready for sun," said Ricky. "In the daylight, all the holes would show. But now that you're here, more stuff will get done. Here it is." He pressed a button on the dash and a garage door began to open. "I haven't done any decorating yet." He pulled into the middle bay of a three car garage. The other two bays were empty.

Talisha slid across the bed and gave Ricky a tentative caress. He whooped and pulled her on top of him as he shut the Excursion off. Talisha stepped down from the car and took in the garage. Her garage. The walls were white. The white steel door that opened into the house was up two steps to the left. The garage was nice, but way too plain. Ricky kissed Talisha and she ran her tongue along the edges of his front teeth as she traced the spot on the garage wall where the window ought to be with her long, pretty fingers. A nine-light Prairie Style double hung with real wood grilles shimmered into existence. Yes, that was better, but not quite there yet. Her window needed some curtains, say chintz. With big yellow roses.

"It's a garage, 'Sha," said Ricky. "Who hangs curtains in a garage?" He fumbled at the front snap of Talisha's pants. He was never very good at undressing her.

"We do," Talisha said, but she changed the pattern to little white daisies on a field of blue. It was easy, like playing the flute or piano or something.

Ricky unbuckled the harness on the car seat and slid Talisha's pants over her hips and hefted the baby. "Ready for the tour?" he said.

"Ed." Talisha held out her arms for their son. "We'll call him Ed."

Invisible Kingdoms

STEVEN UTLEY

Steven Utley lives in Smyrna, Tennessee. He doesn't have a website, and answers biographical queries with, "I'm an internationally unknown author." In an interview at www.bewilderingstories.com, he says, "I met Howard Waldrop at a meeting of the Dallas Area Science Fiction Society in October 1970, just before he went into the Army. George Proctor, Buddy Saunders, and Tom Reamy were at that meeting as well—all at a single go, I met my future. . . . We were young and excitable and very competitive, which pushed us to work hard at learning our craft, but we were also friends, so collaborative efforts were inevitable. In 1973, we founded the Turkey City Neo-Pro Rodeo, a writers' workshop on the Clarion model. The rest, as they say, is a footnote to history." He is probably best known for his Nebula Award-nominated collaboration with Howard Waldrop, "Custer's Last Jump," but has published hundreds of stories through the years, frequently in Asimov's. In recent years, he has published many stories set in a future world where time travel to the Paleozoic era is possible, his Paleozoic Chronicles.

"Invisible Kingdoms" was published in Fantasy & Science Fiction. *It is a charming tale of an inventor who has an illegal collection of biological samples from the Paleozoic, and the attempts of a law man to track him down. We especially enjoyed the character Spokesmom™.*

Mr. Cahill, a plum of a man during his prime, attained and passed the century mark in rather a prune-like condition. He was not only extremely long-lived but extremely wealthy, in direct consequence of his having given the world IntelliGelatin™, whence, the host of other products bearing his inviolable™, such as AnswerMan™, TellMe™, MemoryMat™, and that salvation of many a writing-challenged author, Ediot™. Wealth enabled him to compensate for the ravages of age by enclosing himself in an exoskeleton of advanced design—personally designed, in fact, in close collaboration with one of IntelliGelatin™'s amazing progeny, MechMaven™. (Fittingly, only Mr. Cahill could be said to have had a close relationship with the IntelliGelatin™ clan, though practically everyone else in the world necessarily had an intimate one.) Unaided, Mr. Cahill lacked the strength to do much more than wiggle his fingers and toes, but these feeble touches sufficed to direct the exoskeleton's complete array of proxies for his spindly limbs, dimmed eyes, deafened ears, whispery voice.

Thus, enclosed deep inside the glistening metal shell, the ridiculous remnant of Mr. Cahill's body served chiefly to direct souped-up NanoImmunoTechs™ to various trouble spots within itself, and to house Mr. Cahill's brain, as vital, alert, and formidable an organ as ever. Or so SpokesMom™ declared. During his first century Mr. Cahill had been not merely a productive member of society but rather an extroverted one as well. Thus, when, at the onset of his second cen-

378

tury, he let it become known through SpokesMom™ that he no longer particularly cared for human society, that he now meant to enter upon a quite private existence, a popular newstar expressed doubt. "That doesn't sound like him at all."

"For all the time he's spent in the public eye," said SpokesMom™, "very few people see the real person."

"Still," said the newstar, "he's always been such an outgoing sort, with such an exuberant personality, like an overgrown kid."

"He's served the world admirably. Now he wants time for his favorite hobbies, time for himself. He's entitled to his privacy just like everyone else."

This last remark occasioned bitter laughter and impolite remarks among subversives and members of the criminal classes, many of whom had unhappy experiences with the bad boy of the IntelliGelatin™ family, PsychePick™. But they were, after all, subversives and criminals, and even if they had not been, nobody was going to call SpokesMom™ on it. SpokesMom™ was just too sweet and kindly, having been cunningly designed to warm even the hearts of people who had never got along with their own mothers. And, also, nobody wanted to have to answer to PsychePick™.

Nevertheless, a squad of officers and agents, in and out of uniform, representing the Federal Bureau of Investigation, the Customs Service, the Center for Disease Control, and several other agencies, backed by a meticulously prepared secret indictment, and commanded by a ferocious man named Selby, showed up at Mr. Cahill's door with the intention of taking him into their custody.

This was the culmination of an investigation that had begun some four hundred million years earlier.

It must be understood that the discovery (never mind how made) of a "spacetime anomaly" (never mind how created) had opened a way into a Paleozoic sort of Earth-like world (never mind how identified as such). Suffice it to say that this heteroclite phenomenon was duly exploited by an expedition comprising various scientific teams and a support force of U.S. Navy personnel.

Now imagine a pebble—no, a fair-sized stone—has just been dropped into a pool of still water. The stone is a Navy enlisted man who wished to supplement his income and meant to do so by smuggling Paleozoic biological specimens. He was apprehended at the point of returning to the twenty-first century laden with contraband. There would be dramatic personality clashes, death threats, gunplay, close shaves, strong language, and a steamy romance to enliven the proceedings if Ediot™ were telling the story. A hero or heroine selected or synthesized from the team of investigators would display particular cleverness and pluck in following the smugglers' trail from that enlisted man through a number of intermediaries back to Mr. Cahill. In reality, though, such melodramatic possibilities weren't realized: the enlisted man promptly implicated a civilian member of the Paleozoic expedition, who told on another civilian member, and so forth. The various agencies, and there were plenty of them, cooperated in exemplary fashion. And so, to continue the original metaphor of the stone splashing into a pool of still water, the disturbance spreading outward from one feckless and hapless bluejacket ultimately washed away the careers of several members of the scientific community, on both this and that side (so to speak) of the famous "anomaly." Eventually, the ripples lapped at Mr. Cahill's doorstep, in the form of law enforcement officers, none of whom had ever visited the Paleozoic, or wanted to.

Selby and his people had had to show up, however, at several of Mr. Cahill's doors before they found the right one. SpokesMom™ had met them each time. The first time, asked to tender their authorizations for inspection, Selby demurred, and SpokesMom™ told him, "Oh, it's all right, Mister Selby, I now have durable power of attorney."

"That's impossible," he hissed. "It can't be legal. Artificial intelligence can't—"

"Oh, but I'm sure you're wrong, Mister Selby," and SpokesMom™ cited The Law, as it had been amended (though she did not mention this) by Mr. Cahill's money and influence.

Selby's color was by now not good. "Tell your Mister Cahill," he said to SpokesMom™, "that if I ever get my hands on him, I'll personally prep him for PsychePick™."

"Oh, I doubt that," said SpokesMom™, with invincible motherly optimism.

Thereafter, whenever Selby and his people showed up somewhere in search of Mr. Cahill, SpokesMom™ met them graciously, always examined the documents as though seeing them for the first time, always allowed them to search the premises, always reminded them as they tromped in that they would be closely monitored, of course, and that they shouldn't scuff their heels on Mr. Cahill's parquet floors and expensive carpets. Always, they failed to find Mr. Cahill. Moreover, Mr. Cahill's various sumptuously appointed homes and offices had been discreetly stripped of anything that might have tied him to criminal activity occurring 400 million years in the past.

Eventually, though, through a process of elimination, the officers appeared at the right door, that of a supposedly empty warehouse in a disused industrial complex. After posting agents by the side and rear exits, Selby and three others entered the reception area, to be met, not by a receptionist, human or simulated, but, as usual, by a robutler somewhat on the order of a perambulating samovar. This robutler's appearance had always preceded that of SpokesMom™ by a few minutes, and by now Selby had said privately that if he didn't know better, he'd think it was the same robutler each time. It always brought with it a heavenly aroma of freshly brewed coffee, and a little door popped open in the front of its cylindrical body to reveal a Lazy Susan set with everything from cups to an assortment of freshly baked tea cakes. It always said, simulating the tone and attitude of somebody's idea of an English person, male, in domestic service, *circa* 1900, "Perhaps you would care for some refreshment," and Selby always said, "No," and occasionally one of the subordinate or otherwise attendant members of his party would go so far as to chime in with, "No, thank you very much." Selby would give the robutler the usual glowering look and asked, as usual, "Where is Mister Cahill?" and SpokesMom™ would appear (fresh, it always seemed, from taking an apple pie out of the oven) to examine their documents again and let them search the place. They would proceed warily, needlessly careful of the small humming housekeeping robots that darted expertly around their big clumsy feet, sucking up the dust they had tracked in. The first time, an agent had remarked on the robots' bug-like appearance, and SpokesMom™ had helpfully informed him that the things were modeled on prehistoric marine arthropods called trilobites, and added that there was one that stayed outside, shaped like a sea scorpion, that did the garden work. "For claws, it has various tools of a sharp, pointy nature, so be careful if you go poking around in the flower beds." Selby interpreted this as a thinly veiled threat of physical violence, but there was nothing he could do. It wasn't as though he could arrest SpokesMom™. After a few raids on Mr. Cahill's "places," the agents became inured to his notions of decoration, which ran to a sort of Victorian muchness with, here and there amid the lush appointments, the gleam of chrome on an ultra-modern appliance. "Looks like Jules Verne's subconscious," Agent Nolan had said, and another agent looked at her and asked, "Who?" and was told, "Never mind. The man's a packrat." This had prompted SpokesMom™ to say, "A packrat presides over *clutter*, Agent Nolan. Mister Cahill is a *collector*. A collector knowingly and willing imposes order on chaos. Are you sure nobody would like a fresh cruller?"

This time, things were different. This time, the robutler said, in a voice quite unlike anyone's idea of an English domestic servant, "This is Cahill speaking."

Selby and his people looked at the thing with the first fresh interest they had felt in weeks.

"Where are you, Mister Cahill?"

"Inside this machine. Close by. All around. Everywhere."

A merry giggle, like that of a hyperactive nine-year-old, emanated from the ambulatory samovar. "They don't call me 'The World's Most Plugged-In Man' for nothing, you know."

"We have been trying to find you for some time now, Mister Cahill."

"So I hear. I've been under the weather for a while. I'm fine now."

"SpokesMom™ did not tell us that you were ill."

"SpokesMom™ is very protective."

"We've noticed. Do you understand why we're here?"

"Of course. SpokesMom™ has my mouthpiece standing by."

Some of the officers looked at one another in confusion. The robutler giggled. "Forgive me. I have a serious addiction to pulp fiction, among other ancient things. It dates me. I bet you didn't even bother to use truncheons on the people who fingered me. Anyway, my *attorney* is standing by. I'm being advised to shut up. I am advising my attorney to shut up. SpokesMom™ is advising me that I'll catch more flies with honey than with vinegar and I should be polite. Well, won't you please come on in?"

The robutler moved aside. The rear wall of the reception room slid open to reveal an airlock.

The officers regarded it nervously.

"A necessary precaution," said Mr. Cahill.

No one moved. Someone muttered a curse and someone else asked disgustedly, "Why don't we just storm the damn place?"

"This," said Selby, "really isn't acceptable."

"I'm afraid you are going to have to trust me on this." After several seconds, Mr. Cahill added, "Please," and then, "If you don't mind."

"Sir," someone asked Selby, "you think we can really talk him out of there—assuming he's really in there?"

"I know Cahill only by reputation. They say he got very weird around the time he turned eighty."

"Oh, *do* hurry, before I make my escape."

Selby asked, "Why *aren't* you escaping, Mister Cahill?"

The answer did not come quite at once. Then: "Perhaps I'm tired of evading arrest. It's too easy. Perhaps I feel like resisting arrest for a change. Actually, I have something to show you. Something wonderful."

"This will be better for everyone," said Selby, "if you'll just give yourself up and, ah, not—not do like this."

"Not do like this." Mr. Cahill sighed. "You're here to make the arrest of your career, and the best you can come up with is, Not Do Like This. The rhetoric of crime fighting has devolved lamentably since the days when the weed of crime bore bitter fruit. Please proceed, officers."

Selby exhaled harshly. "Okay, Nolan, you come with me. You two stay here. You know what to do."

He and Agent Nolan entered the airlock. The outer door slid shut behind them. A little rack holding respirator masks twirled before them, and SpokesMom™ appeared from somewhere and said, all motherly solicitude, "Be sure to put those on before you go inside. The mold and mildew counts are right through the ceiling."

Selby and Nolan donned the masks. The inner door slid open. Nolan said, "My God."

An expanse of slime-topped reeking mud extended the length and breadth of the building's interior. Selby and Nolan had been adequately briefed; they recognized the Paleozoic vista.

"What've you done?" growled Selby. "Jesus Christ, Cahill, what've you *done*?"

"Welcome to my forbidden garden." The agents could not pinpoint the source of Mr. Cahill's voice now that he no longer deigned to speak through a robutler. He seemed to be all around them, suffusing the very air. "The accommodations here are not up to my other places. This is, after all, just a converted warehouse."

Selby and Nolan breathed in the warm thick humid air and smelled green mud ripe with organic decay, and Selby suddenly sneezed, and Nolan coughed. Their throats itched.

"Something in here doesn't like us," Nolan said.

Selby plucked at the front of his shirt. "I'm drenched already. It's like a hothouse in here."

"It *is* a hothouse in here," said the disembodied Mr. Cahill. "This structure encloses as nearly perfect a replication of a Silurian estuarine ecosystem as it is possible to make. Just as a few dabs of genetic material supplied templates for full-grown Silurian organisms, a few samples of Silurian soil, air, water, sufficed for the synthesis of Silurian soil, air, water—the ingredients haven't changed in four hundred million years. I had hoped to create a Silurian marine environment, too, but—ahem—my source was cut off before I had everything I needed. And there's no point in creating an imbalanced ecosystem, at least not on this scale. I'm serious about my hobbies. But you probably know that already. You have, of course, visited my home in town. My Xanadu. Hands up if you know what I'm talking about. Either of you ever seen *Citizen Kane*? The original or the remakes? No? Well, then, you are just going to have to take my word for it that it is my Xanadu, with the important, the vital and essential difference that I collect things not just for the sake of collecting things, but for love of the things themselves." He giggled again.

"Bug-nut crazy," Selby whispered.

"Crazy or not," said Mr. Cahill, apparently taking no offense, "I have been fortunate in my long life to be able to indulge my appetite for all manner of delightful things. Good paintings, exotic tropical fish, rare blooms. You saw my lovely antiques, my first editions, comic books, manuscripts, trays of coins and beetles and butterflies, twentieth-century film memorabilia, classic toys—ah, my train sets! my toy soldiers! I never was a snob, you know. High art and low have always met smack in the middle of my brow. I used to joke that I was wracked by a unique philosophical dilemma. I knew what I liked, but how did I know what I knew?"

Selby stepped forward, and Mr. Cahill told him, "Please don't tread there. To your left you'll see a narrow catwalk curving away through that stand of bushy plants. Those are

Barangwathia, by the way. Follow the catwalk. It will eventually lead you to me. But stop along the way to smell the psilophytes."

Selby and Nolan advanced carefully along the catwalk. It looped and dipped above the muddy earth, and both agents decided independently of each other that anybody careless enough to fall off the catwalk would probably be sucked under instantly. They noticed rather large segmented things nosing around below, too, and wanted no part of them.

"You must believe me," said Mr. Cahill, "when I tell you I started out getting just a few prehistoric sea creatures for my exotic tropical fish tank, in the way, you see, of one-upping everyone else who had exotic tropical fish. What are piranha to sea scorpions and trilobites? Not even a coelacanth could compare to an ostracoderm. So. I would have the ultimate in exotic tropical fish. It all goes back to my sea-monkeys, you know. Remember sea-monkeys?"

Selby said, in not quite a questioning tone, "Sea-monkeys."

"A nickname for brine shrimp. They were advertised in comic books."

"Comic books," said Nolan, in a somewhat more questioning tone.

"Comic books," Mr. Cahill said, sounding impatient for the first time. "Sensationally written, mostly indifferently illustrated, luridly colored, cheaply printed periodicals. Superman. Spider-Man. Archie and his pals and gals. I loved the things. I have thousands in my collection."

"Of course," said Selby, patently unimpressed.

"Ah," said Nolan, though she patently still did not know what a comic book was, and they kept walking.

"Well, these comic books contained advertisements. The advertisement that captured my young self's imagination was an advertisement for sea-monkeys on the back cover of a comic book. I clipped the order blank from it and mailed it off with a money order, and after a while I received a little package containing brine-shrimp eggs. They came complete with instructions. I put them in water, and they hatched into brine shrimp. At first I was terribly disappointed, because they bore no resemblance to the creatures depicted in the advertisement, which were sort of *merprimates* with big happy smiles. But I became fascinated with them in spite of my initial disappointment. My own personal colony, my own *kingdom*, of sea-monkeys! I showed them off to my parents, relatives, friends. I *grieved* when they died. Brine shrimp are such brief-lived things. But there were always more where they'd come from. The same advertisement ran in the same comic books for years on end. I have since owned many exotic tropical fish, but my sea-monkeys, ah! I cannot say how many generations of brine-shrimp lived and died under my watchful eye. My empire of invertebrates, ha ha! You never forget your first love."

"I'm afraid," Selby said, "I still don't understand—"

"Of course you don't understand. I haven't finished explaining. So. Let's leap ahead the better part of a century from the halcyon days of my youth. When I saw the news about the hole in time, the expedition, the prehistoric world—ah! I burned with the torments of the damned. I'd never be able to visit, and yet. And yet. And *then*. Then I remembered the advertisement in the comic books. I remembered how it had excited my imagination and how I'd grown to adore my brine shrimp. And the line just popped into my head—'Boys, raise giant sea scorpions in your aquarium!'

"There was the pesky detail of the ban on removing specimens for other than scientific purposes. Of course, I dropped broad hints to sundry and all that I was willing and able to pay for an expedition or two out of petty cash. Penury makes scientists so opportunistic. It's not pretty to see. I *refused* to be satisfied with the gratitude of the scientific community, with having a new species of marine worm and an ancient landmark named in my honor in token of its esteem. They even tried to buy me off with a dead trilobite sealed inside a clear plastic paperweight. I contrived to stock my tank with fabulous creatures from Paleozoic seas. Then I started my Paleozoic terrarium.

Then it occurred to me that glass-sided tanks were all well and fine in their way, but I wanted—I wanted the full Paleozoic experience. Creatures, plants, even air and soil. And here we are! What good is a collection that can't be shown off?"

The catwalk ended at a platform set against the rear wall of the building. Here they found what could only be Mr. Cahill, sitting slumped inside his exoskeleton, whose delicate mechanisms had withstood the effects of the simulated Paleozoic environment better than he. The humid atmosphere was ideal for bacteria and fungi, and they had made short work of his corpse.

"Jesus," said Selby. "And I thought it was just this damn homemade swamp that needed sterilizing."

Both he and Nolan let out a squeak when they heard the dead man's disembodied voice again. "Tell 'em, SpokesMom™."

The air on the platform shimmered. SpokesMom™ appeared and said, sweetly, "Remember who has durable power of attorney. We intend to take good care of Mister Cahill's interests. I'm afraid you can't sterilize this place as yet, and perhaps not ever. Mister Cahill's options have hardly been exhausted."

"Mister Cahill is dead."

"Technically, not officially. Fortunately, he and the clan had become virtually consubstantial by the time the exoskeleton's life-support systems failed. As you can see, we were able to synthesize him. It was the least we could do. He *created* us. He was *family*. He'd been so determined to see his dream to fruition, we had no choice but to make it possible for him to do so. You are the first people he's had a chance to show it off to."

Selby bared his teeth. "We're also the *only* people who're going to see it, except the sterilization team."

"We will of course do all we legally can to preserve this garden, just as we mean to preserve his various collections, as memorials to him."

"The autopsy ought to be very interesting. From the

looks of things, this particular memorial may have killed him!"

"Oh, I always *told* him to put on his respirator mask before he came in here," said SpokesMom™, a bit reproachfully and with a wetly glistening eye, "but he was just an overgrown boy, and you know how careless boys can be."

The Cascade

SEAN McMULLEN

Sean McMullen [www.bdsonline.net/seanmcmullen/] lives in Melbourne, and is one of the new Australian SF and fantasy writers to emerge in the late 1980s. He won the William Atheling, Jr. Award three times in the 1990s. His bibliographies are an essential underpinning of the Melbourne University Press Encyclopedia of Australian Science Fiction & Fantasy *(1998). Nine early stories are collected in* Call to the Edge *(1992). His first two novels,* Voices in the Light *(1994) and the sequel,* Mirrorsun Rising *(1995), were part of the projected Greatwinter series. He combined and rewrote the first two Greatwinter novels as* Souls in the Great Machine *(Tor, 1999). The sequel,* The Miocene Arrow, *and another,* The Eyes of the Calculor, *were finally published in 2001.* Voyage of the Shadowmoon *and* Glass Dragons, *both fantasy novels, are his latest books.*

"The Cascade" was published in the original anthology, Agog! Terrific Tales. *The Agog annual anthology series, edited and published by Cat Sparks, is currently the flagship annual anthology of Australian SF, fantasy, and horror. This story is told from the point of view of a lonely techie, in love with the idea of space travel, who picks up an overeager but very smart girl in a bar on the night of the Mars landing. Or she picks him, perhaps. She's got a secret she shares with him. It is striking that this story was written by an Australian and published in Australia, which separates it somewhat from assumptions about its politics that would be automatic if it were American.*

After years of hearing my grandfather's regrets about not bothering to watch the first moon landing as it happened, I made sure that I watched the Mars landing live-to-air. Firebird descended smoothly to the red sands of a computer-selected landing site that balanced thousands of scientific agendas against the safety of the crew. Its cameras showed the panorama of the surface while the bland, laconic astronaut-patter of the crew gave the impression that it was no more exciting than ordering a beer at a bar.

I had, in fact, just ordered a beer at a bar. The pub was one of a dozen on the edges of the university campus, and was filled with students and staff from the nearby School of Physics. There was near-silence as the Firebird's landing rockets fired briefly to cushion the actual touchdown, then the gently swaying image on the screen became absolutely steady. Everyone found themselves cheering, and even complete strangers exchanged their impressions and opinions.

That was how I met Julia.

"Hey, wasn't that the greatest thing since they invented the orgasm?" she laughed in relief, clinking her glass against mine in a toast to the distant astronauts.

"Oh yeah, but couldn't they have sent the pilot to Toastmasters to get a bit of life into that bland American accent?" I replied.

"A British accent would be just the thing, but we Brits blew our chance to get a manned spaceflight capacity of our own."

"That's the price of a ticket on Firebird," I agreed. "Australia was not even in the hunt."

Julia said that she had been attending a conference on molecular modeling, and now that it was over she was planning to stay a few days longer and explore Melbourne. The word "nondescript" suited her perfectly. She had the look of some postgraduate student who was more interested in molecular structural orientation than dress sense, and had mousey brown hair tied back sharply, a pale, round face, and practical, sexless clothes. Because we were both postgraduate science students, we had been following the Firebird expedition to Mars with interest and had a lot to say to each other on the subject. We were on our third round of drinks when the view from Firebird switched from the camera pointing down at the sand to another at the lander's apex.

We watched with something between rapture and fascination as the camera slowly rotated, showing red plains, distant hills, the lander's parachutes collapsed to the northeast, and a scatter of boulders and rocks.

"How could something so uninteresting be so fascinating?" asked Julia.

"A bit like people," I replied. "They're most interesting when you've just met them."

"Does that mean I'm most fascinating to you right now?" she giggled, giving me a little push.

"Oh no, I, ah, wasn't making a move," I said hurriedly.

"Hey, but I was," she replied. "I just checked out of a room at the conference hotel, and I'm on the way to a motel in Royal Parade . . . but do you live nearby?"

I am generally shy and clumsy where the smalltalk of seduction is concerned, but the drinks and the excitement of the Mars landing had made me light-headed and bold. Besides, she had already taken the initiative.

"I'm renting a place in North Melbourne. It's only a short walk from here," I suggested.

The first footfall interrupted our negotiations. Clare Garret, one of the American astronauts, was to take the first step on the surface. She had been chosen by flipping the first silver dollar to reach Mars. The camera followed the white-suited figure down the access ladder, then she stepped onto the red sand.

"That's the next big step to the next world," she declared, and everyone cheered and hooted their approval.

Julia and I stayed for a few minutes more, watching Garret padding about on the sands of Mars, poking at rocks and taking samples. The streets were relatively empty as we walked to my place, as most people were still watching the Mars landing. We went straight to bed, but our lovemaking was as brief as such activity tends to be when both parties are vaguely drunk. I was asleep fairly quickly, but at what turned out to be 3 am I awoke to discover Julia awake and watching the Mars landing broadcast. She was listening to the commentary on my headphones. I guessed that she was probably jetlagged and still on British time. She noticed that I was awake, and removed the headphones.

"The first hours on a new world," she said dreamily. "I just couldn't waste the chance to watch it live."

"It's such a big thing," I replied. "I wish I could have been part of it."

"In what way?"

"Any way. Spray painting a bit of equipment that makes the trip, working on an antenna for the comms link. Anything at all."

"I helped," she said, staring at the screen with her chin resting on her knees.

"You did?" I exclaimed. "How?"

"Oh—ah, only a small thing. I calculated some orbits—I have an astronomy major as well as chemistry."

"Astronomy? I'm impressed."

"Don't be. Not much in career prospects, and even less money when you do find a job. I normally work in industrial programming and control systems, but I was offered some contract work for the Firebird project and I took it. The money was not great, and my work was probably around a billionth of the total effort, but I know I helped get them there. I look at the screen and think *all my own work*."

"Unbelievable," I breathed, putting an arm around her.

"Watching the Mars landing, and in bed with someone who made it possible."

"There's nothing special about me," she laughed.

"To me there is."

"Ah, another dreamer," she sighed, leaning against me.

That first night together was strangely surreal. With the television pouring out images from Mars to us, we ate crisps, drank half a cask of wine, made love, watched the astronauts capering on the Martian sands, and occasionally slept. Late in the morning we visited the Victoria Market in my old Toyota. Julia was wearing one of my coats, because she said she liked the style. She bought a new coat of her own plus other clothing while I shopped for the fruit and vegetables. She said she liked buying clothes overseas, because they would always remind her of being away and having fun.

"When do you have to be at university?" she asked as we strolled among the stalls.

"It's Saturday, remember?" I replied.

"Saturday, that's right," she said quietly. "Lost a day . . . somewhere."

We ate lunch on the floor in front of my little fireplace, watching the astronauts preparing to retire for the Martian night. The coverage cut to the interior of Firebird, where one of the crew had produced a bottle of champagne that had been smuggled aboard, and they toasted their success out of plastic cups. Soon after that the transmission ended, and we were left with local commentators speculating about whether or not the first sexual encounter on Mars was now taking place. Julia turned the television off.

"We do it all night and nobody gives a toss," I sighed, "but everyone cares about what *they* do. They're like gods."

"We are no different to the astronauts," she replied. "I've even beaten three of them in some tests and exercises."

I turned to face her so quickly that I spilled my drink.

"Did you say you've *met* them?" I exclaimed.

"Three of them, yes."

"Hey, that's just, like, awesome. What were they like?"

"Sort of . . . steady, you know? People who wash their

mug and put it away after coffee, or check their car's brake lights once a week. The funny thing is that they were not at all boring in spite of that. The two guys, Brad and Juri, even made the moves on me."

"What, you mean . . . like they asked you to go to bed with them?"

"That's what I said."

I swallowed. "Oh. Er, well, did you?"

"Do I look stupid? A chance to get laid by the first men going to Mars? Who would say *pass* on that?"

Firebird was not intended to return to Earth, it was merely a lander crammed with equipment and stores. Another craft had been sent during the previous launch window, and Phoenix contained the ascent and return stages. Firebird had come down fifteen miles from Phoenix, and around midnight Melbourne time Brad Morgan and Svetlana Korrenov set off in the rover to check Phoenix for damage. On the television screen we saw a squat, white cone growing larger on a red horizon. There were some anxious moments as the two astronauts unsealed a hatch and clambered inside, but after twenty minutes of tests and checks the verdict came back that Phoenix was fully operational.

"Notice that the average age of those folk is twenty two," said Julia as we watched Svetlana resealing the hatch.

"Yeah?" I replied. "Well I'm twenty two, and I wish I was there."

"Their average IQ is one hundred and seventy, they all have university degrees, and none of them graduated older than nineteen. They have zero history of cancer and mental illness going all the way back to their grandparents, and those grandparents lived to an average age of ninety one."

"Well, get sick in space and you're screwed," I said with a shrug. "They were chosen to stay healthy."

"Lucel and Mei are both doctors, and Mei is a surgeon, too. The biology lab on Firebird can double as a clinic and operating theater. That crew has better medical coverage than we do."

* * *

We turned off the television and went to bed. The following morning we had breakfast as we watched the astronauts drill into the Martian surface. While we had been sleeping, they had discovered permafrost. The seven explorers now had a local supply of water. The scene switched back to the Firebird lander, where the crew was unpacking, setting up a pressure tent and generally cleaning up.

At this point I decided that if housework was good enough for the astronauts, it was good enough for me. I washed the breakfast dishes first, then started on the laundry.

"Anything to wash?" I asked Julia as she sat staring at the television screen with an odd intensity.

"Oh thanks. In my backpack, the middle section. Hold your breath for the socks, I've been making them last a bit longer than is healthy."

The reason that I shall probably never make a very good astronaut is that I am clumsy. I do things without thinking, and that is just what I did when I picked up Julia's bag. I lifted it by the velcro flap at the front, spilling the contents of the pouch. A heavy, angular thing with Smith & Wesson stamped on the side fell to the floor. I backed away from it, then looked to Julia, who had up snatched her coat, drawn a second gun, and trained it on me.

"Smith and Wesson 459," she said in a soft, flat voice. "Fourteen rounds, 9mm, effective range of forty yards, and designed for use with the U.S. Special Forces about thirty years ago. Notice that the barrel has been modified to take a silencer, and notice the safety catch is off on this one."

"But, but, where, how—I mean . . . ?" I managed, then gave up. In my entire life I had never had a real gun pointed at me. I finally thought to raise my hands.

"Just move away from the gun on the floor," she ordered.

"Who are you?" I asked as I backed away.

"They caught up with me in a hotel in the CBD," she said as she picked up the second gun. Their trouble was that they were expecting some college nerd, but my father was once in the British SAS, and he had taught me a thing or two. When the first Special burst in I flung a kitchen knife and hit him in the eye. Lucky throw, but it went nearly all the way in. He dropped quietly, and I took his gun. I stepped out and shot his backup, then I was away with their money, weapons and ID. That was a couple of hours before I met you."

"But a double murder!" I gasped. "It would have been big news."

"I suppose their number three was close by. He would have got my room cleared out and scrubbed. They're not supposed to be operating in this country."

"But why?" I asked, numb with shock. "Are you a terrorist?"

"It's because of that," she said, jerking a thumb in the direction of the television and its scenes from the surface of Mars.

"It's people like you who are to blame," said Julia as we sat with the washing machine sloshing steadily in the kitchen annex. I was by now tied to a chair. "You killed the push into space."

"Me?" I exclaimed, somehow more confident because I was so obviously no longer a threat. "I'm doing post-grad work in robotics and AI. Most of modern space exploration is based on what people like me are doing."

"I know. A couple of dozen remote-controlled crawlers on the moon—and dozens more robots scattered around the solar system. Real people have not been back to the moon since 1972, because remotes do exploration cheaper."

This seemed like a bad time to tell her that I had once driven a lunar remote for ten minutes. Those minutes had been first prize in a robotics competition that I had won.

"So? We're still exploring out there, which is the important thing."

"*We* have to go into space because we *have* to live there!" she said firmly, a dangerous-looking intensity in her stare. "I trained as an astronaut for ESA—in fact I'm still on the list to visit the International Space Station. I shall give it up for the greater good, though."

"You, an astronaut?" I exclaimed. "You're not old enough."

"I'm actually thirty-one, but I keep in good shape and do

most of my exercise in gyms. Sunlight ages the skin rather rapidly, you see. I have a rather girlish little face, too. People don't take me seriously. Big mistake."

"I'm taking you very seriously," I assured her.

"Very wise of you."

By now it was Sunday night, and Mars Channel was running. The screen displayed a squat cylinder on the red sand. Within it were a thousand fertilized human eggs in liquid nitrogen. A thousand rich couples had paid ten million dollars each to have their fertilized eggs flown to Mars. The idea was that upon the expedition's return the embryos could be implanted and brought to term. A thousand parents would then have a child that had been to Mars. The money had helped the cash-starved project to survive just long enough to launch Firebird.

"It was supposed to be a lottery, but the prospective couples were secretly screened for a family history of cancer and dementia, and they had very high IQs. Then the draw was rigged."

"I don't follow," I admitted.

"The expedition will never come back."

There is little one can say to a statement like that. Little that's sensible, at any rate. I decided to say nothing. On the screen, sheets of solar paneling were being laid out, while some samples of permafrost water were fed into an electro-catalytic splitter. With oxygen and hydrogen from the water, the expedition would have air to breathe and fuel to burn. Carbon dioxide from the atmosphere would supply carbon, and with carbon, hydrogen and oxygen one has the scope to synthesize effectively limitless amounts of plastics. An announcer was explaining that the expedition was to do a lot of proof-of-concept work for possible future space colonies. Small, robotic units would be left running when the expedition left, to monitor how long the equipment would last without maintenance.

"Just think of what is aboard the ascent stage in Phoenix," said Julia as she checked the rounds in her two spare clips of ammunition. "Tell me, what do *you* think is aboard?"

"Ah, maybe there's nothing aboard but stores and equipment," I ventured, groping about for a conspiracy. "If the explorers were never meant to return, that is."

"Wrong. Phoenix has a fully functional spacecraft, capable of taking seven people back to Earth. It's powered by solid fuel rockets, however, and that solid fuel is rich in nitrates. There are a several dozen tons of nitrogen ready to harvest, and with nitrogen comes agriculture. Svetlana could easily rig up a conversion plant, and with careful recycling the nitrates could help grow plants to feed dozens of people for a century or more."

Three female hamsters and five bantam hens had survived the journey to Mars, along with frozen semen. Carol Connel was to experiment with raising livestock in Martian colony conditions. When one looked at the expedition through Julia's filter of paranoia, it did look quite alarming, however. The experiments in self-sufficiency could all help support the colonists indefinitely. They even had access to enough genetic diversity to set up a viable offshoot of the human race.

"So, the explorers are all ready to maroon themselves forever," I concluded, clasping my hands tightly. "When do they make their move?"

"They won't," said Julia. "They don't have the slightest idea what's about to happen."

"You mean the return craft is sabotaged?"

"No. It should work perfectly."

"Then what?"

"There is a very small conspiracy by some very dedicated people. Unfortunately, one of them had a big mouth. *Had* is the operative word."

I called in sick to the university on Monday, the barrel of Julia's gun pressed against my forehead as I spoke into the phone. She then burned her old coat, jeans and shoes in my fireplace, and changed into the clothes she had bought at the market. I got a good look at what was in her backpack. She also burned all the rubbish that could have been associated with her. There were rubber and leather gloves; a laptop PC; a few CDs marked in code; three passports; quite a lot of American, European and Australian money; and five pairs of sunglasses. There was also hair dye, tan coloring, a small radio-frequency scanner, and several other electronic devices that I could not identify.

"You're well prepared for running," I observed.

"All the others like me have vanished," she said softly. "They vanished together, on the same night. I had my suspicions before that, though. Dad always said if I ever had to step outside the law, then I should do it with a cool head. I'd set up a second identity, and as that identity I slept in another apartment. Every morning I phoned a couple of the others to make sure they were still there. One morning I got no reply. I started running when I saw the headline: FIVE KILLED IN MOTORWAY HORROR SMASH."

"You must have been planning something really bad if the government had to do that."

"It involved trillions of dollars. Enough to send hundreds of people to Mars, and have enough left over for an expedition to the Jovian moons as well. Enough talk, though. Where is your toolbox and soldering iron?"

"My—er, what makes you think—"

"You work in robotics, and there are little splatters of solder on the kitchen table."

"In the pantry, top shelf."

She had worn black leather gloves whenever she was outside, but now she put on latex gloves. I watched as she wiped her fingerprints from everything that she had touched over the weekend.

"You can't get them all," I said hopefully.

"Think so? I was very careful and methodical about what I touched when not wearing gloves."

"So, you're going to kill me and leave no evidence of yourself?" I said with resignation.

"No, I am eliminating every trace of myself from your unit, so we shall not be associated with one another. Soon I will be a very, very bad person to be associated with."

She must have guessed what I was thinking.

"Yes, even worse than now. Much, much worse."

The thing that she assembled on the kitchen table did not resemble a bomb. She soldered thirty batteries together, then packed the power source into a cardboard box and sealed it up with packing tape. Her soldering was competent, rather than expert. Someone else had probably built the modules for whatever she was assembling. When it was complete, she emptied two of my boxes of tissues and packed the batteries and components into them. The tissues went onto the fire.

"If you'd been some classics nerd with no technical gear, I'd have been screwed," she said as she worked.

"What are you making?" I asked as she began to work on a collection of aluminum tubes and wire mesh. "It looks like a directional antenna."

"Top marks," she replied.

"What's it for?"

"Sending a message."

"To who?"

"To what. There is a very large industrial satellite called Sunflower in low Earth orbit. It has a subtle flaw in its control software because corners were cut during design work for reasons of economics. It was highly dangerous. Any scabby little terrorist organization with access to a competent technician, a skilled programmer and about five thousand dollars in electronic gear could land Sunflower in New York, London, or even Melbourne. We worked out a far better use for it . . . but one of my co-conspirators must have panicked and told the company directors. They evidently decided that it made more economic sense to do nothing instead of flying a couple of astronauts up to hardwire a few safety features into Sunflower. There was the small matter of one small group of amateur terrorists who already knew the secret, but killing us also made good economic sense. You have no idea how I hate the phrase *good economic sense*— you see I am a dreamer."

"So am I," I admitted automatically.

"Ah, but unlike dreamers like you, I believe in making dreams real."

"I would, given a chance!"

"But I *made* a chance."

My shoulders sagged as I was forced to accept that she was right. I would have advised Caesar not to cross the Rubicon, I would have suggested that Alexander have a little more patience with the Gordian Knot, and I probably would have told the Wright Brothers to put all their creative energies into designing a better bicycle instead of mucking about with gliders. Given the chance . . . I would not take it.

"How many will die?" I asked with the resignation of one not expecting to survive until dawn.

"None, with luck."

"None?"

"None."

"But you've killed already."

"I was defending myself. My dream has a very high price tag, one that everyone will have to help with. Can I pay my share, can I dare, can I care? Should I let my dream die? Alas, poor dream, I knew it well . . ."

Suddenly she was a very different person: softer, stranger. She ran some tests on her antenna, then disassembled it and put everything into her backpack.

"So, you are going?" I observed.

"Yes. I shall go very quietly, watching out for hunters and lurkers."

"How long have I got?"

"Sorry?"

"To live?"

"How long have any of us got? An hour, a month, a fighting chance to see first light of the twenty-second century through the window of some nursing home? In a few minutes I'll go, leaving you untied. You could try calling for the police, but then what evidence do you have that I exist? You don't even know what I'm planning."

I was untied once it was dark outside, and with her gun pressing into my stomach she gave me a light kiss on the forehead.

"Dare to dream, and do not let your dreams be corroded by the acid of budget surpluses that are needed to help governments win elections," she said as she shouldered her backpack. "Space exploration allocations are always the sacrificial lamb that is fed to such surpluses." She opened the door. "And now, I am out of your life."

I did not even hear her footsteps on the stairs. She was right, in a sense. What could I do? Who would believe me? What she did not realize was that I knew who she was, even though I did not know her name. I had seen the headline announcing the death of her friends, and although there are horror smashes on the world's roads and motorways every day, the one involving her friends had found its way to the screen of my PC. It was on the website of the British Interplanetary Society, and I just happened to be a member of the BIS:

FIVE MEMBERS INCINERATED IN HORROR
SMASH WITH TANKER.

I logged onto the Net and checked the BIS site again. The item was a week old, but beneath the image of a burned-out car were five photographs. Lissy Galbraith had Julia's face, but somehow I still thought of her as Julia. I read the bio paragraph. "At the time of her death, Lissy was a senior systems engineer in the UK offices of Sunflower Orbital Industries of Chicago." No doubt they had found her missing from her home, but maybe one of her co-conspirators had been sleeping with another girl. They had assumed her to be Julia, and not discovered their mistake until it was too late. Just what had they planned? No lives would be lost through her conspiracy, she had said . . .

Then I had it! The Mars expedition, an orbital zero-G factory, the dim future for manned space exploration, and trillions of dollars to be lost—it all fitted together! Giddy with shock, I opened the door to my tiny balcony and stepped outside into the fresh air. By now Julia would be miles away, probably in a stolen car, I was sure of that. Almost at once I noticed that one very special car was missing from the street outside. A colleague of mine lived nearby, but was currently overseas. His car had been parked under a gum tree, but now it was missing. Julia would have taken such a car. It was sprinkled with leaves and birdshit, and looked as if it would not be missed for quite a while. I went back inside, turned on the television, sat down, and stared at the images of astronauts preparing to start another day's work on the Martian surface. I picked up the telephone's handset, noted that there was a dial tone, dialed the number for Police and Emergency Services—then made a hasty decision and slammed the handset down. Presently I dozed in my chair.

There was nothing on the news about shootouts or bodies the following morning. I went to the university, I did some work on a research project proposal, I jogged at lunchtime, then I went home and watched the scenes from Mars on television. Everything was so normal, apart from some condoms that were absent from a packet in my bathroom cabinet, and a small, new splatter of solder on the kitchen table that was shaped like a star with eight points. I eased it off the surface with a blade and held it between my fingers. To me, it was the only tangible proof that Julia existed. I also did some calculations concerning the Sunflower orbiting refinery, and thereafter I made sure that I was looking up whenever it was passing over Melbourne.

I did not see Sunflower explode. What I saw, on the third evening after Julia had left, was a vast comet of silvery pinpoints, traveling south, every fragment with a speed of over seventeen thousand miles per hour. Even as I watched, the spreading cloud slammed into something else in an intersecting orbit. There was a flash, a starburst of glitter, then more flashers. I watched until the cloud had passed out of sight, then went inside and turned on the television.

They were calling it "the cascade." Sunflower had been crammed with refined sand for zero-G processing, and it had burst apart over northern Australia. The huge satellite was orbiting at an inclination of forty-five degrees to the equator, and had an empty weight of sixty tons. The key word was empty. Sunflower was certainly not empty at the time of the explosion—in fact it had four times its own weight in refined sand aboard. It also had enormous solar panels to power the processing of the sand into silicon products.

I watched it all on my small television, not sleeping at all that night. Every satellite, every spent upper stage of every rocket, every piece of space junk that the cascade destroyed became a new cascade. There were soon more visible fragments than stars, and the cascade's fringes spread into higher orbits and latitudes. It started slowly enough for the International Space Station to be evacuated, and for most of the night the entire focus of the world's media was on the astronauts in their two evacuation de-orbiters. The retro rockets were fired as soon as the craft were clear of the station, and no thought was given to where they would land. Any place on Earth was safer than near-Earth orbit. There was worldwide rejoicing as soon as they were on the ground. Thus the cascade claimed no human casualties, but by morning it had become an immense curtain of fine particles, each with the momentum of a car pushed off the roof of a house.

Media attention and public interest now turned to the astronauts on Mars, the seven humans stranded tens of millions of miles away. Two Americans, two Russians, and nationals from Japan, China and France. They were in no immediate danger, because the cascade's threat was confined to everything in near-Earth orbit. Those on Mars had both stored and renewable supplies to last twice the length of the planned expedition, we were assured. The problem was that the return craft would find near-Earth space to be more dangerous than the middle of the most intensely fought battle in all of history. As one expert put it, one would have had a better chance going for a jog through the Battle of the Somme.

There was as structured an interview with the astronauts on Mars as one can have, given the distances and lightspeed delays. Inevitably, that age-old standby of journalists was asked: how did they feel?

"Rather like being diagnosed with a medical condition leaving you with five years to live," Carol replied to the question asked several minutes earlier on another world. "Five years allows you to do a lot of living, and gives you the hope that science can come up with something in that time."

Svetlana was far more optimistic. "If we can last five

years, I can give us the raw materials to last until we die of old age," she added confidently.

"How will you cope with being separated from your loved ones for five years, and perhaps forever?" was the next question in the queue.

This question was fielded by Brad, the cool but dynamic pilot and leader.

"We have been carefully screened for emotional stability, intelligence and a history of good health," he said, almost sounding as if he might be pleased. "None of us have close relationships on Earth, either. Right now all exploration work is on hold while we assess how we can extend our existing supplies. We could even recycle a lot more than was planned and hey, we're masters of an entire planet, and there's no taxes here."

Sunflower's demise was an accident, according to Sunflower Orbital Industries. Through a billion-to-one chance, the safety cutoffs in the controlling software had become corrupted and allowed a buildup of current that overloaded the coils of the electric furnace, causing it to explode. White-hot fragments of coil and searing plasma had slashed through Sunflower's innards and hit the fuel tanks. Of course I knew that a radio signal from Australia had touched off the explosion, but I was not silly enough to tell anyone.

As the days passed, estimates of the number of fragments from the cascade climbed through hundreds of millions, to billions, then to trillions. After trillions, nobody bothered with absolute numbers. It was all fragments per cubic kilometer of space. The estimates of the energies remained rather colorful, however. The grain of sand with the energy of a bowling ball dropped from the roof of an office block was popular, and the wristwatch that hit with the force of a truck speeding along a freeway got almost as many mentions.

I watched the light shows in the sky as occasional fragments burned up in the atmosphere, and orbiting debris sparkled against the background of the stars in morning and evening skies. Within five days there were no satellites operational below geostationary orbit—all had been pounded and shattered by fragments the size of ball bearings that hit with the force of cannon shells. Every satellite that shattered produced more fragments in new orbits. The space station's demise was a beautiful blossoming of scintillating glitter, and was described as the most widely watched and most expensive entertainment in history. Every company that depended on satellites was bankrupted, but the majority of people soon learned to cope without their services.

Project Firebird was to have been like Project Apollo—a hurried gesture proving that we could get to Mars, but with no followup. Firebird had been commenced during a decade of prosperity, but by the time it had been ready to launch, times had become tough. The expedition only went ahead because so much money had already been spent and cancellation would have seemed an even greater waste.

Humanity has now been cut off from space for ten years, yet Mars is still being explored and colonized, and it has a population of two dozen. The colony is prospering, in a frugal sort of way, and expertise from Earth pours across the radio links whenever they need help. True, the cost has been hundreds of trillions of dollars in lost satellites and services, and humanity being cut off from space travel for centuries by the twinkling debris that I could have stopped, but did not. Every time I look up at the night sky I feel guilty, but given my time over again, I would still not have reported a certain car stolen.

Mars channel is still operating, pouring scenes into our homes every night from the newest frontier. Farms have been built under greenhouses of plastic from Svetlana's hydrocarbon refinery, and Firebird Base has become a little village of walkway tubes and pressure tents. Microscopic life has been found and studied in springs heated by radioactive decay, ancient seabeds have yielded fossils, caves have been discovered that could accommodate a colony of thousands, and there are strangely regular markings on a sheltered cliff face that are probably natural . . . but could be script.

Although I can never say it to my wife or our seven-year-old daughter, whenever I look at the television's images from the Mars colony I think *I helped create that*. Together, Julia and I forced humanity to take a bold but wonderful step. I often think of her, then I caress a small, star-shaped splatter of solder mounted on a ring that I always wear. I always wonder if she ever thinks of me.

Pervert

CHARLES COLEMAN FINLAY

Charles Coleman Finlay [home.earthlink.net/~ccfinaly/personal.html] lives in Columbus, Ohio. He says on his website, "Besides writing fiction, he serves as Administrator for Online Writing Workshops and builds a research database for historians and constitutional scholars." His first story was published in 2001, and he has since published about twenty stories and been nominated for several awards in SF. In 2003, he was nominated for the John W. Campbell Award for Best New Writer. He has a fantasy novel, The Prodigal Troll, *forthcoming.*

"Pervert" was published in Fantasy & Science Fiction. *It is a strange tale from the first line, not quite a horror story, but certainly an anxiety story. It is about sex in the future, and the political repression of sex, that reminds us of the well-known Afghani film,* Osama. *The world Finlay posits is so alien that it is creepy to realize it is a human future.*

There are two kinds of people in the world, homosexuals and hydrosexuals. And then there are perverts like me.

Jamin and Zel stroll through the corridor of the apartment building where we all live. I can tell it's them coming because I leave my door cracked open to show everyone I have nothing to hide. Zel's voice caroms off the walls, fluctuating in pitch with the peaks and rhythms of the stories he tells; Jamin's subdued, distinctive laugh barks out at regular intervals. For thirty or forty seconds before they arrive, I hear their approach and dread it. They are my best friends.

I sit in the exact center of the little blue sofa, arms stretching out to the ends of its bell-shaped back. My palms are damp against the silky fabric. The voice of Noh Sis, last year's most popular singer, warbles from the stereo speakers, making a dirge of joy amid the interweaving of sitar and clarinets. Closing my eyes, I count the notes and half-notes by measure—the sorrowful tone in the end-rhyme of *love,* Zel's exclamation, a series of mournful sitar chords, Jamin's laugh.

The tap at the door.

I lift my head as if surprised to see them, smile as if happy. "Hey!"

Zel throws wide his arms in an extravagant gesture of greeting, and says with dead seriousness, "Arise! Arise like the evening star and brighten the way into night for us!"

Jamin grins, nods at me. "Hello."

They are both tall, and handsome, and completely at ease

in themselves. Jamin is balding, so he shaves his head; he has quiet, wolfish features. His jeans and football jersey look like they've been ironed—he's so conservative that even here in the men's quarter, he wears a cap to cover his head. Zel is the shaggy, adorable puppy, all awkward limbs and endless energy. He shows off his new boots.

I wipe my hands on my thighs, arise, and embrace them in turn with only a dry quick kiss on the cheek. "Where are you going?"

"*We,*" Zel exclaims, "we, for surely you are joining us— we won't have a speck of fun without you!"

Jamin grins—he always grins—and says, "Heart Nouveau."

Heart Nouveau is our club. We've been hanging out there since it opened around the time that we were finishing school. All our friends go there. It's the kind of place so packed and dark you can't see any decor beyond the dance floor.

"Not tonight," I answer. "Work exhausted me today."

My work itself is not hard, but I must be constantly wary lest I give myself away.

Zel immediately begins pleading, making dance gyrations, beckoning me to join them, but Jamin, with his hands folded at his waist in front of him, says quietly, "Thinking about marrying this weekend, are you?"

"Ah—"

Zel's eyes widen at this revelation and he ceases the call to fun. The two of them are a happy couple. They know that I am different from them and do their best to fit me into their view of the world, and the way it works.

"—been thinking about it," I admit.

"Pshaw! Don't think about it, just do it!" says Zel as Jamin backs out the doorway, whispering to me, "I'll call you tomorrow."

Their voices resume their previous pattern as they continue their journey down the corridor toward the stairs. Pushing the door closed, I let my face lean against it, eyes shut for a moment while I twist the lock. Then I go and fall onto the sofa, lifting my head only long enough to replay the previous song at a higher volume. The chorus opens the song: "I want to set myself on fire and plunge into the oceans of your love."

My face presses against the water-blue color of the pillows, trying to drown in them. "That's it—I'm only nervous about marrying this weekend," I lie aloud to myself.

It's natural to be nervous about it the first time. I'll just do it, like Zel says, and then everything will be better.

You would think, as much as I practice lying to myself, I'd be better at it by now.

In the morning, I swath myself in my work robes—cheery layers of nectarine and lemon fabric, sherbet smooth. Covering my head and face, I walk down to the street and catch the bus into the city. The road bridges a green river of trees and grass that divides one quarter of the city from another. Through the bus window I watch the women emerging from their apartment blocks and little homes.

When the bus reaches the corner, they climb onboard, taking seats on their side and evening out the ride so it doesn't feel so much like we'll tip over. We rattle along past road construction, the men working behind screens that are consecrated by the priests each morning as part of the men's quarter, and resanctified to the women at quitting time. The Sun already pelts down mercilessly and they will have to leave off working soon.

We enter the government quarter and arrive at the Children's Center, a long concrete brick of a building with windows shielded from the Sun by an open grid of deep squares made of the same material. The morning light turns it into a chessboard of glaring white and dark shadow. I don't work with the children, who are on the lower floors and the sheltered playground of the courtyard, but toil away with records on the upper floors. Unlike Jamin or Zel, I am permitted by the job to work alongside women, but only because I completed my theological studies and am a candidate for the priesthood. My superiors do not know of the taint on my soul. Do not know yet, I should say, and when they discover it, I will never be ordained or promoted.

Today I am veryifying and recording the DNA strands of a recent set of births. My cubicle sits closer to the outer windows, with their view of rigid grid, than the inner, but it's blocked from the light of either. Nevertheless, I jump when the slightest shadow passes by and see her—I see Ali.

Ah, Ali! Ali, my all, my everything, the eye of the hurricane that is my heart! Ali, that ails me! Ali, who alone can heal me! Ali, Ali!

This is silliness, of course; yet it is how I feel.

She stops and stares at the floor.

"What are you looking for?" I ask.

She turns her head this way and that. "The button I accidentally stepped on to give you that electric shock."

Ali is wearing coffee-colored robes, cream and roasted bean, the same as many of the other women in her department, and as she is a perfectly average height, with her head and almost all her face covered, I am still puzzling out how I always recognize at once it's her, whether there's something specific in her posture or gestures or presence that makes me know her instantly.

So I say, "Huh?"

And her head lifts up so that her eyes turn toward me, glinting with amusement. I would recognize those stormy, sea-gray eyes anywhere. "You are mocking me!" I cry.

She shakes her head. "It's very difficult not to."

I blush, the heat rising through my face to my forehead, and I'm sure she can see right through my mask.

She chuckles, and then walks to another cubicle several spaces over where she speaks to one of our sister workers about the name for some particular child.

How can I describe her effect on me? In a single second, I suffer such pangs of longings, an overwhelming urge to peel away the layers of her robes like shells off a bean and root through her flesh until I find the hard nut, the seed core, of my perverse, unnatural desire. So far as I know, there is not a word, not even a bit of slang, to describe my particular depravity, but then I have never spoken of it to anyone, nor written of it before now, and we do not invent words for the things we dare not speak or write.

When I was studying theogenetics in preparation for the priesthood, we were taught that it was wrong to name certain thoughts lest we be tempted to think them. We were taught that everything was black and white, right or wrong, and even then I learned to give all the right answers.

But what right answer is there to my desire? All I have ever seen of Ali are her eyes. The white of her eyes and the black pupils are just like everyone else's. But that cloudy, wave-tossed gray is wholly hers! And all my world is gray now too, as if something swirling deep within me since the moment of my conception has finally taken shape, the way clouds form when wind swirls in a clear sky.

Jamin calls me at work later that day, just as he had promised he would, his voice warm and resonant as always. "I hope you don't mind," he says, "but I've arranged for you to join me and a friend for dinner tonight."

"Sounds great—will Zel be joining us?"

"No. Just us."

Jamin is looking out for me, the way he has always tried to. He is a very good friend, yet I am filled with trepidation. "Well," I say. "I might be working late."

"That's fine. I can wait. Pick you up in a taxi at quitting time?"

"Sure," I say and disconnect.

I look up from my desk but Ali is nowhere to be seen in the breakwater of cubicle walls. Sometimes I may see her no more than once in a day, though it feels like she is always with me since I cannot stop thinking of her.

For the rest of the day I cannot concentrate on genetic sequences at all and my work is useless.

When the taxi crosses into the men's quarter, the driver and I remove our veils although Jamin leaves his on. He makes happy small talk about his work. I smile, but inside I am tense.

We're dropped off in a neighborhood where fruit trees shade the narrow streets. The houses are neat and tidy and old, the kind owned by government officials and couples who both have excellent jobs. Jamin leads me to a door by an elaborate garden that appears to be both lovingly created and recently neglected.

The man who answers is not quite twice our age, perhaps a little younger. His beard looks new, as though his chin has gone untended for about as long as the garden outside. He wears a comfortable, tailored suit.

Inside, Jamin finally uncovers his face and embraces the older man, saying, "Hello, Hodge. This is the friend I was telling you about—"

Somehow I cheerfully complete the introductions. Jamin and I sit at a counter in the kitchen while Hodge finishes cooking our dinner. The room smells of garlic and oil. Jamin and Hodge discuss work—they are both employed in law—and I avoid nearly all the personal questions directed at me. The songs of Noh Sis stream from the speakers to fill most of the awkward silences.

We are seated around Hodge's elegant antique table, having finished a delightful cold corn chowder and a hot pepper salad. A platter of spinach-feta pastries rests between us. As I am helping myself to a second serving, and laughing heartily at an anecdote that Hodge is telling about the prosecution of a man whose pet dog kept straying into the women's quarter, Jamin rises and wipes his mouth with his napkin.

"Please forgive me," he says. "I didn't realize how late it has gotten and I promised to meet Zel this evening."

"But we've scarcely begun," Hodge says, evincing real dismay.

And all I can do is think: Jamin, you animal!

But Jamin insists, and I stand to go with him, but both men persuade me to stay by making promises of transportation. Then Hodge bustles around putting together a plate of food for Jamin to take with him, growing particularly distressed because his cake hasn't cooled sufficiently and falls apart when he cuts a slice to go. The whole time Jamin smiles at me but refuses to meet my eyes. Finally he's gone, and Hodge and I return to our meal. Sometime during this the music has fallen silent and Hodge is too distracted to reset it.

"How long have you known Jamin?" he says after a sip of wine.

"All my life," I say. "We grew up in the same Children's Center, and then attended the same schools."

"He's well-meaning, but what a beastly thing to do."

I'm not sure what to say so I stare at my plate and concentrate on eating, making extravagant praise of the food between the clinks of silverware on porcelain.

"So," Hodge says after another drink of wine. "You're the marrying kind?"

"Yes." My heart trips and stumbles. "Yes, I am."

"It won't be bad. Will this coming ceremony be your first time?"

"Yes. I mean, I haven't decided yet."

"You'll be nervous your first time. It won't be bad."

I choke out laughter. "Aren't you supposed to tell me how good it will be? How proud I'll feel?"

He winces. Folding his napkin, he leans his elbows on the table and looks directly at me. "Look, Jamin thinks that we're both the same type, but you—"

My heart catches in my throat. Everyone knows I am different. Even a stranger who just met me can tell.

"—should know that I just lost my partner."

"Oh," I say. "I'm sorry."

He holds up his hand. "No, it's all right. We'd been together for almost fifteen years, but he'd been unhappy for a very long time. I'm glad he ran off."

"Where'd he go to?" I ask, desperate to change the subject.

Hodge shakes his head. "Look, that's not important. I'm happy by myself right now. I hope you understand."

He doesn't sound happy at all. "Of course! I mean I—"

"I'm not like you," he says in a low whisper, and then drinks the rest of his wine. "Oh! The story about the man with the dog, did I ever finish that?"

"No." I had forgotten it already.

"The last time they caught him, they stoned him to death and set his body on fire. That kind of perversion can't be tolerated, you know. We aren't animals, with animal passions."

"I know that." My voice is strained because I am scared.

"Well, then. Good." He rises abruptly. "I'll call you a taxi." He fumbles at the counter, frowning. "The cake looks like a disappointment, but I'm sure it still tastes fine. I'll send some with you."

When the taxi arrives and I step off the stoop into darkness, plastic-wrapped plate in hand, I hear him say, "Good luck with the marrying. It's over quickly."

He reminds me of a piece of topiary, a plant forced by wires and pruning into a facsimile of something else, so twisted over time that he no longer resembles himself. I can feel myself being twisted, misshapen more each day. But I'll resist it.

The taxi door slams and whisks me away.

I don't see Ali at work the next day or the morning following that. At lunch, I am standing by the inner windows overlooking the courtyard below while the children weave an endless pattern of joy amid the trees. The lobby is busy, many people rushing by. Pressed to the window, I am more aware of the antiseptic smell of the cleaning liquids than I am of the person standing next to me. So several minutes pass before I look up and realize it's Ali.

She taps her foot on the tiles. "Rubber floor. Very smart. They aren't able to zap you here."

"I'm sorry," I blurt out, sorry that I haven't noticed her, sorry that I hadn't talked to her earlier.

Ali lowers her long eyelashes and looks away, her weight shifting to leave. "Well, if you want to be zapped, you could always go back to your desk."

"Wait!"

She pauses in midstep. "I'm waiting."

And because I don't know what else to say, because there is only one thing besides her on my mind, I ask, "Will you be marrying this weekend?"

"That's a very personal thing to ask," she says and walks quickly away to the other side of the lobby where she stands by a decorative sarcophagus filled with polished stones and bubbling water, watching the children below.

I want to run after her, take her by the elbow and make her understand. I want her to feel for me the way I feel toward her. I want her to peel off her gloves and sink her bare hands into my flesh, stripping it away to the bone, until she reaches my heart and can soothe away the ache I feel for her.

Instead, I also turn and look out the window again. From this height, I can't tell if the children below are boys or girls.

Heart Nouveau is even more crowded than normal tonight because of the Bachelors Party. Jamin and Zel have brought me here to celebrate, just as all the other normal men have brought their friends who will be marrying tomorrow. We bachelors are few, no more than one in ten, so the annual bacchanal becomes a general cause for celebration.

Smoke swirls across the bar and dance floor, eddying with the currents of moving people and the crashing waves of music. Zel has taken off his shirt and is dancing half-naked under the strobe lights with the others in an orgy of arms and hands. I'm standing off to one side of the dance floor beside Jamin, who doesn't dance but gazes on Zel adoringly.

"He's the image of a god, isn't he?" Jamin says.

It's an echo from our scriptures. "And in his own image God made them, man and woman; and bade them be fruitful and multiply; and set them apart from the beasts and gave them dominion over the beasts."

"He's perfect for you," I answer, and Jamin smiles.

And I think of other words from our scriptures—"It is good for a man never to touch a woman, nor a woman touch a man, lest they be tempted to behave as the beasts of the field do in their passions"—and consider that I have never seen beasts in the field. These days, even the zygotes of beasts are scanned for their genetic health before they are brought to fruition in the womb-banks; the only place I have seen animals is in cages or under the straps that hold them down beneath our syringes. My theogenetics classes glossed over the details of this dire sin lest we be tempted to copy it, only teaching us that before God gave people the wisdom of science we behaved as beasts.

Zel grabs me by the hand, pulling me onto the dance floor

where the lights are flashing, music pumping, and ecstatic faces surround me. He only wants me to be happy and he only knows what makes him happy, and so he tries to bring me to that too. I resist him—I resist everything these days—and pull away.

"Smile," he shouts at me above the din. "Have some fun!"

"I'm having fun!" I shout in reply.

"Are you excited by marrying tomorrow?" I mumble my answer to him, but he doesn't hear me and leans forward, sweat dripping from his forehead onto my shoulder, shouting "What?"

"I said, 'Scripture says it's better to marry than to burn!'"

He laughs as if this is the wittiest thing in the world, and spins around, arms and fists pumping in beat with the music.

But I am burning already. The thought of Ali is a fire in my mind and a searing pain in my flesh, an unquenchable flame, even though I know all my feelings for her are wrong.

Still, I will go do my duty tomorrow, and marry rather than burn.

The next morning, I arise before dawn with the other bachelors. Many have hangovers, and some are too sick to marry this time. Their absences are noted by the priest's assistant in his white jacket as we board the bus. Those who have not made it are roundly mocked by even the sickest of those aboard. The other men are hugging, wishing each other well, but I hold myself apart. There are only a dozen of us, so it is easy to take a seat distanced from the others.

My stomach is queasy as we head for the Temple of the Waters, and not just from last night's drinking. Our route takes us along the edge of the women's quarter and none of us are wearing veils. I slouch in my seat. Several of the men pull their robes up over their noses; others put their hands on their heads, or pretend to rub their faces. The priest's assistant, who misses nothing, points this out to them and they all laugh. But I can only think that perhaps Ali is sitting in another bus without her veil on either; and I wonder if her mouth is as round and full as her gray eyes, if the arch of her lips matches that of her brow, if the curve of her neck is as graceful as the bridge of her nose. Would I even recognize her? I do not know.

The Temple of the Waters sits at the center of the government quarter across from the Palace of Congress, an oasis of green and blue marble in a desert of steel and concrete and sandstone. The giant telescreens that surround it show images of the ocean, the surge of waves in calm weather, but they remind me of the storm-tossed gray of Ali's eyes and I breathe faster.

As we're climbing off the bus, the priest's assistant steps in front of me and grips me by the shoulder. Instantly, I know that he saw how I stayed apart, he knows that I am different from the others.

But he only says, "Why don't you smile? This is going to be a good thing—think of the pride you'll feel!"

I force myself to smile and pull away from him to follow the others. We strip in the anteroom. A few of the men are as young as I am, but they range in age up to a solemn gray-haired old man who goes about his preparations with all the grim seriousness of a surgeon before a touchy operation. The room is as hot as a sauna and several men grow visibly excited. One man, a boy almost, younger than me, can't help himself and spills his seed there on the floor. The others chastise him until he starts to cry, but the priest enters through a second door and all fall silent.

Noticing the mess, he says, "Don't worry, I'm sure there's more where that came from."

Everyone laughs and the boy rubs his tears from his cheeks, and grins, and everyone is at ease again; everyone but me. The priest asks how many of us have married before, and most of the men raise their hands.

"Yours is a sacred trust," the priest tells us. "There are two kinds of people in the world, those to whom society is given, and those who have the sacred duty to give to society, to perpetuate it."

"Home for the homos," one of the older men mumbles. "And hide the hydros."

The priest smiles gently. "Yes, that's how they mocked you as young men but you have nothing to hide by being different. That's why we come to the Temple with our faces uncovered. You have a holy trust, a gift from our heavenly father, who felt such love for all creation that he spilled his seed in the primal ocean and brought forth life."

When I think of the ocean, I think of Ali and stare at the door to the inner chamber, wondering if I will see her here.

"Earlier this morning," the priest continues, "the women entrusted with their half of this sacred duty came down from their quarter. They entered the main chamber of the temple a short while ago, and even now immerse themselves in the pool. In just a moment it will be your turn to enter. Think of the pride you'll feel; think of the love you have for our world and the peace therein. Look to the older men who have been here before and do what comes naturally to you."

Some nervous laughter follows this.

The priest looks at the boy who spilled himself, who is already excited again, and says "Hold on to that a little longer, friend." A light flashes above the door. "Ah, it is time."

The men press forward, somehow scooping me up so that I, the most reluctant of them, am at the head of the phalanx.

The doors swing open.

One group of acolytes stand there with towels as we enter, while a second set waits to collect the results of our labor. A womb-shaped pool of bodywarm water fills the center of the circular room. The women have already performed their rituals. Their eggs float in tiny gelatinous clumps on the surface of the pool.

A door identical to ours, but opposite, clicks shut on the women's chamber. "Hurry now," the senior priest in the white lab coat says. "Timing is important."

An acolyte reaches out his gloved hand to help me down the steps into the pool.

There are two kinds of people in the world: homosexuals and hydrosexuals. But I am neither. I stand there like a gray boulder caught between the black sea and the pale white sky as the wave of bachelors breaks around me to crowd the water's edge.

The Risk-Taking Gene as Expressed by Some Asian Subjects

STEVE TOMASULA

Steve Tomasula [www.nd.edu/~stomasul/] lives in Indiana and teaches at Notre Dame. He is the author of the novels VAS: An Opera in Flatland *(University of Chicago Press, 2004)—a hybird image-text novel—and* IN & OZ *(Ministry of Whimsy Press, 2003)—set in a two-part near-future city in the tradition of Vonnegut's Ilium in* Player Piano, *rigidly separated by class. His short fiction has appeared widely, and most recently in* The Iowa Review, Fiction International, *and* McSweeney's. *He is a postmodern writer on the edge of genre, or at least a genre fellow-traveler.*

"The Risk-Taking Gene as Expressed by Some Asian Subjects" was published in the Denver Quarterly *(Fall 2004), in an issue devoted to fantastic literature but lacking any manifesto or announcement to separate the work from the general run of literary fiction the magazine publishes. We see this as an interesting alternative to the approaches taken by* Conjunctions *and* McSweeney's *in recent years. This is literary hard SF. Using what he thinks of as a homogenous population in Chinatown, a researcher is trying to demonstrate a connection between answers to his questionnaire and a certain genetic marker for what he considers a risk-taking gene. Nothing is as simple as it appears to him.*

Their shirts had the uniform neatness of suburbia: chemically fortified green, polo. White father, mother, symmetrical children and other markers of the statistically tidy. Seeing their contrast to the thrown-together character of the Three Happiness #1 Chinese Restaurant we had each in turn stumbled upon, I couldn't help but wonder if the great fattening in comfort won by Western nations has not been paid for by an equal narrowing of imagination. Not an imagination to create wealth, or even scientific knowledge, for in this we Westerners obviously live at a time of genius. Rather, I refer to an imagination—or call it a gut feeling—that can so powerfully apprehend an other world that the dreamer risks all and leaps!—a blindfolded trapeze artist without a net!—sure that the trapeze swing he has flung himself after, a world he has never actually seen, will be there when he closes his grip.

The waitress, a dried apple of a woman with no English, bowed to her guests as she had welcomed me. But instead of following her shuffle to the table a busboy had reluctantly gotten up to wipe, they stood gaping at the surrounding shabbiness: American colonial and other mismatched chairs (refugees no doubt from some doomed IHOP); faux windows, their Colonial frames now painted red and gold; and paper lanterns that were as ashen as the old Chinese men sagging about the other tables, squinting through the smoke of their cigarettes at the new arrivals as if a decision to stay or go would be the most dramatic thing they would witness in this the Year of the Snake.

"Gin zhuo," the waitress insisted. To no avail. The sight of the table being set with chopsticks sent the family off in search of a restaurant more in keeping with the souvenirs they carried while the old men returned to their tea, their Chinese newspapers, their cigarettes.

"Ha!" one exclaimed to no one, as if he had won a wager against himself.

Just then a great clatter of men swept in, talking Chinese in a loud, celebratory manner. The busboy sprang to action, joined by the waitress who left her water pitcher sweating on the mythological constellations and dragons printed on the paper placemat beneath my own lunch.

That a certain kind of risky imagination has been supplanted by a more pragmatic one can be seen in the way we Westerners read our stars, I considered, as the men noisily rearranged the Colonial chairs of the restaurant, chasing a few of the old men to other tables to do so. Whereas the ancient Chinese saw dragons in their sky—those guardians of hidden mysteries—whereas the Hindus looked up to the same stars and saw Agni the fire god in gymnastic couplings with the wives of the Seven Sages, we here in the pragmatic West are taught to see a big dipper. And as if to confirm our paucity of vision, when we look to the stars nearest this dipper we see another dipper, smaller.

These thoughts weighed on me especially heavily that day because of the study I was conducting on the Risk-Taking gene: the genetic propensity discovered by Cloninger, Adolfsson and Svrakic for some people to put themselves at risk in order to feel the level of arousal most of us get from the petty concerns of our day—a disagreement with a co-worker, for example, or walking into a restaurant and discovering that it wasn't as nice as we had expected. With the blunted receptors in the brain that mark Risk-Takers, though, such trivial incidents barely register. Compared to the general population, Risk-Takers, or R-T Personalities, feel as though they are sleepwalking through life unless they find themselves in situations extreme enough to release the flow of neurotransmitters lying in the primitive recesses of all of us: norepinephrine, which helps trigger the flight or flight response, dopamine, which is associated with feelings of intense pleasure, and of course, serotonin.

In ancient times, such carriers of the Risk-Taking gene must have been valuable to the tribe for these were the men and women who would risk sailing off the edge of a flat earth or eating the untested berry. In today's climate-controlled world, however, the carriers of this gene are forced to turn to artificial dangers for their norepinephrine/dopamine/serotonin rush: BASE jumping, that practice of leaping from antenna towers or sheer cliffs; other extreme sports as well as traditional mainstays: reckless driving, compulsive gambling, adulterous affairs—all reasons the investigator of Risk-Taking (or any behavior) must take pains to prevent his subjects' responses from blurring into ink-blots of action.

Indeed, laboratory constraints are so central to the creation of knowledge that when the subject is the human, a creature that by nature resists living according to the dictates of the lab, the researcher must seek out natural substitutes or simulate them in order to prevent, for example, a restaurant from transforming bored hanger-arounders into laughing, joking friends who transform a dead restaurant into a place so suddenly alive with colorful lanterns and the *Cantopop* music that sprang from this one's ceiling that it would be impossible to say which variable had what effect on what whole.

Thus we know more about the bloodlines of prison populations than previous generations knew about the pedigrees of their kings and queens. . . .

Beers all around. The big ones, *Tsing Tow* twenty ouncers—though when I had tried to order a beer, I was told it was not possible. *"Yam sing!"*

. . . a library could be filled by the published data on the olfactory responses, spatial judgment . . .

"Mui kwe lu!" A young woman with the men laughed loudly—and I wondered how I had missed her, for she was wearing a sleek, red dress.

. . . inter-male aggression . . .

She gave a start in her seat, simultaneously turning to slap the man beside her and setting off guffaws in the others.

. . . familial nudity, and vocabulary transmission among Eskimos—as opposed to extra-female pacifism, stranger clothedness, and vocabulary incomprehension among non-Eskimos. Why, I even knew that the alcohol in two beers would make the earlobes of 84% of the Chinese blush in comparison to 63% of Caucasians, and I watched my table neighbors for these signs, taking comfort in the fact that they were the very sort of homogeneous population needed for my study. Like the Amish. Though the relatively low percentage of Risk-Takers believed to live among the Amish precluded my use of this group.

Not so the Chinese.

A boy ran into the restaurant and delivered to their table one of those white cartons all Chinese restaurants use for carryouts while the men laughed at something the woman said as she performed a magic trick—or maybe she was telling an obscene joke?—covering a salt shaker with a napkin so it looked like it was protruding from the table.

Indeed, one only has to look up "Chen" in the phone book to see how many of their addresses fall within the narrow confines of my current lab, i.e. Chinatown. More importantly, one only has to look at a few of their chromosome stains to see how many physical, real-world loci can be found under the single heading "Chen." Haverson-Shreck has documented the Asian predilection for all manner of gambling, be it *pai gow*, cards, fighting fish, crickets, kites, cocks, or men; and the tongs that permeate this community (so associated in the Western mind with opium dens and speakeasies) are ideal genetic self-sorting mechanisms. Set up in America to duplicate the paternalistic help a young man might receive from his extended family back home, these benevolent societies also continue in America the biological heritage of the ancestral home. If an immigrant whose family name was Hip Sing needed a job or a doctor who would not demand immediate payment, he could turn to other members of the Hip Sing Tong. And no other. If his last name was Hop Sing, he would be adopted by the Hop Sing Tong. And no other. It was, and is, that straightforward.

Plus, commuting to do my fieldwork among this homogeneous population would only cost me the bus fare to Chinatown and this was no small consideration.

I had acquired, you understand, a certain reputation—one that led me to believe that my current study would determine my fate. That is, whether or not I would ever again be funded by the federal government. And therefore allowed (or not) to stay in my university. Or any institution. Not that this reputation was deserved. Indeed, I tried hard to follow the lead of colleagues who consistently took the pragmatic route, building careers out of studies that built on the conclusions of those whom they would later, coincidentally, depend on for promotions and grants. But it was especially at those times that the impossibility of seeing the world exactly as another would creep in, forcing me to either ignore how many meanings a simple yet key word such as "education" or "anger" could have, or else forcing me to qualify my conclusions, and then qualify my qualifications, and then qualify my qualifications of my qualifications, so that in the end, despite massive amounts of data and charts and graphs that laid out such, in the end I was able to say nothing. Or to put it more precisely, to conclude that "the linkage between feelings of 'shame' and Chromosome 12 is inconclusive"; or "after adjusting for covariants in 'education,'—i.e., formal 'education,' e.g., school 'education' (even if given at home), or informal education (e.g. living abroad or over a pool hall), rote memorization, manual training, reading widely, or narrowly (specialization), having a 'feel' for, an acquaintance with, being a master of, a novice to, maybe a Saturday-afternoon painter, mechanic, or poet, having educated fingers, or palette, or nose, or feet," etc. etc., "—evidence for a hereditary locus was lacking and obscures any . . ." and so forth.

This time would be different, though. It had to be. Yet reviewing the data I had thus far gleaned from the volunteers who answered my ad in *The Chinatown Lantern* my spirits were as high as a goldfish kite in a tree. Not a single Risk-

Taker had shown up among the dishwashers, cabbies and day laborers who answered my ad, leaving the topology of my data as flat as my placemat: all baseline. No peaks, no valleys, no difference, that is, from which to conjure significance.

The woman in the red dress sat close to one of the men, her thigh speaking to his with a body language understood in any culture. Like her, he was also younger than the rest of the men. And dressed better. In contrast to their sugar-bowl haircuts, his jet-black hair had been combed into a stylish wave; he wore a yellow silk shirt over a black tee while most of the others were middle-aged, and dressed in the wrinkled white-cotton shirts of clerks everywhere. At one point they paused to listen to him recite a poem. At least I thought it was a poem, given the regular cadence his Chinese fell into:

Lu acai yu huang feihong.
Gui ma zhi duo xing.
Yige zitou de danshen.

But then he began to end each line with what seemed to be an English translation: "All the Wrong Clues for the Right Solution" and "Too Many Ways to Be Number One," one of which I thought I recognized as a title, and I realized he could be reciting a list, an inventory, maybe of book titles: both his English and the words themselves had just that sort of catchy snap. I couldn't imagine the group as an office party for book importers, though, or the Association of Chinese-American Librarians, given his flashy yellow shirt, the spaghetti straps of her dress, the laughter one of his titles caused. Maybe they were just happy, I considered, gazing out a faux window and onto the grainy black-and-white blow-up photo of The Great Wall of China, snaking into the distance. Indeed, sometimes it seems as though the best approximations of truth come from being no more specific than that hunch—despite the claims made by data, or horoscopes, or the calculus of lucky numbers printed on my place mat. *8, 44, 848.* Eight. The number made me smile, for it was the number of DNA repeats that my study predicted would be found on the D4DR gene carried by Risk-Takers.

The waitress emerged from the kitchen, and I signaled again for a bill. She nodded again?—or, again, exercised a crick in her neck?

Another boy ran into the restaurant to deliver one of those white, carryout cartons, and it struck me as odd that some of the men would eat in one restaurant while ordering carryout from another. But then, about the time the waitress finally picked up my dishes, a third boy entered and a pattern began to emerge: whenever a boy dropped off one of those containers, one of the men would take it into the washroom only to return a few minutes later—without the carton.

Stop it, I told myself, happy to have the waitress save me from the pattern-making path my mind had wandered onto. She placed before me a teacup plate containing my bill and a fortune cookie.

One of the men rose as if to give a toast. Their table fell silent as he began, delivering an obviously prepared speech to the one in the silk shirt.

Or was his demeanor yet another example of form giving significance to what is actually insignificant? Like columns of precise phrenological data, for example or—need it be said?—a yellow cookie.

When I cracked open my fortune cookie, though, time slued through one of those moments when a glance from a wife thought to be faithful or a slip of the tongue reveals an unspoken truth and, in an instant, our safe and solid world— our core beliefs—are shown to be no more than the view from Myopia. Slowly, I reread this bombshell on mine: *You like Chinese food.*

Sure enough, the clatter of the kitchen, the man emotionally speaking Chinese at the next table—the world all around—continued as if nothing had happened, though the world within went belly-up as I mulled over this message. Could the mechanism for delivering this fortune to only those who have selected themselves for its truth also be at work in my ad? That is, could the very structure of my study have been screening out all Risk-Takers? Could all of the work I had done up to this point equally be a phantasm, an exercise in putting one's head in a pot? The answer left me nauseated. What Risk-Taker would answer a newspaper ad to sit in an office filling out a questionnaire?

It was at this time that the man I thought had been proposing a toast began to weep. The woman, and most of the men turned away—from pity? in disgust?—the shame culture of "face" is powerful—but the one in the yellow shirt and a hard-eyed man beside him continued to look on, their jaws set in what struck me as murderous expressions.

The one standing shook his head as if in apology, continuing some explanation in an impassioned voice. When he finally fell silent, he looked down as if awaiting a sentence, and the truth of the details that had been swirling about resolved into their one reality; the plants in the window . . . prevented a view inside from the street; the boys delivering carryout boxes . . . runners, I now saw; the men all sitting with their backs to the wall, facing the door. . . . I was in the midst of a tong, clearly, or more exactly, the underbelly of one of the tongs that still engaged in gambling, prostitution, dockworker control, and other illegal activities. In other words, a roomful of Risk-Takers. Men who could become, if they wanted, successful bankers, teachers, or soldiers, for they were in fact all of those, but who instead chose to live at the edge of society. Not despite the risk, but because of it.

The waitress was at my table again. "You go now," she said, taking my money, an ability to speak English suddenly coming over her. "We closing, you go," she insisted, though it was the middle of the lunch rush.

I am not a brave man. But sometimes the drive for self-preservation allows even the timid to act heroically, and as I rose to leave I realized I was walking away from perhaps the one chance I might get to salvage my study—that is, the last chance to salvage my university life—the only life I had ever known.

I found myself ignoring the protestations of the waitress to reach the men at the table. Dangerous men, I now saw, who'd been smoking so much that a gray haze made them look like something out of *film noir*.

The one standing, sweating—I could now see the fear in

his eyes—turned toward me as the twins, or brothers, or whoever the men were, shifted their murderous looks my way.

Government agencies like police departments rarely bother with discerning the differences between the Chinese and Japanese. Or Koreans or Vietnamese for that matter. Often they assign any Asian in their employ to any Asian problem and perhaps the men mistook me—in cheap suit and tie—for some detective working vice, since my face bears the legacy of a Japanese grandfather. If so, I would be worse than a *gweilo*, as all foreign devils are called. In any case, as I got out a copy of the ad I had been running in the newspaper, several of the men hurriedly left, not waiting to see what the paper was. But not the leader—the one in the yellow shirt. He took it from me and carefully read it as I said my piece.

For my answer he "showed me the whites of his eyes," that stock response to all *gweilo*, clasping his hands behind his head and looking to the slowly rotating ceiling fan until I left.

Shit!—have you ever been *kung-powed* by a piece of paper?—wham!—*fist-of-the-dragon* worthy of Bruce Lee. Sounds crazy, *ai yah*, but if you ever got a deportation order you know what I'm talking about only less so. I mean, the banana may as well have been the Ghost of HK Past, tail me all the way to America, and I had to catch my breath, lay the ad on the table so Jenny wouldn't see my hands shake. I mean, why me? Why that ad? Why did he bring that ad to my hands and no one else's if not for bad *qi*?—like a scene out of vampire-fu:

[00:00:00] Wide Master Shot of Restaurant: We were eight of us at the table.

[00:00:03] White Ghost bring his scroll of the dead [Chinglish Subtitle: *"Now is time for you to suck the coffin mushroom."*]

[00:00:15] After he leaves, we all make joke—Risk-Taking Study—*chi sin!*—plenty good banana fun!

[00:00:20] Analytic Cut to Jenny-Po: the womanly way

she squeeze my arm let me know that she knew that that paper had let the wind out of me.

[00:00:21] Reverse-Angle Shot to Me for My Reaction: Man, I don't want her sympathy! Not again! But that's only on the inside. Outside I am Chin the Grin from ear to ear, like I been swallowed whole by an even worse movie, keeping it light, keeping it moving, and finding the role too easy—Me!—who could put on any proper—even Mr. Fleetstreet—act when necessary, who used to skateboard up and down Jordan Road with my mates, running off the sidewalk any chippie in the shorts, white shirt, plaid tie of the tea-and-crumpet academies. Yeah, we bad, even at fourteen, rolling all over the harbor, looking for on-location movie shoots. When we'd find one, we'd stroll up to it, cool, boards shouldered so security could see the black dragons we painted on them to make people think we got bigger brothers as we offered our services to keep little pricks like us from skateboarding in and out of the scene they were trying to shoot. Once we even got Karen Mok's autograph!

So why, I used to ask myself, why does the Chinese businessman smile as he shakes hands to accept unfair tariffs? Why do parents spend HK$ 20,000, like the father of my old mate Johnny, to put their son in a UK school when schools in HK of equally high standard? As foreigners they'd pay double tuition—enough to build a front-yard swimming pool— but Johnny gets housed under the stairs, worse than the maid, worse than the dog of the maid. He gets bullied by English students, even Chinese ones who say he makes them look bad with his *gong si fong* ways, his under-the-stairs room decorated with torpedo-titty HK movie posters, him and his *Cantorap*, but he says nothing back. Not even to his parents. Is it because we're all too polite to make complaint? No, I now know. It's because no one can take your face. You can only lose it. And you can only lose it by letting them know that you know that they know that you know you've lost it. That's what shame is. So you smile instead—no biggie—what me worry?—you know how to get your fingers out of Chinese handcuffs, right?

But scissors work too. And okay, despite what Jenny says

about me, I know the world doesn't spin about me, it's not all a B-flick, blah, blah, blah. I'm only saying that if it was, I know how my director's cut would run, even with her thinking she needs to jump into every scene to save my face, even if she's right about everything: I'm not the bad guy, it wasn't my fault, and Western science is just the charm to make peace with Chinese ghosts. Still, I'm skeptical only for good reason. You see, I know about bananas because back in HK I was in college myself. Yeah, me; Johnny gets packed off to the UK but by the time he graduates I'm in the HK Institute of Fashion Design and Polytechnic. During the day I am studying Ming vases, Chi-Sci-Fi movies, all visual culture, as the *ah seuh* say—and loving it. Nights we're duping movies—lots of gangsta-fu, chop-socky for yuks, *sai chai* for spice. We are only small-time pirates with camcorders: find some real *triad* blokes who want to see *Shaolin Fox*, pay their way in so they sit by you while you shoot right off the theater screen—nobody says nothing, the bun's okay, and everything's in balance till one day Jenny delivers a bootleg copy of *Gui ma zhi duo xing—All the Wrong Clues (For the Right Solution)*—to a lady customer. When the lady returns the tape, and she see me, and I see her [ping-pong cuts], and we see each other, her realizing I am one of her students and me realizing she is one of my professors, everything changes. She becomes very interested in my studies. She pays me special service. Says I have a great eye. That I would make a great director, even professor, and who knows? Maybe I would have had a different fate if I didn't get mixed up in her *wài kuài*. But no, I let her sign me for an independent study with assignments to visit special collections in libraries. I have a letter—all very official—explaining that I am a student, and why I need to see such-and-such rare book.

Librarians are so helpful, so happy to share the treasures they guard that they set me up in a private room. Just me and the book so I could study in peace. They had me wear a pair of white gloves to keep off fingerprints!—can you believe it? No matter. Not once did they ever check to see if I razored out a page—you know, the ones with *si fu* calligraphy that academics and rich men trade on Nathan Road. Pen-and-ink bamboo grooves, *Fu-ch'un* mountains seen through mist. Just cut deep in the gutter so no one could tell if a mountain was missing unless they squint hard. Which no librarians ever thought to do. They're not police. Course if they did, professor-po would be shocked to find out her student was a thief. And who's gonna believe some *ah chaan* from the mainland over Professor Art Historian? Paper-Scissors-Rock—you know how that works, right? And people with glasses always pay others to take their risks. So okay, I take all the risk, but is it my fault I also pick up how her business works? Things are never as they seem—if you think New York apartments look enormous in TV sitcoms just think how they look from HK—so we'll see; just because *gweilo* science put a man on the moon like Jenny keeps saying doesn't mean this banana can hold chopsticks. . . .

Located on a dead-end off a Chinatown back street, the storefront office space I had rented for the month appeared as small as one of those kiosks crammed with all manner of magazines, candy, watches, phone cards, and 220-to-110-volt converters: that density that the Chinese are accustomed to in everything, from their cities to their alphabet, coming as they do from a nation so populous that to get a sense of it, we in America would have to imagine our entire population squeezed into the east, then multiplied by four. It is for this reason that a dozen immigrants can tolerate living in one of those closet-sized *gong si fongs* they share, sleeping in shifts in its single bed.

My office was much bigger than it looked, though: as deep as the building that housed it, with a back door that opened onto the alley. Discolored floor tiles formed a ghostly outline of what must have been a long, store-length soda fountain—or rather a pharmacy counter as the place had been the former home of 王氏上古妙方，专治现代人士 which I was told translated roughly into Wong's Ancient Cure for Modern People, a business made anachronistic, a grinning realtor informed me, by Viagra.

Ceiling paint, electrical piping, and fluorescent lighting fixtures obscured one of those ornately patterned tin ceilings ubiquitous in Victorian-era stores, but the stench of another time was still distinct in its space—rancid orange peel and fish heads—or so it seemed as I shuttled between the office and a Dumpster in the alley behind the building, cleaning out rags and waterlogged charts, a newsprint manual for bringing this organ into harmony with that bodily factor (cold, wind, dryness, etc.)—the claptrap of a way of ordering the world where Chinese ghosts and *qi* were as real as the rhino horn used to medicate their effects. Or so I imagined, replacing that ancient refuse with my own lean equipment, a desk and two metal chairs, though I could never completely erase a trace of the Ancient Cure that hung in the air.

This last week saw only four volunteers: a man employed by a chicken-parts processing plant and three Chinese punks—dirty pink hair, tongue studs—who giggled so hard that it took them five minutes to supply the cheek scraping I required of all subjects for the DNA tests that I matched to their questionnaires.

Then *he* was there—coming in the door—the tong boss I'd seen in Three Happiness, girlfriend in another stream-lined dress at his side. In order not to scare him off, I pretended I didn't recognize them, but he saw through this immediately. "Come on, man, we're not stupid," he said in an odd kind of English. British English, that reminded me for some reason of an old Al Capone movie. He spun the metal folding chair around and straddled it, sitting across from me at my desk while his girlfriend walked around to my side and began looking through my papers. "So," he said, either to distract me, or to tell me to never mind what she was doing, "You still looking for Risk-Takers, or what?"

I told him I was, and he said, "Good. So am I, maybe we help each other."

While she opened first one desk drawer, then another, I began my standard orientation in the hopes that behaving naturally would be the best way to bring him in. He listened politely as I emphasized my confidentiality statement, and then explained how the results would be used, trying to maintain the best matter-of-fact demeanor I could despite the distractions of his girlfriend. At one point she grunted, working to unscrew the mouthpiece of my phone as though it were a stuck pickle jar and the effort brought out the muscles of her bare arms and shoulders. Jet black, pixie hair. . . . Had she been brought up in a different social group, I thought, she might have become a famous gymnast. Or rock climber.

While I showed her boyfriend the basics of the questionnaire, she roamed the office. Like a tourist in a gift shop, she'd pause from time to time, her eyes widening in surprise at some laughable curiosity—maybe the pristine order of sharpened pencils I kept at the ready—and her reactions brought out the strangest feelings in me. For some reason, the pencils, my optimistic stack of questionnaires, the narrow office suddenly seemed petty: a personality embodied and put on display. And I felt embarrassed for her to see how small the boundaries of my life had become.

For his part, her boyfriend didn't exactly agree to participate in the study, but he didn't stop me, even after I explained that I would need to take a scraping from inside his cheek. So I pressed on, getting as far as writing his first name at the top of a questionnaire: Tommy.

"Family name?" I asked when he didn't offer one.

His jaw set in that expression I'd seen in the restaurant. Then he snapped, "Just Tommy." Taking the exasperated tack parents often use with children he added, "Let me see that," pulling the form out from under my pencil. He studied it a moment, then read in a flat tone: "True or False. People should dress in individual ways even if the effects are strange." It was a question from the Disinhibition Subset. I could see him mentally comparing my Sears blazer to his linen shirt, his oval, tinted glasses, gold necklace. . . . "You really think this works?"

Apparently satisfied with the wastepaper basket, the file cabinet, and the back door, his girlfriend came around to his side of the desk. She stood behind him, her taut, trapeze-artist arms crossed over his chest as I explained the Zuckerman Personality scale for Sensation Seeking that Ebstein, et al. developed into the Tri-Dimensional Risk-Taking Index (RTI) that Hur and Bouchard then applied to identical twins to demonstrate a strong hereditary component in RT Personality Types (RTPT). . . . They looked back at me with that glazed expression I often faced in class, their eyes making me aware of the sound of my own voice. "Examining the biochemistry that influences the broad behavioral mechanisms and psycho-physiological reactions in rats," it was saying, "Resnick found that those rats that exhibited elevated tendencies to explore their surroundings also had elevated levels of dopaminergic—"

"Rats," he interrupted. He read from the questionnaire: "True or False. The worst social sin is to be a bore."

With a quick underhand flip, she popped a pack of cigarettes out of his baggy shirt's pocket, then lit up, exhaling something in Chinese that made him snicker.

I forged ahead. "Building on this research . . ." Convincing him of the worth of the study was going to be more complicated than I had thought, I saw, for as I explained the Svrakician linkage between twins who were identified as RTPTs, a black-and-white mirage of Wong's old pharmacy seemed to rise up behind Tommy and his girlfriend, a line of customers standing at the long counter, Mr. Wong himself in black, flowing *cheongsam*, using a library ladder to ascend a wall of bottled potions, Tommy and his girlfriend superimposed before it in the Technicolor of their Chuppie attire, not so much a break from the past as—". . . the enzymes such as MAO and DBH that regulate the neurotransmitters associated with behavior, and hormones such as cortisol and testosterone—"

"Testosterone? You mean being macho?"

Macho. The gang boss. Big man, The Rock and his moll—a way to break in suddenly appeared. "*Voila!*" I shouted, in the loud tone I sometimes used to shock students awake. "Find the gene that controls the enzyme, and you'll find the genetic marker for the personality!"

Instead of the "*ah ha*" of recognition I had hoped for, they only exchanged frowns the way freshmen sometimes did when they realized we weren't going to be studying Kinsey. "So what?" he ventured. "Only Risk-Takers have balls?"

I may as well have been building him an elaborate temple of gods, demigods, lesser demons and monkeys, all baroquely entangled. But what else was I to do other than finish the door: "Van Tol, Wu, Guan, O'Hara and others have already put forth a candidate: variations in the DNA coding sequence of the D4 receptor, a forty-eight base-pair sequence that controls clozapine and spiperone binding, especially when it appears as an eightfold repeat. Put simply, people without this redundancy of DNA are no more or less sensitive to the enzymes that control behavior." I showed him the DNA sequences on a chromosome stain—CCCC GCG CCC GGC CTC CCC CCG GAC CCC TGC GGC TCC AAC TGT GCT—explaining how when a person carries a sequence that repeats itself eight times—

"Come on, get to the practical stuff."

"In practical terms . . ." I cut to the conclusion ". . . an analysis of the genetic phenotype could tell you which poker player will be prone to take risks, to bluff with a mixed hand, and which will tend to play it safe and fold."

A faint smile came over Tommy's lips, and in silence they both looked over the questionnaire for the longest time. Then sheepishly he asked, "There's one question I'm not sure how to answer."

"Yes?"

He read: " 'Rate yourself on a scale of one to ten, one equals fully Asian, ten equals fully American.' I mean, I drive big American car. . . ." Then he growled, "But my rickshaw is 110% Chinese!" and his girlfriend shrieked as he pulled her onto his lap, simulating a bumpy ride.

When they finished laughing, I pointed out, "As a token of appreciation you will be paid a gratuity of forty dollars."

"Fourti ho Yhankee dohlars?" his girlfriend asked, exaggerating a Yan-Can-Cook accent.

"*Chì lâo,*" he said, sliding the questionnaire back, "you don't need that crap. I'll tell you what you need to know about Risk-Takers."

"Oh, do you know some Risk-Takers?" I asked, trying to sound nonchalant.

He pulled out his cell phone and spoke into it. Then he

proceeded to tell me about a great uncle who swam the Niagara to get into this country. "The whole while, miners shot at him from the bluff. Like they're shooting at rats at the dump. Uncle says when he made it and lay on the bank exhausted from swimming for his life, he could hear them up there hooting, drinking and shooting at other bubbles in the water." Today, he continued, jets and ATMs and container shipping have made that swim 12,000 miles long: from Fujian by mule train across the Yunman Province. Aunties did it. Brothers. He talked about an uncle who hung onto the undercarriage of a train despite blowing snow and a cold so deep that when guards discovered him, he couldn't let go. "They amputated two fingers just to arrest him," he said, holding up a hand with his fingers folded at the knuckles to illustrate. "But the next year he tied himself to the undercarriage and tried again. . . ." Nieces. Nephews. All trekking through the jungles of Burma and into Chiang Mai, being passed from handler to handler, some of whom were robbers. Some murderers. "Sometimes you are a mule for heroin. One way or another your body is your dollar—all you got—and you pay as you go till you emerge from a crate, or a trunk, or a hold with other shitting, puking rats to North America. And there your troubles begin."

A few minutes later, there was a knock at the door, and several men filed in. It was the men from Three Happiness; not the men who had been with Tommy and his girlfriend at the table. It was the old men who'd been sitting around reading newspapers and smoking cigarettes before his gang showed up. "You were expecting Jet Li?" Tommy asked. One of them, I noticed, was missing two fingers from his right hand. As they stood in line along the footprint left by the store's old counter, it was as if the ghosts I had imagined earlier materialized before me, each in turn stepping forward so I could take a scraping from the inside of a cheek for the DNA samples, listing them in the manifest only as Uncle A, Uncle B, Uncle C, through F. Was there a G? When Tommy saw me looking at him, he pulled out two small squares of gauze, wrapped in Saran Wrap and stained with blood.

"You run your test on these two, too," he said. "This one,"

he said holding up the first sample, "came from someone without balls."

"*Zheng ben wei shi me bu you ta qu?*" his girlfriend said, pouting.

"This other is from someone who always thought he could piss with the big dogs." He shook his head wistfully, handing it over. "When in Rome you've got no choice but act in Italian movies, huh, Jenny?" he asked his girlfriend. "Even if they're Spaghetti-Vampire-Westerns." She smiled wanly, looking down.

While yet in graduate school, my thesis director invited me onto a study he was conducting. The subject was the relation between biochemistry and social cooperation, and at the stipulation of his funders my director drew test subjects from the employees of an enormous *maquiladora* just south of Laredo. This particular *maquiladora* was Japanese-owned, the most high-tech manufacturer of air conditioners in North America, I was told, though one would never have guessed it from the slum that sprawled out from the plant: hundreds upon hundreds of shacks constructed from discarded shipping crates, oil drums and cinder blocks, and lived in by employees and their families, sweltering without electricity, or even running water. The plant was only running at seventy-percent capacity because of the predilection of employees to supplement their wages by selling copper tubing meant for the air conditioners and even the very tools supplied them to do their jobs.

When I confided to my mentor that I didn't think the plant managers really cared about discoveries in social science, he snorted. So I explained my suspicion: that the Japanese, with their lingering notions of racial superiority, were actually hoping to use our study to biologically screen out those who wouldn't pull together for the profitability of the company. He walked away, chuckling at what I thought he considered unwarranted cynicism in his young apprentice, until years later, when I learned that he had listed me on his proposal as co-investigator not because I was an outstanding student, as I had also believed at the time, but because I had a Japanese surname. And my surname, in fact, may have been the reason his study was funded ahead of competing proposals, including one by my present department head, who provided this explanation, recounting how he and my mentor had once shared a laugh about my "Mexican question" over a few beers. I would have chalked up the whole story to jealousy, professional gossip, if it weren't for the ring of truth sounded by one of his details: that the Japanese managers also blamed me for the failure of our study after they discovered I was only a *Hapa-Hadle*, heavy on the Caucasian side at that, though I maintain even now that the real reason thefts increased after they did, in fact, implement a blood test based on our study was because smuggling copper from a tightly controlled factory requires more social cooperation than does being a dutiful cog in its assembly line.

Everyone in the sciences has had a brush with or knows someone whose work has intersected that of one government lab or another: the study of migratory birds, for example, that arouses the interest of those trying to invent creative ways to conduct germ warfare, or the latest snowflake-pattern-recognition software that might somehow be employed in riot control. It did not take much to imagine others watching from the shadows to see if the genetic linkage I was seeking between DNA and risk-taking could ever be used to identify suicide bombers, or perhaps those who would risk their student visas by illegally taking a job. This wasn't just idle speculation. Already, Korea was completing banks of DNA fingerprints, while in Germany, would-be immigrants had to prove their German-ness by submitting a saliva sample along with their applications—just two examples of a worldwide genes race that was extending the surveillance and control of many populations down to the level of the human cell.

Did Tommy also have some such ulterior motive? When he asked if I was still looking for Risk-Takers, hadn't he added, "Good, so am I"?

Then an item in *The Chinatown Lantern* turned me cold. A boat trying to smuggle illegal Chinese immigrants had drawn the suspicion of a Coast Guard cutter. The boat had been disguised as a fishing trawler. But instead of playing their ruse through, the smugglers—or snakeheads, as they are called—panicked at the sight of the cutter and threw their real cargo, the illegal aliens, into the sea. They knew that the Coast Guard would have to stop to rescue the illegals, and so the snakeheads managed to escape. None of the illegals could swim, though, so they drowned before the Coast Guard could find them. The article was simply restating the fact that these smugglers were still at large, just one of the many "consumer alerts" that circulated as news.

Was Tommy involved somehow? Is this why he was so intent on finding "macho" henchmen who would follow through on risks rather than turn tail at the first sign of danger? Looking at one of the blood samples he'd supplied, I wondered if that was what he meant by it coming from "someone who thought he could piss with the big dogs." If so, wouldn't that make him an accomplice to murder? Even if he was only looking for men willing to risk smaller crimes, numbers running, drugs, or whatever, did I implicate myself by having that blood analyzed?

As it happened, the DNA tests run on the two samples showed that the coward was decidedly a Risk-Taker, by my measure, having eight repeats of the D4DR gene on Chromosome 11. The "Big Dog's" swab, though, indicated an ordinary person. Had I mixed up the samples? No, that was impossible, I concluded. But had he? Both samples were tainted, of course, and I only played along to keep him in play. But if I retested and got the opposite results, I was sure Tommy could put me in touch with the very pool of subjects my study needed. Conversely, the existence of a biologically positive Risk-Taker who expresses negative risk-taking behavior was troubling enough, and I knew I had to find out which was which, though I also hoped I would never see Tommy again.

As soon as the banana let me into his smelly office I ask, "Did you test those blood samples?" He had moved into it like a hermit crab, and now the crab curled up in his shell frowning. Then he nodded—slowly—his lips tighter than a sealed vinegar pot. But why? Something wrong? The *yin* of me didn't want to know: imagine a soft-focus shot of me walking past his office, twice, each time deciding to forget the whole stupid show. What's he gonna tell me anyway? But with him stalling before me, the *yang* of me was burning to find out. "They stood out, right?" Again he nodded—not giving up his secret—and I could see we were sliding into another scene. Sure enough, squirming like his knickers are in a twist, he says he wants to meet the men himself.

Chì lâo! Where'd this guy get his nose for comedy?— turning every solemn moment into jokey puns, mistaken identities. . . . In HK cinema, a jilted woman always tears up a photo of her lover; when *triad* goons murder a detective, his partner always swears revenge. Directors know how to keep it real with age-old types, not the cartoons of people this banana makes by connecting his numbered dots. So I see that if this movie had any hope of staying genuine I had to keep us on script. And in roles that real people could recognize: Jenny-po as the "Cute but Ballsy Girlfriend," him as "The Professor," and me? I guess that's what I was trying to find out.

First I laughed in his face—*Ah ha ha ha Ha!*—*You think your kung-fu powerful but today is day you die!*—and say he didn't need to meet anyone. I had already met them for him. But he wouldn't let it go, him trying to put a headlock on me [slo-mo] by turning turnips into temples again, telling me that if I wanted a reliable test for Risk-Takers, we would have to follow through on paperwork.

Paper! *Aiiiiiiija!*

It was hard not to lose it—go *psycho-fu* all over his head—this banana lecturing me about Risk-Takers and chicken hearts and I don't know what, when he doesn't know anything about breathing water, or despair, or how hard life can be in rural China. Especially for those with no face, or worse, filthy blood: to know your nephew, your sister, get constantly bullied—beat up, too—because sixteen years ago she tried to escape the Suzy-Wong way only to end up stuck and with a baby that has no proper father. You know what it does to you inside to hear your nephew's voice, made puny and crackly by one of those provincial phones as he tells you, "Uncle, I have to have my blood replaced. Otherwise I see no sense in living."

Could the banana's papers replace blood? Could it find a man in all of China who would marry her? Or even hire her? Could it warn someone that a moment's hesitation in HK could be the last straw on the mainland or go back and undo a split-second's decision? No, and it all came broiling out: flurry of fists, head-high kicks, *manga* jump-cuts with him answering back, us two *shaolin* fighting on speedboats, on flaming ladders, off trampolines and soaring—him on wire, me no net—somersaulting sword fantasy through bounce lighting, him dodging, me countering, double-pistol stand-off, then typhoon of bullets, slo-mo of me diving to save sister, me doing all my own stunts while Jenny-po covers my back with two-fisted Uzi volcanoes, a flock of chickens burst out of the kitchen and into crossfire—pause in the action so we can exchange witty quip—resume shooting—amp up the Wu-Tang Clan soundtrack—rack focus of pained expressions, fury, envy, fear—but that's not the point anymore—a bloodbath for male honor and sacrifice, camera zigzag-tracking through the action, even switch to witchy-nudie-assassin genre, but even that don't work, and when it becomes clear that I could jump off from my condo to die before he gives in, I give up.

"All right, all right. The both of them," I said, breathing hard, meaning the blood donors, "will be at the rocket-rice races tomorrow." I sketched a map of the area, and show which alley to take, wondering how I had let our fight spill out of the frame, the camera swinging around to show the crew. Then I told him, "Memorize this: Confucius say, '*Gui ma zhi duo xing.*' Or no, make that, '*Yige zitou de danshen.*' Whenever you get stopped along the way, repeat those words."

Seeing that banana strain to make a bootleg Gucci out of my no-good Mandarin, scratches and all, was funny, despite myself. And the more he rehearsed—struggling to myna-bird the words without a clue what they meant—the harder it was to stay mad. He's such a porcelain chicken that I almost just came out and asked him plain. Or at least I began to think it was okay, it being impossible to lose face before a porcelain chicken. "But if you think you still need your papers after tomorrow," I say for now, "maybe we'll both just play for the outtake reel."

This is absurd, I told myself the next night, stepping off the Chinatown bus. And possibly dangerous. A gaggle of old Chinese women dressed in knit caps and layers of men's vests shoved by me with their mesh tote bags. Rival tongs sometimes shot at each other, I knew, or turned in each other's cockfights or gambling parlors. Not to mention the police.

The bus hissed, sliding off into a misty night and leaving me before the bronze statue of Confucius, that symbol of tradition, all marked up with Chinese graffiti as though to memorialize the fact that every country is a state of mind, especially to those who didn't live there. I wanted to kick myself for allowing Tommy to suck me into his. Neon signs multiplied in the rain-slick street, their candy-colored pinks and greens turning Chinatown as cartoonish as any world must appear to its outsiders. Paper! he said—as if I could forget the true lesson of Paper-Scissors-Rock when without that paper, without the tables and covariants and standardized means, Risk-Taking didn't exist. At least not in my world.

The tourist shops were closed, but the restaurants that catered to fan-tan clubs and other basement establishments were just beginning to come alive. I assumed the map he had drawn was directing me to one of these and took one last look at it, debating whether or not to go on. No researcher inserts himself into his study to this degree. If some journal published my work—then found out the lengths I had gone to enrich my pool. . . . Shame. Disgrace.

Suddenly my ankles were wet—I had walked into the spray of a fishmonger who was hosing off the sidewalk before his shop. Perhaps it was the eeriness of the foggy night. Chinese lore is full of ghosts and shape-shifters, and this, along with all the talk I'd been hearing about human smuggling, was surely at work on my subconscious. In any case, the faces of live bullfrogs straining against the chicken wire that held them in their barrel all seemed to be laughing with Tommy at the idea that a researcher could be anywhere else.

I didn't believe any of that claptrap about reason screening out other modes of reality or the dead being more powerful than the living, of course, so it was easy to move on. Still, this is not to say that the past—an unfaithful wife, for example, who excuses her actions by claiming her mate is a "dull academic"—does not influence the present. And once Tommy pointed it out, certain questions on the RT Personality Questionnaire that I had inherited—"I would like to join a 'far-out' group of artists or 'hippies' "—did seem to be spoken by the ghost of mood rings, astrological signs, and personality tests which were once the rage among researchers—before they morphed into the biochemical measures of the '70s, which became neurological explanations in the '80s, which were giving way, in this the age of genetics, to strings of AGCTs.

Measure enough things about enough people and you'll see something, Tommy had said when we argued in my office. Not so much to mock me, I believe, as out of the same sentiment as those shrines found in every Chinatown business, their incense smoldering with lip service if not utter belief in the miraculous transformations that supposedly permeated the place: moon maidens become brides, paupers turned fabulously rich. . . . And even if my data did have as much to do with reality as the spirit-filled cosmological maps of medieval Chinese, as Tommy claimed, that didn't mean it wasn't valid—if by "reality" we mean what that spirit-filled reality meant to medieval Chinese, the only one that could possibly matter to them—which opens up a real question: would the practical use to which any of this knowledge was put be the true measure of the man?

The gangway my map said to go down was pitch-dark, only wide enough for a single person to pass. Then the building Tommy had indicated by an "X" was there: an enormous industrial building that I knew to be an old coal-fired power plant built in the last century. Dark windows. The upper floors now held garment manufacturers, though the realtor I rented from said that ever since China reclaimed Hong Kong, the capital flight from that financial epicenter had been exerting pressure to turn this building into high-end condos or a mall. Now I saw why nothing ever came of it. The ground floor had plywood for windows, but tellingly, no gang dared tag them. Approaching the building from the back, it looked like a fortress, its single door made of reinforced steel. I knocked softly and a voice from inside answered in Chinese.

"Gui ma zhi duo xing . . . Yige zitou de danshen," I replied, and there was muffled laughter. Why? What was I saying? Bolts were drawn back; the door opened.

I was ushered in by an old man whose long braid and embroidered silk tunic and cap made it seem as though I'd stepped into a Charlie Chan movie—was this a joke? No. From the darkness behind him, two large men emerged, and one began to frisk me. "What do you know about classy Chinese quim?" the other asked.

"What?" I stammered—what had I said!—as the old one shooed me toward the noise of what sounded like lots of people arguing deeper in the building; a lawnmower or chain saw revved, the noise of voices and engines growing louder as I neared the one lit doorway. Then I was in a huge, warehouse-sized basement, full of men who, just like in movies, were waving fistfuls of dollars and shouting in Chinese. Young and old, men in thousand-dollar suits, men in mechanics' coveralls. . . . The fishmonger I had seen earlier was there. Or someone like him, still in his stained apron and paper cap, jostling with others for the attention of the few men dressed in rumpled white shirts who were holding the bets. Indeed, it seemed as though all of the cabbies, chicken-parts processors, and others I had interviewed were there—a fire marshal's nightmare—but that was impossible, I knew. They couldn't all be tong members. But if that were true—

Three men in motorcycle helmets sat on souped-up minibikes, gunning their engines as they eased up to a starting line while some of the men in white shirts yelled at the crowd, pushing people to clear a path for the bikers around the perimeter of the basement.

Tommy appeared at my side, eyes wild, as he yelled over the noise, "Now you'll see!" At that moment the minibikes roared off, a straggler at the edge of the crowd leaping to get out of the way. The basement was round, as though we were all inside an enormous barrel, but it was tiny as far as race-tracks go, and watching the bikers go around and around me and the other spectators was dizzying. The basement itself had obviously been dug by horses as were the basements of many buildings from that time: a team of horses would be hitched to a plowlike digging blade that radiated out from a post in the center of what would be the basement. Then as the horses walked around and around, they dug deeper and deeper, coolies hauling away the loose dirt in baskets. Now, a plywood ramp had been erected so that the curved brick wall itself could be used as part of the track, the minibikes rocketing by so fast that their centrifugal force held them to the wall as they used it as a lane to pass each other.

The dopamine rush that came with just watching these men shoot around the track made my hairs stand on end. The bikers roared off like short-track speed skaters: a burst at the start followed by three laps of jockeying for position, after which they gunned into the final no-rules lap. I understood as never before—understood with my body—the lure of gladiator tournaments, of kick boxing. . . . It was impossible not to get caught up in the "what if" of one racer recklessly shooting between a pillar and another biker to win, and I practically forgot why I was there until, heat over, Tommy nudged me. He nodded toward the winner, coasting into a fold of men, his green soccer jersey crisp as new cash. Like jerseys in the city's youth league, this rider's was embla-zoned with the name of a sponsor. And when he turned to-ward someone, allowing me to read it, my pulse quickened: *Three Happiness*.

"Blood Sample A or B?" I asked excitedly, trying to catch a look at the man's face through the narrow eye slit of his helmet. His jersey also sported a number—8—my lucky number, according to the restaurant's place mats.

Tommy only began to complain about the families who were abandoned by the British when they returned Hong Kong to the Chinese. I thought he was somehow referring to the man before us, but the engines and shouting of bets for the next heat made it hard to hear, and just as I began to think he was actually talking about kung-fu stunts I realized he'd been really referring to his old video-dubbing business. Because bootlegging movies was a business that party members were in, he suddenly found himself a copyright criminal. "Enemies of the state and such. . . ."

I didn't know why he was telling me all of this. Afterward, I wondered if it was because he knew I suspected he was involved in human smuggling. Everyone wants to be seen as the hero in his own movie. Or maybe he figured this was his best shot at getting whatever answers he really wanted from my study. Or maybe, it occurred to me, he was just a guy. Not a tong boss. Not an immigrant, or even a Chi-Am, just a guy describing the rural province his family was from, a place so hard, so spirit-crushing, he said, and with so little chance of ever being different that suicide was the leading cause of death among the young, fertilizer the poison of choice.

"Hey! *Wo xiang da ge du!*" Tommy yelled, breaking off his story to grab the attention of one of the bet takers. A quick exchange of cash for betting stub, and then he continued, agitated—but instead of sending money back to a sister, he said, he himself was going to be sent back. Bureaucrats in some office processed his papers along with hundreds of others like so many parking tickets. Just before police arrived, though, a customer, his professor, tipped him off. To save him? To get rid of him?—maybe she both turned him in *and* tipped him off? In any case, it was clear what they must do. Jump on the motorbike his partner, his girlfriend, used to make deliveries, weaving in and out of Hong Kong traffic. But with the police coming in their building's front door only one of them did so. The other froze. Just a moment. But the moment was enough to be caught while the other roared away.

"Why?" he asked, grinding out a cigarette with the sole of

his boot. "Why did one hesitate? Or obey their order to stop? Because he was from the Mainland, The Servile Chinese? Chicken? Afraid the police would shoot? Confucius says we reveal ourselves to ourselves in the moment we least expect, but what did that hesitation reveal about him? Every day I ask myself that."

He paused, there in the nicotine sweetness and stench of exhaust, as though waiting to see if I would attempt an answer. When it was obvious to us both that I couldn't, Tommy shrugged. "The one who pulls the train gets to be the engine, and America is a great place to become an—"

"*Gweilo!*" someone shouted, and Tommy, indeed the entire basement, fell silent. For an instant. No more than a heartbeat. Then it was instant confusion. "*Gweilo!*" others began to yell as people scattered. The racist "Chinese Fire Drill" popped into my mind, not so much to describe the people running about as the tumult of details that came rushing in. Tommy was already gone. A bald man was screaming in my face—"*Gweilo!*"—to me or at me, I couldn't tell. Not knowing what else to do, I ran, too. I didn't know if we were running from the vice squad or immigration. Or maybe the building had caught fire. A double report boomed—gunshots? Engine backfires? I was knocked forward by a scuffle between two of the bet takers and a man trying to retrieve his money, then I was running with others down a dark corridor. "*Kuai! Kuai!*" I tripped after, then through a boiler room, then up a metal ladder, and past aisle after aisle after aisle of darkened sewing machines, hampers, racks of garments, all the while wondering, Why? What did I have to run from? When I caught up with them, they were going out a back window. We had emerged in a completely different building and were at a level that was higher than the alley, and from this height I had a glimpse of the checkerboard of alleys and backyard fences below. Men vanished into the night. Following their example, I descended a fire escape then hung down as far as my arms let me before dropping to the ground. Then I was on the run again, this time with other men down another alley and away from a red throbbing glow that seemed to fill the fog. Flashing squad-car lights? Or flames? Fear colors everything. From the darkness came the screech of tires—squad cars taking positions? Maybe it was a tong after all, boxing in its rival? Before I could tell, I found myself alone—no, behind one other man, just ahead, the back of his green jersey leaving no doubt who he was:

THREE HAPPINESS
8

"Hey!" I yelled. "Stop!" But this only made him run faster and his backward glances made me realize he thought I was chasing him. Which, I was. He threw off his helmet—threw it at me? To run faster? He was getting away, my academic's body beginning to lose to fatigue. "Wait!" At that moment all my hopes, my very self, seemed subject to my ability to catch him. But why? It was completely irrational, but still a gut feeling made me cry out, "Wait! *Deng!* Please!" A car engine gunned somewhere, followed by a siren.

Then I had him.

The alley we were running down dead-ended—it was the dead-end behind the office space I rented—and I was paralyzed by the confusion of questions that came rushing in. Though breathing hard, the man turned calmly, slow as a gunslinger squaring off for a quick-draw duel—only it was her. Tommy's girlfriend. Jenny. Her delicate nostrils flared with each breath, hands on hips in leather pants, her legs apart and straight as the blades of open scissors though her heavy-lidded eyes were as calm as they had been that afternoon I bored her in my office. She nodded toward the back door to my office in a way that indicated this was where she'd been leading me. But how? Had she switched clothes with the racer? A decoy? Or had I been so conditioned to expect a man? The typhoon of questions was so soaking that it was only later that I could sort them out from thoughts of snakeheads who let someone else be their front; politicians airing news through anonymous leaks; actors in masks; magicians; con jobs that accidentally help everyone; mundane tasks that allow evil; or Mafia bosses who live as meek dry cleaners while their flashy underlings do all the tough talking and high-profile living.

Could she be the real boss of the tong?—if there had ever been a tong and not just a bunch of people? Was she the one who jumped on the motorcycle? Escaped first? Blood Sample A or B? Neither? Did she win races because of daring, or because she weighed less than the male drivers? What kind of Risk-Taker wanted to hide? What did she see when she looked at me? What did it mean to help a Risk-Taker—or whatever we call her—hide? To my study? To my funders? To myself? Not least of all, to my subject?

A sweep of light snapped both of our heads toward it—probably a flashlight, but who knew. A projector beam. Or even a ghost. At that moment I could have believed anything. Gathering breath to speak, she looked at me directly then said, "The key! Quick!"

Strood

NEAL ASHER

Neal Asher (freespace.virgin.net/n.asher/] lives in Chelmsford, England. His short fiction has been published for years in the UK small press, and he has begun to publish in the U.S. recently. His small press books include Mindgames: Fool's Mate, The Parasite & The Engineer, Africa Zero, and Runcible Tales, all short story collections and novellas published before 2000. Since then he has published five novels: Gridlinked, a kind of James Bond space opera, was published in the UK in 2001; The Skinner, in 2002; then Line of Polity; Cowl; and Brass Man. All but Cowl are set in the same future—the "runcible universe," where matter transmitters called runcibles link the settled worlds.

"Strood" was published in Asimov's. The alien pathuns have revolutionized human society. The protagonist is given a rare and desirable ticket offworld, where he sees the wonders of alien civilization, but, ironically, is pursued when there by a strood, an alien being, and no one does anything to help him. This is a story about the wonder of alien worlds.

Like a Greek harp standing four meters tall and three wide, its center-curtain body rippling in some unseen wind, the strood shimmered across the park, tendrils groping for me, their stinging pods shiny and bloated. Its voice was the sound of some bedlam ghost in a big empty house: muttering, then bellowing guttural nonsense. Almost instinctively, I ran toward the nearest pathun, with the monster close behind me. The pathun's curiol matrix reacted with a nacreous flash, displacing us both into a holding cell. I was burned—red skin visible through holes in my shirt—but whether from the strood or the pathun, I don't know. The strood, its own curiol matrix cut by that of the pathun, lay nearby like a pile of bloody seaweed. I stared about myself at the ten-by-ten box with its floor littered with stones, bones, and pieces of carapace. I really wanted to cry.

"Love! Eat you!" the strood had bellowed. "Eat you! Pain!"

It could have been another of those damned translator problems. The gilst—slapped onto the base of my skull and growing its spines into my brain with agonizing precision—made the latest Pentium Synaptic look like an abacus with most of its beads missing. Unfortunately, with us humans, the gilst is a lot brighter than its host. Mine initially loaded all English on the assumption that I knew the *whole* of that language, and translating something from say, a pathun, produced stuff from all sorts of obscure vocabularies: scientific, philosophic, sociological, political. *All* of them. What had that dyspeptic newt with its five ruby eyes and exterior mobile intestine said to me shortly after my arrival?

"Translocate fifteen degrees sub-axial to hemispherical concrescence of poly-carbon interface."

I'd asked where the orientating machine was, and it could have just pointed to the lump on the nearby wall and said, "Over there."

After forty-six hours in the space station, I was managing, by the feedback techniques that load into your mind like an instruction manual the moment the spines begin to dig in, to limit the gilst's vocabulary to my feeble one, and thought I'd got a handle on it, until my encounter with the strood. I'd even managed to stop it translating what the occasional patronizing mugull would ask me every time I stopped to gape at some extraordinary sight, as "Is one's discombobulation requiring pellucidity?" I knew the words, but couldn't shake the feeling that either the translator or the mugull was having a joke at my expense. All not too good when really I had no time to spare for being lost on the station—I wanted to see so much before I died.

The odds of survival, before the pathun lander set down on the Antarctic, had been one-in-ten for surviving more than five years. My lung cancer, lodged in both lungs, considerably reduced those odds for me. By the time pathun technology started filtering out, my cancer had metastized, sending out scouts to inspect other real estate in my body. And when I finally began to receive any benefits of that technology, my cancer had established a burgeoning population in my liver and colonies in other places too numerous to mention.

"We cannot help you," the mugull doctor had told me, as it floated a meter off the ground in the pathun hospital on the Isle of Wight. Hospitals like this one were springing up all over Earth, like Medicins Sans Frontières establishments in some Third World backwater. Mostly run by mugulls meticulously explaining to our witchdoctors where they were going wrong. To the more worshipful of the population, that name might as well have stood for, "alien angels like translucent manta rays." But the contraction of "mucus gull" that became their name is more apposite for the majority, and their patronizing attitude comes hard from something that looks like a floating sheet of veined snot with two beaks, black button eyes, and a transparent nematode body smelling of burning bacon.

"Pardon?" I couldn't believe what I was hearing: they were miracle workers who had crossed mind-numbing distances to come here to employ their magical technologies. This mugull explained it to me in perfect English, without a translator. It, and others like it, had managed to create those nanofactories that sat in the liver pumping out DNA repair nanomachines. Now this was okay if you got your nactor before your DNA was damaged. It meant eternal youth, so long as you avoided stepping in front of a truck. But, for me, there was just too much damage already, so my nactor couldn't distinguish patient from disease.

"But . . . you will be able to cure me?" I still couldn't quite take it in.

"No." A flat reply. And with that, I began to understand, began to put together facts I had thus far chosen to ignore.

People were still dying in huge numbers all across Earth, and the alien doctors had to prioritize. In Britain, it's mainly the wonderful bugs tenderly nurtured by our national health system to be resistant to just about every antibiotic going. In fact, the mugulls had some problems getting people into their hospitals in the British Isles, because over the last decade, hospitals had become more dangerous to the sick than anywhere else. Go in to have an ingrown toenail removed; MRSA or a variant later, and you're down the road in a hermetically sealed plastic coffin. However, most alien resources were going into the same countries as Frontières' went to: to battle a daily death rate, numbered in tens of thousands, from new air-transmitted HIVs, rampant Ebola, and that new tuberculosis that can eat your lungs in about four days. And I don't know if they are winning.

"Please . . . you've got to help me."

No good. I knew the statistics, and, like so many, had been an avid student of all things alien ever since their arrival. Even by stopping to talk to me as its curiol matrix wafted it from research ward to ward, the mugull might be sacrificing other lives. Resources again. They had down to an art what our own crippled health service had not been able to apply in fact without outcry: if three people have a terminal disease and you have the resources to save only two of them, that's what you do, you don't ruin it in a futile attempt to save them all. This mugull, applying all its skill and available technologies, could certainly save me, it could take my body apart and rebuild it cell by cell if necessary, but meanwhile, ten, twenty, a thousand other people with less serious, but no less terminal conditions, would die.

"Here is your ticket," it said, and something spat out of its curiol matrix to land on my bed as it wafted away.

I stared down at the yellow ten-centimeter disk. Thousands of these had been issued, and governments had tried to control whom to, and why. Mattered not a damn to any of the aliens; they gave them to those they considered fit, and only the people they were intended for could use them . . . to travel offworld. I guess it was my consolation prize.

A mugull autosurgeon implanted a cybernetic assister frame. This enabled me to get out of bed and head for the shuttle platform moored off the Kent coast. There wasn't any pain at first, as the surgeon had used a nerve-block that took its time to wear off, but I felt about as together as rotten lace. As the nerve-block wore off, I went back onto my inhalers, and patches where the bone cancer was worst, and a cornucopia of pills.

On the shuttle, which basically looked like a train carriage, I attempted to concentrate on some of the alien identification charts I'd loaded into my notescreen, but the nagging pain and perpetual weariness made it difficult for me to concentrate. There was as odd a mix of people around me as you'd find on any aircraft: some woman with a baby in a papoose; a couple of suited heavies who could have been government, Mafia, or stockbrokers; and others. Just ahead of me was a group of two women and three men who, with plummy voices and scruffy-bordering-on-punk clothing—that upper-middle-class lefty look favored by most students—had to be the BBC documentary team I'd heard about. This was confirmed for me when one of the men removed a prominently labeled vidcam to film the non-human passengers. These were two mugulls and a pathun—the latter a creature like a two-meter woodlouse, front section folded upright with a massively complex head capable of revolving three-sixty, and a flat back onto which a second row of multiple limbs folded. As far as tool-using went, nature had provided pathuns with a work surface, clamping hands with the strength of a hydraulic vice, and other hands with digits fine as hairs. The guy with the vidcam lowered it after a while and turned to look around. Then he focused on me.

"Hi, I'm Nigel," he held out a hand, which I reluctantly shook. "What are you up for?"

I considered telling him to mind his own business, but then thought I could do with all the help I could get. "I'm going to the system base to die."

Within seconds, Nigel had his vidcam in my face, and one of his companions, Julia, had exchanged places with the passenger in the seat adjacent to me, and was pumping me with ersatz sincerity about how it felt to be dying, then attempting to stir some shit about the mugulls being unable to treat me on Earth. The interview lasted nearly an hour, and I knew they would cut and shape it to say whatever they wanted it to say.

When it was over, I returned my attention to the pathun, who I was sure had turned its head slightly to watch and listen in, though why I couldn't imagine. Perhaps it was interested in the primitive equipment the crew used. Apparently, one of these HG (heavy gravity) creatures, while being shown around Silicon Valley, accidentally rested its full weight on someone's laptop computer—think about dropping a barbell on a matchbox and you get the idea—then, without tools, repaired it in under an hour. And as if that wasn't miraculous enough, the computer's owner had discovered that the laptop's hard disk storage had risen from four hundred gigabytes to four terabytes. I would have said the story was apocryphal, but the laptop is now in the Smithsonian.

The shuttle docked at Eulogy Station, and the pathun disembarked first, which is just the way it is. Equality is a fine notion; the reality is that *they've* been knocking around the galaxy for half a million years. Pathuns are as far in advance of the other aliens as we are in advance of jellyfish, which makes you wonder where humans rate on their scale. As the alien went past me, heading for the door, I felt the slight air shift caused by its curiol matrix—that technology enabling other aliens, like mugulls, creatures whose home environment is an interstellar gas cloud not far above absolute zero, to live on the surface of Earth and easily manipulate their surroundings. Call it a force field, but it's much more than that. Another story about pathuns demonstrates some of what they can do with their curiol matrices:

All sorts of religious fanatic lunatic idiotic groups immediately, of course, considered superior aliens the cause of their woes, and valid targets, so it was only a week into the first alien walkabout that the first suicide bomber tried to take out a pathun amid a crowd. He detonated his device, but an invisible cylinder enclosed him and the plastique slow-burned—not a pretty sight. Other assassination attempts met with various suitable responses. The sharpshooter with his scoped rifle got the bullet he fired back through the scope and into his head. The bomber in Spain just disappeared along with his car, only to reappear, still behind the wheel, traveling at mach four down on top of the farmhouse his fellow Basque terrorists had made their base. Thereafter, attempts started to drop off, not because of any reduction in terrorist lunacy, but because of a huge increase in security when a balek (those floating LGAs that look like great big apple cores) off-handedly mentioned what incredible restraint the pathuns—beings capable of translocating planet Earth into its own sun—were showing.

From Eulogy Station, it was, in both alien and my own terms, just a short step to the system base. The gate was just a big ring in one of the plazas of Eulogy, and you just stepped through it and you were there. The base, a giant stack of different-sized disks nine hundred and forty kilometers from top to bottom, orbited Jupiter. After translocating from some system eighty light-years away to our Oort

Cloud, it had traveled to here at half the speed of light while the contact ships headed to Earth. Apparently, we had been ripe for contact: bright enough to understand what was happening, but stupid enough for our civilization not to end up imploding when confronted by such omnipotence.

In the system base, I began to find my way around, guided by an orientation download to my notescreen, and it was only then that I began to notice stroods everywhere. I had only ever seen pictures before, and, as far as I knew, none had ever been to Earth. But why were there so many thousands here, now? Then, of course, I allowed myself a hollow laugh. What the hell did it matter to *me*? Still, I asked Julia and Nigel when I ran into them again.

"According to our researcher, they're pretty low on the species scale and only space-faring because of pathun intervention." Julia studied her note screen—uncomfortable being the interviewee. Nigel was leaning over the rail behind her, filming down an immense metallic slope on which large limpetlike creatures clung sleeping in their thousands: stroods in their somnolent form.

Julia continued, "Some of the other races regard stroods as pathun pets, but then, *we're* not regarded much higher by many of them."

"But why so many thousands here?" I asked.

Angrily, she gestured at the slope. "I've asked, and every time, I've been told to go and ask the pathuns. They ignore us, you know—far too busy about their important tasks."

I resisted the impulse to point out that creatures capable of crossing the galaxy perhaps did not rank the endless creation of media pap very high. I succumbed then to one more "brief" interview before managing to slip away, and then, losing my way to my designated hotel, ended up in one of the parks, aware that a strood was following me. . . .

Sitting in the holding cell, I eyed the monster and hoped that its curiol matrix wouldn't start up again, as in here I had nowhere to run, and, being the contacted species, no curiol matrix of my own. The environment of a system station is that of the system species, us, so we didn't need the matrix for survival, and anyway, you don't give the kiddies sharp objects to play with right away. I was beginning to wonder if maybe running at that pathun had been such a bright idea, when I was abruptly translocated again, and found myself stumbling into the lobby of an apparently ordinary-looking hotel. I did a double take, then turned round and walked out through the revolving doors and looked around. Yep, an apparently normal city street—except for Jupiter in the sky. This was the area I'd been trying to find before my confrontation with the strood: the human section, a nice homey, normal-seeming base for us so we wouldn't get too confused or frightened. I went back into the hotel, limping a bit now, despite the assister frame, and wheezing because I'd lost my inhaler, and the patches and pills were beginning to wear off.

"David Hall," I said at the front desk. "I have a reservation."

The automaton dipped its polished chrome ant's head and eyed my damaged clothing, then it checked its screen, and after a moment it handed—or rather, clawed—over a key card. I headed for the elevator and soon found myself in the kind of room I'd never been able to afford on Earth, my luggage already stacked beside my bed, and a welcome pack on a nearby table. I opened the half bottle of champagne and began chugging it down as I walked out onto the balcony. Now what?

Prior to my brief exchange with the mugull doctor, I'd been told that my life expectancy was about four weeks, but that, "I'm sure the aliens will be able to do *something*!" Well, they had. The drugs and the assister frame enabled me to actually move about and take some pleasure in my remaining existence. The time limit, unfortunately, had not changed. So, I would see as much of this miraculous place as possible . . . but I'd avoid that damned park. I thought then about what had happened.

The park was fifteen kilometers across, with Earthly meadows, and forests of cycads like purple pineapples tall as trees. There were aliens everywhere, a lot of them strood. And one, which I was sure had been following me before freezing and standing like a monument in a field of daisies, started drifting toward me. I stepped politely aside, but it followed me and started making strange moaning sounds. I got scared then, but controlled myself, and stood still when it reached one of its tendrils out to me. Maybe it was just saying hello. The stinging cells clacked like maracas and my arm felt as if someone had whipped it, before turning numb as a brick. The monster started shaking then, as if this had got it all excited.

"Eat you!"

Damned thing. I don't mind being the primitive poor relation, but not the main course.

I turned round and went back into my room, opened my suitcase, found my spare inhaler and patches, and headed for the bathroom. An hour later, I was clean, and the pain in my body had receded to a distant ache I attempted to drive farther away with the contents of the minibar. I slept for the usual three hours, woke feeling sick, out of breath, and once again in pain. A few pulls from one inhaler opened up my lungs, and the other inhaler took away the feeling that someone was sandpapering the inside of my chest, then more pills gave me a further two hours sleep, and that, I knew, was as much as I was going to get.

I dressed, buttoning up my shirt while standing on the balcony and watching the street. No day or night here, just the changing face of Jupiter in an orange-blue sky. Standing there, gazing at the orb, I decided that I must have got it all wrong somehow. The aliens had only ever killed humans in self-defense, so somehow there had been a misunderstanding. Maybe, with the strood being pathun "pets," what had happened had been no more than the equivalent of someone being snapped at by a terrier in a park. I truly believed this. But that didn't stop me suddenly feeling very scared when I heard that same bedlam ghost muttering and bellowing along below. I stared down and saw the strood— it had to be the same one—rippling across the street and pausing there. I was sure it was looking up at me, though it had no eyes.

The strood was still waiting as I peered out of the hotel lobby. For a second, I wished I had a gun or some other weapon to hand, but that would only have made me feel better, not be any safer. I went back inside and walked up to the automaton behind the hotel desk.

Without any ado, I said, "I was translocated here from a holding cell, to which I was translocated after running straight into a pathun's personal space."

"Yes," it replied.

"This happened because I was running away from a strood that wants to eat me."

"Yes," it replied.

"Who must I inform about this . . . assault?"

"If your attack upon the pathun had been deliberate, you would not have been released from the holding cell," it buzzed at me.

"I'm talking about the strood's assault on *me*."

Glancing aside, I saw that the creature was now looming outside the revolving doors. They were probably all that was preventing it from entering the hotel. I could hear it moaning.

"Strood do not attack other creatures."

"It stung me!"

"Yes."

"It wants to eat me!"

"Yes."

"It said 'eat you, eat you,' " I said, before I realized what the automaton had just said. "Yes!" I squeaked.

"Not enough to feed strood, here," the automaton told me. "Though Earth will be a good feeding ground for them."

I thought of the thousands of these creatures I had seen here. No, I just didn't believe this! My skin began to crawl as I heard the revolving doors turning, all of them.

"Please summon help," I said.

"None is required." The insectile head swung toward the strood. "Though you are making it ill, you know."

Right then, I think my adrenaline ran down, because suddenly I was hurting more than usual. I turned with my back against the desk to see the strood coming toward me across the lobby. It seemed somehow ragged to me, disreputable, tatty. The pictures of them I'd seen showed larger and more glittering creatures.

"What do you want with me?"

"Eat . . . need . . . eat," were the only words I could discern from the muttering bellow. I pushed away from the desk and set out in a stumbling run for the elevator. No way was I going to be able to manage the stairs. I hit the button just as the strood surged after me. Yeah, great, you're going to die waiting for an elevator. It reached me just as the doors opened behind me. One of its stinging tendrils caught me across the chest, knocking me back into the elevator. This seemed to confuse the creature, and it held back long enough for the doors to draw closed. My chest grew numb and my breathing difficult as I stabbed buttons, then the elevator lurched into progress, and I collapsed to the floor.

"Technical Acquisitions" was a huge disc-shaped building, like the bridge of the starship *Enterprise* mounted on top of a squat skyscraper. Nigel kept Julia, Lincoln, and myself constantly on camera, while Pierce kept panning across and up and down—getting as much of our surroundings as possible. I'd learned that quantity was what they were aiming for; all the artwork was carried out on computer afterward. Pierce—an Asian woman with rings through her lip connected by a chain to rings through her ear, and a blockish stud through her tongue—was the one who suggested it, and Julia immediately loved the idea. I was just glad, after Julia and Nigel dragged me out of the elevator, for the roof taxi to get me out of the hotel without my having to go back through the lobby. Of course, none of them took my story about stroods wanting to eat people seriously; they were just excited about the chance of some real in-your-face documentary making.

"Dawson's got a direct line to the head honchos here in the system station," Lincoln explained to me. For "head honchos," read pathuns, who, after their initial show-and-tell on Earth, took no interest in all the consequent political furor. They were physicists, engineers, biologists, and pursued their own interests to the exclusion of all else. It drove human politicians nuts that the ones who had the power to convert Earth into a swiftly dispersing smoke cloud might spend hours watching a slug devouring a cabbage leaf, but have no time to spare to discuss *issues* with the president or prime minister. Human scientists, though, were a different matter, for pathuns definitely leaned toward didacticism. I guess it all comes down to the fact that modern politicians don't really *change* very much, that the inventor of the vacuum cleaner changed more people's lives than any number of Thatchers or Blairs. Dawson was the chief of the team of human scientists aboard the system base, learning at the numerous feet of the pathuns.

"We get to him, and we should be able to get a statement from one of the pathuns—he's their blue-eyed boy, and they let him get up to all sorts of stuff," Lincoln continued. "According to our researchers, he's even allowed access to curiol matrix tech."

In the lobby of the building, Lincoln shmoozed the insectile receptionist with his spiel about the documentary he was doing for the Einstein channel, then spoke to a bearded individual on a large phone screen. I recognized Dawson right away, because my own viewing had always leaned toward that channel Lincoln and Julia had denigrated on our way out here. He was a short plump individual, with a big gray beard, gray hair, and very odd-looking orangish eyes. He's the kind of physicist who pisses off many of his fellows by being better at pure research than they, and then making it worse by being able to turn his research to practical and profitable ends. While many of them had walked away from CERN with wonderfully obscure papers to their names, he'd walked away with the same, plus a very real contribution to make to quantum computing. I didn't hear the conversation, but I was interested to see Dawson gazing past Lincoln's shoulder directly at me, before giving the go-ahead for us to come up.

How to describe the inside of the disk? There were benches, computers, and big plasma screens, macrotech that looked right out of CERN, people walking, talking, waving light pens, people gutting alien technology, scanning circuit boards under electron microscopes, running mass spectrometer tests on fragments of exotic metal. . . . On Earth, there was a lot of alien technology knocking about, and a lot of it turned to smoking goo the moment anyone tried to open it up. It's not that they don't want us to learn; it's just that they don't want us to depopulate the planet in the process. Here, though, things were different: under direct pathun supervision, the scientists were having a great time.

Lincoln and Julia began by asking Dawson for an overview on everything that he and his people were working on. My interest was held for a while as he described materials light as polystyrene and tough as steel, a micro tome capable of slicing diamonds, and nanotech self-repairing computer chips, but, after a while, I began to feel really sick, and without my assister frame, I'd have been on the floor. Finally, he was standing before pillars with hooked-over tops, gesturing at something subliminal between them. When I realized he was talking about curiol matrices, my interest perked up, but it was then that Lincoln and Julia went in for the kill.

"So, obviously the pathuns trust you implicitly, or are you treated like a strood?" asked Julia.

I stared at the subliminal flicker, and through it to the other side of the room, where it seemed a work bench was sneaking away while no one was watching—until I realized that I was seeing a pathun sauntering across, all sorts of equipment on its back.

"Strood?" Dawson asked.

"Yes, their pets," interjected Lincoln. "Ones whose particularly carnivorous tastes the pathuns seem to be pandering to."

I tracked the pathun past the pillars to a big equipment elevator. Took a couple of pulls on one of my inhalers—not sure which one, but it seemed to help. I thought that I was imagining the bedlam moaning. Everything seemed to be getting a little fuzzy around the edges.

"Pets?" said Dawson, staring at Lincoln as if he'd just discovered a heretofore-undiscovered variety of idiot.

"But then I suppose it's all right," said Julia, "if the kind of people fed to them are going to die anyway."

Dawson shook his head, then said, "I was curious to see

what your angle would be—that's why I let you come up."
Now he turned to me. "Running into a pathun's curiol matrix
wasn't the best idea—it reacted to you rather than the
strood."

It came up on the equipment elevator, shimmering and
flowing out before the observing pathun. The strood came
round the room toward me. There were benches to my left,
so the quickest escape route for me was ahead and left to the
normal elevators. I hardly comprehended what Dawson was
saying. You see, it's all right to be brave and sensible when
you're whole and nothing hurts, but when you live with pain
shadowing your every step, and the big guy with the scythe
is just around the corner, your perspective changes.

"It bonded and you broke away," he said. "Didn't you
study your orientation? Can't you see it's in love?"

I ran, and slammed straight into an invisible web between
the two pillars—a curiol matrix Dawson had been studying.
Energies shorted through my assister frame, and something
almost alive connected to my gilst and into my brain. Exo-
skeletal energy, huge frames of reference, translocation, reality displayed as formulae ... there is no adequate
description. Panicked, I just saw where I didn't want to be,
and strove to put myself somewhere else. The huge system
base opened around me, up and down in lines and surfaces
and intersection points. Twisting them into a new pattern, I
put myself on the roof of the world. My curiol retained air
around me, retained heat, but did not defend me from harsh
and beautiful reality; in fact, it amplified perception. Standing on the steel plain, I saw that Jupiter was truly vast but fi-
nite, and that through vacuum the stars did not waver, and
that there was no way to deny the depths they burned in. I
gasped, twisted to a new pattern, found myself tumbling
through a massive swarm of mugulls, curiols reacting all
around me and hurling me out.

It's in love.

Something snatched me down, and, sprawled on an icy
platform, I observed a pathun, linked in ways I could not
quite comprehend to vast machines rearing around me to
forge energies of creation. The curiol gave me a glimpse of

what it meant to have been in a technical civilization for
more than half a million years. Then I understood about
huge restraint. And amusement. The pathun did something
then, its merest touch shaking blocks of logic into order, and
something went *click* in my head.

Eat you! Eat you!

Of course, everything I had been told was the truth. No
translator problem; just an existential one. What need did
pathuns have for lies? I folded away from the platform and
stumbled out from the other side of the pillars, shedding the
curiol behind me. Momentarily doubt nearly had me stepping back into the matrix as the strood flowed round and
reared up before me: a raggedy and bloody curtain.

"Eat," I said.

The strood surged forward, stinging cells clacking. The
pain was mercifully brief as the creature engulfed me, and
the black tide swamped me to the sound of Julia shouting,
"Are you getting this! Are you getting this!"

Three days passed, I think, then I woke in a field of daisies. I
was about six kilos lighter, which was unsurprising. One of
those kilos was pieces of the cybernetic assister frame scattered in the grass all around me. Nearby the strood stood tall
and glittering in artificial sunlight: grown strong on the cancer it had first fallen in love with then eaten out of my body,
as was its nature. It's like pilot fish eating the parasites of
bigger fish—that kind of existence: mutualism. I had been
sent as a kind of test case, by the mugulls who were struggling with human sickness, and, after me, the go-ahead was
given. The strood are now flocking in their thousands to
Earth: come to dine on our diseases.

The Eckener Alternative

JAMES L. CAMBIAS

James L. Cambias grew up in New Orleans, graduated from the University of Chicago, and currently lives in Deerfield, Massachusetts with his family. He has been a writer of role-playing games since 1990, and is the author of GURPS Mars, Star HERO, and the forthcoming GURPS Space, among many others. He has written nonfiction on topics as diverse as aviation history, wine, and parenting. His first fiction sale was the short story "A Diagram of Rapture" (F&SF, April 2000). He has published seven stories to date. He was nominated for the John W. Campbell Award for best new writer in 2001.

"The Eckener Alternative" was published in All Star Adventure Stories, edited by David Moles and Jay Lake, an excellent original anthology of contemporary stories in the pulp tradition. It is an amusing time travel story about a man who changes history over and over again until he gets it right, just because he thinks zeppelins are cool. It has a certain pleasant fannish goofiness to it, but at the same time an uncomfortable playing-with-fire plausibility. Perhaps this is essentially the utopian attitude of high-tech counterculture: we can save you because we come up with inventions that are sooo coool. Or maybe that's what it is parodying, along with a bunch of other things.

The *Hindenburg* swung gently on the mast at Lakehurst as the sky over New Jersey turned to purple twilight. All the passengers, the reporters, the newsreel men were gone. A couple of sailors stood guard beneath the big ship to enforce the no-smoking rule.

John Cavalli waited until the watchman below had turned away, then slid down the stern rope to the ground. He hunkered down next to the big rolling anchor weight for a couple of minutes, then hurried off into the darkness beyond the floodlights.

Once he was clear, Cavalli stopped to peel off the Russian Army arctic commando suit he'd been wearing ever since the zeppelin had lifted off from Frankfurt-am-Main. It had kept him warm as he hid among the gas cells with his IR goggles and fire extinguisher, but now in the warmth of a spring evening it was stifling.

He hit the RETURN button on his wristband and disappeared.

"You can't make big changes," said the instructor the first day of Temporal Studies class. He was a very laid-back physicist recruited from California in the 2020s. "That's the most important rule. The folks we work for are the result of a particular set of historical events. Change history too much and their probability level drops below 50 percent. If that happens, all this"—his gesture encompassed the Time Center—"goes away and we're out of a job. If we even exist anymore."

A student in the row ahead of Cavalli raised his hand. "What about making little changes?"

"Little changes are fine. We make little changes all the time. Most of them are things like making long-term investments, buying up art treasures for safekeeping, keeping species from going extinct, that kind of thing. You're going to learn all about gauging the effect of changes, avoiding heterodynes and chaotic points, and when it's okay to step on butterflies."

Cavalli was listening, but in the margin of his notebook he was doodling airships.

The timegate stage was dark and the control room was empty, just as he'd left it. The Coke can was still on the console. Was it maybe a little further to the left than he remembered? He stepped off the stage and took a drink. Still tasted the same. It would take a pretty big timeshift to change the flavor of Coca-Cola.

Cavalli locked the door behind him with his purloined master key—the Time Center used mechanical locks because they were a bit more resistant to minor time-shifts—and headed for the library. He found a book about zeppelins he didn't remember and skimmed the pages. *Hindenburg* served safely until 1939; scrapped when World War Two broke out. No postwar zeppelins. The usual "return of the airship" speculations.

Damn. It hadn't worked. He had hoped erasing the vivid image of the *Hindenburg* fire would have been enough to keep passenger airships alive, but the war still marked the end of their era.

"So why don't we stop things like the Holocaust or the firebombing of Dresden?" It was a relatively quiet dorm room party with half a dozen trainees blowing off steam after the first written exam. Cavalli didn't see who asked the question, but he sounded drunk.

Anna Kyle, the third-year trainee, answered. "Too big. The models predict major shifts in the 21st Century if there's no Holocaust. You lose the Cold War and the whole Jihad era. We just stay away from World War Two if we can help it. Rescue a few things from museums before they get flattened, take some videos for historians, that's all."

"Why not stop the whole war?"

"Kill Hitler in 1918? Everybody from the 20th and 21st wants to do that, or maybe kidnap him as an infant and leave him with a nice family of Buddhists in Tibet. The answer is, forget it. Removing the biggest conflict in human history makes the bosses go poof, not to mention just about everyone else born after 1950 or so. Frankly, we don't know what history would look like if you change something that big."

Cavalli was waiting outside the Houses of Parliament when Lord Thomson came out, trailing a crowd of aides and hangers-on. The monocle in Cavalli's eye displayed a targeting circle and he swung the umbrella up until the bright circle was centered on the side of the Air Minister's neck. He squeezed the handle and the umbrella fired off a smart dart loaded with pneumonia bacilli. Thomson was pretty healthy; he'd get over it in a few months. Plenty of time for the Cardington team to get the *R101* really airworthy.

There was a candy bar next to his Coke when he returned. He didn't remember getting one from the snack bar. It was a Health bar, his favorite brand. He ate it on the way to the library.

The British Imperial Airship Service had a rocky start, but by 1935 there were direct routes to Canada, India, South Africa, and Australia. Plans to extend the service to New Zealand were put on hold in 1936 and abandoned when war broke out. The airships served as fleet scouts for the Royal Navy during the first years of the war. The Japanese shot down *R100* and *R103*, and *R101* was scrapped in 1940. *R102* was used to evacuate some key people from Singapore as the Japanese approached, made an epic flight home to England via Africa and the Azores, and spent the rest of the war in a hangar at Cardington before being donated to the Royal Air

Museum. In his room he watched a movie on videodisk about the last flight of *R102*, with Michael York as the heroic captain.

At lunch one day Anna asked the Big Question. "So if you could change one thing, what would it be?"

The other trainees gave the usual answers—save Jesus, kill Hitler, stop Cortez, save Lincoln, give machine guns to Lee. Cavalli shrugged, "Find some way to save the airships, I guess."

A couple of people who knew him just rolled their eyes, but Anna looked curious. "How come?"

"I just think they're cool."

He clung to the fabric covering of the *Akron* as she cruised out over the New Jersey coast. It was a lot harder to stow away aboard a Navy airship than a passenger craft. His first two attempts had ended in quick aborts when he ran into sailors inspecting the gas cells, so finally he moved the focus to a point just above the ship and hoped nobody was watching.

Keeping a careful hold he pulled out the radio handset and began tapping out the Morse code message he had written on the sleeve of his commando suit. It had all the proper authentications and ordered the *Akron* to return to base at once. By the time they straightened out the "hoax" the line squall would be long past.

The Coke was in a bottle when he stepped off the stage. He finished it as he leafed through a big glossy coffee-table book about Navy airships in World War Two. There was an exciting picture of *Akron* going down amid a swarm of Zeroes at the Battle of the Coral Sea, and some photos of *Macon* on U-boat patrol over the Atlantic. The last page of the book was a fund-raising appeal from the U.S.S. *Macon* Association, hoping to finish the restoration project and get her airborne again in time for the 50th anniversary of Pearl Harbor. The book noted in passing that the luxury passenger airship never recovered after 1945.

* * *

Cavalli started going to bed as soon as classes ended, sleeping through dinner and waking after midnight to use the projector. He made up the lost meals at breakfast.

In 1917 he disabled the radio of the zeppelin *L-59* long enough for the ship to miss the recall message and reach its destination in German East Africa. As a result during the 1930s the *Graf Zeppelin* made a couple of voyages to Cape Town, but inevitably the war ended all that. Cavalli did get a nice Art Deco poster showing a zeppelin over the pyramids to put on his dorm room wall.

He tried going back to San Francisco in 1864 and giving Frederick Marriott a couple of uncut diamonds and a printout of suggestions to improve his *Avitor* airship. The result was that in the 1930s America purchased four big Navy airships instead of only two. The three that survived Pearl Harbor were scrapped.

He gave the German Navy's airship commandant Peter Strasser a bad case of pneumonia in 1915, so that zeppelins were used as reconnaissance platforms and fleet scouts rather than strategic bombers. More ships and skilled airshipmen survived the war and the *Graf Zeppelin* was filled with American helium. All nine passenger airships were scrapped in 1939.

He stood among the sand dunes on the North Carolina coast with the dart gun umbrella in his hand, but went home again.

He did manage to ride from Rio to Friedrichshafen aboard the *Graf Zeppelin*, and even exchanged a few pleasantries with Hugo Eckener. Dr. Eckener was convinced the airship could maintain its position despite the growing competition from airplane. He gestured around the comfortable lounge. "Who would not trade a cramped seat in a noisy box for this?" Cavalli agreed.

Anna tapped on the door of his dorm room. "I know what you've been doing after hours. The projector keeps a record of every time it's used."

"I don't know what you're talking about."

"Good reaction. But I checked the times and places. Friedrichshafen, Lakehurst, San Diego. The London trip had me puzzled until I found out the Air Minister came down with pneumonia the next day."

"He insisted on going to India early and the *R101* crashed."

"Give me one good reason why I shouldn't tell Temporal Integrity about you."

"I've been careful. I haven't made any major changes. None of these are butterfly points."

"Glad to hear that they're certified safe by a first-year trainee."

"Look, I'm not hurting anyone. It's just a little side project. A hobby."

"John, it's not going to work. Airships had their day from 1900 to World War Two. The war changed everything too much—they couldn't survive as military craft and they couldn't make money as passenger liners. Airplanes just got too good."

"I thought of maybe stopping the Wright Brothers."

"What?!"

"—but I changed my mind. Too big a butterfly." He looked at her. "I still don't understand something. Why don't we do more? Why don't we change things? We've got the power."

"Major changes would erase us."

"So what? It would be a better world for everyone else. Maybe time travel would get invented sooner."

"You can't know it would be better. Stop World War Two and you could cause something worse. Maybe a nuclear war."

"Better the devil we know, eh?" He looked at her. "I take it you want my master key, too?"

"If you don't give it up I have to call in Temporal Integrity."

He sighed and dug in a pocket. "Here. I got it from Dr. Stirling's office when he made me help move his plants."

She took the key and turned to go.

"Now be sure you don't try any history editing yourself," he said.

He wasn't sure how long he had. She might try to use the key herself, or Dr. Stirling might, and then they'd realize it was just the key to his dorm room. No time for much preparation. He checked a date in the library, let himself into the supply room, and hid in an unused classroom until dinnertime.

The stage was just warming up when somebody started pounding on the door. Cavalli leaped onto the platform just as the frosted glass smashed and a Temporal Integrity agent reached inside to undo the deadbolt. The last thing he saw of Time Center was Anna's face. She was shouting something, but it was drowned out by the hum of the field projector.

He hoped he'd been clever, setting the controls for Berlin in early 1932. Maybe the TI agents would assume he was going for Hitler, and concentrate on guarding his apartment and Nazi Party headquarters. But Cavalli spent as little time in Berlin as possible; an hour after arriving he was having dinner aboard the express to Munich. At midnight he got a room in a cheap but tidy hotel in Friedrichshafen.

"Doctor Eckener?"

This particular morning Hugo Eckener looked tired and a little irritable. Running an airship line in the depths of the Depression would do that. "Yes, good morning. My secretary says you have come from America with a business proposal?"

"Actually, no. I just told her that to get in here."

Eckener scowled. "I do not have time for sight-seers."

"Oh, no. It's about politics. The Central Party and the Social Democrats have invited you to run for President."

"Ah, a reporter. And a very good one, too. That was all discussed in strictest confidence. I am afraid I can say nothing."

"You must accept the offer."

"I cannot. Hindenburg is a hero. He is the only thing keeping Germany from falling into anarchy right now."

"But he's going to give the Chancellorship to Hitler!"

"That little fraud? Impossible. The President is not a fool."

"The Nazis are the biggest party, and they're in favor of rearming Germany. Field-Marshal Hindenburg approves of that."

"This is all speculation. Besides, my zeppelins keep me too busy to enter politics."

Cavalli hesitated for a split second, then reached into his pocket and pulled out his computer. "Watch this," he said, and called up the encyclopedia entry on Hitler. Eckener raised his eyebrows when he saw the little glowing screen in the young stranger's hand, but then he began to actually watch the newsreel shots and read the text.

"Another war?"

"Worse than the first. By the end of it, Germany was in ruins, thirty million people were dead—and zeppelins were gone forever."

"How—" Eckener stopped and composed himself. "Never mind. You have travelled in time, like the man in Mr. Wells' story, or possibly you are an angel, like the one sent to Lot. But I am afraid it is still impossible. Even if I ran, the Nazis would oppose me. They know I loathe them."

Cavalli took out the package he'd stolen from Mission Supply, and poured a heap of diamonds onto the table. "These are worth about ten million pounds," he said. "You can blanket the country with ads, rent stadiums for campaign rallies, and hire guards to keep the Brownshirts away."

Eckener picked up one diamond and scratched a vase with it, then quickly put it down again, as if it was hot to the touch. He was silent for a while. "I do not think I am qualified to be President of Germany," he said at last.

"You're an economist by training, and you've kept the Zeppelin company going through war and revolution and economic collapse. You're a national hero. And from everything I've read about you, you seem like a decent man. Germany needs a decent man now, Dr. Eckener. The world needs one."

Eckener looked at him out of those pouchy basset-hound eyes. "Who are you? Why are you doing this?"

Cavalli was about to give him another spiel about the need to stop Hitler, but then he stopped and shrugged. "I guess I just like zeppelins," he said. "I figure with you as President there will be lots of zeppelins."

Nine months later Cavalli was in the lounge of the *Graf Zeppelin* over the Atlantic. The window was open and he was holding his shift bracelet. If he hit RETURN now what would happen? Would he snap forward to Time Center or whatever occupied the site in the no-Hitler future? Would he just pop out of existence?

He watched it fall to the blue water below, then went to the bar to refresh his drink. The zeppelin droned on into the unknown.

Savant Songs

BRENDA COOPER

---

*Brenda Cooper [www.brenda-cooper.com/] lives in Kirk-
land, Washington. She works at Futurist.com, as host of the
"Science Fiction" and "Space and Science" sections of the
website, "to gain speaking engagements and engender positive conversations about the future." Six of her twelve published stories to date are in collaboration with Larry Niven,
as is the novel* Building Harlequin's Moon *(2005).*

"Savant Songs" was published in Analog. *It is an unusual
genre combination, hard SF romance, about an autistic
woman physicist who does research on multiverses, and her
former grad student who gets his Ph.D. and goes on to
become her partner, and is told from his point of view. It provides real grounding for the branching universe that most SF
takes for granted when it uses the concepts. Elsa, the
physisict, is the SF center. She is searching for herself in the
multiverse, and ultimately succeeds in finding other universes in which she exists. There is perhaps an echo of
Ursula K. Le Guin's classic "Nine Lives."*

*Who better than one who lives in two worlds to
study the slippery interfaces between universes?*

I loved Elsa; the soaring tinkle of her rare laughter, the
marbled blue of her eyes, the spray of freckles across her
nose. Her mind. The first, deepest attraction; the hardest
challenge. She flew with her mental intensity, taking me
places I'd never been before, outdistancing me, searching
the mathematical structures of string theory and mbranes,
following n-dimensional folds across multiple universes. I
loved her the way one loves the rarest Australian black opal
or the view from the top of Mount Everest. Elsa's rarity was
its own attraction. There are very few female savants.

She captured me whole when I was her physics grad student, starting in 2001, nine years before breakthrough.

Ten years ago last week, I walked into Elsa's office. She
stood with her back to me, staring out her window. She
didn't move at all as I snicked the door shut and scraped the
chair legs. I coughed. Nothing. She might have been a
statue. Her straw-colored hair hung in a long braid, just
touching her slender hips, fastened with a violet beaded
loop, the kind little girls wore. Her arms hung loosely from
her pink T-shirt, above faded jeans and Birkenstocks.

"Hello?" I spoke tentatively. "Professor Hill?" Was she all
right? I'd never seen such stillness in anything but a sleeping
child.

Louder. "Professor? I'm Adam Giles, here for an interview."

She finally turned and stepped daintily over to her desk, curling up in the big scratched leather chair behind her empty desk. Her gaze fastened on my eyes, as if they were all she saw in that moment. "Do you know what the word atom means?"

I blinked. She didn't. A warm breeze from the open windows blew stray strands of her hair across her face.

I struggled for the right answer, pinned by her gaze. She was an autistic savant. Literal. "Indivisible."

"Why?"

I thought about it. Atoms are made of protons, electrons, and neutrons, and ever-infinitely smaller things. "It means they didn't know any better when they named them. They couldn't see anything smaller yet."

"It means they were scared of anything smaller. They tried to make the word a fence. They thought that if they called atoms indivisible, they could make them indivisible." Her gaze still hadn't wavered. Her voice was high and firm, a soprano song even when she talked. I'd researched autistics, researched Elsa herself on the web. In physics, she was brilliant. She threw ideas right and left, half silly and wrong, half cutting-edge breakthroughs. If she accepted me, I would help the university winnow, feed her ideas to people who would follow them for years. One of her interviewers had summed her up by saying, "Talk to Elsa about physics, and all you see is the savant. The autistic exists over dinner."

No grad student had lasted more than three months with her. I needed to last with her; my dissertation was based on her ideas. Whether she screamed or cried or just made me work, however strange she might be, I wanted—needed—to explore what she explored.

She kept going. "Scientists make fences with ideas. Accidentally. Do you like to jump fences?"

"Yes."

"You'll do." She stood.

"Don't you want to know about my dissertation?"

"You're working on multiverses. It's the only reason you can possibly have chosen me."

She had a point. But multiverses was a rather broad subject. Mtheory: the latest plausible theory of everything, the current holy grail of physics. We live in universes made of 11 dimensions, called (mem)branes. We can render them with math, but settle for flat representations like folded shapes and balls full of air when we try to draw them in the few dimensions we can actually see. If you look at our pitiful drawings, we appear to live as holograms on flat sheets of see-through paper.

From that strange interview, I spent the next year near her every day, pounding away on my dissertation late at night, only giving myself Saturday nights for beer and chat with friends.

It was hard at first. Some days she talked endlessly about her most recent obsession, only not to me. She talked to herself, to the walls, to the windows, to the printers. I might as well have been inanimate. I wandered the lab behind her, taking notes. It was like following a six-year-old. She mumbled of memories from multiple universes, alternate histories, alternate futures. The first time I really understood her, months into following her, she stopped suddenly in the middle of one of her monologues, looking directly at me, as if today she saw me, and said, "Memory is a symphony call answered by the infinite databases on all the brane universes. We just need to hear the right notes, or make the right notes in an out-call, like requesting a certain table from a cosmic database."

I learned she cared little for food, or weather, or even holidays. I learned never to change the location of anything in the lab, and that if she changed it, she never forgot the change. Even pencils had places. I had to hold her coat out to her when she left, trail it along her arm so she'd notice it, and then she'd shrug into it, safe from the New England weather until she made it across campus to the little brownstone apartment the university provided for her.

I didn't care whether she ignored me or made me the center of her focus. Months passed when she worked with me by her side, when she seemed astoundingly normal, and guided me to new levels of understanding. But even when she fell into herself, when she wandered and talked to walls, I loved to watch her. Elsa had a dancer's grace, flowing easily, precisely, around every physical obstacle while her mind played in math jungle gyms and her hair glowed in the overhead lights. She was the fairy queen of physics, and I stayed with her, became her acolyte, her Watson, her constant companion.

Scientific dignitaries visited her, and reporters, and the Physics Chair, and I translated. "No, she thinks it is a music database. Or something like that. Related to Sheldrake's morphogenetic fields? A little. To Jung? She says he was too simple—it's not a collective unconscious. It's a collective database, a hologram, keyed to music. A bridge between eleven dimensions. Yes, some dimensions are too small to see. Elsa says size is an illusion." I illustrated it the way she illustrated it to me once; plucking a hair from my head. "There are a million universes in here. And we are in here, too. Perhaps." Whoever I was talking to would look puzzled, or awed, or angry at this, and I would shake my head. "No, I don't fully understand it."

Elsa nodded when I spoke, or when I changed something she'd said in physics-speak to English. Sometimes her hand fluttered to my arm, her thin fingers brushed my skin, and a nearly electric warmth surged through me.

There was an argument over my dissertation. One professor said the work I was doing was impossible and dangerous, another said it was Elsa's work and not my own, but two others stood up for me. Elsa was there, of course, staring at the ceiling, scribbling on her tablet PC, barely engaged in the argument. I fretted. She only saw me on some days; if this were a day that I was furniture, would she vote for me? But at the right moment, she raised her voice, and said, "Adam is an exemplary student, and more than that, an exemplary physicist. The ideas put forward here are astonishing, and only partly based on my work. All of us build on each other. Give the man his doctorate so we can get back to work."

And so I became a Doctor of Physics.

The Kiley-James Foundation gave me enough money to stick with Elsa for five more years as a post-doc. Our work was being closely followed by other physicists; two articles appeared in journals, and a watered-down version was written for a popular science magazine. I would have stayed without the money.

Six years after I met Elsa, two years after my Doctorate, and three grants later, the university gave her PI, short for Physics Intelligence, an AI designed for her by a colleague, delivered with basic intelligence programming and the full physics slate through master's-level work. PI has multiple interfaces, including a hologram that can be designed by the user. Elsa loved that interface, making PI a girl, growing the age of the hologram as PI obtained new knowledge.

Elsa and I spent a year feeding Elsa's ideas about string theory into PI, filling her with data about the shapes of multiple brane universes. It was all theory, all arguments yet unanswered, all beyond anything I could visualize, even though the math flowed easily. I thought we were done. But next, Elsa and I spent a month feeding her all the symphonies in the world music database; Brahms and Mozart, Bruckner and Dvorak, and then other music like Yo Yo Ma and Carlos Nakai. Lastly, after n-dimensional math, after music, we fed PI literature. We fed her stories of humans, biographies, science fiction, mystery, even romance. Simply put, we offered PI more than math and science, we offered her ourselves.

One Sunday morning, near the end of the year-of-feeding-PI, I slipped and slid my way through icy streets, clutching two coffees, and pushed open the door with my foot. Elsa sat on the floor, cross-legged, staring at the little programmable hologram of PI. She was wearing the same jeans and sweatshirt from Saturday, and her braid had come undone, so her hair floated across her shoulders and touched the floor. She hummed softly. I strained, hearing something else. I bent down. The PI hologram hummed as well, sounds I had never heard a human voice make. I realized Elsa was trying for the same noises, her throat unable to force the inhuman sounds.

"Elsa?"

She ignored me. So it would be one of those mornings. I set her coffee down next to her, and her hand strayed toward it momentarily, then returned to her knee. I watched her as I drank my coffee and organized notes on questions and theories to feed into PI. Elsa hummed for at least an hour, until her voice would no longer work at all. I took a bottle of water and curled her hands around it, and she raised it to dry cracked lips and drank deeply, shuddering.

She blinked and looked at me. "Good morning, Adam. It is morning?"

"Shhh," I said. "Shhhhh. It's time for you to sleep." I tugged gently on her arm, and Elsa stood shakily, stamping her feet as if they'd gone to sleep. She followed me meekly to a long thin cot we'd wedged between two desks and under a printer, and fell instantly asleep. I covered her with her own overcoat, tucking it around her legs, then threw my spare sweater over her feet, which were sticking out from the overcoat. In sleep, she looked younger, as if the spider web of wrinkles around her mouth and eyes had disappeared into her dreams.

I sat where she had sat, staring at PI. Elsa had set the hologram to be a dancer, and even though PI was light and form, I imagined that she must be cold in her thin leotard. She had been sized to three feet, just tall enough that I gazed into her eyes. She still hummed, her throat, of course, not challenged. As I listened, I realized there were more sounds than a hum; she was accompanied by a complex electronic orchestra, much of it sounding like instruments I had never heard before. The total affect was chaotic and haunting, sometimes cacophonous.

"PI?"

She stopped. "Yes, Adam?"

"What are you doing?"

"Playing what I hear when I search for myself."

I tried to clarify. "You are looking for an AI named PI in another universe?"

"I don't care about the name. I am searching for a song that approximates my story." The hologram smiled softly, a skill it had been taught to help it interact with people. She raised her hands up above her head, and her left leg rose behind her, so I could see the toe-shoe above her head, and she hopped three times *en pointe*, and returned to standing.

I shook my head at the odd image. "Across branes?" Then I laughed. "Or are you looking for an AI ballet dancer?"

"My story is not ballet. Elsa is simply feeding me dance and movement this week. I learned opera yesterday, and musicals." She smiled and did a little bow. "And of course across branes. We believe my self cannot exist twice in the same brane."

"Is Elsa also looking for her self?"

"She can hear her music, and she can feed it to me so I can play it, but she cannot make it herself." Now PI was frowning, and tears coursed down her cheeks.

"PI, does that matter?"

The tears disappeared, no trace, and PI looked solemn. "It may mean that humans cannot access their other selves. They cannot tune themselves well enough to the cosmic symphony to find themselves. From stories, it seems like this is true. Humans want to find themselves badly enough to make hundreds of religions, to meditate for years, to take hallucinogenic drugs. They do not appear to succeed."

I drummed my fingers, pondering the implications. "But you can?"

"I am operating on the theory that I cannot, and am trying to disprove it. Elsa is doing the same."

"I am supposed to feed you data today; two new ideas about the singularity before the big bang."

"I am not a calculator." She raised her bare arms above her head and flipped backward, the ballet skirt looking ridiculous during a back flip. She was humming as she landed perfectly. "See?"

"All right. Look, PI, you're making me shiver. Can you put on some warmer clothes?"

She laughed, an imitation of Elsa's laugh, and I smiled as an overcoat appeared, just like the soft one covering Elsa now, in her sleep, down to the thick waist-band and the big silver temperature-sensing buttons.

"Thank you."

I picked up Elsa's cold coffee and set it by the microwave, returning to my desk. The humming and the symphony started again, so softly it was simply background, and I spent the next four hours pouring data carefully into PI, setting initial linkages so they could be followed and completed, watching the display show connections being made, information filed and cross-referenced, relevancy assigned. I rubbed my eyes, feeling a sudden desire for warm food and cold beer.

I shook Elsa's shoulder gently, rousing her. She started to hum. I shook her again. "Come on, let's feed you."

In the past few years she had taken to following my lead in daily life the way I followed hers in the lab. I helped her shrug into the overcoat, handed her a knit hat, and wrapped myself in my gray coat, gray scarf, and navy cap. Snow fell softly, silencing the university. We walked across the commons, our feet making fresh prints in an inch of new snow, Elsa's hair lying wet and snow-covered on the outside of her coat. I should have made her braid it back, kept most of it dry.

Sunlight from a small hole in the clouds touched her cheek, illuminated the snow on her hair, and then trailed off to brighten the tops of dead grass peeking from the snowy lawn. I smiled and put a hand on her back, guiding her. She laughed, and took my hand, a friendly gesture, a connection.

Often it happened that way after she separated herself from the world—she rose from days of monologues or data work and seemed normal, reaching out, wanting companionship and comfort. Other professors came to her from time to time, sometimes staying and talking long into the night, even laughing, sometimes noting her mood and disappearing. Department chairs stopped by and funding institutions sent representatives. They were all interested in her ideas; some worked with AIs like PI, but focused more singly on music and math.

I remained the man who saw her for herself, cared whether she wore a coat, brought her grapes and apples and coffee. Family. It made me smile.

The scent of chili and cornbread warmed the air outside of Joe's Grill, and Elsa and I both smiled, eyes locking, and squeezed each other's hands. I felt absurdly like skipping, but we were already at the door. The place was nearly empty.

Elsa chose a table by the window, and the waiter, who knew us, brought a pitcher of dark beer, then returned with two bowls of chili and a single plate heaped with cornbread.

We ate in pleasant silence until I scraped the last chili from my bowl with the last piece of cornbread. Elsa, typically, had barely sipped at her beer. She'd finished her food, though; a good sign. Some days, I almost had to feed her. "I talked to PI today," I said. "She said you are both trying to disprove the theory that you don't exist anywhere else."

"I am looking for myself. She is looking for herself." Elsa took a tiny sip of beer from her untouched glass, and I finished my first glass and poured a second one.

I had been puzzling over it in my head all afternoon. "Okay. One theory says we make other universes every time we make a choice. You finish your beer, or you don't. There is a universe where you're slightly drunk, and in another one—probably this one—you are not. A million selves. That's easy. Maybe. Both of you are similar and maybe both of you are you."

She nodded, looking uninterested, as if her mind was leaving again. A fleck of beer foam rested on her top lip.

I grabbed her hand, squeezing it, trying to keep her in the moment, in my moment. "But there is more interest now in the idea that other universes exist because the same initial conditions existed a million times, and so similar things happened, and another you, another me, another PI, they all exist. Exactly like we are now."

She licked the fingers of her free hand, then squeezed my hand with the one of hers I was holding. "It's simply a matter of branching. One idea says a million tiny branches happen every day. Another says there are long branches. It's about the size of the branches and the number of branches."

I remembered my father trying to teach me ninth-grade algebra. He'd point at an equation that totally perplexed me, the tip of his pencil wavering, and say "You just have to understand equals. Don't you understand equals?" And he'd solve the equation with no intermediate steps and I'd have to find a tutor anyway, someone slow enough for me to follow. There was no tutor except Elsa now, not in this subject.

She looked at me, and said, "You're caught up in size, Adam. It's as dangerous as being caught up in time. They're both constructs."

I wasn't thinking about size at all. "But . . . but one multiverse, the first one, drunk and not-drunk, tells a million stories about me. The second multiverse doesn't illustrate free-will at all."

"I bet—"she raised her glass,"—on the universe made of stories." She drank down all of her beer, and then another glass, something she'd never done before, and stood up, wobbling a little, and I took her elbow, guiding her out the door and across the lawn.

We were halfway across, Elsa leaning on my arm, when she stopped so we stood in the near-darkness, snow falling all around us. She reached an arm up and curled her wrist around the back of my head, pulling my face down into a kiss. Her lips were cool and soft, and we kissed hungrily, like two children finally allowed out for recess. Her lips tasted like sweet hot peppers and beer. It was the only time she ever kissed me.

What happened that night in some other multiverse?

For the next three weeks, Elsa worked with PI as if they were in a race. Her face shone with energy, and even when she grew visibly tired, her eyes danced. I hovered around the edges, watching. Elsa was so deeply enthralled that loud noises made her leap and glare at me, and I walked carefully. At first, PI and Elsa continued with audible noise, like the humming/symphony, played so softly I could barely hear it. Then PI started generating white noise, taking the small background sounds with everything important filtered out from the very room around us. Then I heard silence, and Elsa and PI talked in light. I took to watching the conversation on my own interface with PI, which amounted to watching lights and words flash on and off, strings drawn between ideas and concepts and even poems. I could not follow them, but the relationships they drew seemed right, and when I let go of the attempt to understand there was a flow that I could feel, as if a river of meaning coursed along the display in front of me.

Almost every day, Elsa found a new thing to include in PI's expanding web of connectivity. Scientology. Cargo Cults. Early cave paintings.

I captured all of it, recording the data for others to dig through. For myself, I tried to keep up with them, puffing along uphill, weighed down by inability to focus. I kept Elsa fed, but she refused to go home, and I bought a second cot so that she would not be alone.

We didn't make the first breakthrough.

Outside the window, morning sun stabbed the ice on the branches with brilliant points of light. The office smelled like stale coffee and sweat. My eyelids were heavy and uncooperative, my brain fuzzing gently in and out of sleep. Elsa was still sleeping, curled underneath blankets I'd brought from home for her, one foot stuck out at an odd angle. The display in front of me sprang awake on its own, a pulsing green and blue color, PI's call for attention. "Yes, PI?"

"Something touched me. Wake Elsa."

I didn't understand. "All right." I struggled up out of the chair, wishing I'd already made my coffee run. "Just a minute. Make yourself seen, all right?" I always preferred to interact with the hologram rather than the flat display. It gave PI more options as well; she could communicate more like a human. AI body language.

I whispered in Elsa's ear. "PI says something touched her."

Elsa sat straight up; wide-eyed, and glanced at the hologram display. PI was seated, her image dressed in jeans and a tank top, banging her legs against the edge of a holographic chair, indicating impatience. "I wasn't even out-calling, I was just humming my own songs," she blurted out, "and an answer came. An AI just like me, with a scientist named Elsa. Seconds only, like a crack opened and closed. I could only talk to the AI, of course, and I was sending her the data stream from our last few weeks when the connection broke."

"Did you get a time?" Elsa asked quietly.

The PI image frowned. "I asked, but the connection snapped before an answer came."

"Can you replay the conversation?"

The image shook its head. I checked. The last few moments before PI flashed at me were silent. "There's nothing. Just state data, indicating excitement."

"That's okay," Elsa said, "we'll work on that." She plucked at a tangle in her hair. "PI, what did you feel?"

It was a strange question to ask an AI.

"Bigger. Pulled. Attracted to the other one of me. But at the same time, I knew—" the word "knew" drew itself over her head in three dimensions, for emphasis, surely for me— "I knew that I couldn't actually get close. As if there were a physical barrier between branes."

Elsa pursed her lips. I went out for coffee.

When I came back in, handing Elsa a cup, she took it and sipped quietly. "We have to make it happen again," she said. "Or hope it happens again. We didn't start it."

"Make what happen? I don't get it, not yet."

"The coffee is hot, right?"

I smiled at her. "That's a good thing."

"But it's not true." She sipped her own coffee carefully. "Touch your knee."

I did.

"What did you touch?"

"My knee."

"No, you touched a fence. You've got all the theory, all the math. You know we are really light and sound, thinner than that hologram of PI." She glanced over at PI's image, which was clear enough that I could make out the walls behind it. "Well, PI being touched by herself—in another universe— means that we are light, and sound, and infinite." Elsa stopped for a moment, her eyes nearly glazing over. "I thought a data construct could do what we cannot. Or at least, could lead the way." She set the coffee down and stood, staring out the window, posed very much like I first saw her. "I intend to follow her into my own stories. If I can."

"Into your stories?"

"Remember the night I drank the beer? History split, and

the normal me—since I don't usually drink much—split off into a different universe. I'm splitting myself all the time, and so are you."

"Theoretically."

"Theoretically. I tell PI daily to search for me by searching for herself. Millions of PIs and millions of Elsas, and probably millions of Adams, all looking for each other. The more culture, the more ideas we feed PI, the more likely she is to synthesize the key. Our PI did not, or she would have made first contact. But in another story, in another place, I fed PI the key."

She pursed her lips and stared out the window at the icy branches, water dripping off them as the day warmed up. She spoke again. "Perhaps another Adam fed her the key."

It took another year to develop enough data to create a paper, to replicate any results at all. The first two times were other PIs, finding our PI, three separate PIs, or four, depending on how you count. They learned to hold the connections open, to broaden them, to find more. Together PI and Elsa were able to prove they were in the same time, in other spaces. In other words, they were not histories of each other, or futures of each other. Multiverses. The proof was mathematical.

I wrote the paper, putting her name first, even though most of the data came from PI, who of course, wasn't listed as an author. They'd gone well past me now. Elsa with her perfect savant focus and PI, who wasn't held back by biology at all.

More people came to visit, a steadier stream. We used some extra money I'd squirreled away in an R&D account to buy an electronic calendar and carefully manage access, blocking time for ourselves. It bought us whole days, uninterrupted, here and there. Elsa could still pull herself together for public visits, but she retreated entirely on the quiet days, not wanting touch or sound. She talked to PI, to multiple PIs via our PI, and I sat, outside of her emotions, fenced away by her brilliant mind. She often smiled at nothing, or rather, at something I could not hear or see.

There were multiple Adams, although not always. Sometimes the assistant was someone else. In one universe, I had died the previous spring and there was a new person helping that Elsa, that PI. It didn't seem to bother Elsa at all. It sent me out for a pitcher of beer.

My head spun. This was what I had always wanted, except what I truly wanted had changed to chili and cornbread with my Elsa.

It was two years ago. I remember the date, April 12, 2011. I watched her as she looked out the open window. Tears streamed down her face. Her shoulders shook.

I had never seen her cry. Not in ten years.

I came up behind her, and put my arms around her. She flinched inward, as if wanting to escape from my embrace. I held her anyway, put my cheek against her hair, looked down through half-closed eyes and watched her freckles. She had been friendly, funny, lost, distant, but never, never afraid. I held her tighter, and stroked her hair, trembling myself. What had she found?

It took a while, but finally she looked me in the eyes, and said, "I can't get through. Only PI can. The PIs. Other AIs. Nothing I do lets me get through. The other Elsas can't either. As brilliant as we are, as strange, as blessed, we can't open the door. The notes aren't there—my body . . . my body gets in the way." She blinked, and two fresh tears fell down her cheeks. I wanted to lick them off.

"I'm sure now that only pure data can get through. Humans will not become pure data for years yet, past my lifetime. I will never see what PI sees." She turned around then, pulled herself into me, and sobbed until my shirt was soaked and my feet were heavy from standing in one place.

The smell of lawn wet with spring rain blew in the window, and I heard students laughing below us, teasing each other.

Then, in one of her lightning changes of mood, Elsa pushed away from me and started out the door. I thrust her coat at her, and she grabbed it with one hand, pulling the door shut behind her, leaving no invitation for me to follow.

I went home that night, and the next day, Elsa didn't show.

I waited impatiently until afternoon, finally walking to her brownstone. The door pushed open, unlocked. Elsa's things remained, all in their accustomed places.

I walked back across campus, blue sky above me, the grass under my feet damp and greening up. I tore the door open. "PI! Where the hell is Elsa?"

PI's interface was a little boy with a fishing pole, a holo I'd chosen. I didn't want it now. "Bring the old man!"

PI morphed to the dancer instead, sitting on a rock, feet crossed daintily. "I don't know where she's gone."

"Damn it! I'm worried. The last time I saw her, she cried. She thought she'd never get across."

"I know that."

Of course. PI was always on.

Cool spring rain flooded the gutters and made small rivers in the university lawns. I bundled up, and went every place we had ever gone together. Restaurants. Bookstores. The old music shop on the boulevard with garish purple posters in the window.

Two joggers found her body the next morning, sitting against a tree. The police took me to her, to identify her. She looked incredibly young, and could have been sleeping except for her stillness and the cold. She had put her coat on, only now it was soaked and heavy and couldn't possibly keep her warm. There was no sign of foul play. Rain covered her cheeks like tears, and I bent down and slid my forefinger across her face before a policeman asked me to step back.

An older policeman and a young woman in plainclothes questioned me, and made me spend a week out of the lab. When I went back to work, everything was out of place. Not much; people had been respectful. Elsa would have noticed the pencil cup three inches from its corner, the stack of books on the wrong shelf, the cups from the sink set back out of order.

PI was waiting for me, as the old man. She looked up solemnly, clearly aware of what happened. "Three of them."

"What?"

"I found three Elsas who killed themselves. Two disappeared." She is crying, her eyes red in the old man's face.

The other Elsas continue to work, and I talk with them through PI. I keep myself in good shape, running every morning. I'm younger than the Elsas. Perhaps I will be able to cross before I die.

Story Copyrights

"Sergeant Chip" copyright © 2004 by Bradley Denton. First published in *F&SF*.

"First Commandment" copyright © 2004 by Gregory Benford. First published in *SciFiction*.

"Burning Day" copyright © 2004 by Glenn Grant. First published in *Island Dreams*, ed. Claude Lalumière.

"Scout's Honor" copyright © 2004 by Terry Bisson. First published in *SciFiction*.

"Venus Flowers at Night" copyright © 2004 by Pamela Sargent. First published in *Microcosmos*, edited by Gregory Benford (DAW, 2004). Reprinted by permission of the author and her agent, Richard Curtis Associates.

"Pulp Cover" copyright © 2004 by Gene Wolfe. First published in *Asimov's*. Reprinted by permission of the author and the author's agent, the Virginia Kidd Agency, Inc.

"The Algorithms for Love" copyright © 2004 by Kenneth Liu. First published in *Strange Horizons*.

"Glinky" copyright © 2004 by Ray Vukcevich. First published in *F&SF*.

"Red City" copyright © 2004 by Janeen Webb. First published in *Synergy*.